A FERRIE TALE

DAVID T. BEDDOW

ARCHWAY
PUBLISHING

Scripture taken from the King James Version of the Bible.

Archway Publishing books may be ordered
through booksellers or by contacting:

Archway Publishing
1663 Liberty Drive
Bloomington, IN 47403
www.archwaypublishing.com
1 (888) 242-5904

ISBN: 978-1-4808-6533-4 (sc)
ISBN: 978-1-4808-6534-1 (hc)
ISBN: 978-1-4808-6535-8 (e)

Library of Congress Control Number: 2018909648

Print information available on the last page.

Archway Publishing rev. date: 04/26/2019

To Sue

FRIDAY, NOVEMBER 22, 1963

New Orleans was enveloped in fog, sprinkles, and wind on the morning of November 22, 1963. In the packed, musty fourth-floor courtroom in the 1910 Beaux-Arts "new" courthouse at 400 Royal Street in the French Quarter, David William Ferrie sat at the defense table with mob boss Carlos Marcello—the accused—and Marcello's closest colleague and personal attorney, G. Wray Gill. Also at the table was Marcello's big-city trial lawyer, Jack Wasserman.

Ferrie cut an intriguing figure in this regal space. He was above-average height, about six feet. He weighed 190 pounds, was in good shape. When he stood, his back was ramrod straight, military straight. He was well-dressed. His skin was dusky. But, at the same time, his russet hair plainly wasn't natural. And the color of the hair on the top of his head didn't quite match the color of the hair above his eyes—they had distinctly different hues. His left eyebrow was a millimeter higher than his right eyebrow. For decades after this eventful Friday, Ferrie was re-membered by court watchers and jurors because of the odd mix of formal carriage and peculiar features.

Observers also never forgot how fidgety he was, constantly shifting around in his chair, his left leg pumping up and down like an oil derrick on amphetamines. He paged through papers, twirled his pencil, darted his eyes about. His facial muscles were tense, his eyes brooding.

Ferrie's skittish demeanor stood in square contrast to the controlled, calm appearances of Gill, Wasserman, and Marcello.

Though known in New Orleans as a quirky man, Ferrie had earned a position as a key pillar in the Marcello mob network. Marcello and Gill valued his varied talents. He had a complicated and muscular brain that they put to good use by assigning him a myriad of odd and difficult jobs. Particularly handy was Ferrie's facility in operating all manner of airplanes. A former commercial airline pilot, he frequently flew privately for Marcello.

The north star in Ferrie's life was his faith, even though his mob ties caused him to perform a legion of sinful acts. He'd studied at two seminaries as a young man, where he excelled intellectually and developed a deep knowledge of the Catholic belief system, including its liturgical principles and rituals, major dogmas and doctrines, and sacraments. Because he was unable to conduct his personal life in ways that were consistent with church tenets, however, he never graduated from seminary and never became a priest sanctioned by the Vatican.

Nevertheless, Ferrie regularly said masses in his apartment, dressed in a purple cassock and swinging a thurible burning incense, for a small flock of like-minded believers. Over years of study, he'd become an adherent of "Old Catholic" theologies and enamored of the writings of St. Augustine of Hippo, who saw life as a constant—sometimes fierce—battle between God and the Devil. He prayed daily to Mother Mary that his iniquitous conduct fell on the right side of this battle.

\\\\

President John F. Kennedy's scrappy brother Robert, the US attorney general and an ardent foe of organized crime, had energetically sought to get Marcello since the bitter cold day JFK was inaugurated. Days after becoming attorney general, with JFK's acquiescence, RFK forcefully and without warning deported Marcello, who was an illegal alien even though he'd lived in the country since he was a baby. Marcello was roughly hustled out of the country. Two months later, though, courtesy of pilot Dave Ferrie, Marcello clandestinely returned to the United

States. Marcello's lawyers thereafter used litigation to avoid redeportation.

RFK's pursuit of Marcello deeply irked him and his principal colleagues, particularly Chicago boss Sam Giancana, for they had helped ensure JFK's victory in 1960. In return, JFK was supposed to lay off the mob—and had also committed to helping it get its Cuba casino empire back. But neither was happening. JFK cryptically messaged Giancana in early 1963 that things would get better in the second term, but, after three years of experience trying to work with the Kennedys, the mob didn't believe him.

With his deportation efforts bogged down by legal maneuvering, RFK sought a different tack to take Marcello down. He'd now charged him with committing a criminal fraud on the United States by offering up, for years, a bogus birth certificate. That charge had been the subject of the proceedings on the fourth floor of the Royal Street courthouse since November 4. The trial was finally wrapping up on this dank Friday.

By early afternoon, the wind beginning to whine through a crack in a small window in the otherwise quiet courtroom, the case was ready for the jury. The defense team, however, wasn't worried about the jury's verdict. Marcello wouldn't be convicted by his New Orleans "peers," some of whom relied on him in one way or another for their livelihoods. Leaving nothing to chance, Marcello's associates had offered one of the jurors a handsome financial donation if there were an acquittal.

Marcello, Gill, and Ferrie *were* anxious about other things that day. Their minds were on Dallas, a part of Marcello's territory.

At a few minutes after one o'clock, as the judge, Herbert Christenberry, was reading the instructions to the jury, he was handed a note. He read it over twice, readjusted his reading glasses, licked his lips, and matter-of-factly relayed the news in the note. "Ladies and gentlemen, I'm enormously sad to report that the president has been shot in Dallas and is feared dead." The jurors, prosecution team, and spectators, in unison, drew in their breaths. Marcello, Gill, and Ferrie did their best to do the same and to look surprised.

After an awkward minute or two of quiet murmuring and rustling in the courtroom, Judge Christenberry spoke again. Slowly addressing the jury, choking on his words, he reported, "My friends, I have no words of wisdom for you, I'm sorry to say. Tragic, just tragic. By God's grace, let's each say a private prayer for the president and his family. And for us all."

Ferrie bowed his head. *Eternal rest, grant unto him, O Lord.*

"Amen," the judge said after a minute of silence. "Okay. We have been at this trial for three weeks, and it *is* Friday afternoon. My preference would be to send you off to deliberate and see if we can get this done so we can go home and grieve with our families without distraction. I would understand, however, if you weren't up to this task at this time and would rather wait until Monday. What say you?"

The jurors looked around at their colleagues. One said he was ready to continue. The others nodded in agreement.

Judge Christenberry finished the instructions and sent the jury off to deliberate at 1:45 p.m. A verdict of acquittal was announced at 3:30.

\|\|\|\|

The victory party for Marcello had been in the works for several days. It wouldn't be canceled, or even toned down, because of JFK's murder.

Marcello's consiglieri commandeered the entire bar at the historic Hotel Monteleone on Royal Street, on the southwestern edge of the French Quarter. The hotel had been founded by a Sicilian shoe maker in 1886. The Monteleone was a favorite of Marcello's, who was Sicilian by blood.

The hotel's Carousel Bar was a New Orleans institution. Its circular bar rotated like a merry-go-round, adorned with an immense umbrella that twirled along with the bar as it turned. The umbrella had happy alternating broad green and yellow stripes, running from the center to its outer edges. The patrons at the bar sat on one of twenty-five blood-red, swiveling padded stools. The bar made a full rotation every fifteen minutes, turning on two thousand steel rollers.

On the far side of the bar was a cozy lounge area, like a big living room, with soft chairs and wood tables. A large model ship was perched on a windowsill overlooking Royal Street.

The walls of the bar held cartoonish circus-related paintings, the most prominent one being of a colorful carousel anchored to a curved rocker board, poised to lift off like a hot-air balloon, a flamboyance of flamingos off to the side.

The Carousel Bar had attracted a host of eclectic people over the years, particularly authors. Ferrie frequently felt the ghosts of William Faulkner and Ernest Hemingway, who had been regular customers, in the bar. Mississippi writer Eudora Welty was a frequent reveler here. Truman Capote composed while sitting at the bar. Tennessee Williams mentioned the Carousel Bar in his plays *The Rose Tattoo* and *Orpheus Descending*. The hotel and bar appeared in Ernest Hemingway's short story, "Night before Battle."

Drinks were on the house. And the Carousel Bar's signature drink, the eye-opening Vieux Carré, laced with Hennessy cognac and Sazerac rye, was flowing like honey. George Oechsner Jr., the manager of Pat O'Brien's on nearby St. Peter Street, had supplied trays of potent, heavily rummed hurricanes, a Pat O'Brien's invention served in glasses shaped like hurricane lamps.

A dozen topless girls from the Sho-Bar and the 500 Club sashayed through the crowd.

"It's like being in Tits-burg, Dave," a pie-eyed Wasserman said to Ferrie. "Or Hooterville!" Ferrie didn't crack a smile. He was nervous about his next assignment, which would have to be initiated that evening.

Marcello had the sway to bring in Kid Thomas, Sweet Emma Barrett, and George Lewis from a brand-new group called the Preservation Hall Jazz Band to play their special style of jazz— Dixieland infused with ragtime, blues, and traces of music written to support eighteenth-century quadrilles. The grandson of the hotel's founder, William Monteleone, was in attendance. William was active in the anti-Castro community, which the mob was aggressively supporting. William's anti-Castro colleague and public relations man Ronnie Caire was sycophantly following him around the bar.

Marcello presided, grinning ear to ear. Known as the "Little Man" because of his five-foot-two frame, he was now sporting his trademark sunglasses, which hadn't been allowed in the courtroom.

Ignoring the celebration, Ferrie and Gill huddled in the corner of the lounge with a third man, talking seriously and shunning the Vieux Carrés and hurricanes. They had work to do. The third man William Guy Banister was a former FBI agent turned private investigator and bag man for Marcello. The three reviewed the assignment. Ferrie then left the bar and slipped into a phone booth in the Monteleone lobby. He called Dallas. The call was short but animated.

Heading for the hotel's front door, he was greeted by a distraught but elegant-looking middle-aged woman. "Oh, my God," she blurted out. "It really happened." She repeated "Oh, my God" over and over until Ferrie grabbed her shoulders and gently shook her quiet.

"Dr. Mary, ma'am, you gotta get outta here. I'm okay, just fine. But I need to get going, need to get on the road."

"Where to?"

"You don't want to know. Just, ma'am, please—lie low for a while. Stay away from the lab." They hugged like friends who thought they would never see each other again.

"Be careful, Dave." Dr. Mary was antsy. Her voice shuddered.

Ferrie slipped her a note in a Town and Country Motel envelope and then shot out onto Royal Street and caught a cab.

\\\\

The next ten hours were harrowing for Ferrie. The cab took him to his home on Louisiana Avenue Parkway. He briefly watched the assassination news on his black-and-white, sixteen-inch Motorola TV while he gathered up a small, already-packed satchel. Two of his friends and occasional roommates Layton Martens and John Irion were there, glued to the screen. They barely noticed his coming and going.

Ferrie prayed briefly in his back room. "I beseech You for strength and for wisdom that I'll be able to endure this situation and be able to handle it in a way that will bring Glory to Your name."

He grunted goodbye to his friends and slipped into his newly purchased 1961 baby-blue Comet station wagon.

Ferrie's orders were to drive straightaway to Houston. In other circumstances, he would have flown himself to Houston, but he'd been directed to go by car. A private, unscheduled plane flying late at night into Texas the night of the assassination could have drawn attention.

However, he was prepared to do some flying later in the weekend. A de Havilland Dove—a rugged, twin-engine British monoplane—had been positioned at Scholes Field on Galveston Island, ready for him to fly an escape mission south to Guatemala on Saturday or Sunday, if necessary. But whether this would be necessary was still unclear. Based on the public reports, only Lee Oswald had been arrested. That Oswald, a callow young man with aimless ambition, was arrested wasn't a surprise. But there still was no news about the second shooter.

While most of the country was glued to the unprecedented wall-to-wall television news coverage and beginning to mourn the death of the young president, Ferrie was about to take a nerve-racking, 358-mile drive across the countryside of western Louisiana and East Texas to Houston through a pounding rainstorm. He had no confidence he'd get back to New Orleans alive. They might silence him as they were planning to do with Oswald.

Ferrie didn't make this trip alone. He wanted traveling companions, for company to be sure, but also so they could bring his

Comet station wagon back to New Orleans, were he called on to leave Texas by air.

But most important, his companions would corroborate his cover story for this odd trip, "if slap comes to tickle," he told them. They didn't know the real purpose of the trip, but they knew Ferrie did a lot of unusual and confidential jobs for the local mob. They were used to memorizing cover stories when they went on adventures with him.

On his way home from the Monteleone, Ferrie thus had had the cab backtrack and pick up twenty-four-year-old Alvin Beauboeuf, his closest heterosexual friend, in front of Joseph Kohn Middle School, which was near Al's home on Alvar Street and not far from the historic and creepy St. Vincent de Paul Cemetery. Al had roomed in the past with him.

From Louisiana Avenue Parkway, Ferrie and Al drove to pick up another buddy, Melvin Coffey. Ferrie had known Melvin for almost ten years and spent time with him several times a week. At Melvin's place on North Pierce, also not far from a well-known New Orleans cemetery, St. Louis No. 3, he turned on the TV to check on the latest news from Dallas.

This was a long-planned trip mixing business and pleasure, Al and Melvin would say. They were getting out of town to relax by hunting, fishing, and drinking. They were also going to take a look at a Houston ice-skating rink. The unlikely premise for looking at the rink was that Ferrie was considering buying it. He needed something to do after the Marcello trial, and he needed income, the story would go. A man from Houston had told him about this business opportunity.

Ferrie made two calls from Melvin's home phone. First, he called a payphone number at the Winterland Ice Skating Rink in southwest Houston. No answer. He then made a reservation for the three of them at a Houston motel owned by Marcello.

This was all happening at a frenetic and terrifying pace. "I need a bite before we hit the trail," Ferrie declared to his two friends. His favorite restaurant outside the French Quarter was John Paul's, near Moisant Field in Kenner. It catered to pilots. The three had ribeye steaks. Ferrie, smoking a cigarette, talked to a few of the pilots he knew there to get an update on the weather.

The ribeye made him feel more focused and ready to go.

After finishing up with a slice of pecan pie, he announced, *"Laissez le bon temps rouler."*

It wasn't until nine o'clock the night of JFK's assassination that Ferrie and his two friends left the environs of New Orleans for Houston. They took US 90, first heading south to Houma and then northwest to Lafayette. At Lafayette, Route 90 turns due west toward Texas, passing through the southern part of Acadia Parish near Evangeline and directly through the last city of any size before Beaumont, Texas—Lake Charles. The streaking Comet was battered by rain and, when there was a break in the rain, by bugs on the windshield. Al sat in the passenger seat. Melvin was in the back seat, sipping rye whiskey.

At Lake Charles the three men stopped to gas up and use the bathroom at a service station.

"Al?" Melvin asked. "Don't you know a good-time gal here?"

"Shit, you're right. Dave, can we stop for fifteen minutes?"

"Fuck no. Keep your scummy pants on, Casanova. I'm screwed if we don't get our asses to Houston ASAP."

They juddered into Texas and made it to Houston at 3:15 a.m., driving straight to the Winterland Ice Skating Rink.

Winterland was a popular landmark in southwest Houston. It was just two miles south of the exclusive River Oaks neighborhood, home to wealthy Texas oil men like W. Howard Lee and Oscar Wyatt, who, along with their peers in Dallas, were the de facto governors of the state. Winterland was housed in a huge building with a giant pair of skates encased in cement out front. Buzzing with activity during the day, it was quiet and lifeless in the middle of the night. Ferrie stepped out of the car, crunching the gravel as he walked past the cemented skates.

"What the fuck are you doing?" Al complained. "I'm beat, let's go to the motel. There ain't nobody here."

Al and Melvin didn't know, but Ferrie had to make absolutely sure that nobody was there. He jiggled the large handle on the front door. Locked. He walked the entire perimeter of the facility. Nobody around. *Maybe our second shooter was hiding out somewhere until tomorrow,* he imagined. They'd come back to the rink later in the day.

Ferrie then made several calls from the outdoor payphone at Winterland. The first call was to Gill. Gill and Banister were still awake in Gill's large office in the Pere Marquette Building, awaiting his call and nervously drinking too much Old Taylor bourbon.

"Keep checking the rink tomorrow as you meet with Rolland," Gill said. "And go ahead and pull the trigger with Ruby. So to speak."

"I already talked to him briefly from the Monteleone but'll call him again in a few minutes and talk in more detail."

"Remind him of your conversation in October in Dallas. You know, about his sister and his fucking dog."

"I bet he brings it up first."

Ferrie pushed the hook switch down, slipped in a few more dimes, and dialed the Carousel Club in Dallas. Jack Ruby owned and operated this second-tier burlesque and strip club, though it was ultimately controlled by Marcello. Ruby would be at the club even though it was approaching four in the morning and even though it was closed for the weekend because of the assassination.

Funny I've just driven from the Carousel Bar and now I'm calling the Carousel Club, Ferrie thought to himself.

A crusty-voiced man named Larry picked up the phone, sounding surprised that someone was calling so late. Larry Crafard, a former carny, worked as a jack-of-all-trades for Ruby.

"Jesus Beverly Christ, who's calling at this hour?" Larry crackled.

"None of your goddamn business," Ferrie said. "Need to talk to Jack."

Ruby walked into his office from the dim bar to get the phone.

"Hey, Jack, we told you the Oswald plan would work."

"Schmuck got caught, though," Ruby responded. "Now it's fuck-me time—you sure we have to do this?"

"Everything'll be fine. Everyone wants Oswald dead. You got the seven grand from Jones, right?"

"Yeah. That'll get the IRS off my *tuchus*. Not that it'll matter if I'm fried."

"They'll really call you Sparky then." Ruby's nickname, which had followed him around since childhood, was *Sparky*. It annoyed him.

"Asshole."

"You ready to go?"

"I guess. I went over to the cop station tonight to see how hard it was to get in. They just waved me in. Every cub reporter on the planet was in the building, roaming about anywhere they wanted to. They brought Oswald right out in the goddamn hallway on the third floor and then again in the basement. Hard to believe, even for Texas."

"Good you can get in so easily."

"I can get in, no problem—every cop there knows me. But letting all those reporters in? And parading Oswald around like he'd just won best in show? You goddamn got me. Shit, I even brought my gun, made sure I could get in with that."

"Gill wants it done before they transfer Oswald to the county jail," Ferrie instructed Ruby.

"Just promise me again that Eva and Sheba will be okay. Please, Dave—my old friend."

Ruby was a surprisingly emotional guy for a small-time gangster and strip-club operator.

"Of course—as long as you just take this one for the team, Jack. Marcello's word is gold, he won't let you go down. And you know I'd never screw you after all we've been through. Key West. Cuba. Jacksboro Highway. The Egyptian Lounge. *Jada*."

"Yeah. I know I got no choice. I've already felt out my main guy about the transfer. Sergeant Dean. Just keep your eyes on the boob tube."

Ruby hung up. *Oswald has to be silenced soon,* Ferrie thought, *before he wises up and figures out he's been set up. He's already telling the world he's a patsy.*

The boys finally checked into Marcello's Alamotel, room 19, several miles away on South Main. The motel had a geographically inaccurate slogan: "Remember the Alamo-TEL!"

"We're sleeping till the crack of noon, boys," Ferrie said.

After sleeping in Ferrie made several calls from the motel, two to friends he knew at New Orleans radio stations—WDSH and WSHO—to see what they knew about the assassination. They knew nothing he didn't know. And one call to the Town and Country Motel to ask the same question of Marcello's brother Anthony, who ran the motel. Same answer.

Ferrie then knelt and recited David's plea for mercy in Psalm 51, the "Miserere."

"Have mercy on me, God, according to thy lovingkindness: according unto the multitude of thy tender mercies blot out my transgressions. Wash me thoroughly from mine iniquity, and cleanse me from my sin." Feeling cleansed, he gathered up the boys.

They spent Saturday afternoon at the rink, mainly hanging around and waiting. In support of the cover story for the trip, Ferrie spoke a couple of times to the manager, Chuck Rolland, about the financial costs of operating the rink. He told Rolland he was interested in buying the place but needed to do his due diligence. He also spent more time on the rink's payphone. One of the calls was to follow up with Ruby. He also checked in with Gill.

He and his buddies didn't skate. The second shooter never appeared at the rink.

Because the second shooter was a no-show, there was no need to go to Galveston to fly him out of the country. Ferrie had been told to leave the de Havilland Dove there if he didn't need it that weekend. It would be picked up by another Marcello pilot after things had cooled down in Texas.

But he'd promised Galveston to the guys. Al and Melvin had never been to this decadent, not-very-nice beach town. So, they still went, driving the fifty miles southeast Saturday evening, with a brief sightseeing stop at NASA's Manned Space Center requested by Melvin.

They roamed around waterfront bars Ferrie knew from earlier visits while flying for Eastern Air Lines, though there were few revelers out and about on that sad night. The three men each slept well, lulled by the waves crashing against the seawall by their motel, the Driftwood. In the morning, they headed back to Louisiana.

Ferrie's decision to go on to Galveston was also prompted by news Gill had passed on to him through the Winterland payphone. His fellow Marcello foot soldier and amateur detective—the seamy Jack Martin—had disclosed to the FBI, Gill said, that Ferrie knew Oswald and had spent considerable time with him the previous summer. He also said that Martin was circulating a false story around New Orleans that Ferrie's Tulane University library card was found on Oswald by the Dallas police.

And a startling story was starting to spread around the Quarter, Gill had revealed, that Ferrie had hypnotized Oswald to shoot Kennedy. Gill didn't know where that story was coming from. Probably from one of Ferrie's young male acquaintances.

Gill had advised Ferrie to take his time getting home.

\|\|\|

When Ferrie finally returned to New Orleans a few days later, he became the first person to be arrested as a suspected conspirator in the assassination of JFK. Though the evidence against him was too thin to hold him at that time, he came under sharper suspicion toward the end of the remaining thirty-nine months of his life. Just days before he was to be rearrested in February 1967 for JFK's murder, Ferrie was found dead in his apartment. He was wearing what appeared to be a white shroud, grasping a plain olive-wood crucifix.

INTRODUCTION

Dave Ferrie was only thirty-two-years-old when he landed in New Orleans in 1951, but he'd already had a lifetime of experiences.

From an early age in his hometown of Cleveland, Ohio, Ferrie began to display an energetic tangle of remarkable characteristics—a conspicuous intellect, a sharp memory, an endless curiosity about all things scientific and historic. By the age of eight, he could read music. He learned how to hypnotize people at ten, spoke decent French and Spanish by twelve. His fertile mind soaked in information "like a lost Arab sucked in water at an oasis," his mother Burdette often said. "A true polymath," his father James would say.

A profound commitment to religion filled him around the time he hit puberty, inspired by Burdette, who was a devout Catholic. The Ferries were "Black Irish" Catholics—"Black Irish" because they had dark rather than the more traditional pale complexions of the Irish. He attended an all-male Jesuit high school, Saint Ignatius, on West 30th Street in the Ohio City section of Cleveland. By the time he entered Saint Ignatius, Catholicism was the guiding light in young Ferrie's life. He set a goal to become a priest.

After high school Ferrie enrolled in a Jesuit college, John Carroll University. But after two rocky years—he was a champion debater and wrote for the school newspaper there but, at the same time, "wants attention and distinction," was "lacking in common sense," and was "hard to direct or control"—he switched to a seminary to pursue his great ambition. He chose Saint

Mary Seminary in East Cleveland, six miles from John Carroll. By Rockefeller Park. Archbishop Edward Hoban, who oversaw Saint Mary as Coadjutor Bishop of Cleveland, was immediately impressed by the depth and sincerity of Ferrie's faith. But, over time, the archbishop became concerned about him, for he was displaying some unwelcome characteristics.

First, Ferrie was experiencing homosexual urges. These had creeped up on him during his time at Saint Ignatius and grown stronger at John Carroll and at seminary. He had confessed this sin to a priest at the seminary. While he restrained himself on most occasions, he had several casual encounters with fellow students that were discovered by teachers.

At the same time, he'd become increasingly hyperactive and anxious. Vibrant though relatively calm as a kid, his mind began to run faster and faster in late adolescence. *Maybe it was the way the frontal lobe in his brain had finally formed,* he wondered. *Or maybe his neurotransmissions were out of balance.* Whatever the reason, thoughts constantly ricocheting around his head, he grew perpetually restless by the time he entered Saint Mary. This condition, which never left him during the rest of his time on Earth, exploded into irrationally impulsive acts during periodic times of sharp stress.

And, though he could feel his brainpower continuing to swell, he also began worrying incessantly, particularly about his health. Seemingly out of nowhere, he became convinced that cancer cells were running around his body.

After two years Archbishop Hoban dismissed Ferrie, deciding that he didn't have the correct temperament to become a priest nor the ability to comply with the church's moral code.

Ferrie took a break from his religious studies to finish his college degree, earning a BA in philosophy from Baldwin-Wallace College, which was close to his family home, while also student-teaching at nearby Rocky River High School, close to Lake Erie. With a college degree in his pocket, he reentered seminary, this time Saint Charles Seminary in Carthagena, near the Indiana border.

Saint Charles had been founded in 1861 by a conservative Catholic sect called the "Missionaries of the Precious Blood." This small sect, formed at the direction of Pope Pius VII in 1814 to inject more spiritualism into the church, focused on devotional study, asceticism, and good works. Ferrie excelled at studying and was admired for his intellect. He also performed good works. But Ferrie eventually was asked to leave there for reasons similar to those that drove him from Saint Mary, doubts that he'd be able to live a holy, much less an ascetic, lifestyle. He also was found lacking in humility, a cardinal trait of these "Missionaries."

Deeply depressed that his goal of becoming a priest had been dealt an apparent fatal blow, Ferrie impulsively took a grave step—he attempted suicide, a clumsy but genuine attempt at hanging himself.

After a few days of emergency treatment, Ferrie hyperactivity began to slowly kick back in. But he remained gloomy and anxious, and the several years of mental pressures were taking a toll. By his twenties the rare disease of alopecia universalis, which is triggered by stress, had seized his body. His immune system attacked his hair follicles. He was rendered bald in all places where hair was supposed to grow. He compensated by wearing toupees and wigs—and fake eyebrows, which were often the first thing people noticed, depending on the care he took in attaching them on any given day.

\\\\

Though Ferrie never officially entered the priesthood, he believed in his heart of hearts that he'd earned and deserved the status of a priest. He kept the robes and priestly accoutrements he'd been given at Saint Charles. He began conducting masses for small groups of believers.

\\\\

James Howard Ferrie was a respected public servant in Cleveland. He'd worked his way up from patrolman to captain and then chief of detectives in the Cleveland Police Department. At the same time, Mr. Ferrie had also earned a law degree, and his father and brother were public servants as well, high-ranking members of the Cleveland Fire Department. As part of the successful Ferrie clan, Dave Ferrie was expected to do well and serve the public.

But James Ferrie knew his son was different from the rest of the family in numerous ways and wasn't cut out for a life of public service. He loved the boy, though, and wanted him to be happy and engaged.

The Ferrie family had lived at 17302 Laverne Avenue in the West Park area of southwest Cleveland since 1928—a mile and a half from Cleveland Hopkins Airport. As a teenager Dave Ferrie spent many hours watching landings and take offs at the airport. He'd long been fascinated with planes and flying.

To direct him away from his continuing despondency after Saint Charles and the suicide attempt, his father set his son up to take flying lessons at Sky Tech Airway Service at Hopkins.

Ferrie was immediately facile as a pilot, and flying became an obsession. He earned his pilot license the day after the Fat Man atomic bomb was dropped on Nagasaki, Japan, ending World War II.

As his father had sought, the endeavor of flying would keep depression at bay for most of Ferrie's life.

He soon began teaching students himself. He got a part-time job teaching aeronautics at the all-Catholic Benedictine High School, about ten miles away in East Cleveland. In 1947 he became an effective and well-regarded instructor of Civil Air Patrol cadets—young wannabe pilots. Some of his Benedictine students participated. Ferrie was surprisingly effective. A local aviatrix named Jean Naatz said that he did "more for the Civil Air Patrol than anyone else had for many years." He was "an excellent pilot." She also observed that he "had an extremely high IQ and could almost be described as a genius."

To support this new vocation, James Ferrie bought his son a seventy-five-horsepower, blue-and-white Stinson 105 monoplane, a nifty little airship with a range of 350 miles.

Ferrie's young students included earnest pilots-to-be, such as sixteen-year-old future moonwalker Neil Armstrong, whom he worked with at a grass airfield near Wapakoneta, an Ohio CAP landing site, using an Aeronca Champ, a light monoplane made in nearby Hamilton. Ferrie's serious students, though, weren't as much fun for Ferrie as the many convivial rakes he had, boys who wanted to be pilots just to be cool and get girls. He began hanging out with some of the convivial boys, including twenty-year-old James Lewallen, whom he'd reconnect with in the early sixties in New Orleans.

Ferrie was familiar with the seedier sides of Cleveland, having found various places to indulge his escalating sexual fancies. One night in 1949, he took some of the good-time Charlies out on the town. After a few too many rounds of Carling Black Labels, the boys announced they wanted girls. Though not *his* thing, he knew where to take them.

News of the boys going to houses of prostitution soon found its way back to their parents. Ferrie was kicked out of the Ohio CAP and ostracized by his new friends at Hopkins. To stave off another serious bout of depression, he decided to seek out other cities in other states to do his flying and teaching, places that may be less interested in the private lives of their pilots and CAP instructors.

He decided to head south. Southerners, he'd heard, though holding traditional values, were hospitable, reverent, and politely restrained.

||||

At the large Streamline Moderne Greyhound station on Chester Avenue in Cleveland, the first southbound bus he found was heading to Tampa, Florida. Tampa sounded like a nice place to Ferrie. It had a pleasant subtropical climate, a solid economy, two airports, an air force base—and was just twenty-five miles from festive Gulf of Mexico beaches. He decided to give it a go. He got a job in Tampa without much effort as an insurance examiner. This mundane-sounding job was surprisingly interesting to Ferrie and taught him sleuthing skills that would come in handy later in his life.

Tampa at the time was a buzzing hive of organized crime activity, led by both Santo Trafficante Senior *and* Junior. The mob's Tampa headquarters were in a part of the area called Ybor City. Ferrie soon discovered Ybor City. An ethnically-mixed area, with grand social clubs established by workers brought to town in the late nineteenth century to work in Tampa's Cuban-cigar industry, Ybor City was more interesting to Ferrie than downtown Tampa, Clearwater, or St. Petersburg, which were whitebread and unimaginative though much more upscale.

Mob activities began in Ybor City for expected reasons in the 1920s, to provide the many immigrants with prohibited alcohol, but they were later fueled by the incentive to control the ubiquitous "bolito" establishments around the city. Bolito was an immensely popular working-class lottery game, using one hundred numbered balls mixed in a bag and then selected by players. Rival mobsters fought fiercely in the 1930s to control this industry, with Trafficante Senior winning out during World War II over Anglo and Italian competitors. From there the Trafficante empire boomed.

Ferrie began hanging out at the Yellow House and Dream Bars, each of which ran mob-sanctioned bolito games. He made acquaintances at those Ybor City establishments that led to some minor investigating assignments for the Trafficante family, including looking into places with *un*sanctioned bolito games. His brainpower became readily apparent to the organization. He was asked to undertake research on Cuban politics for Trafficante Junior, who'd gotten a bug about Cuba. Inspired by the Cuba connection to Ybor City, Trafficante Junior became intensely interested in doing business in Havana. One opportunity quickly seemed obvious—reviving and dilating the fledgling gambling industry there, like the Chicago mob was doing in Las Vegas.

He'd met several times in 1948 over in Daytona Beach with the exiled former president of Cuba, Fulgencio Batista, who was plotting a return to Cuba. Trafficante Junior offered to help, in return for Batista's support of his possible future business activity in Cuba. Informational briefings prepared by Ferrie aided these efforts.

Ferrie came to respect what he viewed as the mob's underlying commitment to family, colleagues, and order. And its acute anti-Communism, fueled by the Cold War, connected particularly strongly with him. Communism was anathema to Catholicism because of its atheism, rejection of private property, and violation of subsidiarity. Popes had expressly condemned this socialistic philosophy since the *Rerum Novarum* in 1891.

In Ferrie's uniquely wired mind, the mob's tendencies toward violence could be justified in many cases by its commitment to the community and the common man.

He was developing a "just war" philosophy, similar to beliefs held by many conservative Catholics, including many of his teachers at Saint Charles Seminary. He discovered and came to revere *The City of God* by Saint Augustine of Hippo. Saint Augustine wrote that "wise men" on the Earth sometimes had to "wage Just Wars" in order to vanquish the Devil and gain citizenship in the City of God. Perfection didn't exist on Earth, so "Just Wars" were allowed where necessary to avoid "unjust wars." Violence was justified by God in certain cases, he understood Saint Augustine to say, such as to respond to past or present aggression and to restore order and property.

These words of Saint Augustine resonated with him:

> Christ's servants, whether they are kings, or princes, or judges, or soldiers, or provincials, whether rich or poor, freeman or slaves, men or women, are bidden, if need be, to endure the wickedness of an utterly corrupt state, and by that endurance to win for themselves a place of glory.

Ferrie returned to Cleveland when he learned his father was dying. His father's death laid him low. In a rush to chart a new course focused on flying, he turned to the US Air Force. Joining quickly became an urgent obsession. He could get away from Cleveland and spend his time flying—and, at the same time, be a warrior in the Cold War. Flushed with this new ambition, he impetuously wrote President Truman's Commander of the First Air Force, resident at Mitchel Field, trying to impress him with exuberance and tough talk.

"There is nothing I would enjoy better than blowing the hell out of every damn Russian Communist, Red, or what have you. We can cook up a crew that will really bomb them to hell. I want to train killers, however bad that sounds. *It is what we need.*"

With the Korean War approaching, the Air Force needed pilots. But not so badly that it would accept Ferrie after this batty letter. While his language was exaggerated, it did reflect how his exposure to the Tampa mob and his continuing study of Catholicism had changed him.

Dejected but still looking for another way into the world of aviation, Ferrie applied to Eastern Air Lines' training program. With so many experienced pilots going into the Air Force, there was a shortage of pilots available for Eastern. With its standards bent to capture more applicants, Eastern accepted him into its program.

He performed adequately in Eastern's program, though things didn't always go smoothly. His piloting skills were good, but he wasn't as disciplined as the trainers would have liked. "He has a tendency to talk his way through flight school rather than follow the procedures," one trainer wrote. Another said Ferrie could be "odd at times." Where he stood out was in the non-flying parts of the program, particularly public speaking and customer relations, relying on skills he'd developed practicing to be a priest. Eastern wanted its pilots to be well-rounded and capable of involvement in community affairs and communicating facilely with passengers.

Ferrie got his wings.

He was assigned to the newly-named LaGuardia Airport in New York City, but he'd become enamored of the South and requested reassignment there. Eastern happened to have a slot open in New Orleans, and they offered it to Ferrie.

Pleased with this assignment, he flew his Stinson 105 monoplane down to New Orleans's elegant Lakefront Airport, which jutted out into the estuary known as Lake Ponchartrain, resting on six million cubic feet of landfill.

His start as a pilot for Eastern in New Orleans was successful. In particular, he proved to be a team player by speaking to civic groups and at travel agency events on behalf of the airline. His good work was reported up the Eastern corporate chain. At the same time, background checks had uncovered troublesome evidence of some of his irregular lifestyle choices. But the good outweighed the bad for Eastern, at least at that time. He was fully embraced by the company.

On May 23, 1953, the president of the airline—the famous World War I flying ace Eddie Rickenbacker—sent Ferrie a glowing letter of commendation. Rickenbacker had reviewed Ferrie's file, as was his custom with all new pilots. The reports on Ferrie's technical capabilities as a pilot were positive, but the Eastern investigators noted in some detail his personal defects and strange habits.

On his copy of the letter to Ferrie, Rickenbacker wrote, "This man bears watching."

CHAPTER 1

"**D**ave, whatcha doing?"

"Napping on the couch."

"Right. You won't even nap when you're dead."

"Won't need to sleep in Heaven. You know—all that holy energy."

"We'll see."

"What's up, Dutz?" It was unusual for Dutz to call Ferrie.

"Just wondering if you're coming over to the Quarter tonight. I'd like to talk to you about something."

Dutz Murret ran a gambling club in the French Quarter for New Orleans mob boss Carlos Marcello. Ferrie was an occasional player at the club, favoring games of the mind, like five-card stud, over games of chance, like roulette.

"Sure. I'm meeting a guy at the 500 Club at ten. I can swing by before then."

New Orleans had proved the optimal place for Ferrie to start a new life and put his depressive troubles behind him. The city was tolerant, friendly, fun. Life was musical. A hundred years before he took up residence there, the *Daily Picayune* summarized the New Orleans heartbeat—"Everyone in this good city enjoys the full right to pursue his own inclinations in all reasonable, and unreasonable, ways." The DNA of New Orleans was reflected in many of its large gaggle of nicknames. The Big *Easy*. The Land of *Dreams. Story*ville.

The City that Care Forgot.

The sobriquet the *Crescent City* not only derives from the graceful curve in the Mississippi River that borders the French

Quarter but also from the sensation that surrounds "crescent moons." For centuries, a crescent moon caused joy and a sense of adventure, for it was the first step from new moon to full moon. It heralded the birth of new light in the sky. It was greeted, not uncommonly, with irrational celebration.

"The thing about this town," Ferrie observed to a friend and colleague eight years later, *"the craziest things make perfect sense."*

\\\\

It was May 13, 1955, Friday the thirteenth, when Dutz called. Ferrie was in the middle of celebrating mass in his apartment. There were only five members of his flock present, a mishmash of sinners and outcasts, but he was in full priestly regalia. A purple cassock with a white apron and white sleeves adorned his body. A triple-peaked biretta, also purple, rested on his reddish wig.

He had erected a small mahogany altar in his cramped apartment, in front of a dark curtain with a large crucifix pinned to it. A credence table, with a chalice and a paten perched on top, sat nearby. Two thuribles burned incense.

On this day Ferrie's mass focused on the Catholic teaching of salvation through good works.

Focusing on the crucifix, Ferrie fiddled with his rosaries, respectfully bowed his head, and genuflected. He then turned to face his flock.

"It's not enough simply to say 'I believe' and then go home and do nothing," he preached. "The Bible, in Matthew seven, verse twenty-one, says, 'Not everyone that saith unto me, Lord, Lord, shall enter the Kingdom of Heaven; but he that doeth the will of my Father which is in heaven.'"

He spoke of the good-works project he'd committed himself to. "My friends, here's my testimony.

"I'm taking a philosophy course at Tulane. My professor mentioned that experiments on the brain were being done at the Medical School by a doctor there named Heath.

"My curiosity was piqued. I went over there. From the observation deck, you could see men, prisoners from the state mental health hospital, hooked up to wires and electrodes." Ferrie's voice softened. "They seemed groggy, probably drugged.

"A famous cancer doctor named Alton Ochsner—you've probably heard of his hospital and clinic—was watching as well," he continued. "He and I spoke at some length. I could feel something special about him. He has an aura, a kind of godly aura. He talked about his quest to cure cancer in a penetrating way that touched me deeply."

Dr. Ochsner played in the big leagues in New Orleans. He'd once been given the highest honor the city bestowed—Rex, King of Carnival—and was well-connected around the rest of the country and in Latin America. He worked resolutely and genuinely for the poor. He'd gained international fame by being the first person to link smoking tobacco to lung cancer.

A renowned surgery professor at Tulane University and New Orleans Charity Hospital, Dr. Ochsner and four cofounders opened a clinic in 1942, modeled on the Cleveland and Mayo Clinics, on Prytania Street in the Touro section of uptown New Orleans. They formed the Ochsner Medical Foundation a few years later. A year before this sermon, the Foundation had added a new five-story hospital on Jefferson Highway near the Mississippi River, six and half miles from the French Quarter. This sparkling facility—called the Ochsner Foundation Hospital—brought state-of-the-art medical technology on a large scale to New Orleans for the first time. With this resource, coupled with the Ochsner Clinic on Prytania, the city and Dr. Ochsner were able to recruit high-flying young doctors from around the country, including Dr. Mary Sherman, who would later play an important role in Ferrie's life.

"Dr. Ochsner's mission in life is curing cancer, which he believes is an earthly embodiment of Satan's evil. Ever since God banished him from heaven, Satan—Lucifer—has been trying to destroy mankind, the children of God. God, we know, will eventually be victorious in His eons-long battle with evil when

Jesus returns, but until then we need to fight Satan where we can. That is what Dr. Ochsner's doing. It's what we all must do.

"I believe I myself have had cancer. But God, the Almighty, so far has kept me safe. To honor Him, I've committed—like Dr. Ochsner—to try to find a cure for cancer. In any way I can. Playing a small part in this journey will be my salvation.

"Find *your* path to salvation," Ferrie implored his handful of congregants.

"Go forth, my brothers and sisters. And look around you. See the trees, the rivers, the stars. In each and every one of these, you can see the Master's hand. God is immanent in this world. Bless you all."

As was his custom, he ended the mass in Latin.

"*Ite, missa est.*"

The small flock responded in unison, "*Deo gratias.*"

Ferrie shook their hands as they left his apartment.

His homily about his personal mission to cure cancer was true. He spent many hours of his off-duty time mixing chemicals in beakers, dissecting white mice, weighing and examining extracted tumors, and studying cuts of tissue under microscopes. He would identify abnormal cells and tissues and test various solutions on them.

He had read volumes and volumes on oncology, on cell growth and mutation, and on viruses that may cause cancer. He followed scientific journals, particularly from the National Cancer Institute, and the ongoing work of cancer scientists, especially Sydney Farber, who was doing groundbreaking work on childhood leukemia and working on a new treatment process called *chemotherapy*. His amateur research efforts thus were not clueless, though hardly likely to generate any real advances in the science.

Ferrie lived in Jefferson Parish, just above River Road—ten miles west of the French Quarter—in one of four small apartments in the cream-colored stucco house at 209 Vinet Avenue, a one-story house that sat sideways on its lot, the four apartment doors facing the side of the house at 211 Vinet. It had a good-sized backyard.

This was a tightly knit neighborhood in the mid-1950s. The residents informally referred to it as "West Jefferson." The same families had lived there for several generations. The houses weren't big or expensive, but the neighborhood was well-kept and safe.

Jefferson Park was nearby, and Dr. Bloom's innovative Magnolia School to the south near the river was a shining example of how to train disabled citizens to lead productive lives. Getting to downtown New Orleans was easy on public transportation.

Ferrie had become a well-known figure in West Jefferson. Physically, he was hard to miss. As a commercial airline pilot, he'd developed an erect posture, which made his head of faux auburn hair and patchy eyebrows even more noticeable. Just knocking around the neighborhood on a day off, he often applied his wig and eyebrows with little care, which sometimes made him look more like a Mardi Gras reveler than an off-duty pilot. In his worst moments, he looked like he'd adhered tufts of carpet to his head and brow.

Notwithstanding his occasionally peculiar appearance, the neighbors enjoyed Ferrie's company. He was friendly. And, given his unnaturally broad range of knowledge and interests, he was always engaging. His job as an Eastern Air Lines pilot seemed exotic.

He volunteered to mentor teenagers interested in flying and had helped expand the local Civil Air Patrol in New Orleans. Serving first as commander of the CAP unit at Lakefront Airport on Lake Pontchartrain, he was now training students at the closer Moisant Field in Kenner. He'd successfully recruited a number of boys from the neighborhood into the CAP program.

Neither his neighbors nor the New Orleans CAP knew about Ferrie's past problems with the Cleveland CAP.

The neighbors *were* aware of Ferrie's deep religious convictions and his amateur masses. His readily-apparent and vigorous conservative Catholicism was a concern for a few in the neighborhood, which predominantly was made up of Huguenot descendants, but most saw his spiritual side as a good thing.

His annual trips to local hospitals to deliver toys to sick children at Christmastime were well-known and respected in the neighborhood. He planned to go to the new Crippled Children's Hospital that year to do the same. He was also known to volunteer time at Loyola University's Holy Name of Jesus Church, by Audubon Park. Ferrie enjoyed working with the nuns there— and always marveled at the divinely carved, Carrara marble alter, which, emblematic of New Orleans, had been paid for early in the century by a local brewer.

Neighbors also were impressed with his talk of earning a PhD in psychology from a school in Italy and eventually becoming a social worker or counselor after his pilot days. They liked the fact he spoke to civic groups.

The chink in Ferrie's relationship with his neighbors was the junky condition of his residence. Outside the front door of his Vinet Avenue apartment, along the side path, there often were unusable tools, buckets, and trash. His part of the shared backyard resembled a landfill, usually containing rusty cages, burned-out appliances, an ancient grill, and more trash. At times, there'd be a mangy-looking monkey in one of the rusty cages. Unpleasant odors radiated from inside the house, caused by smelly laboratory mice and old cigarette butts. The few neighbors who'd been inside were taken aback by what they saw. Wall-to-wall clutter. Not just mice and cigarettes but also beakers, syringes, test tubes, books, dirty dishes, religious paraphernalia, maps, flight manuals, all manner of old furniture.

Though he was a likable neighbor in other ways, most adults went out of their way to avoid getting too close to his residence. His crazy array of interests and darting mind had proven to be too inconsistent with good housekeeping.

Neighborhood teens, on the other hand, were drawn to him and his unusual experiments. Although he focused mainly on laboratory mice and an occasional monkey, the neighborhood boys would bring him stray dogs and wild animals to work on.

\\\\\

Later on that warm and partly cloudy May day, after cleaning up from his mass, Ferrie left his apartment for the French Quarter. He walked up Vinet toward Jefferson Highway to catch a Tulane bus to Canal Street. Neighbor Earline Chaix was walking the other way toward the Magnolia School. Mrs. Chaix was always pleasant to him.

"Where you headin' Cap'n Ferrie?" she kindly asked.

"Greetings, ma'am. I'm heading out to Moisant Field. I'm training twenty cadets now. Have some really good ones."

"Good for you. You're doing God's work, keeping those boys off the streets and giving them useful things to do. Just be careful."

"Yes, ma'am."

"I hear you're speaking at the Ladies Day lunch."

"Looking forward to it. Roosevelt Hotel, a month from today."

"I'll be there."

"Excellent. You have a good day."

Ferrie didn't want to tell her where he was *really* going—the French Quarter, to a gambling joint to meet a mob operative and then to a burlesque club to meet a fellow homosexual.

He bought a NOPSI ticket for seven cents and boarded an eastbound bus, which bumped along Jefferson Highway past the 1838 Greek revival Rosedale house and then followed Claiborne Avenue to Canal Street. Ferrie jumped down to terra firma there, trolleyed down Canal to Burgundy, and zig-zagged through the Quarter to Dutz's place of business.

The Lomalinda, near the Hotel Monteleone, was one of several gambling establishments controlled by Carlos Marcello. This particular club's daily operation was managed by Charles "Dutz" Murret, a former local sports star and current part-time criminal. He ran a couple of small handbooks, where racing bets were taken, for Marcello—at 128 Chartres Street and 837 Iberville—but the Lomalinda was his big ticket.

Dutz was fifty-four, athletic-looking, and good natured. As a young man, he'd been a professional boxer. After a short-lived boxing career, he became a manager for a number of well-known local boxers, including the spunky Hill brothers—Red and Louis. It was during this time that Dutz became involved with the New Orleans mob.

Athleticism ran in Dutz's family. His son "Boogie" played outfield for two years in the St. Louis Cardinals organization. His daughter Joyce married the captain of the Tulane football team. Dutz periodically still tried to help out and promote young, promising boxers.

An active Catholic like Ferrie, he'd been happily married for many years to the former Lillian Claverie. Lillian, the daughter of a streetcar conductor whose mother had died when Lillian was young, grew up in New Orleans. She had one sister, a difficult woman named Marguerite.

In contrast to Lillian's single, long marriage, Marguerite had been married three times, the second time to a man named Robert Edward Lee Oswald. She had two children by this man. Her third marriage had ended in a brutal court case.

Dutz worked days as a longshoreman with the Checkers' Union Local No. 141B. The Lomalinda was his more lucrative occupation, though. Running an illegal gambling club for the mob paid well but wasn't easy. He had to have financial and managerial skills in addition to serving as a bouncer, peace-maker, and arbiter when customers were unhappy with their luck or had been overserved.

Like numerous other establishments throughout Louisiana, the Lomalinda had illegal slot and pinball machines. It was the illegal distribution of these machines that had made Marcello powerful and wealthy.

The Lomalinda, however, had much more than just slots and pinball machines. Its most popular games were poker, craps, and roulette. The club also offered *vingt-et-un*, a Cajun version of blackjack. As a bow to the storied history of gambling in New Orleans, there was one oval table used for the old French card game *faro* and a more elaborate table used for the game *bagatelle*, a billiards-like game using ivory balls and wooden pins guarding six holes.

With foreign-looking, mustachioed croupiers and filterless Gitanes Brunes for sale, the club had an exotic and mysterious feel.

It hadn't taken long after Ferrie had moved to New Orleans for him to meet Dutz in the whirlwind of the French Quarter. Ferrie had gravitated toward seedy places of entertainment, which, in New Orleans, were often run by the local mob. He and Dutz had many mutual friends.

Dutz greeted him warmly at the front door of the Lomalinda. They sat down with cold Jax beers. Ferrie recognized Dutz's immediate mob boss, Sam Saia, sitting at the bar. Saia, chubby-cheeked and usually ill-humored, watched over the Lomalinda for Marcello and operated the organization's main handbook, located at Felix' Oyster Bar on Iberville Street.

"*C'est bon*," Ferrie said, eyeing his bottle of Jax.

"The best beer on the planet."

"Everything okay with you, Dutz?"

"Splendid. The Marcello guys are good to work for—as long as you don't piss them off."

"I did a little work for the Trafficantes in Tampa a few years ago. They played rough when they needed to, for sure, but they provided a lot of help to the regular Joes over there, including jobs. I was comfortable working for them mainly for that reason."

"Mr. Marcello could probably use a guy like you. But for now, Dave, I'd like to ask a personal favor."

"Fire away."

"It's family stuff. Lillian and I got a nephew, about fifteen or so, who needs some help. Guidance. He's smart—I think he could go somewhere. But he's been royally screwed up by Lillian's sister, who is fucking certifiable. My sister-in-law spends most of her time looking for the next husband. The family's always broke. Kid was born here, but the mother's moved around a lot since then."

"Why do I have a bad feeling about this?"

"No need, just relax. The kid's staying with us for a spell while the mother works some things out. He'd been living at an apartment with his mother above a bar on Exchange Place, not too far from here. Between Canal and Iberville. But that's kind of a rough place for a kid. Was hanging out with some bad hombres."

Exchange Place, created in 1831 as Exchange Passage to facilitate a rear entrance to the Merchant's Exchange at 126 Royal, was always a sketchy part of the Quarter. In the 1800s it was the location of New Orleans's main dueling academies. At the time Oswald lived there, Exchange Place ran rife with low-level mob and gambling activities.

"I'm kind of impressed with the boy," Dutz continued. "And I think you would be too. He reads a lot, works out, seems pretty serious. A bit of a wisenheimer, but he ain't gonna be perfect being raised by that shrew."

"What do you want me to do with this kid?"

"Take him under your flying wing, so to speak. Get him into your boy-scout airplane thing and teach him some discipline— teach him how to be a pilot. I know he'd like that. And I know he'd be serious about it.

"He's desperate to get in the Marines when he turns eighteen and then to get the hell out of Dodge. But that's not going to happen unless he gets some direction."

"I don't need a bad apple in my cadets."

"He's not a bad apple. Not yet anyway. He had a rough spot when he was twelve or thirteen, living in the Bronx. He's been a pretty straight arrow since then, knock on wood, but he's surrounded by trouble."

"The Bronx?"

"His mother dragged the family up to New York City several years ago. She had a son from her first marriage living in the Upper East Side at the time. He told the mother he could get her a job in New York. She went up there, took the family. They lived with this guy, John Pic, and his wife for a bit and then rented a couple apartments in the Bronx, one near Yankee Stadium, one near the zoo. Mrs. Oswald got a job at a place that made hose. She spent most of her time either working or looking for a man. This kid had nobody to make him go to school. The truancy police put him in a juvie hall for a while."

"Did he do bad stuff?"

"Not really, mostly just skipping school. He did one thing that was more funny than bad. He ditched a few days of school and somehow got up to the Canada border and begged his way into Canada so he could see what another country was like. Sounds pretty industrious, right?"

"Debatable."

"The only sorta bad thing he did was take some shots at their apartment building on 179th in the Bronx with a BB gun. No real damage, but the Jew landlord was pissed. I talked to the boy about it later. He said he was just bored. He *did* say he was a great shot."

"Terrific."

"He's a good kid, Dave. The stuff he reads is right up your alley. Philosophers and political shit. He gets along fantastic with my daughter Marilyn. And she's a schoolteacher, doesn't suffer fools. I can guarantee he won't give you any trouble."

"All right, Dutz. Give me a month or so, have him meet me on the tenth at Moisant, at the back hanger. Nine in the morning. What's the kid's name?"

"Lee. Lee Oswald. Named after his late father. Robert E. Lee Oswald. Hopefully, young Lee can live up to that heroic name."

"You mean take up arms against the president?"

"Funny. No. I mean do something honorable, be somebody. By the way, Lee never knew his father. He died before Lee was born. The poor bastard literally was nagged to death by my bitch sister-in-law Marguerite. Literally—*nagged* to death!"

"Sounds like he's better off now."

"No shit.

"*Lee* is a clear, strong name," Dutz continued, "but then they gave him a kooky middle name, *Harvey.* They were probably thinking of the Firestone tycoon who'd just died. But kids used to call him Bugs Bunny because of that name. You know, after the invisible rabbit. From that Jimmy Stewart movie. He hates the name. Don't call him Harvey."

Ferrie left the Lomalinda and headed into the heart of the French Quarter, which had become wondrous, almost sacred ground for Ferrie.

The Quarter was laid out in grids by French royal engineer Adrien de Pauger, on riverfront ground surrounded at that time by cypress swamps, after the Great Hurricane of September 11, 1722. Pauger's *Plan de la Nouvelle Orleans's* detailed sixty-four-block design—covering a half of a square mile—laid out a rectangular pattern surrounding three sides of an open square, a *place d'armes* later named Jackson Square. Because of this plat, the Quarter also came to be known as the "Vieux Carré," the "Old Square." Pauger borrowed the crux of this historic creation from the work his boss Le Blond de la Tour had done for Mobile and Biloxi.

The French Catholics who gradually flowed into the French Quarter in the 1700s were imbued with a joie de vivre not practiced by the Puritans, Quakers, Baptists, or Anglicans in British Colonial America. Many of the new French residents of New Orleans moved over from French-controlled Mobile, bringing the fun of Mardi Gras with them—by the 1730s Mardi Gras was openly celebrated in the Quarter. Though life was difficult on the frontier, a tradition of pleasure, parties, and good food began early in the life of the city.

Spanish control of New Orleans a century later brought raucous fiestas and exotic foods, only embellishing the free and joyous spirit of the locals. Though appropriately called the French Quarter, given its origins, the architecture in the area was distinctly Spanish—Iberian flat-tiled roofs, Mediterranean colors, intricate Moorish-influenced ironwork.

Ferrie walked a block up Iberville and then weaved to the right through the dancing crowds on Bourbon Street, where the pulse of the Quarter bounded. The busy street was named for France's House of Bourbon, just as the alcoholic drink was. There was a rhythm to Bourbon, cacophonous music resounding throughout as usual. Locals and tourists mixed operatically in a sea of aimless jollity. Saints and sinners. Gifted and strangely dressed buskers were on most every corner, some playing music—like Harmonica Slim blowing his Hohner Marine Band—some juggling or telling fortunes. He could see Ruthie the Duck Girl, trailed by several tottering ducks, roller skating across Bourbon on Bienville Street. Banjo Annie waved at her. Higglers all around.

Unique to New Orleans and the French Quarter were impromptu brass band parades. You could turn any corner at any time of day in the Quarter and have a good chance of running into a roving brass band. These bands typically would have a "main line," which was the primary band, playing trumpets, tenor saxophones, and sousaphones. And thumping bass drums. There would be a "second line" behind the "main line" made up of random folks following along, dancing, perhaps twirling an umbrella or waving a handkerchief. In most cases, the "second line" typically would be marching to the beat of a snare drum. An array of other instruments also could be in the "second line," not uncommonly including Irish bagpipes.

Ferrie saw a small band following Ruthie, up Bienville from Chartres Street. He liked marching in night parades like this one but couldn't do so this night.

He met his old friend and former roommate Mike Wakeling at the Sho-Bar on Bourbon, a few doors from the Old Absinthe House. The Sho-Bar, previously known as the "Circus" and then the "Puppy House," was one of the oldest strip clubs in the United States. Of all the strip-burlesque houses in the Quarter, the 500 Club and the Casino Royale were the only peers of the Sho-Bar, though the Old French Opera House was just a notch below in quality. Like these three establishments, the Sho-Bar was ultimately controlled by Carlos Marcello. It was operated by Marcello's one-eyed brother Pete.

This particular night was a big one for the Sho-Bar. Its world-renowned main attraction was the headliner—Blaze Starr. Warming up the crowd in advance was Harold Baptiste's jazz trio. And then Hotsy Totsy, "the Aqua Queen," who stripped in a stage set designed to replicate the Fountain of Youth.

One-eyed Pete Marcello was working the room. He greeted Ferrie.

Both Ferrie and Wakeling were homosexuals, but that made them only more interested in what went on in the Sho-Bar. They loved the whole show—the dancers, the costumes, the music, the corny special effects, the comedians, the singers. The Sho-Bar was always merry. Tonight would be even more special.

After the Aqua Queen's signature act, Lenny Gale performed a hokey comedy routine, and the legendary Lou Norris sang a couple of songs.

Waiting for Blaze Starr to come on, Ferrie said to Wakeling, "I had an interesting meeting with Dutz over at the Lomalinda. He wants me to mentor his nephew. This kid sounds like the kind of young man we could have fun with."

"All right," Wakeling said. "Be careful, though. Dutz comes off as Mr. Nice-ass, but these Marcello guys have a whole other side if you fuck around with them."

"That's CK, baby. I'm not an idiot."

"Jury's out on that. And what's CK?"

"Common Knowledge. You need some CK in life."

Blaze Starr came out to a standing ovation. She had radiant red hair and stunningly jaunty breasts. She was draped in a beaded black lamé gown—Ferrie had heard she made her gowns herself.

Blaze was a natural entertainer, mixing salacious dances with funny, off-color stories.

"She should be ticketed for a moving violation," Ferrie joked.

Blaze began building to her big finish by gracefully tucking a long-stemmed rose between her mesmerizing boobs, leaning back, and blowing the petals slowly and sensually across the vast expanse of her chest.

The big finish that night was her trademark "exploding couch." She became increasingly worked up as she danced. She appeared to get so sexually aroused that she had to stop and lay down on a couch, fanning her face with her right hand. From a device in the couch, smoke began to billow out from between her legs. Then an electric fan blew red paper streamers up from the bottom of the couch. A spotlight climbed up Blaze's legs and stopped just below her waist—it looked like a "blaze" was coming from her crotch. Then the lights faded to darkness.

Ferrie and Wakeling, along with the rest of the crowd, feverishly chanted, "Blaze, Blaze, *Blaze*."

The lights came back up, and Blaze was gone. The show was over.

"Now that's a genuine ecdysiast!" Ferrie shouted to Wakeling over the crowd din.

"You took the word right out of my mouth," Wakeling shouted back.

Ferrie hadn't noticed before, but there was a VIP table close to the stage. Carlos Marcello, wearing sunglasses and a neat business suit, was sitting there with Santo Trafficante. A third man at the table stood up to clap, the man with the godly aura—Dr. Alton Ochsner.

CHAPTER 2

Oswald arrived at the back hangar at Moisant Field in Kenner at 9:00 a.m. sharp on a hot Friday morning. Moisant had replaced the smaller Lakefront Airport in 1946 as the main commercial airport serving the city. Though larger, Moisant lacked Lakefront's class.

"Lee Oswald?"

"Yes, sir."

Ferrie shook Oswald's hand. "Nice to meet you. I'm Dave Ferrie."

They chatted casually, sizing each other up.

Expecting a kid who looked and acted like other kids he'd known who'd lived around Exchange Place, Ferrie was surprised by Oswald. He found a spick-and-span, ruggedly handsome young man, polite and articulate. He had some odd characteristics, though. He wouldn't look you in the eye, he mainly stared at his feet. He spoke in a robotic, monosyllabic way. He seemed devoid of emotion.

Even with his plodding way of speaking, Oswald nevertheless exuded self-confidence, even overconfidence, Ferrie sensed.

\|\|\|

Ferrie showed Oswald around the airport and gave a brief lecture on the person it was named for.

"John Moisant. This guy was an early stunt flyer, had no connection whatsoever to New Orleans except for crashing his plane near this land in 1910. Was trying to win a prize for the longest flight that year. He died on the way to the hospital. Typical Big Easy thing to name something important after someone like that, a fatuous swashbuckler."

The conversation moved quickly to political theory, a keen interest of both of them. Oswald was reading an imposing variety of political philosophers from all over the spectrum, including Proudhon, Marx, Engels, Rousseau, Montesquieu, Paine, Locke, and Camus. He'd read the Federalist Papers. And Ayn Rand. *Interesting guy*, Ferrie thought. *Very interesting.*

Oswald sat in on a lecture Ferrie gave on avionics that day to the Moisant Field CAP squadron. He spoke up several times, asking good questions. Ferrie *was* impressed with Dutz's nephew, at least enough so to sign him up for the full cadet program.

Oswald asked if the program included any firearms training.

"Jesus no, Lee. Guns and flying don't mix, at least not for us civilians. We're not preparing to swoop in and retake Dien Bien Phu. Think discipline and focus."

"Aye-aye, scoutmaster."

"But if you're interested, I can show you some of my own guns. At my apartment."

\|\|\|

Oswald began cadet training a few weeks later. Though Ferrie's squadron was located at Moisant, the new wannabe cadets were trained at Lakefront.

The Lakefront facility was fantastic. The 1934 terminal was the finest Art Deco structure in the South. Eight large Xavier Gonzalez aviation-themed murals decorated the upper floor of the two-story atrium, and the walls were adorned with rose-, cream-, and beige-colored marble paneling. In addition to the Art Deco terminal, there were tennis courts, a swimming pool, and a dance hall. And the complex included hotel rooms and VIP suites. Amelia Earhart had rested in one of the VIP suites on her way to California to kick off her final flight.

Ferrie had moved his Stinson 105 over to Lakefront from Moisant Field for the training. With the money coming in from

Eastern, he'd bought a second plane, a slightly lighter machine known as a Taylorcraft L-2. It was also temporarily docked at Lakefront. He'd eventually return them both to Moisant.

It wasn't a short trip out to Lakefront for either Ferrie or Oswald, but the Lake Forest line eventually got them there.

Oswald began basic cadet training with dedication. He was given a uniform, which he promised to pay for in a week. With help from his Uncle Dutz and his older brother Robert, and with his own paper route, he paid for the uniform on time.

Training meetings happened three times a week. Oswald attended all of them. Ferrie was there for most of them as well, teaching at various times. After two weeks the cadets who had taken the courses and were deemed to have "graduated" to the next level were allowed to actually fly with an instructor. Oswald's short flight around Lake Pontchartrain was with instructor Ferrie.

The next step for the cadets after the introductory flight was a weekend bivouac, to provide some basic training in survival skills such as setting up a camp and building a fire without matches. These basic instructions would help these city boys if they ever had to ditch a plane away from civilization. It also served as a bonding experience for the cadets and their instructors.

Oswald's introductory bivouac was at a place called Abita Springs, a straight shot across Lake Pontchartrain, on a Wednesday in July. Ferrie was able to borrow a car through Dutz, and he picked Oswald up at Moisant. As the crow flies, Abita Springs is only twenty-five miles across the estuary, but a causeway being constructed to span it wasn't quite finished. They thus had to drive sixty-five slow miles around the western side of the lake, across Jones Island, turning east toward Abita Springs at the small city of Ponchatoula. Being confined in the car for so long gave Ferrie and Oswald a couple of hours to chat.

Oswald reeled off the places he'd lived. New Orleans— Pauline, Alvar, Congress, and Bartholomew Streets; Sherwood Forrest Drive. Dallas, Ft. Worth, and Benbrook, Texas.

Covington, Louisiana. Manhattan. The Bronx. Back to New Orleans—French and St. Mary Streets. Exchange Place.

"Quite the ramblin' man. But tell me this—what do you want in life?" Ferrie asked.

"Not much of a clue. Join the Marines, I guess. And I gotta get outta this fucking country, at least for a while. I wanna see other places. I wanna see how other people think, how they live, how they make a living, how they have fun."

"I need to do more of that too."

"You know what Camus said? 'You can't create experience. You must undergo it.'"

"Shit, my cadets are always quoting Camus to me."

"Huh?" Though well-read, Oswald had little sense of humor.

"Forget Camus. What about day-to-day stuff? You got a girlfriend?"

"That's not even on my radar. That gene hasn't kicked in."

"Impressive you know what a gene is."

"Dutz subscribes to *Nature*. I skim some of those journals. Lots of articles lately on DNA."

"The 'double helix.'"

Ferrie smiled as they chugged through Covington and approached Abita Springs. Oswald oddly went stone silent, staring out the window at a rare forest of longleaf pine trees that edged the campsite.

They were the last to arrive. Fifteen or so cadets were putting up tents, and three of Ferrie's fellow instructors were already barking orders. It was August and filthy hot. Most of the group sported white T-shirts and military-looking pants. A few of the instructors wore helmets with insignias to reflect that they were in command.

Ferrie and Oswald immediately joined in the group's activities.

The instructors showed the cadets how to pitch tents and dig latrines. The cadets learned how to make fires without matches, starting with a spindle stick on a natural fireboard. Oswald was a self-assured though clumsy worker.

The cadets were directed to cook chicken and corn on the cob over grills one instructor had brought. Ferrie told some piloting war stories before lights-out.

Ferrie and Oswald shared a tent. "Not a lot of brain power in that group," Oswald condescendingly said. He then dropped off to sleep seconds after hitting the sleeping bag. Ferrie stayed up for a while watching him sleep.

On the drive back, Ferrie asked Oswald about his family. He didn't get along with his mother, he said. As Ferrie had heard from Dutz, and as Oswald confirmed, Mrs. Oswald was selfish and inattentive. She was prone to irrational outbursts and was often frantic and needy, Oswald reported. The only good thing about her was that she wasn't around much.

Oswald related one illustrative family incident from the early 1950s when Lee and Marguerite were living with John Pic and his family in New York City. Mother Marguerite had been having sharp arguments with John's wife Margy, whose mother was the owner of the Pic apartment. One day things reached a boiling point—over which TV program to watch. Marguerite exploded at Margy, threatening violence. Margy responded in kind. Oswald was whittling with a pocket knife at the time and pointed it at Margy, which silenced her. But his mother didn't stop, became dangerously aggressive. He punched her in the face. She fell backward. Oswald waved the knife around, he said, to keep Marguerite from coming back at Margy.

"Just another day in the Oswald family. John kicked us out. And I haven't had much of a relationship with my mother since then."

"You went to the Bronx from there?"

"Couple places in the Bronx. Sheridan Avenue, I believe. Then East 179th. That's when I met the Rosenbergs."

"Really? Julius and Ethel?"

"Yeah. I took a handout from them. Interesting stuff in it about Marxism. My first exposure."

"Amazing."

"Didn't really like New York. They made fun of me, my accent. Laughed at my clothes."

"You look fine to me."

"They won't be laughing when I become a big shot."

A tittle of cheekiness, Ferrie thought to himself. "Tell me more about the Big Apple."

"I skipped a lot of school, just read stuff at home and watched TV. They threw me in some kinda youth house for about three weeks in '53 'cause I was a *truant*. That place was freaking scary—full of bad kids, some who'd murdered people. The good thing is that they had a social worker look at me, she said I had 'superior mental resources.' I'll always remember that phrase.

"Then back to good old N'Orlins last year."

Oswald talked about his full-brother Robert, who was five years older. Robert survived the family dysfunction, joined the Marines, and just finished up a tour in Korea. He'd received his sergeant's stripes. Oswald liked his brother Robert, wanted to follow in his footsteps.

Uncle Dutz and Aunt Lil served as surrogate parents for him, Oswald confirmed. He almost certainly would have been in real trouble by now, even in jail, he admitted, if it hadn't been for Dutz and Lil.

Ferrie drove toward Moisant Field, where he'd picked Oswald up the morning before, but kept going on to his apartment on Vinet, to show off his guns and to visit further. Parking the car on the street, they walked down the north side of the house to Ferrie's apartment door. Entering the apartment, Oswald paused as he looked around. Even though he was raised by a mother with inept housekeeping skills, he'd never seen anything quite like this. *Is Ferrie having a garage sale in his apartment?* Oswald wondered.

The place was in its usual state of disorder and curiosity. Oswald picked up a wooden crucifix that was resting on a side table. And then a biretta. "You a church deacon or something?"

"Catholic priest."

"Catholic? So you report to the pope?"

"That's what they say I'm supposed to do."

"That's weird, man. Catholics are a little scary to me."

"Yeah?"

"It's like they appear to be Americans but they have a secret life controlled by the pope."

"So true. So true. Just don't tell anybody else."

"What's the smell?"

Oswald's nose led him to the white mice, dozens of them in several crowded cages. A few were dead. Beside the cages were microscopes, scales, laboratory beakers.

"Welcome to my humble abode," Ferrie said. "Don't mind the mice. I have some scientific hobbies that involve playing around with these dirty rotten bastards that nobody wants anyway."

"Where are the guns?"

Ferrie went through the kitchen to a locked closet. Inside were three serious pieces, a Beretta Model 59 Mark IV battle rifle and two Colt Python revolvers, and a couple of hunting rifles, Winchester M12s.

"Grab a couple and let's go out back," Ferrie proposed.

In the back yard, Oswald cradled the Beretta. He rubbed the barrel. "Christ, this feels good. Can hardly wait to play with the really big ones in the Marines."

"No shooting here. But next time we'll go to the range over at Honey Island Swamp. You been there?"

"Never heard of it."

"Ah, you gotta go. There's something really strange about that Swamp. They have animals there you won't see anywhere else. Weird reptiles that look like a cross between chimps and alligators. And I heard they have a rapacious swamp monster, like a huge gorilla, though I'm a little skeptical. In any event, there's a hell of a shooting range there."

Back in the house, Ferrie offered Oswald a drink. Unusual for a kid from the streets, he hadn't yet tried alcohol. "A glass of milk, please."

Ferrie obliged but poured a shot of Old Taylor for himself.

He joined Oswald on the couch. "Well, quite a weekend, don't you think?"

Oswald nodded.

"What do you like to do for kicks, Lee? You can't read and exercise all the time."

"As I said, just trying to get the hell outta the Big Easy. The fun and games can wait."

Ferrie fancied himself an expert in hypnotism, which he'd studied and practiced since he was a preteen. He'd hypnotized several young men in recent years, to loosen them up. Now it was Oswald's turn.

"Ever been hypnotized?"

"What? Of course not. That's just an idiotic magic act by snake-oil salesmen. It's not real."

"It's real. I can do it. I'm serious. Been doing it for years."

Skeptical, Oswald agreed to humor Ferrie.

This should relax this stiff, Ferrie thought.

Oswald sat on the couch, and Ferrie pulled up a chair right across from him. "Stare into my eyes. Don't blink."

"*Jawohl, mein Führer.*"

"Now, extend your right arm, palm up."

Ferrie slapped down on Oswald's palm and said softly but in a commanding voice, "*Sleep.*"

With Oswald acting sluggish, he made his move. He tousled Oswald's hair and then pulled his face closer. He attempted to press his lips on Oswald's. Groggy, it took Oswald a few seconds to figure out what was going on. His eyes popped wide open.

Pulling loose and jumping up, Oswald roared, knocking over a 1920s French art deco lamp Ferrie's parents had given him. He landed a right hook on Ferrie's jaw. Wild-eyed and menacing, he pounded him in the face, alternating his fists, until Ferrie was bloodied.

He harangued Ferrie. "Fucking fruit, weirdo. Jesus-shit. How does it feel to be such a freak?"

Oswald glared witheringly. He then glanced over at the Colt Python revolvers, took a step toward them but stopped. His mouth went from angry and grim to a smirk, and he turned his eyes back on Ferrie. He held the smirk for a full minute, staring at Ferrie the entire time, and then left, running all the way to Jefferson Highway to catch a bus.

Ferrie wouldn't see Oswald again for almost a decade. During those years, Oswald would get his wish to get out of New Orleans to visit far-away places.

\\\\

Wasted and wounded, Ferrie staggered to his feet and made his way across the apartment to his closet. Wading through the mess, he pulled out the purple robe and a red scarf. Wrapping himself in these vestments, he limped over to his makeshift altar.

He knelt and looked up to the ceiling with his arms outstretched and palms facing up.

"O Lord Jesus Christ, Redeemer and Savior, forgive my sins, just as You forgave Peter's denial and those who crucified You. Count not my transgressions, but, rather, my tears of repentance. Remember not my iniquities, but, more especially, my sorrow for the offenses I have committed against You." As he did daily, Ferrie also prayed to Mother Mary for forgiveness and salvation.

\\\\

Ferrie's long interest in conservative theology had developed into a captivation with the rituals and doctrines of "Old Catholicism." The direction the church had taken in the previous eighty-five years repelled him. Since Pope Pius IX's First Vatican Council, which proclaimed the pope's infallibility, the church had become more centralized and controlling of its members. Instead of priests determining the best ways to develop a direct connection between the individual and God, Pius IX sanctioned a system where the individual would relate to God only through the pope and the pope's rules.

The post-Vatican I church, Ferrie came to believe, placed a counterproductive stranglehold on all aspects of the priests' ministry and parishioners' personal lives. He was guided, instead, by the teachings of the Declaration of Utrecht in 1889, which was the manifesto of Old Catholics. The declaration embraced what it said were the original traditions of the church, which focused on a personal and direct relationship with God. Divine revelations could flow nonstop from God to the individual. Remarkably, Old Catholic dioceses allowed priests to marry. *Why not? The very first pope, Saint Peter, was married.* They also were more tolerant of individual lifestyle choices. *Didn't Jesus consort with a prostitute and have his feet anointed by a sinful woman?*

In Ferrie's mind Old Catholic theology, like the teachings of Saint Augustine, elevated good works over personal flaws— "fault[s] of men" could be overcome by "word and deed," the 1889 Declaration had said.

Old Catholic leaders tweaked some of the details of the mass. For example, priests faced their congregations not the altar and the cross. And most of the service was said in the local vernacular, though there continued to be some Latin catch phrases.

Ferrie adopted these tweaks in *his* masses, and he followed the more flexible pre-Vatican I approach to believers' comportment. But he didn't reject the Vatican and Roman Catholicism altogether, as many Old Catholics did. His masses were otherwise traditional, with the Eucharist being central and the other six sacraments well-recognized. He still revered and prayed to the pope as the grand leader of the church, while at the same time believing him to be fallible and not the ruler of all aspects of believers' lives. He closely studied the Roman and Baltimore Catechisms, Catholic missals, papal declarations, and Catholic scholars, both ancient and modern. His dream remained to be a Vatican-certified priest.

Though, with the exception of his *versus populum* orientation and frequent speaking in English, Ferrie's masses were largely standard, in New Orleans everything is done a little differently.

So, over the several years he'd been in the city, he'd often mixed in some aspects of a religion that pervaded the citizenry, Voodoo. Given his ever-curious brain, Ferrie had exposed himself to the New Orleans Voodoo tradition. Not a true Voodoo believer by any means, he *was* intrigued by some of the rituals and the spiritualism of its adherents. He occasionally finished his sermons with the phrase "*ayi bobo*," a Voodoo version of "amen."

Voodoo incorporates aspects of Christianity, Ferrie had been surprised to learn. Like Christians, adherents of Voodoo believe in one supreme God. Voodoo has a counterpart to the virginal Mary called *Aida Wedo* and a version of Saint Peter called *Legba*, the guardian gatekeeper. Catholic and Voodoo priests worked together in Africa to improve conditions for the people there.

After Ferrie's prayer to Mother Mary, Ferrie shut his eyes and knelt silently as if in a Voodoo trance.

CHAPTER 3

Three years later, as Ferrie was praying alone, the silence was shattered by the harsh *tringg tringg* of his phone. It was Dutz. Out of the blue. They hadn't spoken since Ferrie's dust-up with Oswald.

Hopefully, he thought, Dutz didn't know about the come-on to his nephew. It quickly became clear that he didn't.

"Dave, long time. Look, I've mentioned you to Saia, and Mr. Marcello's heard about you from his network around town. I told Saia you'd probably be interested in helping us out."

"What do they have in mind?" Ferrie asked, relieved.

"Nothing real specific now, but the organization always has a need for clever guys like you."

"You're too kind, *mon ami*."

"And the Little Man knows about your flying. That's the big thing for him. If he likes and trusts you, he may eventually have you fly him around, be one of his pilots. No surprise, I'm sure, but he takes some trips he wants no one to know about. *No* one. He has access to planes, but he's short on pilots who are smart enough to keep their traps shut. He's pretty generous with guys that help him *and* keep quiet."

"I'm pretty good at sealing my lips. I'm not going to sink any ships, Dutz."

"Huh?"

"Loose lips sink ships."

"Right. Look. I know you're a big-time Catholic—much more serious than me. You wouldn't have a problem working with the mob, though, would you?"

"Well, obviously, it depends on what they want me to do. But you'll remember that I did a little work for the Trafficantes in Tampa—Ybor City. Some investigations and shit like that."

"You won't be surprised to hear that Marcello spoke with Trafficante Junior about you. Senior died, you know. Only sixty-eight."

"I heard. Junior probably wouldn't remember me."

"He's got a mind like a steel trap. And, c'mon, Dave, people tend to remember you."

"Must be my charm."

"If you're up for helping, you'll be getting some assignments soon."

"Okay. You know where to find me."

||||

It didn't take long. "The Marcello guys are ready to see you," Dutz said over the phone a few days later.

"Jeez. Okay. What's the gig?" Ferrie was ready, willing, and able to help, mainly because he was broke. Had been spending too much of his Eastern Air Lines paycheck entertaining young friends in the Quarter.

"They don't tell me much. I don't know. Just meet me at the Lomalinda at seven thirty tonight. Work?"

"Sure."

"One other thing. Thanks for helping Lee out a few years ago. Guess where he is now?"

"No idea."

"In freaking Japan. Marines. He got his wish to get far away from this place. Been in California, Florida, the Philippines. Having the time of his life—shit, he met John Wayne on Corregidor."

Thank Jesus he's almost seven thousand miles away.

"Last time I saw him was at my apartment after the bivouac. He wanted to see some of my guns."

"He's going places now, I'm sure of it," Dutz said.

||||

Ferrie eagerly entered the Lomalinda that evening. Dutz was sucking on a Pearl beer and had already ordered one for him. "The best beer on the planet," Dutz said.

"Of course."

The two men chatted and took a few swings at bagatelle.

They then left the Lomalinda, walking up Royal to St. Louis Street. Passing Antoine's Restaurant, they reached Bourbon Street and the 500 Club, just a few blocks up Bourbon from the Sho-Bar. Like the Sho-Bar, the 500 Club was controlled by Marcello. In fact, Marcello had a small office at the 500 Club, on the second floor looking down at customers as they rounded the bar in the entryway and entered the main showroom.

The 500 Club's shows revolved around nearly naked women, with some comedy and crooning mixed in. But, more so than the other strip joints in the Quarter, it also was a serious musical venue. It was one of the first substantial jazz clubs in the Quarter, opening in the 1940s. It was operated by a well-known local musician named Leon Prima.

Leon and his jovial younger brother Louis were born in the French Quarter of Sicilian parents. Both were successful band leaders and skilled trumpet players. In the 1920s Leon led a well-known local band called the Melody Masters. He played with many jazz greats of the time, including Jack Teagarden— "Mr. T." During World War II, Leon and Louis moved to New York City to lead a big band and play their trumpets. Louis began singing as well then, in a unique raspy and comic way. Though he focused on jazz numbers, he had a penchant for singing the occasional Italian folk song.

The brothers moved back to New Orleans in the early fifties. Louis got a regular gig at the Sho-Bar, singing with his boyish young wife Keely Smith and blowing his horn. The Sho-Bar described him as "The Man Who Plays Pretty for the People!" Leon, however, decided he liked managing clubs better than playing—he'd operated the Shim-Sham Club at 227 Bourbon in the thirties—so, he cut a deal to run Marcello's 500 Club.

With Marcello's blessing, Leon upgraded both the music and the girls sides of the 500 Club to meet the hard competition radiating from across St. Louis at 501 Bourbon. When Leon took over the reins of the club, that hot corner had housed the Casino Royale, a burlesque house operated by a former stripper and torch singer named Stormy Lawrence. Stormy's feature act was the luminous Evangeline, "the Oyster Girl." Voyeurs, eyes agog, would marvel as Evangeline's spectacular body, topped off by dyed viridescent hair, rose from a giant oyster shell. She'd then dance around the stage suggestively, softly fondling an oversized pearl. Shuttered in 1957 over a dispute with the landlord, the Casino Royale was replaced by a new, high-octane jazz club called Dan's Pier 600. Dan's featured a brilliant thirty-five-year-old jazz trumpeter named Al Hirt.

At the time Dutz and Ferrie paid this visit to the 500 Club, Louis had moved to Las Vegas with Keely to perform on a regular basis at the Sahara. He was becoming nationally known. He and Keely did play at the 500, however, whenever they visited New Orleans. They always performed their jazz-campy version of "That Old Black Magic." When his brother and sister-in-law were in town, Leon liked to open for them with his bawdy cover of "I Wish I Could Shimmy Like My Sister Kate."

Keely Smith's star had risen along with Louis's. Nineteen fifty-eight was a landmark year for both of them. Their "That Old Black Magic" became a Top 20 hit and was nominated for the first-ever Grammy for Best Group or Choral Performance. Keely's maiden solo effort, "I Wish You Love," was also nominated for a Grammy, the first ever for Best Female Vocal Performance. Less joyous for the couple that year was their marriage, which was being rocked by an affair Keely was enjoying with Frank Sinatra. Keely had met Sinatra at the Sahara during a set with Louis in the hotel's lounge.

Though not there this particular night in 1958, Louis was always a presence at the club—pictures of him were on the walls, and his hits, like "Sing, Sing, Sing," first made famous by Benny Goodman, rang out between acts.

Leon greeted Dutz warmly and guided him and Ferrie to a back table, past several strippers milling about in lingerie looking for tips. Marcello was sitting at a large table with an elegant-looking man. Dutz was visibly nervous to be in the presence of his ultimate boss. He had few occasions to deal directly with Marcello. But Marcello rose and hugged him. "My brud-da," he said.

Marcello shook Ferrie's hand.

"I heard a lot about you, Ferrie."

Marcello had heard not only about Ferrie's piloting skills but also about his native intelligence, spirited curiosity, and prolific energy. Santo Trafficante gave Ferrie good grades for his work in Ybor City. Trafficante had highlighted his skills and balls as an investigator—and his loyalty.

"You a smart guy, Ferrie," Marcello said. "I hear dat. You a good flyer, too. I need a flyboy with some brains."

The other man at the table with Marcello was his lawyer and close advisor, G. Wray Gill. Gill was a distinguished looking gray-haired man with a slight turkey neck. He wore a dark, well-tailored business suit. He was quietly polite, exuding an air of authority and intelligence.

He and Marcello had developed a strong professional and personal relationship in the late 1930s. Gill was a prominent criminal law attorney in New Orleans until he took on a case for the local chapter of the NAACP to represent a black man accused of murdering a deputy sheriff. The defendant, a twenty-year-old from northern Louisiana named Jerome Wilson, had been convicted of murder, but Gill got the conviction overturned on appeal. Before Wilson's retrial commenced, he was dragged out of his northern Louisiana prison by local whites and brutally murdered with a hammer.

The murder was praised by Louisiana's governing elite, including Senator Huey Long, who said in an interview the day after the murder, "This nigger got hold of a smart lawyer somewhere and proved a technicality. He was guilty as hell."

Gill, the "smart lawyer," thereafter was blacklisted by most of white Louisiana, so he turned to Louisiana's undersociety, including the mob. Marcello had been moving up the mob chain at the time and increasingly used Gill's services. These days, they were practically joined at the hip.

"Ferrie, you could help our family of workers around dis great city," Marcello argued.

"Yes, sir."

"I'm just a small business guy, Ferrie. I sell tomatoes. The best tomatoes. You like tomatoes?"

"Love them, sir. Particularly the Creoles. *Molto* delicious."

"I sell da satsumas in the fall. People love dem little sweet rascals."

"Including me, sir. The New Orleans orange. You know they were originally from Japan and brought over—"

Dutz elbowed Ferrie to shut him up.

"I got udder businesses too, Ferrie," Marcello said. "Ferrie, listen. You can do it all in America, get rich and enjoy life. As Governor Huey said a long time ago, 'Every Man a King' in this country. We gotta help America, Ferrie. We could use an *omu* like you."

Gill spoke up. "We have businesses in other places in Louisiana and over in Texas, from Dallas and Houston down to Laredo on the Mexico border. But we are seeing some big headwinds coming our way. There are folks in Washington on a battle charge to tie us into being part of a larger network of organized crime."

"I've read about Bobby," Ferrie said.

"He a little bitch shit," Marcello said.

Marcello and his fellow mob leaders were deeply concerned about RFK's crusade against organized crime.

"This Mafia stuff won't last, but it could be a nuisance for a while," Gill said. "As you'll see, Dave, our businesses are improving the lives of thousands of the good citizens of Louisiana and Texas.

"The *other* headwind may be more serious," Gill continued. "*Communism*. Communism is spreading like the Spanish flu did in 1918. It's wildly contagious. You've seen it in Eastern Europe. You're starting to see it in Southeast Asia—that Russkie and Chink puppet General Giáp has forced the French out of an important country over there, Vietnam. And *now*, Dave, the Commies are right off our shores. As we speak, they're trying to take over Cuba. You've heard of Fidel Castro?"

"Sure," Ferrie responded. "But Castro's no Communist. He's a freedom fighter, right? Batista's the brutal guy. I've even thought about trying to help Castro."

"Slow down, Captain. You wanna be locked up like those guys in Brownsville?

"Nobody knows Cuba better than Mr. Marcello and his colleagues," Gill continued. "The hotels and casinos are only part of their businesses there—they have much more. Here's what we know. Batista threw Castro in jail for a while. Castro had been a rich spoiled kid, but he turned into a socialist farmworker in college. Prison was a shock to his system, apparently. He came out a full-on Communist."

"Jesus, really?"

"Batista made two mistakes. For one, he didn't execute the bastard. And then he just let him go. Bye-bye, have a nice life. Un-fucking-believable."

"Dat Castro is now like Lucifer, Ferrie. Duh *Diavulu*," Marcello said.

"But, sirs, President Eisenhower isn't going after Castro."

"Ike doesn't know that Castro's a Communist," Gill said. "But Ike's not the shiniest coin in the Trevi Fountain. And his CIA director's been focusing his time on Guatemala, Iran, and screwing fancy women around the world. In any event, the government doesn't have the resources that we have down there."

"Not even close, Ferrie," Marcello said.

"Castro had to leave Cuba after he got out of jail," Gill said. "He went to Mexico. But he's back in Cuba now. Batista couldn't catch him when he returned with his other comrades. And old

Beno currently has no fucking idea where Castro is, just somewhere in the mountains. We believe Russia is providing some
assistance to Castro and his band of losers."

"He can't beat Batista, sir," Ferrie asserted.

"I don't think so either," Gill replied, "but we have to be
vigilant."

Ferrie nodded.

"Bottom line," Gill said. "Cuba goes Commie, we lose a shit-
ton of money and power."

"We've got an offer for you," Gill continued. "We'll give you a
monthly retainer. I'll discuss the details of that with you later.
And there'll be extra payments for some special projects."

"Thank you, sir. Assignment?"

"We want two things from you, for now. First, as Mr. Marcello
suggested, we'll need you to do some flying for us. We know you
own a plane or two and have access to others. Mr. Marcello owns
some as well. This flying will be here and there around the country, maybe up to Canada once or twice, maybe Cuba as well."

"Cuba? Shit! Yes, sir."

"Beyond that, we would like to be able to call on you on occasion to check out some people around town. They say you know
the town and the Quarter pretty well."

"I get around."

"Good." Gill finished up, "I want to meet with you in a few
days. At my office. I'm in the Pere Marquette Building. You
know, where Common crosses Baronne, close to the Roosevelt.
Or at Mr. Marcello's main office, at the Town and Country Motel
out on Airline Highway—Mr. Marcello does his serious business
there, it's too crazy here in the Quarter. I'll call soon, Dutz gave
me your phone number.

"We'll try not to interfere with your job at Eastern," Gill
continued.

"I'm flattered by all of this, gentlemen."

"Unless you have questions now, just wait for my call," Gill
said.

"We have big work, Ferrie. Big work. We happy for your help." Marcello said.

"*Grazij.*" Marcello bowed.

"*Di nenti,*" Ferrie replied.

Ferrie wasn't persuaded that Castro was as bad as Marcello and Gill made him out to be. *But they're the bosses,* he told himself.

Marcello and Gill each hugged Leon Prima as they began to head out.

llll

An astonishing, chestnut-haired stripper was dancing erotically on the stage, wild orgasmic noises coming from her throat, in only the scanty top half of a faux prison uniform. She played with her G-string, pushing it down to her knees with her back to the crowd. She pretended to make love to a stripper pole. Even Ferrie paused to take a long look.

"Who is that?" Ferrie asked Prima.

"She calls herself . . . '*Jada.*'"

CHAPTER 4

Gill called Ferrie three days later. "Come out to the Town and Country."

"In Metairie—Airline Highway, right?"

"1225. Just before Maple Ridge."

"Give me an hour to finish something?" Ferrie was in the middle of dissecting a mouse.

"I need you to meet someone. Come to Marcello's office in the building out back. Behind the pool. Knock on the door marked 'Employees Only.'"

Ferrie was excited. *This could be the beginning of new adventures—and the greenbacks could be put to good use.*

The Town and Country Motel, as its Airline Highway address suggested, was on the way to Moisant Field. The motel was in the midst of a "miracle mile" of other cheap motels, gas stations, sketchy strip joints, billboards, parking lots, and trashy bars. It was a one-story, L-shaped building with a diner-style restaurant and covered carport entryway. Its large, red, white, and yellow three-section sign displayed "Town" and "Country" in large cursive letters. Marcello's office was in a separate nondescript gray cinder-block building out back past the pool.

The motel was run for Marcello by brother Anthony.

The Town and Country was just five miles from Ferrie's Vinet Avenue home. He conveniently got there by hopping on the Clearwater and Airport buses.

Gill opened the "Employees Only" door to Marcello's office on Ferrie's knock. It was bare-bones inside, with no suggestion that an important man worked there. Inside were several cluttered rooms and a sweet-looking middle-aged lady behind a typewriter. She greeted Ferrie, identifying herself as Dorothy Ott.

Gill introduced Ferrie to a man who would begin playing a pivotal role in Ferrie's life. "Dave, meet Superintendent Guy Banister."

"Nice to meet you, sir."

Banister was tall and, like Gill, distinguished looking, though handsomer. He not infrequently was mistaken for Gregory Peck around town. His soft but slightly twangy northern Louisiana accent was reflective of his roots just below the Arkansas border.

He had a striking biography, starting out as a policeman in his hometown of Monroe. He thereafter joined the FBI and was present when John Dillinger was shot in the back of the neck and killed in the alley by Chicago's Biograph Theater in 1934.

Banister became a favorite of J. Edgar Hoover's. Hoover sent him to the FBI's New York office before World War II to head an investigation of the American Communist Party.

His FBI service took him from New York to Montana, Oklahoma, and Minnesota. He later returned to Chicago, where he served as special agent in charge. He retired in 1954 to New Orleans and joined the New Orleans Police Department as assistant superintendent.

"Guy helps us out when he can," Gill said. "He could use your help on a few assignments Marcello has requested."

Gill left Banister and Ferrie to themselves.

Banister got straight to the point. "I've checked you out. I know about the young boys. I know about the mice and the cancer stuff. I know about your Catholic shit. More important, we know about your flying prowess. We've talked to Rickenbacker."

"Know that the 'young-boys' story surely's been exaggerated," Ferrie said. "I can explain."

"No need. I frankly don't give a fuck. What matters to me is that by all accounts you're a resourceful guy with some useful talents. I also know you hate Communism, like we do. Assholes."

"Commies present an existential threat to our freedoms. Sir."

"Mr. Marcello has asked me to go above and beyond my official duties to help him protect our fair city against these radicals. There are leftists in our midst. Not many, but, like cancer, they could metastasize if we don't snuff them out."

"Smart analogy."

"The first thing we need you to do is help us identify the most potent lefties in town. Start at the colleges—Tulane, Xavier, and Loyola. There are some smart-ass kids there who fantasize about being radicals. These jack offs would be harmless except that more dangerous professional Commies are slipping into town to recruit them. You'll need to get in there and identify the worst lefties at the schools and then identify the pros pulling their strings. We'll take care of them from there ourselves, or have DA Dowling do it."

"Sounds like fun."

"Fun's the word. To make it even more fun for you, you'll be working with one of our finest bad guys—Jack Martin."

"Heard of him," Ferrie said, without ardor.

"You know he's basically a creep."

"I've heard him called worse."

"No surprise. But if you know anything about him, you know he's good at this kind of thing. We're going to have Martin take the lead on this little project and do the bulk of the work, but you need to be involved. Later . . . soon . . . you're going to have other things to do. Bigger."

"Bigger is always better. Next steps for now?"

"I've set up a meeting for you and Martin. He'll give you more detail. Meet him tomorrow at the Sho-Bar at two. Believe me, you'll have no trouble finding him. He'll have a limey tweed hat on and a rye whiskey in front of him. Will be sitting at the bar."

"I don't have to wear a hat, do I?"

"You can wear whatever you want."

"Hats are tough for me, with my fake hair and all."

"I'm sure," Banister said. "Look, this Martin project is important, but, as I mentioned, Mr. Marcello has a higher-priority assignment for you. We'll talk about that in a few days. When we do, bring a map of Cuba with you."

"Yes, sir." Ferrie naturally was intrigued.

Gill closed the meeting. Ferrie left, noticing the sign on the back of the door. *Three Can Keep a Secret If Two Are Dead.* He never forgot that baleful message.

〽️

Ferrie wasn't accustomed to going to the Sho-Bar during the day. Saluting the doorman the next afternoon, Ferrie entered the unusually quiet burlesque house. Passing from the daytime brightness to the darkness of the club, his eyes took a few seconds to adjust, his pupils expanding to let in more light.

The bar counter extended from the street side of the club all the way to the stage. Sitting midway down, wearing a small trilby hat with a multicolored band and slim red feather, was Jack Martin. Ferrie looked askance at him.

One-eyed Pete wasn't there this early in the day. The strippers were from the junior varsity. No Blaze Starr. They were competent, though, and actually raunchier than the prime-time crew, bending every which way to the music. But their dances lacked class and creativity. In contrast, the varsity dancers had themes, humor, and tricks. Verve.

The team slated to dance at the Sho-Bar that night was especially strong. The sign out front on Bourbon Street announced that the prime-time show would feature Hotsy Totsy, "the Aqua Queen"—whom Ferrie had seen with his friend Wakeling—along with superstar Kalantan, "the Heavenly Body," who'd performed an exotic Afro-Cuban dance in the 1955 movie *Son of Sinbad* starring Cliff Robertson and Vincent Price.

Ferrie shook Martin's hand and took a seat at the bar. Jack Martin looked like a B-movie stereotype of a gumshoe detective. His trilby hat sat high on his head, the tweed brim tipped up away from his face. He had a large forehead, dark circles under his eyes, scruffy wisps of hair on his chin—the sunken look of a face that frequently had a bottle attached to it.

Martin's scruffy appearance belied the fact that he *was* a cagey investigator. His street skills had been honed over years of criminality. In a clipped way, Banister had described Martin to Ferrie as being "highly observant" and "quick witted."

Martin had a multipage rap sheet under his erstwhile name Ed Suggs—theft, robbery, carrying a concealed pistol, impersonating an FBI agent and an army colonel, impersonating a doctor, disturbing the peace, vagrancy. In one odd period of his earlier life, he'd taken up performing illegal abortions in Houston—until one of his patients, a young woman named Helen Nichols, died. Martin was indicted for murder but fled the state before being prosecuted.

In addition to Houston, he'd been arrested in Fort Worth, Galveston, San Diego, and Los Angeles over the years.

After moving to New Orleans as "Jack Martin," supposedly a writer and newspaperman, the local authorities got to know him quickly. In police reports he was described as "crazy," "a mental case," an "odd character."

Marcello's folks also came across Martin. They immediately recognized a potentially useful asset, even though he was a loose cannon who'd have to be watched and managed. The mob network was particularly intrigued when Martin's wife Mae checked him into the psych ward on the third floor of the Charity Hospital two days before Christmas 1956. She told the doctors Martin must have dementia because he'd "played Russian roulette." After treatment he was discharged a month later into the care of his wife, with a written diagnosis that he had a "sociopathic personality" and was "antisocial."

Being "crazy," "mental," "odd," "sociopathic," and "antisocial" wasn't disqualifying, by any means, for gangster work.

The long counter at the Sho-Bar was a landmark in the Quarter. It was made from a mammoth western red cedar grown three thousand miles away on Vancouver Island, Canada. Running his hand over the top of the pinkish brown wood bar, Ferrie believed he could sense souls who had leaned on the soft cedar in joy and sorrow, in grief and celebration. For a few seconds, Ferrie forgot where he was and why he was there, distracted by a prayer running through his head. Then Martin spoke.

"You know the goal. We get the left-left-leftiest of the lefties out of this town. Here's what I'm working on. Your buddy Dutz has found us four college-aged kids who'll hang out around Tulane and Xavier—for a price, of course. I've told these boys also to check out LSU-New Orleans, as well as Loyola, but to focus on Tulane and Xavier.

"We've checked these four guys out," Martin continued. "They're good. Two of them went to school with Dutz's nephew Lee Oswald. You know him?"

"Yep. He made an impression on me. Literally."

"The two Oswald guys are named Ed Voebel and Al Campbell—went to Beauregard Junior High with him. Not a bad school, serves mainly Lakeview, but it gets some Quarter kids like Oswald and these guys, as well as gang members from the Irish Channel. The Quarter boys fight with the gangs while the rich Lakeview kids watch. In any event, Voebel and Campbell, and presumably Oswald, grew up pretty quickly there."

"I hope they have personalities. Unlike Dutz's nephew."

"They'll do fine. They're going to find the loudest-mouth junior Commies and pretend to be *simpatico*. They'll invite them *and* their 'mentors' to meet at a 'safe house' Guy has rented on Louisiana Avenue Parkway, not too far from both Tulane and Xavier—near Roman and Toledano Streets. Radicals get orgasms when they hear talk of 'safe houses.'"

"Then what?"

"We'll be there in the next room with Banister. Campbell is the brains of the foursome. He'll try to get a guest to say something that sounds treasonous or like he's going to incite violence. Then Guy'll come out with his badge, wave it around, and arrest the bastard. He'll give them a choice of leaving the state or getting locked up."

"Good times."

"We're also going to have a couple of Guy's cops driving around off and on around the colleges, undercover. If our boys hear extreme Commie talk on campus, they can call Guy through his secretary Delphine. She can always find Guy—especially at night, if you know what I mean. If he likes what he hears, he can radio the cops and have the lefties arrested on the spot."

"Convoluted but might work."

"But things never go as planned, so that's one of the reasons Guy wanted you on board with me. You'll help me get the lay of the land and keep an eye on how things are going. We'll surely be calling some audibles. You know, like in football."

"You can be Y. A. Tittle."

"Good old LSU boy. MVP in the most boring game in history, '47 Cotton Bowl. Zero-to-zero tie."

"I'm from Cleveland. I'd rather be Otto Graham. Professional athlete of the year!"

"Sure, whatever floats your boat. Couple more things. *Número uno*—the Marcello guys know you can hypnotize people. At the 'safe house,' when we have some of these assholes there and we aren't getting what we need for an arrest, Guy wants you to step in. Pretend you're a lefty, chat up the most serious lefty there. And then hypnotize the guy. We'll get him to confess his sins."

"You know hypnotism doesn't always work. Some guys can resist it. I've seen it, believe me."

"It could be worth a try. *Número dos*—"

"Yep?"

"Guy knows you're working on a PhD in psychology. Fucking impressive, by the way."

"*Pasib*, comrade."

"Do your studying at the libraries at Tulane and Xavier when you can. And then keep your eyes and ears open there, maybe meet some students, see what you can pick up."

"I'll need to renew my library cards."

As Ferrie lifted himself off his bar stool, Martin announced, "Banister wants to see you at the motel tomorrow morning. Ten thirty."

Ferrie left Martin at the bar. He shaded his dilated pupils against the sun as he shuffled out to Bourbon Street. His plate was getting full between the Martin work, some Eastern Air Lines trips coming up, and whatever flying project Marcello and Banister had up their sleeves.

||||

At the Town and Country that next late-spring morning, Banister's one agenda item was Ferrie's other assignment. When Ferrie arrived, toting a map of Cuba, Banister wasted no time. He met Ferrie out in the parking lot, ushered him to his Chevy Bel Air, and drove the eight miles down Airline Highway to Moisant Field.

"I need to see your planes."

CHAPTER 5

Fidel Castro was born into a wealthy family near the eastern end of Cuba on August 13, 1926—a Friday the thirteenth. After a normal though not trouble-free childhood, he was sent at age nineteen to boarding school in Havana, a Jesuit institution called *Colegio Belen*. He moved from there after a few months to the University of Havana to study law.

Though apolitical before university, Castro became immersed in the student left-wing movement while studying law. He was elected president of the radical, anti-imperialist Federation of University Students, which was focused on halting any and all US involvement in the Caribbean. Castro became particularly interested in student efforts designed to preserve the independence of the Dominican Republic and Colombia.

Castro made his first public splash in November 1946 in a speech at an annual ceremony commemorating the anniversary of the 1871 execution of eight young medical students by the Spanish. The ceremony took place in the Colón Cemetery in the exclusive Havana suburb of Vedado, seven blocks from the Malecón boulevard and seawall by the ocean. The students' bodies had been unceremoniously dumped on the land that later became Colón.

The speech relentlessly condemned the administration of Cuban president Grau. That administration, Castro said, was grossly corrupt. Grau's ministers were stealing public funds while thousands of people were starving, he thundered. Castro shocked the gathering by declaring that certain high-ranking government officials were running violent gangs in the country.

Suddenly, Castro was on the front pages of Cuba's main newspapers, on the country's political map. Over the following eighteen months, Castro hyperactively joined the left-leaning Party of the Cuban People, the *Partido Ortodoxo*, attempted to join in an expedition to protect the Dominican Republic, led a student protest over the government killing of a student, and travelled to Bogota, Colombia, as part of a student group sponsored by Juan Péron to support the Colombian Liberal Party in its fight with the governing Conservative Party.

Two years after his maiden speech in Vedado, Castro took a break to marry a fellow student, the daughter of a prominent politician, the wealthy mayor of a city in eastern Cuba. In a turn away from his growing revolutionary career, Castro accepted an offer from his new father-in-law to pay for a three-month honeymoon in New York City. Castro and his new wife, Mirta, initially stayed at the Waldorf Astoria on Park Avenue and then moved to a brownstone at 155 West 82nd Street, east of Amsterdam Avenue, owned by Mirta's brother.

Castro developed a love for professional baseball and T-bone steaks. He rented a white Lincoln Continental. Foreseeing years of struggle in Cuba, Castro indulged in the finer things America offered. Including jazz music, a creation of New Orleans. Castro had enjoyed jazz since he'd moved to Havana. In New York, he frequently traveled up the island to Harlem late at night to listen to great black jazz artists performing at places like the Sugar Cane Club at Fifth Avenue and 135th and the cavernous Savoy Ballroom on Lennox Avenue. And Clark Monroe's Uptown House, 198 West 134th. Monroe's was a particular favorite, the informal home of the "Bird," bebop saxophonist Charlie Parker.

Castro mingled with many young Americans, both black and white, at Harlem clubs like these on this trip and on a shorter return trip he made after graduating from university in 1950. Including with a young black Harvard-trained lawyer named William T. Coleman Jr. Castro and Bill Coleman ran into each other more than a handful of times in Harlem clubs. They enjoyed each other's company and shared a robust attachment to jazz. Sometimes joined by Nelson Rockefeller—an American royal and an ardent music lover—Castro and Coleman relished the talents of Hazel Scott, Cab Calloway, Lionel Hampton, Duke Ellington, and Coleman's friend Lena Horne. In his memoirs written at the end of a storied career, Coleman remembered Castro as being "affable, witty, mercurial, and unpredictable." Castro, however, clearly was "not a crazy man," Coleman wrote.

Serendipitously, in 1964 Bill Coleman became the senior Federal investigator looking into the possible involvement of Castro and his government in the assassination of President Kennedy.

Back in Cuba in the 1950s, Castro was introduced to the writings of Karl Marx. He studied *The Communist Manifesto* and *Capital: Critique of Political Economy.* He was particularly inspired by Marx's essays in *The Eighteenth Brumaire of Louis Napoleon*, which emphasized the role an individual can make in the course of history.

Castro's antigovernment activism increased geometrically. He decided to run for the Cuban House of Representatives, but the election was scrapped after a successful coup in 1952 by Fulgencio Batista, backed by the army. In 1940 Batista had become the first nonwhite President of Cuba. He'd been out of power since 1944, spending most of his time in Daytona Beach fishing, bike-riding, and plotting his return to Cuba. Eliminating Cuba's parliamentarian government, Batista assumed the role of military dictator.

Concerned about this attack on Cuban democracy and about Batista's right-wing politics, Castro and 150 other associates, including his brother Raul, naively tried to overthrow Batista the next year. Their poorly planned attempt to attack the Moncada Barracks near Santiago de Cuba bordered on the comical. Castro was imprisoned on the large Cuban island Isla de Pinos, a former pirate hideout.

Castro was released after only two years as part of a general amnesty plan Batista thought would solidify his public support. Escaping to Mexico, Castro regrouped with many of his former associates and with some new partners, most notably a former medical student turned revolutionary, an Argentinian named Che Guevara. Castro and Che met for the first time in Mexico City in June 1955.

In late November 1956, Castro gathered eighty-one associates, including Raul and Che, boarded a leaky sixty-foot, Brooklyn-built motoryacht named *Granma* in Tuxpan, Mexico, and headed to Cuba to try to join a rebel uprising in Santiago de Cuba. The uprising fizzled before *Granma*, slowed by a norther, landed after seven days on rough seas. The landing was at Playa de las Coloradas, south of Belic. Batista's troops knew of the landing and found the Castro group at a town called Alegría del Pío, inland from Cabo Cruz and the Vargas lighthouse. The invaders had trudged ten miles from the sea over unique land marked by uplifted marine terraces and cliffs to what became a fateful, bloody battle. Castro and thirteen comrades miraculously escaped Batista's men, leaving sixty-eight rebels killed or captured. The government troops didn't think it worth the effort to chase this small band of ragged men into the mountains.

This thirteen-man group, which included Raul and Che, spread out into the dense Sierra Maestra Mountains and began a guerrilla war against Batista.

Castro's guerrilla war gained steam in the last few years of the 1950s. Batista should've been able to easily swat the rebels away, but Castro and his band were adept at using the jungles for protection. And they'd secretly procured heavy artillery from the Soviet Union, which was looking for a foothold in the Western Hemisphere.

The mob was concerned. Its investments in Cuba had become an important part of the overall enterprise. The mob controlled a casino empire in Cuba—overseen primarily by Florida mob boss Santo Trafficante, along with a Jewish gangster named Meyer Lansky—that was even bigger than the one it had in Las Vegas. The mob had started in Havana with the Tropicana Club and the San Souci. After 1955 the Habana Riviera, the

Sevilla-Biltmore, the Capri, and the Havana Hilton had opened. These facilities were grandiose. Stunning.

The Tropicana in particular attracted celebrities and politicians, in part because of its scantily clad and voluptuous showgirls, known as "*Los Diosas de Carne*," who often danced on outdoor catwalks placed among royal and old man palms. Carmen Miranda and Josephine Baker periodically performed in the indoor Crystal Arch. Nat King Cole performed there as well and was a bigger star in Cuba than he was in America. Lena Horne, Bill Coleman's friend whom Castro had met in Harlem, regularly sang at the Tropicana.

In addition to the financial benefits to the mob, the splendid Havana casinos enhanced the mob's influence in important circles of power in the United States. Havana had become a hot spot for fun, escape, and adventure for the elite. The rich and influential came down to the island. Frank Sinatra was enticed to invest in several casinos, tying him in further than he already was to the mob's organization. Superstars Errol Flynn, Marlon Brando, George Raft, and Ernest Hemmingway were regular visitors.

Important American politicians traveled to Havana as well, frequently on junkets paid for by lobbyists. A young United States Senator named John F. Kennedy was brought to Cuba by Trafficante. While there, JFK—traveling with his friend Senator George Smathers of Florida—was treated to a call-girl threesome at the Comodoro Hotel. Trafficante was ever the gracious host.

The mob cemented relations with Batista by investing in the declining but iconic 1930 Hotel Nacional de Cuba. With the mob's money, the hotel became a national treasure.

As Castro gained strength, the mob needed to know whether its lucrative Cuba operation was at risk. Trafficante and Lansky agreed to gather information on the ground, hiring undercover operatives to tramp through the jungles and learn what they could. Marcello took on the job of surveilling the situation from the skies.

\\\\

Banister was directed to manage Marcello's new Cuba assignment and to fully utilize Ferrie. And his planes. Both the Stinson Voyager and the Taylorcraft L-2 were light utility planes that could fly low and quietly, perfect for air surveillance. The Stinson Voyager was a single-pilot, two-passenger braced monoplane developed right before the United States entered World War II. The Taylorcraft, also a light World War II-era aircraft, was designed specifically for observation. A short takeoff and landing plane capable of using rough runways, it also accommodated a pilot and a companion.

Ferrie took him up for spins over Lake Pontchartrain in both the Taylorcraft and the Stinson.

"Love 'em," Banister said after they'd returned to the ground. "These can travel about 300 to 350 miles before refueling, right?"

"Yes," Ferrie responded. "Impressive research, sir.

"What's the plan?" he then asked after a brief pause.

"We appreciate you meeting with Jack Martin. Spend as much time as you can with him over the next month or six weeks. Help ensure he's got his little project under control. Make sure he hasn't drunk himself off the rails.

"Thereafter," Banister continued, "you're going to shift your focus. Continue to keep an eye on Martin as you can, but your main priority is going to be Cuba."

"I've got the map in my back pocket."

"Mr. Marcello needs some eyes on the prize down there. Some eyes from the sky."

"I *am* flying to Cuba?"

"You got it. Could be fun."

"Roger that."

"We need you to get intelligence on Castro and his thugs, how strong they are, where they're heading. That kind of thing. You should be able to see them, flying low. We can't find out anything useful from anybody, including our friends in the CIA."

"I'm not sure what I can find out that they can't."

"You'd be surprised. We'll go over the details later."

"A lot more detail, I hope."

"Sure. For now, I can tell you you'll only have to make a few trips to the Pearl of the Antilles. After that, your priority is going to be to train others to go down there. Mr. Marcello's getting some other light aircraft. We'll keep those at Lakefront. You'll train these wannabe flyers at a field not far from there and then set up a system of regular surveillance over Cuba using these guys and the planes."

"This is a lot to digest."

"Of course. But we do need to get you going pretty soon. Batista appears to be getting flummoxed by Castro. We need to know what we're dealing with. I can tell you the Little Man is not happy."

"Naturally," Ferrie said. "I hear Batista's weaker than people thought he'd be."

"Start drawing up some plans to hop down to Key West. We have a guy down there who knows Cuba well. He'll help you plan the details of your flights and then help analyze what you've seen. I'd use the Taylorcraft."

"This'll be a doddle," Ferrie said with a tinge of sarcasm.

"Duck soup. Gill wants to get together with us to discuss this in more detail. Let's meet a week from today at his office at the Pere Marquette, ten o'clock. In the meantime, relax as much as you can. Except you gotta make sure Martin's not fucking up."

"All right."

"Now, a little preview of where exactly you're going. Unfold your map." Pointing at the map, Banister said, "Focus on this— the town of La Plata on the southern Caribbean coast. Just below the rebels' mountain range, the Sierra Maestra. There'll be some fireworks there."

CHAPTER 6

Ferrie met several times with Martin and the four paid fake-students at Tulane and Xavier during May and June of 1958. With some success, he tried hypnosis on a few junior-league lefties at the "safe house" on Louisiana Avenue Parkway. He studied at the Tulane library and, chatting with students, got a few leads for Martin.

At the Tulane library, instead of studying for his PhD, Ferrie read through every book the library had on Cuba. At home, using Eastern Air Lines maps, Ferrie planned various air routes to Key West, each of which would require at least three refueling stops for his Taylorcraft. On his Cuba map, as Banister suggested, he focused on the area around La Plata, from the sea up to Pico Turquino, which Ferrie had learned was the highest point in Cuba at 6,476 feet.

As scheduled, Banister and Gill met Ferrie at the Pere Marquette, a modern Gothic, eighteen-story building built in 1925. Gill's office was on the seventeenth floor.

Ferrie was exhaustively briefed by Gill with up-to-the-minute information on the current situation in Cuba. The mob had picked up some new information from a source close to Batista's head of the joint chiefs, General Cantillo, Gill related. Batista was impatient with the irregular and disorganized skirmishing, which was being won by small groups of Castro's guerrilla fighters. He was ready to mount a full-on offensive on Castro's stronghold in the Sierra Maestra. Enough is enough, Batista had concluded.

The source close to General Cantillo passed on a request to his mob contacts for help in providing Cantillo with real-time information on the location of Castro's fighters. The general desperately needed covert surveillance by air and a rapid-fire system for communicating information to the ground commanders.

Ready to go, Ferrie took vacation time from Eastern. He left Moisant Field for Key West just after the Fourth of July in the Taylorcraft, stopping in Fort Walton Beach-Destin, Gainesville, and West Palm Beach for fuel. Ferrie flew low over the eighteen-mile barrier island where the Town of Palm Beach was located, admiring the large oceanfront mansions with their shining azure pools. He spotted Joe Kennedy's classy estate near the northern tip of the island and Marjorie Merriweather Post's blatantly opulent, faux-Mediterranean Mar-a-Lago further south. He then buzzed over Miami Beach, noticing the sweeping Fontainebleau and more traditional Eden Roc Hotels. Passing over dozens of small tropical cays south of Homestead, he marveled at the ruins of Henry Flagler's early-twentieth-century "eighth wonder of the world" between West Summerland and Bahia Honda Keys and just south of Lower Matecumbe Key. *The railroad that crossed the ocean.* Unimaginably at the time, Flagler engineered the first physical connection between Miami and the southernmost town in the continental United States, Key West, in the first decade of the century. Flagler's railroad over the Florida Keys was blown asunder in 1935 by the strongest hurricane in American history.

Key West International Airport was tucked in the southeast corner of this spirited small island, named *Cayo Hueso* by Spanish settlers. The Spanish chose this term, "bone island" in English, because the island was littered with the bleached bones of Native Americans when they arrived. The bones of the losers of some ancient battle.

Banister had told him to cab from the airport on through the town to the A&B Lobster House at the main harbor. A&B was one of the first sizable restaurants on the island, opened in 1947 by Upper Matecumbe Key friends Alonzo Cothron and Berlin Felton. *A and B.*

But Ferrie asked the cab driver to first swing over to the south end of Front Street so he could see the stately 1891 red-brick Custom House. The Naval Court inquiry into the sinking of the USS *Maine* in Havana harbor during the evening of February 15, 1898, Ferrie knew, was held there on the second floor. That inquiry occurred quickly after the disaster, with fifty-nine survivors of the explosion appearing in person in Key West. The court concluded that a mine had destroyed the ship, but it couldn't determine who was responsible. The American public, though, blamed Spain. This suspicious event ignited the Spanish-American War, which set Cuba on the course that eventually led to the current tumult.

At the A&B, located at the other end of Front Street, Ferrie climbed the stairs to the restaurant, which jutted out over the water. July is hotter in Key West than it is in Cuba. Ferrie was sweating by the time he reached the top stair. As he'd been instructed, he told the young lady at the front reception desk that he was meeting a man named Sparky.

The young lady—who announced she was Berlin's daughter Clarenda—took Ferrie to a man sitting on a candy-apple-red, naugahyde-cushioned chair at a table covered with a white table cloth, drinking an iced tea and deep into the house specialty, Oysters Rockefeller. "You must be Dave Ferrie," the man said, standing up, extending his right hand. Sparky was an outgoing, well-dressed man in his mid-forties. His toned arm muscles were evident when he shook Ferrie's hand. "Pleased to be working with you. I heard you're not a *schmendrik.*"

"I take it that's good, Sparky," Ferrie said.

"Could be worse. Look, whatever clown's told you to call me Sparky should go to hell. I hate that fucking name. My sister, God bless her, called me Sparky when I was a kid and it stuck. Sparky is a goddamn horse in a shitty comic strip. Don't call me that."

"Sure. I'll call you whatever you want."

"The name is Jack."

"Nice to meet you, Jack."

"The last name is Rubenstein. But I don't use that long Jewish name. I live in Texas and I like the place, for the most part, but it's full of wingnuts and ignorant anti-Semites. I'm a proud Jew, but I'm also practical—I have good businesses in Dallas. Mainly titty bars but tits with class. The Silver Spur. The Vegas Club. The city calls them 'dancehalls,' but they're well aware of what kind of dances they do.

"Unlike some of the Jews in Dallas who run businesses, I'm out and about around town all the time. I network—it's good for business. But it's prudent if the city cowboys and oil suckers don't know I'm a Jew."

"I knew the bigots there didn't like Negroes . . . but Jews?" Ferrie asked.

"Funny story for you. One night a well-known oil guy was in my Dallas club, loudly complaining about Jews. I went over to his table and asked him nicely—he was a good customer—to tone it down. He said to me, 'Jack, c'mon, you know I like Jews—orange Jewwwz, apple Jewwwz, tomato Jewwwz.' Even I laughed at that one."

"Hilarious."

"But most of the Jew things I hear are ugly, not at all funny. It's just a fact that a lot of the crackers in Texas hate Jews. I don't shit know why. Christ, Jesus was a Jew."

"Makes no sense."

"Nope, but *que será será*. In any event, I shortened the name Rubenstein so no one could tell if I'm Jew, gentile, Pagan, Canadian, Martian, whatever."

"To?"

"My friends, enemies, strippers, other coworkers in Texas—even the Jew ones—call me Ruby, Jack Ruby."

CHAPTER 7

Ruby and Ferrie stayed at the Flagship Motel and Restaurant, a stone's throw from the Custom House. Glowing signs advertised "Breakfast Served All Day" and "Cocktail Bar." The Flagship—festooned with Coca-Cola signs outside and a mock ship funnel on the roof—had a whimsical look that belied the fact it was one of Key West's better motels. Adding to the whimsy, the Flagship Restaurant offered curb-side service for diners on the go.

Ruby spread detailed maps of Cuba out on the breakfast table at the Flagship the next morning. Pointing to the same spot Banister had pointed to a few weeks earlier, he said, "Batista has a large force led by Major Quevedo ready to attack from the south. Here, at La Plata, tomorrow morning. Batista believes this should put Castro away. Castro appears to have only about three hundred men in the area, but no one knows for sure. That's where you come in."

"I buzz around, take some pictures?" Ferrie asked. "Radio you with what I see?"

"Right. Check the mountains above the river, see how the rebels are deployed. Assembled together? Split into divisions? Snipers in trees?"

"Okay."

"You'll also need to eyeball Batista's men—they're not exactly Patton's Third Army. Do they look serious, organized, well-drilled? Or just going through the motions? You should be able to get a sense."

"My fuel'll only last so long."

Ruby had things well-planned. "Just east of La Plata is the bigger town of Santiago de Cuba. There's an airport there right along the Caribbean, named for some old revolutionary—Maceo Airport. We've made arrangements for you to refuel there as you need to. Just land and head for the fuel tanks. Your code words are *silver spur*."

"What if I go down?"

"I've got a friend who ran a club in Dallas. He's running the Tropicana in Havana now for some of Marcello's friends. He and I have been to hell and back. He'll do anything for me. If you get in any trouble, find a way to contact the Tropicana and ask for Lewis McWillie. You'll be fine."

Ferrie scribbled *Lewis McWillie, Tropicana* on a Flagship Motel napkin.

\|\|\|\|

The next morning Ferrie took off from the Key West International Airport and, after crossing one hundred miles of the Atlantic, scissored across the northern coast of Cuba at Caibarien and then traversed the heart of the island to the Caribbean. He circled south and east around the tip of Cabo Cruz and the Vargas lighthouse—the area where Castro came ashore in the ship *Granma* to start the revolution in 1956—and then sped north, crossing the southern coastline between La Plata and Santiago de Cuba. He crossed the Sierra Maestra and flew back to the Caribbean at La Plata.

Batista's men were coming ashore at the mouth of the La Plata River.

Running low on fuel, Ferrie touched down at Maceo, refueled, and flew west along the ridge to Bayamo. He executed a dozen passes south around the planned battle area, which indeed was in and around the village of La Plata. He refueled twice. He radioed Ruby frequently.

As the government troops were getting their footing on land, Ferrie could see rebel troops positioned in separate small groups in the mountains encircling the village. Single rebel snipers were scattered about, strategically looking down on the village and surrounding beach. Ferrie could see that the rebels had blocked the key roads up the mountains with tree trunks and rocks. The rebels looked locked and loaded. Determined.

In contrast, the government troops appeared overconfident and casual as they dug trenches in the sand. Some were laughing. Some were smoking cigarettes. A few even appeared to be catching some shut-eye in the warming sun.

"Looks like Quevedo's troops are walking into a trap," Ferrie radioed to Ruby.

It was too dangerous for Ferrie to fly after dark. He headed back to Key West at dusk. Ruby met him at the airport.

"I got a pretty good look. You heard my radio signals. If Batista was looking to roll up the Sierra Maestra and have a knockout blow, it's probably not going to happen."

"I passed on your intelligence. I think the intelligence had an impact. General Cantillo had ordered Quevedo to hold some troops back but now's going to have him send them in in a second wave. Batista still seems confident."

"I'm not sure I'd be."

"There's only so much we can do. They say Cantillo doesn't want any more air intelligence. Apparently, he believes that a plane flying around distracts or even scares his troops. Marcello has agreed to hold us back, for now anyway. Quevedo has told headquarters he's got a handle on the situation and the second wave will work."

"Send a message from me that it ain't gonna."

"Nah, too late. That's the plan. We've done our job. I don't usually drink, but let's do a few mojitos in hopeful anticipation of a victorious Batista."

After too many rummy mojitos and cigarettes at the Brown Derby at the southeast corner of Southard and Whitehead Streets, and a surprisingly good night's sleep at the Flagship, Ferrie made the three-stop trip back to New Orleans. There he learned the attack on La Plata had utterly failed. This humiliation was made worse by the shocking defection of Major

Quevedo—who was a school friend of Castro's—and a few other officers to Castro's side.

\|\|\|\|

Ferrie had to put in a few days' work for Eastern, flying typical routings back and forth to Houston and Austin. And he had to tend to all the other activities in his life—dissecting mice, celebrating Catholic masses, catching up on the Jack Martin project. Ferrie worked it out with Banister that he'd spend just one day a week, Saturday, training new pilots for Cuba.

That training had taken on new importance after the La Plata debacle. The Saturday session was twelve hours long, starting at 5:30 a.m. This secret activity naturally couldn't occur at Lakefront or Moisant. Marcello associates of Gill and Banister had secured from friendlies in the Department of Defense the use of an inactive military field along the Intracoastal Canal 10 in Michoud, fifteen miles east of New Orleans. This facility had been used by a War Department contractor Higgins Shipbuilding to build Liberty Ships during World War II. FDR visited the facility in 1942. It was used during the Korean War to build tank engines. By 1953 the Michoud Field—its fifty-five-hundred-foot runway, semicircular turnarounds at each end, still intact—was deactivated. It laid unused until being commandeered by the mob in 1959.

Ferrie was a confident trainer. "I only need an hour to teach you how to land on a beach. In half a day, I can teach you to land on the back of a hog."

To prepare for his July flight over Cuba, Ferrie had studied Castro and his rebellion with the manic intensity with which he did everything. Castro, he came to see, wasn't trying to overthrow a dictator to restore democracy. Castro had indeed been fully converted to Marxism. He was aiming to establish a *Communist* government in Cuba. Though Ferrie had initially supported Castro, he'd turned full circle. With a born-again religious fervor, he now fully agreed with Marcello and Gill that Castro had to be defeated at all cost.

The cadets could sense Ferrie's fervor. Ferrie was an imposing figure on the tarmac, dressed in black military fatigues, black boots, and a black beret. On these Saturdays Ferrie took special care in applying his eyebrows and short-cropped toupee.

Ferrie started each training day with bombastic lectures on the importance of the mission and the terror the cadets and their families would face if Communism weren't defeated. "America stands at a crossroads," he'd say. Ferrie would then drill the cadets on the art of flying light aircraft and on Cuban geography.

After La Plata the scope of the mission expanded beyond just air surveillance. By mid-September some cadets began flying to Cuba with crates of arms supplied by cronies of Banister's. They used the Marcello planes from Lakefront. Flying low over Batista's troops in the Cuban hinterland, the Ferrie-trained pilots air-dropped the crates.

All of these troops, whether heading to Cuba for surveillance or to drop crates of arms, passed through Jack Ruby in Key West.

The Castro insurgency in Cuba had bobbed up and down like the stock market. After the loss at La Plata, Batista's troops regrouped and rebounded for a time, in part because of the weaponry dropped by Ferrie's cadets.

Batista nearly destroyed the Castro insurgents at the Battle of Las Mercedes in the Sierra Maestra in late July. But Castro masterfully avoided defeat. He sent a message across enemy lines to Batista's General Cantillo declaring that he was ready to negotiate a surrender. Castro asked for a temporary cease-fire. Incomprehensibly, General Cantillo agreed. During the "negotiations," Castro's troops slipped back into the mountains. Though they had been pinned down by superior numbers, Castro and his rebels escaped. Fuming, the American mob called Batista on the carpet. Batista, though, remained confident. "We still have more people and more firepower," Batista told Santo Trafficante.

With a new lease on life, the rebels regained strength through the fall of 1958. Moving northwest in the middle of the country, they took several cities and secured control of the Cauto River plain. Castro then split his troops into three columns, one under the command of Che Guevara, as they traversed the Escambray Mountains.

As success now seemed possible, other rebel groups that had been Castro rivals decided to join together under him. This was troubling news, because one advantage Batista had had was that the rebels hadn't been unified. The consolidated rebel forces then headed for Santa Clara, the important capital of Las Villas Province, 160 miles from Havana. These forces remained divided into three columns. Castro planned to merge the columns, including the newly joined competitor rebels, after a three-pronged assault on Santa Clara.

The mob was so spooked by these developments that Banister was ordered to have Ferrie himself return to Cuba just after Christmas Day and make a surveillance flight over the midlands to see what he could find out directly.

Were Castro and his now larger consolidated team of rebels successful in taking Santa Clara, they'd have a straight shot to the capital.

Ferrie met Jack Ruby again at the Flagship on Front Street in Key West. They had come to like each other and had a lively evening over dinner at the A&B. Ferrie took off from Key West International early the next morning, December 30, flying toward Cuba.

His flight over Cuba's mountainous Alturas de Santa Clara was tricky. He made numerous passes over the target area, the Los Villas Province, stopping for fuel this time at the airport in Cienfuegos, "*La Perla del Sur*," on the southern coast. Scything northeast up the gut of the island, Ferrie could see hundreds of rebel troops taking over the garrison in the town of Yaguajay, forty-seven miles from Santa Clara. Flying west toward Santa Clara, he spied other rebels approaching Santa Clara.

Ferrie flew over and past Santa Clara. He could see a government train chuffing east from Havana, presumably carrying government troops from Havana toward Santa Clara.

He radioed the news to Ruby. A crucial battle was coming at Santa Clara. And Castro's army—now better-armed after the sacking of the garrison at Yaguajay—was going to be evenly matched with Batista's oncoming fighters. The sun falling, Ferrie beat it back to Florida.

Ruby met Ferrie at the Brown Derby. The bar was full of submarine sailors from the nearby Naval base. Ferrie downed a rum and Coke with lime—a "Cuba Libre." They reviewed Ferrie's intelligence in more detail. And Ruby talked about his new club, the Sovereign on Commerce Street. The next night in New Orleans, Ferrie downed several Cuba Libres with Banister at the Monteleone's Carousel Bar.

Thursday, New Year's Day of 1959, was a fateful day for millions of people, including Ferrie. As he'd predicted, there had been a crushing clash at Santa Clara several days after Christmas. Under the leadership of Che Guevara, the rebels defeated the Batista troops and the Santa Clara police. The rebel victory was made easier by Batista's decision to hold most of his troops back to protect Havana. Che had earlier been able to derail and capture the train Ferrie had seen from the air. It'd been chock full of artillery, which added to the rebels' firepower.

News of the victory at Santa Clara rapidly reached Havana. Batista heard the cheering crowds in the streets of Havana on New Year's Eve and knew the increasingly reenergized and rearmed Castro fighters were heading his way. His troops in Havana were beginning to waver. The United States pulled its support for Batista.

Three hours into the new year, Batista and forty supporters and family members boarded a plane at Camp Columbia, the large base on the outskirts of Havana, and fled to the Dominican Republic. On the second day of the new year, with the city's commandant giving up, a cavalcade of Castro soldiers marched into Havana. Banister and Ferrie were ordered to stand down, at least for the time being.

Castro's grip on Cuba, however, wasn't yet ironclad. Through January and February, Batista loyalists, helped in some cases by

Ferrie trainees, Ruby, and McWillie, dropped bombs from small planes on cities, including Havana, and incendiary phosphorous on sugar cane fields.

But Castro's position only strengthened as his new government survived these attacks. He closed the casinos.

Castro's coup d'état would affect the rest of Ferrie's life in a profusion of perilous ways.

CHAPTER 8

For a year after Castro's victory and the closing of the casinos, the mob was stunned into inaction—as were the US government and the angry Cuban exiles in Florida. As a result, for Ferrie, 1959 was a year of relative calm and normality, at least what passed for calm and normality in his restless world. The storms would come and toss Ferrie in all directions in the 1960s.

Ferrie's apartment in the Vinet house had become an intolerable nuisance to his neighbors. He, in turn, had become increasingly concerned about the attention some of his mob and lifestyle activities may get in this close-knit community. With spare time now on his hands, he decided to move his odd mishmash of stuff, including mice cages and religious gear, to a different, smaller apartment at 704 Airline Park Boulevard, closer to Moisant Field. A neighborhood of blue collar workers and singles.

Ferrie also put more effort into his duties with the Civil Air Patrol during the last year of the 1950s. Training new pilots continued to be rewarding for Ferrie. And it provided opportunities to make new friends to pal around with.

The opportunity to focus more energetically on his religious activities also reinvigorated him. He restarted his periodic masses, which his small flock had missed. And he regularly bussed the ten miles back and forth to the Holy Name of Jesus Church at Loyola University to assist the priest and nuns there. He had developed close bonds at Holy Name in the past and was excited to renew them. He read everything he could about the new pope, John XXIII.

As Ferrie's calm year was winding down, an unexpected and happy event affected his life. One of Ferrie's traditions was to donate toys in December to sick kids as part of a Jefferson Parish toy drive. This year, as in the previous years since December 1955 when the Crippled Children's Hospital opened, the toys were to be donated and distributed there. This new facility was adjacent to the large and mysterious US Public Health Service campus, on Henry Clay Avenue along a Mississippi River levee near the Audubon Zoo in "uptown" New Orleans.

The main structure on the Public Health Service campus was a striking five-story pentagonal building topped by a dome 130 feet high. Six tall white columns fronted the structure. Since 1929 this majestic landmark had been a welcome-to-New-Orleans symbol for eastbound barge captains who had just completed negotiating the sharp camel-hump turn of the Mississippi by the Ochsner Foundation Hospital. But what went on in the structure was a complete unknown to these captains—and, for that matter, to almost everybody else.

Ferrie brought his toys to the hospital a week before Christmas. He'd purchased most of them at the Little Toy Shop, near the river in the Quarter.

The children were gathered in the lounge on the third floor to greet the donors and receive the gifts. Several other toy donors were there as well. Doc Souchon, a physician *and* a jazz performer, was alternately strumming his guitar and his banjo for the kids.

The nurse in charge welcomed Ferrie and introduced him to a young, one-legged boy and to a young girl lying on a gurney. A middle-aged woman was already chatting with the children. Ferrie introduced himself. She was named Mary Stults Sherman. She was elegantly dressed and polished-looking. Her right foot was tapping to Doc Souchon's music. She told Ferrie she was a doctor.

Ferrie and Dr. Sherman chatted casually. Her specialty, she said, was orthopedics, but her real passion was cancer research. She often worked directly with Dr. Alton Ochsner, who had recruited her to come to New Orleans from the University of Chicago.

She mentioned, not entirely jokingly, that she spent more time with laboratory mice and monkeys than she did with humans. She was trying to understand what caused cancer tumors by performing experiments on these animals. She was particularly focused on the connection between certain viruses and cancer.

Dr. Sherman captivated Ferrie. He could tell from the first short paragraphs she uttered that, in terms of brains and class, she was head and shoulders above anybody else he'd ever met. Even Dr. Ochsner. But, at the same time, she was easygoing, was easy to talk to. Although he was an amateur scientist, and she operated at the highest professional levels, Ferrie and Dr. Sherman talked spiritedly about the mission to cure cancer.

Ferrie described his own research with white mice. His work was pedestrian and amateurish, he acknowledged—mainly finding tumors and then injecting different solutions into them to see what happened. He'd read about possible viral connections to cancer, but he didn't have the resources to seriously research such exotic theories.

"Ma'am, it seems like most cancer researchers don't believe cancer can be caused by viruses. But that's not true, right?" Ferrie asked.

"Right. It's not true. Nor is the virus theory new. In fact, there was a doctor before World War I who figured out that a common tumor in chickens was caused by a virus."

"Dr. Peyton Rous?"

"Very good, sir. Go to the head of the class."

"And later Dr. Rous worked on some rabbit virus, if I remember correctly."

"You got it."

Dr. Sherman continued. "I'm particularly interested in picking up on some work a friend of mine named Sarah Stewart has been doing at the National Institutes of Health related to a type of mouse virus that works as an agent to take mouse leukemia and turn it into a glandular cancer. Sarah and her partner have written an article on this."

"I've read it—in a cancer journal," Ferrie said.

Dr. Sherman was duly impressed by his knowledge of this arcane subject and by the fact that he read the *Journal of the National Cancer Institute*. She'd remember his name.

"I have to run," Dr. Sherman said. "Thank you for the stimulating conversation, Mr. Ferrie. Perhaps we can continue this at some point."

"It would be my pleasure, ma'am."

"Godspeed."

"Thank you again, Dr. Mary," the nurse in charge said.

As the doctor disappeared down the hallway, the nurse turned to Ferrie. "Everyone calls her Dr. Mary. She's an angel."

CHAPTER 9

On Thursday evening, October 15, 1959, JFK gave a speech at the Louisiana Democratic Party dinner in New Orleans, intimating without much subtlety that he'd be running for president. The dinner was in the International Room at the Roosevelt Hotel. There were one thousand guests, Al Hirt played at the dinner, and the dueling female piano players from Pat O'Brien's performed later, privately, for JFK and his entourage.

JFK chose Louisiana to float this balloon because he believed the state could be important for him in the 1960 election, with its ten electoral votes and proximity to twenty-one more in Arkansas and Missouri. Louisiana's Democratic leaders, particularly Camille Gravel, had helped JFK in his unsuccessful effort to secure the vice president nomination in 1956. If he kept their support and, most important, locked down that of Governor Earl Long, Huey's younger brother, he could win Louisiana in 1960. Governor Long hadn't supported JFK in 1956 and had felt at the time that Gravel had acted against his wishes.

To help gain Governor Long's support this time around, JFK had decided to make this important speech in Louisiana in front of the governor and the party. It would be difficult to win Louisiana without the governor's help.

Rather than being with his wife that evening, Governor Long was accompanied by his new mistress Blaze Starr. What the governor didn't know was that Blaze and JFK had spent time together in Washington. At some point during the evening, Blaze and JFK slipped off the dance floor and had a quick sexual encounter in a closet at the hotel. Looking for Blaze, Governor Long found the closet and opened the door. Blaze nervously told him she slipped into the closet to readjust her undergarments— she *didn't* tell him that JFK was in there too, hiding behind some boxes. Had Governor Long seen him, JFK's chances to win Louisiana, perhaps the presidency, would have greatly suffered.

After that evening in the Big Easy, the world was on notice that JFK was likely to run for president. He formally announced his candidacy on the second day of 1960. In the historic Beaux-Arts US Senate Office Building, Caucus Room SR-325, JFK pledged to work "to maintain freedom and order in the newly emerging nations" and to "end . . . Soviet gains [that] threaten our very existence."

JFK's main rival for the Democratic nomination was the liberal and feisty senator from Minnesota, Hubert Humphrey— the "Happy Warrior." Humphrey had blasted onto the national scene with a fiery pro–civil rights speech at the 1948 Democratic Convention in Philadelphia. "My friends, to those who say that we are rushing this issue of civil rights, I say to them we are 172 years late. . . . The time has arrived in America . . . to walk forthrightly into the bright sunshine of human rights."

Kennedy was viewed as the moderate even somewhat conservative candidate.

JFK and Humphrey were set to brawl in thirteen primaries. Of the thirteen, two were do-or-die tests for JFK. Wisconsin would show whether he could win in a left-of-center region of the country, an area Humphrey called home. West Virginia was the ultimate trial, though. Many West Virginians were wary of electing a man who may have more allegiance to a foreign potentate, the pope, than to the Constitution.

CHAPTER 10

The grand, smoothly curved Fontainebleau Hotel, sand-wiched between Indian Creek and the Atlantic Ocean at the bend of Collins Avenue on the edge of what had been Millionaire's Row in Miami Beach, sat on the very land where tire tycoon Harvey Firestone's opulent but tasteful Harbel Villa once sat.

For Firestone, Harbel Villa was a retreat to relax by pursuing temperance, good health, and, in particular, intellectual contemplation and discussion. Firestone entertained leading thought leaders of his time, including Thomas Edison, Henry Ford, Charles Schwab, Cyrus H. K. Curtis, John Golden, and President Herbert Hoover, on this narrow spit of limestone and sand. Charity was also a mainstay of the estate. The Firestones frequently opened up Harbel Villa for events for local groups and churches, sometimes using the part of their property that extended over to the west side of Indian Creek, as they had on March 5, 1931, for the Women's Association of the Miami Community Church. At that event Firestone brought out one of his vanity possessions for the children, an elephant named Rosie. He also at one time kept a Liberian dwarf hippopotamus, one of the few in America, at Harbel Villa—a reclusive little fellow named Billy. For reasons never disclosed, Firestone gave Billy to President Coolidge in 1927. Coolidge passed Billy on to the National Zoo, where he became the father of nearly every dwarf hippopotamus born in this country.

Harbel Villa's successor, the Fontainebleau, offered a glitzy, *not* very tasteful contrast. Little intellectual debate happened there. It catered to movie stars, gangsters, and thousand-dollar hookers. The hotel wasn't opened to charitable events unless, of course, the charity paid handsomely. The only exotic animals were humans. Miami Beach had morphed in only thirty years from a quiet, peaceful enclave into the entertainment capital of the east coast. Fun, sun, guilty pleasures.

On the first Saturday morning of the spring of 1960, one of the most celebrated men in America awoke in a Fontainebleau penthouse suite beside a jarringly sensuous brunette. Frank Sinatra, world-class entertainer and amateur hoodlum, looked over at Judy Campbell, who was just beginning to stir.

"After a night like that, Jude, I'm thinking we should get back together."

With sleep still in her sapphire eyes, Judy softly declared, "No way, Francis. Whatever sweet talk you may throw my way, I know you'll still keep fucking any broad you can as long as she's under sixty and has a pulse. Maybe even up to seventy."

"You must have me confused with somebody else, doll."

Judy sat up in bed, scrunching her eyes at the sunlight streaming in through the sheer curtain. The top sheet fluttered down from her chin to her waist. She'd been sunbathing by the pool for several days in a bikini. Surrounded by soft brown skin, her bare breasts glowed white and bright. *Headlights,* Sinatra called them.

"Francis, you'll always occupy a corner of my heart. Always. But hon, after six years of that worthless, horny, two-bit actor husband of mine sneaking around on me, I'm done with philanderers. *I* want to have some fun for a while. Meet some new people, some good guys. Live a little. And maybe, at some point, I'll meet Mr. Right. Even then, though, you and I can still have our visits."

Sinatra lit a cigarette and let her have a drag. "If you say so, sweetheart."

"*Ti amo, tesoro.*"

"*Sí, lo so.*"

He kissed her gently on the lips.

"All right, babe, let's talk about tonight," Sinatra said.

"Another drag please."

He passed the cigarette back to Judy. "You'll have a front row seat at the show. When it's over, I want you to meet another big-shot friend of mine. He isn't pretty like Jack, though he's got more clout than Jack'll ever have, even if he gets elected."

Sinatra had introduced Judy to JFK at the Sands in Vegas in February. He'd been filming the movie *Ocean's Eleven* there with his friends known as the "Rat Pack"—Dean Martin, Peter Lawford, Sammy Davis Jr., and Joey Bishop.

"Name?" Judy asked.

"It's like something out of a Dashiell Hammett detective story. Sam Flood. He wants to meet you and, I'm telling you, he's a good guy for *you* to know. Do me a big favor and go out with him a few times. I guarantee you'll like him—and the high-cotton places he'll take you. He'll be at the party later tonight in the Poodle Lounge."

"Only for you, Francis."

"If you keep your thing going with Jack, you'll find that the Senator may value your connection with Sam. Sam could help him big time in the campaign."

"I'd do anything to help Jack."

"He's really hooked you."

"Oh, yeah. Line and sinker too. What gal wouldn't be hooked? Gorgeous guy! Fuck-me smile! Obscenely green eyes! Filthy rich! If he weren't married, I could see something really happening with him quickly. I know he digs me. A girl can tell.

"Jack and I've talked almost every day since Vegas. That guy's smooth as Mulberry silk, with that sexy Boston accent. We finally made love, Francis. In New York. A few weeks ago, at the fricking Plaza Hotel! He's a short-timer in bed but, wow! It was super exciting being with him."

"I *have* heard he's doesn't have my—shall we say—durability in the bedroom."

"Few do, my love. Few do. Maybe he was just stressed. He's getting really tied up with campaign stuff. I won't get more private time with him for a few weeks. And when that time comes, Katy bar the door, baby."

"Look, I love the guy too. Just don't go off the deep end with him. He screws around for sure, but he's not leaving that high-class wife of his, at least not as long as he's in politics. He knows better than anyone that she's got a corncob up her ass—she adds sophistication, though, to a guy who comes from a sketchy family."

"The Kennedys? Sketchy?"

"All the money comes from the old man Joe's bootlegging. He's a crook—also a serial adulterer and, believe it or not, loved the Nazis. Admired Hitler."

"Whatever. He sired a *muy caliente* son."

"The Kennedys are *nouveau riche* Micks. The Boston Brahmins won't have anything to do with them. That's why the old man's trying to buy the presidency. And that's why Jack needs Jackie. She's old money, the daughter of a silk stocking from Southampton. She fucking speaks French."

"Well . . . maybe. But he clearly gets a lot of ass that's not hers, I can tell you that."

"You don't know the half of it, darling."

"I know more than I want to."

"Back to more immediate matters. The program starts at six fifteen. There'll be a card with your name on it on your seat."

\\\\\\

Sinatra showered and dressed. The last of his Timex television specials was being taped that night, and he was unusually tense about the show. Elvis Presley was performing—for the first time since getting out of the Army. There was a lot of pressure on Sinatra to ensure everything went well. Timex and ABC had ponied up a staggering $125,000 for Elvis's appearance.

Fellow Rat Pack members Joey Bishop, Sammy Davis Jr., and Peter Lawford would be lending aid and comfort to Sinatra by appearing in the show.

Sinatra had been against having Elvis on the show. From different generations, he and Elvis had become rivals. Sinatra was dismissive of Elvis's "rock 'n' roll" music. It had no style, Sinatra believed. Particularly annoying to Sinatra this evening was that he wasn't just going to introduce Elvis. They were actually going to perform together—dueling back and forth between Sinatra singing Elvis's "Love Me Tender," a shitty teenager song in Sinatra's view, and Elvis crooning Sinatra's "Witchcraft." Sinatra was convinced Elvis would ruin "Witchcraft."

The Tom Hansen dancers would provide several finely-choreographed dances to keep things calm. Daughter Nancy would appear throughout the show. She'd make sure things ran smoothly.

Sinatra had invited celebrity friends to the taping, including Miami Beach regulars Gary Cooper, Joan Crawford, Liberace, and Joe DiMaggio. A large contingent of Elvis fans would be there as well. Elvis's crooked agent "Colonel" Tom Parker—who was actually an illegal immigrant from the Netherlands—had had Elvis travel to Miami on a train, making whistle-stops to adoring crowds along the way. Many Elvis fans had followed the train to Miami Beach.

As Sinatra began to turn the knob on the door to leave the suite and go greet Elvis, he swiveled back to Judy and her still-exposed "headlights."

"Jude, didn't your dick ex-husband make a movie with Elvis?"

"The creep's best work! He was the only person, Francis, so far anyway, ever to sing a song along with Elvis in a movie. A real foot-stomper nobody's heard since called 'We're Going to Move.'"

"Small world, huh? I'll probably be the first to sing with Elvis on TV." Sinatra left and went down to Le Ronde, where the show was being taped.

The dueling duet was awkward for Sinatra but went well enough and was a hit for the live audience. Elvis was his usual "aw shucks" Mississippi self, buoyed by hundreds of overstimulated postpubescent girl fans in the crowd. Sinatra masked his annoyance well, grinning through the banal lyrics of "Love Me Tender" and Elvis's disrespectful rendition of "Witchcraft," which included a painfully out-of-place finishing flourish.

Sinatra offered to have a drink with Elvis before he left with the Colonel. As they crossed the lobby of the hotel, trailed by several Rat Pack members, they were called into a raucous bar mitzvah being held in one of the ballrooms. Taking advantage of the free drinks, Sinatra, Elvis, and their small entourage posed for pictures, making the young man's celebration uniquely memorable.

\\\\

The Poodle Lounge after the show was electric. The sense of relief after taping this special show was palpable.

The setting of the Poodle Lounge added to the fun. On the walls were murals of erotic paintings by the eighteenth-century French artist Jean-Honoré Fragonard. Except that the female faces had been replaced with the mugs of poodles.

While Elvis didn't show up at the Poodle Lounge, the other big stars from the taping were there, joined by Dean Martin and Juliet Prowse, who were smoking Chesterfields and drinking straight-up Tanqueray, Sinatra's favorite gin. Hotel owner Ben Novack and his trophy second wife, a former fashion model named Bernice, weaved through the crowd, greeting each guest like a best friend. The Lounge's charismatic host, Ahmed Boob, was there too. Rumor had it that Novack had won Boob in a card game from actor Omar Sharif.

A half-dozen prostitutes—most cultivating a sexy girl-next-door look—were sensually snaking through the crowd. Novack allowed them in on the condition that they wouldn't directly proposition a customer. They were known around the hotel as "food-and-beverage" hookers. While in the Poodle Lounge, they were limited to seeking dinner or nightcap dates with a willing man. Thereafter, off premises, they were free to offer any favors they wanted to.

Sinatra, obviously a little buzzed, took Judy by the arm to meet Sam Flood.

Flood wasn't what Judy had expected. He was an older, ruddy man who was attractive in a kind of life-well-lived way. A gentleman, he took her hand and sandwiched it between both of his. It was a privilege to meet her, he said—she was beautiful, some man should shower her with diamonds and pearls. He made an impression.

"Please, I hope that wasn't inappropriate," Flood said.

"Are you kidding? Girls like compliments. Shower away!"

"I would very much be honored to see you again and get to know you. Frank has told me so much about you."

"I'd be delighted, Mr. Flood."

"Splendid. And call me Sam. Please. I'll reach out to you through Frank in a few days, if you don't mind. Now, I have some business to attend to."

He kissed her hand. Judy noticed his piercing eyes, never diverting from hers.

Another man, who introduced himself politely as "Santo," took Flood away. Flood bowed to Judy before he left.

Santo Trafficante and Sam Flood left the Fontainebleau and went next door to the equally elegant Eden Roc Hotel. Entering Harry's American Bar, they spotted the men they had come to see.

Carlos Marcello stood up and greeted them.

Sam Flood responded, "Carlos, good to see you." As was his custom, Marcello wore a nice suit and, even though the bar was dark, sunglasses. With him was John Roselli, an elegant-looking, silver-haired man—also wearing sunglasses. An outgoing and cheerful man, Roselli was the only one of Marcello's three peers to call him "Little Man" to his face. Marcello was not fond of this moniker that had followed him around since he was in his twenties.

These four mob kingpins controlled the country's organized crime network. Trafficante ran most of Florida. Roselli, though originally a Chicago mob leader, had been sent west to oversee

LA and, increasingly, Las Vegas. Sam Flood, whose real name was Mooney "Sam" Giancana, was the mob boss in Chicago and controlled other parts of the Midwest as well. He also had strong influence over New York. Marcello—New Orleans and parts of Texas.

Among these four equals, Giancana was first. The four reported to "the Commission," the mob board of directors comprised of representatives of the main mob families and chaired by Carlo the "Godfather" Gambino. The Commission only periodically got involved in the day-to-day operations of the four men sitting in Harry's American Bar this day.

"Sinatra's gal clearly didn't recognize me. I can tell you, though, she's really something. Better than Sinatra described. I can see why JFK is risking his political future to get some of that," Giancana said, a broad smile on his face. "Wow!"

"Da thunderbolt?" Marcello asked. Marcello talked like a semi-literate day laborer.

"Sounds like the thunderbolt, Sam my friend," Trafficante said. "You been struck."

"Nah," Giancana responded. "C'mon. She's good-looking. But no love at first sight. Just doing my job."

"There's still smoke coming out of your ass," Roselli joked. "You *do* look a little moony, Mooney."

"*Improbabile.*"

"What is da next step with this *puttana*?" Marcello asked.

"I'll start courting," Giancana said. "She's leaving for New York tomorrow. I'll send five dozen red roses up there. And I'll keep them coming. Frank'll tell her I want to call her, and then I'll unleash the charm.

"She's meeting and screwing JFK in DC in early April," Giancana continued. "Right after the Wisconsin primary. By that time I'll have softened her up and she'll see me after that. That'll be about the time old man Kennedy'll come calling on us for help. This gal will be the direct channel to JFK. That's a big deal and, bonus, it would allow us to bypass that prick brother Bobby. Little fucker."

"*Strunzo.*" Marcello spat on the floor.

"Bobby'll have to get off our backs if—when—we help Kennedy win."

"God help us if that Quaker pussy Nixon wins. You can't believe a word he says. Even Ike doesn't trust him."

"And ya can't buy 'im," Marcello said.

"Not since Checkers," Trafficante agreed.

Giancana had ordered a round of limoncellos. "A toast," he said. "*Cento di questi giomi!*"

"Â saluti!" the other three powerful men shouted in unison.

"To Sam bedding Kennedy's girlfriend!" Roselli raised his glass.

Giancana smiled and raised *his* glass. The others did too.

"*Isa, isa, isa.*" Lowering their glasses, they said in unison, "*Cala, cala, cala.*" Touching the glasses to their lips, "*Accosta, accosta, accosta.*" They then gulped down their limoncellos and banged their glasses on the table.

CHAPTER 11

The Wisconsin primary on April 5 was the first pivotal Kennedy-Humphrey showdown. Humphrey was seen as the natural favorite. Wisconsin had a history of progressivism going back to "Fighting Bob" La Follette, the presidential candidate of the Progressive Party in 1924. La Follette was either Wisconsin's governor *or* senator for the first twenty-five years of the century. Many of Wisconsin's voters thus were historically wired to be receptive to Humphrey's liberal philosophy. The state, moreover, bordered Humphrey's home state of Minnesota.

On the other hand, JFK had a better campaign staff and much more money. He also had the good fortune that 40 percent of Wisconsin's voters were Catholic. JFK was the first serious Catholic contender for a major party's presidential nomination since New York Governor Al Smith in 1928.

His Wisconsin campaign got an improbable boost from a new campaign song sung by his friend Frank Sinatra. Sinatra had changed the words to his Oscar-winning song "High Hopes" for JFK. His new recording of the song was put out on 45 rpm records and distributed around the state. "Nineteen sixty's the year for high hopes. Come on and vote for Kennedy, vote for Kennedy, keep America strong—Kennedy, he just keeps rollin' along."

JFK won surprisingly easily in Wisconsin on a wave of Catholic votes, including from Republican Catholics who crossed party lines to vote for him. JFK got a large crossover vote in particular from the Fox River Valley area of the state, the late

Senator Joe McCarthy's home base. McCarthy had had close connections with JFK's father Joseph P. Kennedy Sr., a fellow extreme anti-Communist, and was the godfather of RFK's first child. Republican Catholics also turned out for JFK in Milwaukee and Green Bay.

The substantial Catholic population of Wisconsin was further motivated by the devious activities of a JFK political operative named Paul Corbin. Corbin oversaw a dirty operation pretending to question JFK's qualifications to be president because of his Catholicism. Several days before the election, Corbin had a mailing sent to thousands of Catholic families in Wisconsin urging them not to vote for "an agent of the Pope." The mailings were postmarked from Humphrey's home base, Minneapolis, Minnesota. This prank fueled the rush of Catholic voters, angry at Humphrey, to JFK.

The funds to support Corbin's mischief had funneled up from Chicago.

With the upset win in Wisconsin, the Democratic Party establishment began to stand up and take JFK more seriously. They saw a custom-built candidate to take on Vice President Richard Nixon, the inevitable Republican candidate. JFK was handsome, youthful, humorous, eloquent—qualities that the dour and loose-jowled Nixon was lacking.

JFK had it all. Almost. From the Democratic National Committee's perspective, the one blemish, notwithstanding the Wisconsin victory, *was* his religion. JFK's Catholicism had worked in his favor in heavily Catholic Wisconsin, but much of the country, the DNC believed, would hesitate to vote for a Catholic, as Al Smith had learned thirty-two years before. Many Americans had a serious unease with a religion that, they believed, saw the pope as the ultimate authority. Would a Catholic president secretly follow the pope's directions instead of the Constitution?

An old joke from 1928 about Al Smith's unsuccessful run for the presidency against Herbert Hoover was recirculating. Before that election, Protestant ministers had warned voters that if

Smith won, the pope would move to America and take over. The story went that the day after Smith's loss in the general election, Smith sent a one-word telegram to the pope— "Unpack!"

The do-or-die test for JFK was the May 10 primary in West Virginia. West Virginia was 98 percent Protestant. Many West Virginians had never even met a Catholic. Humphrey had strong supporters in the state, including West Virginia's new and already powerful US Senator Robert C. Byrd. The *Washington Post* predicted JFK would lose West Virginia due to the "issue of religion."

West Virginia had been artificially created eighty years after the end of the Revolutionary War by being cleaved off of Virginia during the Civil War. Comprising ubiquitous mountains and hills, forty-six rivers and thousands of streams, creeks, forks, and licks, and impossibly narrow valleys, its largely Scotch-Irish population was profoundly religious and more insular than most of America. Certain parts of West Virginia were so isolated that the residents still spoke an English dialect passed down from their ancestors that sounded more like Scottish-flavored Elizabethan English than modern American English. You would hear "aye" for "yes," "haint" for "ghost," "wherefore" for "why," "chide" for "scold," "het" for "upset," "mader" for "tomato." The Shakespearean word "afeared" was still commonly used.

The only significant numbers of non-Protestants in the state were the Eastern Europeans and Greeks who had been brought in during the first two decades of the twentieth century to work in the coal mines, the lifeblood of the state. These immigrants were largely Eastern Orthodox, a religion that rebuked Catholicism after the sacking of Constantinople in 1204.

West Virginia had turned solidly Democratic after FDR and the New Deal paved the way for the mines to be unionized. FDR had famously met with poor coal miners, faces smudged with black carbon, in Elm Grove, West Virginia, a suburb of Wheeling, during the 1932 presidential campaign.

JFK and his main advisor, brother Bobby, believed West Virginia was winnable if key political bosses in the state came to see that supporting JFK was in their personal interests. JFK and surrogates, including youngest brother Teddy, brother-in-law Peter Lawford, and FDR Jr., would attempt to convince them with political and policy pleas. NFL football players Sam Huff and Joe Stydahar—both former football stars at West Virginia University—would use their local celebrity power to be influential.

More was needed though, JFK and RFK knew, but much of that "more" would have to come in private settings involving covert operatives.

Joseph Kennedy had met with Sam Giancana in Chicago shortly before the Wisconsin primary to see what the mob might be willing to do to help make his son president. The price for the mob's help, Joe Kennedy was told by Giancana, was that JFK, as president, would call the dogs off of him and his colleagues—particularly his most rabid pit bull Bobby.

In 1957 JFK had been appointed to a new select committee organized to investigate the influence of the mob on the big labor unions. The committee chair was Senator John McClellan of Arkansas. RFK was assigned to be chief counsel of what became known as the "McClellan Committee" and given an unusual degree of power to set the agenda, schedule witnesses, and undertake much of the questioning of witnesses himself.

RFK was aggressive to the point of becoming almost unhinged in some of the hearings. He was overbearing and badgering in questioning labor union witnesses, who were the committee's original focus. In 1958 the committee switched its focus to the mob, which it frequently referred to as "organized crime"—or the "Mafia."

RFK got increasingly fired up as he learned more about the mob. He summoned Sam Giancana and Carlos Marcello to DC for questioning. He also brought in their mob colleagues Anthony Corrallo, Anthony Provenzano, Joey Glimco, and Vito Genovese from New York and Chicago. They all refused to answer substantive questions, invoking the Fifth Amendment.

Dismantling the mob became RFK's crusade. He wrote a book *The Enemy Within* about this national problem that was published as JFK was announcing his campaign for president.

It was readily apparent to anyone who knew the Kennedys that Bobby would be a key player in a JFK administration, perhaps even attorney general, though he was too young and not qualified for that job. To gain Giancana's support for the Kennedy campaign, Joe Kennedy had to assure him that RFK would be reined in and that the Kennedys would go soft on the mob if they won the White House. They had to focus on more important things, particularly freeing Cuba, Giancana instructed Joe. Without disclosing the details of this deal to RFK, JFK told his father that he was fully on board.

JFK returned to Washington the day after the Wisconsin primary to begin preparing for West Virginia. On Friday the private phone line in his Georgetown home rang.

"Can't wait to see you, Jack." It was Judy Campbell. "I'm at National Airport now."

"I wasn't sure you would show. I didn't hear from you last night."

"I'm such a fluffhead, Jack. I missed the plane. So I went out with Uncle Armand and some of his friends last night. Had dinner at the Persian Room at the Plaza. My body gets moist all over when I think of *our* time at the Plaza.

"And we saw Count Basie at Birdland—on Broadway!" Judy added.

Uncle Armand was actually the brother-in-law of Judy's uncle. Armand Cerami was a well-off owner of two popular fish restaurants north of Miami Beach, in an area called Sunny Isles. He was well-connected to the Trafficante organization. Unbeknownst to Judy, Uncle Armand was fully informed of Judy's connections with both Giancana and Kennedy and had been assigned to keep an eye on her for Trafficante and his colleagues. The mob left little to chance.

Judy congratulated JFK on Wisconsin.

"That was a damn big step," JFK said. "But we have bigger ones to come, darling. Why don't you get your pretty little bottom over here?"

Judy taxied to Georgetown. She was dressed in an elegant black suit and new mink coat. JFK welcomed her with a kiss on the cheek.

Jackie was out of town, as she often was. However, JFK wasn't alone. A tall man was there finishing up some business. The man introduced himself to Judy as William Thompson. Judy learned later that he was a wealthy railroad lobbyist and long-time rake-about-town with JFK. Thompson stayed for dinner, served by a young waiter. JFK and Thompson monopolized the conversation, talking mostly about campaign strategy. They were both confident that JFK could win West Virginia on May 10 and that that would doom Humphrey. All stops had to be pulled out, though, they agreed.

The lobbyist left after a couple of after-dinner drinks. He gently placed a large manila envelope on the petite console by the front door.

JFK showed Judy around the house. It was long and narrow with tall ceilings. The décor was flush with soft floral prints, and, not surprisingly given Jackie Kennedy's urbane taste, there were several pretty pieces of antique French furniture.

Judy and JFK made love. They fell asleep in the same bed, something Jack and Jackie seldom did. JFK was energized in the morning. "Sex relieves my migraines," he disclosed matter-of-factly. "Nothing else works."

He had to get going, he said. He was flying to West Virginia that day, followed by quick campaign jaunts to Indiana and Arizona.

"Judy, before I leave, I need a favor from you. Francis tells me you've met a man named Sam Flood."

"Yes."

"He happens to be a family friend. Francis said you may be seeing him soon in Chicago."

Surprised that JFK knew this, Judy said, "Yes indeed, Mr. Know-It-All. In fact, I'm taking a train there tomorrow."

"I would be grateful if you'd give him something." JFK went to the hall closet and pulled out a small satchel. "He's giving me some advice on the campaign in Illinois and I need to get some material to him," JFK said.

"Sure. I must confess—I don't know much about Mr. Flood, except he's a real gentleman and he's so kind to me. I like him. But I won't get romantic with him if you don't want me to."

"No. That's fine if you want to, sweetheart. He's a good man." Judy kissed JFK goodbye.

Someone on JFK's staff had booked a room at the Mayflower Hotel near the White House for Judy for that night. She grabbed a drink at the Town and Country Lounge, J. Edgar Hoover's favorite lunch spot, and went to bed.

The next afternoon she boarded the overnight Chicago Express No. 9 at Union Station, arriving at Chicago's Grand Central Station at 7:40 a.m. She kept the satchel nearby at all times.

Picking Judy up at the station, Sam Flood told her his real name. "My parents were immigrants from Sicily. I'm known in most places, particularly in Chicago and other big cities, as Sam *Giancana*, a Sicilian name reflecting my Sicilian blood. I use the last name 'Flood' in other parts of the country where folks aren't as keen on us Sicilians—you know we're all criminals!"

\\\\

In the following weeks, Giancana and his associates sent trusted colleagues into West Virginia, each with suitcases packed with cash.

The mob money was needed. As of mid-April 1960, an initial JFK lead in West Virginia—mainly based on his good looks— had completely evaporated. The decline was largely because many West Virginians, now turning their attention in earnest to the election, were learning for the first time that JFK wasn't a Protestant.

On April 12 Dr. Norman Vincent Peale spoke in Charleston, the state capital, forcefully questioning whether a Catholic should be put in charge of the country. Dr. Peale, author of *The Power of Positive Thinking* and a well-known Methodist preacher, believed that the Catholic Church was "a political organization." He said that *no* Catholic, including JFK, could "withstand the determined efforts of the [Catholic] hierarchy to work its will in American political life." The Rev. Dr. Billy Graham, a false reputation for political neutrality to protect, worked behind the scenes to stir up Protestant anxiety.

RFK aggressively ran JFK's West Virginia campaign. He and brother Teddy landed in Charleston on April 6 to set up shop. That afternoon they met at the Hotel Kanawha on Post Office Square, which became the JFK state campaign headquarters, with seventy campaign workers from twenty-eight of the southernmost counties in the state. They flew over to Clarksburg that same afternoon to meet with campaign workers from the twenty-seven other counties. The next day FDR Jr. arrived in West Virginia to visit a handful of key areas of the state, including the southern coal towns of Madison and Logan on Saturday. These industrious towns were where the voters' concern about Catholicism was the most severe.

JFK began a three-day tour of West Virginia coal country on Thursday, April 25. He moved south from Huntington through the small villages of Lavalette, Wayne, Crum, and Kermit on the way to Williamson in Mingo County. Williamson stood on the Tug Fork, a shallow tributary of the Big Sandy River. The Tug Fork provides the border between West Virginia and Kentucky. JFK met with residents of Williamson and crossed the Tug Fork to meet some Kentuckians. He then hopped in a private car and was driven the thirty-four miles northwest to the capital of coal country, Logan.

Logan was a bustling small city of 4,185 people with two primary streets located on a sliver of valley land along the muddy Guyandotte River. It was squeezed tightly between two small but sharp mountain ranges. Logan was the county seat of Logan County.

Logan County was home to the Hatfield clan, which had feuded with the McCoy family across the Tug Fork in Kentucky for most of the second half of the nineteenth century. It also was the birthplace of the world-renowned stripper Blaze Starr. Indeed, other than actress Joanne Dru, and perhaps the late Hatfield family patriarch Devil Anse, Blaze was the county's most famous native.

Introduced by his 317-pound Logan campaign chair, Claude "Big Daddy" Ellis, JFK spoke from the Logan County Court House steps. He gave what had become his stump coal-industry speech. "There is no industry," he began, "which has suffered more from government neglect in the last eight years than the coal industry."

The town's citizens turned out en masse to see JFK, a rare out-of-state celebrity to visit Logan. There was a carnival atmosphere. Most of Logan's business and professional elite was there, as was Henry Hatfield, the grandson of Devil Anse. Henry controlled dozens and dozens of votes in Logan County, including a few from residents of the Hatfield Cemetery in the tiny nearby village of Sarah Ann—pronounced locally as "Sar-ey Ain." RFK and brother Teddy had already met with many of the county's leaders, including with Henry Hatfield and his wife Jean at their hillside home in Sarah Ann.

"Big Daddy" Ellis's enthusiastic support for JFK had been fueled by a gift of $50,000 from JFK agents.

After his speech JFK and his entourage of staffers and press cut through the court house to Jefferson Street and proceeded past the three-story, full-block McCormick's Furniture Store to Main Street. He walked two blocks down Main, shaking hands and signing autographs in front of the ornate, late-1930s Logan Theater. JFK turned right on Cole Street, passed the eighty-room Pioneer Hotel, and then pivoted left on Stratton Street, Logan's other principal street, which ran parallel to Main.

JFK stopped for lunch and another short speech at the town's premier restaurant, the Smoke House. Owner Albert Klele greeted him. JFK posed for pictures with Klele and waitress Vera Runyon as well as numerous Smoke House customers. Those pictures would adorn the walls of the Smoke House for decades thereafter.

But not all was right in Logan for JFK. Strong local factions concerned about JFK and supportive of Humphrey didn't participate in the festivities. They were holed up talking strategy for defeating JFK in the city's best hotel, the Aracoma, which was large enough to front on both Main and Stratton Streets. A key power broker in Logan County Raymond Chafin was leading the pro-Humphrey efforts. Chafin was chairman of the Logan County Democratic Party.

Prominent local jurist Judge C. C. Chambers was there too. Judge Chambers, a former KKK organizer, shared the view of Dr. Peale that JFK would put his loyalty to the pope above his loyalty to the United States. The judge was also put off by his pretty-boy appearance, rich-kid upbringing, and fancy-pants demeanor. *All foam, no beer*, Judge Chambers believed.

JFK left Logan to meet up with FDR Jr. and tour a string of other southern West Virginia towns, but two JFK backers stayed behind. Giancana men. They were efficient and effective in carrying out their assignment to ensure the support of local politicians for JFK. In just a few days in Logan, they easily had determined who the anti-JFK power brokers were. Raymond Chafin plainly was a key one.

As chairman of the Democratic Party in the county, Chafin could turn out nearly half of the county for a candidate. He could also buy votes, often with moonshine rather than money, and he was able to save the good citizens the trouble of actually having to show up at the polls. Their votes could be cast for them by so-called "Lever Brothers." In coal-country West Virginia, "Lever Brothers," named after the maker of soap products, were dishonest precinct workers who flipped levers of the old voting machines on behalf of bribed voters.

Giancana's men had a productive visit with Mr. Chafin at his home in Cow Creek near Omar, about ten miles from the town of Logan. They were up front in asking him what he needed to turn his support to JFK. Chafin said, "thirty-five."

By "thirty-five" Chafin meant $3,500. The Giancana men left two suitcases behind as they drove the fifteen minutes to the Pioneer Hotel, gathered their remaining luggage, and moved on to Welch, Bluefield, and Princeton.

The Chicago gangsters had interpreted "thirty-five" to mean $35,000. Their world was much different from Chafin's.

While Chafin was a crooked politician, and gladly accepted the $35,000, he also was a man of his word. He'd earlier been bought off by the Humphrey camp. Humphrey's fee, however, wasn't anywhere near $35,000. True to his sense of personal integrity, Chafin returned Humphrey's money after he switched his support to JFK. In Logan County, there *was* honor among thieves.

Mob money was similarly being doled out in other counties, particularly in the southern half of the state.

Mr. Chafin announced his support for JFK before the May 10 election. Logan County was locked in for JFK, as were the other southern coal counties. When May 10 came, JFK won the West Virginia primary with 61 percent of the vote. Humphrey won only five of the state's fifty-five counties.

The next day the *Logan Banner* correctly reported that the election involved a "spree" of "flagrant vote-buying, whiskey flowing like water, and coercion of voters. . . . You name it."

Humphrey's candidacy had effectively been defeated. The West Virginia primary victory was an essential step in the election of the country's first Catholic president.

CHAPTER 12

JFK lost the popular vote in a majority of states in the November 1960 general election. But he won almost 40 percent more Electoral College votes than Richard Nixon did, mainly by winning razor-thin margins in Illinois and Texas. Mob largesse was the difference in Giancana's home state, Illinois, particularly in Cook County, and in several Texas counties bordering Mexico.

Many Americans, including Richard Nixon and President Eisenhower, believed that JFK had pinched the election. Reporter Earl Mazo of the *New York Herald Tribune* agreed. A friend of Nixon's, Mazo investigated and wrote a series of articles arguing that the Illinois and Texas results were "fishy." Immediate recounts were held in these and several other states. Results were changed in only one state, however—Hawaii flipped from Nixon to Kennedy. Further efforts by Republicans in Texas were futile because LBJ would never have allowed Texas to go to Nixon. He hated Nixon more than he did any of the Kennedys.

Illinois, though, could've presented a real possibility for the Republicans to get a different result. Out of almost eight million votes cast, JFK won by only eighty-eight hundred votes. An investigation almost certainly would've revealed some Cook County shenanigans beyond simple vote-buying, which was difficult to challenge. But, in the end, even if it turned out that Nixon in fact had won Illinois, JFK still would've been the president-elect. By taking Louisiana, Arkansas, and Missouri, JFK had enough electoral votes—six more than needed—even without Illinois.

The Kennedy endeavor to secure Governor Long's support thus was well worth the effort. JFK was particularly thankful to Blaze Starr's tight lips and to the large boxes that provided a hiding place in the Roosevelt Hotel closet.

Though his election as president wasn't officially challenged, JFK nevertheless was seen throughout his presidency by many— white, high-school-educated males in the South in particular— as a pretender to the throne.

Unwittingly, Judy Campbell had played a consequential role in the election as a facilitator of the private pact between the mob and JFK. JFK now had to keep his part of the bargain.

He celebrated his victory at his father's fifteen-thousand-square-foot mansion on the ocean in Palm Beach, bought in 1933 from the Wanamakers of Philadelphia department store fame. The mansion was built by the legendary South Florida architect Addison Mizner, builder of other historic Palm Beach homes and the father of Boca Raton.

Not all that surprisingly for a Kennedy, JFK's father kept the estate's original name, *La Querida*, Spanish for "the mistress."

\\\\

Organized anti-Castro activities were finally beginning to move forward in various corridors of power in America. The CIA had concluded that Castro had to be taken out. It was mapping out a battle plan for a US-backed invasion. Congress increasingly was taking notice of the Castro threat as well. And the mob was ramping back up to take on Castro and reclaim its casino empire.

Exile groups, too, were getting reenergized and were working together more effectively to try to take their country back as Castro's grip on Cuba tightened. Five of the most substantial groups had formed the Frente Revolucionario Democratico in Mexico in the spring of 1960. With the help of the CIA, the FRD formed a military wing called Brigade 2506.

By November 1960 the FRD was expanding into the United States, setting up shop not only in Miami but in several other southern cities. In that month the FRD leadership sent a former Cuban diplomat named Sergio Arcacha Smith to New Orleans to start an FRD chapter there and raise money and recruits for the cause. As Arcacha Smith told the *Times-Picayune* upon his arrival, "We are hoping that everyone in New Orleans will help us to get rid of Castro."

Arcacha Smith opened the New Orleans FRD office at 403 Camp Street, known as the Balter Building, a five-story masonry building with wrap-around balconies on each floor. It had facings on Camp Street, Poydras Street, and Saint Charles Avenue. This building was quaking with mob, radical right, and anti-Castro activity. It was owned by Colonel Bluford Balter, a leader of the New Orleans chapter of the American Nazi Party and rabid Commie-hater. A worshipper of Huey Long, Balter had placed portraits of the assassinated governor and senator by the elevator on each floor. Right-wing Colonel Edwin Walker rented space in the building. The segregationist Citizens' Council was housed in suite 323.

Because it harbored a menagerie of potential incendiary schemes, the Balter Building was monitored regularly by the FBI, which had offices across the street.

Arcacha Smith was able to lease office 207. Two floors above, on the top floor of the Balter Building in suite 432-34, were the offices of Guy Banister, now a private investigator focusing on work for Marcello. Banister, a friend and occasional business partner of Balter's, represented a bridge between mob and anti-Castro forces. He was instrumental in arranging space for the FRD.

As a committed anti-Communist, Banister welcomed his new anti-Castro neighbor in the Balter Building with open arms. Arcacha Smith, well-educated and worldly, quickly gained Banister's respect and support. He soon introduced Arcacha Smith to a man named Orlando Piedra. Piedra had been the head of Batista's Bureau of Investigation—the Cuban National Police. He'd come to New Orleans earlier that year and was leading a low-key life, helping the anti-Castro effort while staying under the radar because of his notoriety. Cuban agents could be hunting down Batista officials, Piedra knew, particularly officials who had been involved in prosecuting and punishing rebels.

Piedra was wealthy, which allowed him not only to fund the broader cause of conquering Communism, where he often worked closely with Banister, but also to help individual exiles and their families in need of financial support—including Arcacha Smith and his family. He became a generous though not close friend of Arcacha Smith's.

Marcello's well-oiled machine had vetted Arcacha Smith even before he arrived in New Orleans. Banister was fully briefed on the results.

Sergio Vicente Arcacha Smith was born in Havana in 1923. He was raised in the affluent Vedado district of the city, where Castro made his first splash. Vedado extended to the Malecón, the strip of Havana by the Atlantic Ocean. The Malecón's sordid clubs, bars, and gangs pulled the young Arcacha Smith their way. He enjoyed slipping away from his wealthier friends and learning life lessons from some of the less law-abiding young men and women in town. Timorous-looking on the outside, Arcacha Smith was born with a taste for adventure.

In his teens, he was enrolled in a Jesuit high school in Havana, *Colegio Belen*, where he was briefly a classmate of Fidel Castro's. Arcacha Smith's parents, though, became increasingly worried about their son's unwholesome tendencies. They pulled him out of *Colegio Belen* after a few months and sent him to the Havana Military Academy. He graduated from the Academy in 1940.

After World War II, Arcacha Smith studied international law at Columbia University in New York. He returned to Cuba thereafter and joined the Cuban diplomatic service in 1951. He was first assigned to Bombay, India, where he met and married a Pakistani woman named Shelia. After a few years, he left the diplomatic service and spent time in Venezuela, New York City, and Miami pursuing various business ventures.

Arcacha Smith's life experiences helped produce a well-informed, elegant gentleman. And he looked the part. Rather than being scruffy like a revolutionary, or resembling an assassin, Arcacha Smith looked like a cross between Hercule Poirot and David Niven.

Beneath his dapper and gentle exterior, though, Arcacha Smith *was* a committed radical and ruthless activist, with street smarts from his early years on and around the Malecón and with sophisticated smarts from his diplomatic days and world travels.

Moreover, few who observed Arcacha Smith realized that he was highly proficient with a wide range of weaponry, a proficiency he'd honed at military school and later in the army.

In 1959 Arcacha Smith joined a group in Cuba formed by former prime minister Manuel Antonio de Varona to overthrow Castro. When that effort failed, Varona and Arcacha Smith fled to Miami. Varona and several other former high-ranking Cuban government officials also in exile formed an anti-Communist group in Miami that later became part of the FRD. The FBI became aware of Arcacha Smith at that time. In a report to Director J. Edgar Hoover, the agent monitoring Arcacha Smith described him as "one of the more conspiratorial Cuban exile leaders."

Varona admired Arcacha Smith. It was Varona who made the decision to send Arcacha Smith to New Orleans.

Not long after Arcacha Smith's move to New Orleans, Marcello directed Banister to work with him and the FRD, something Banister was already beginning to do, having immediately bonded with Arcacha Smith. Marcello also directed that Ferrie, with his knowledge of Cuba and experiences there, be involved in this renewed effort on Cuba.

In early March 1961, Banister and Ferrie met for coffee at Mancuso's Restaurant and Bar, just down Camp Street from the Balter Building, at Lafayette Square in the corner of a building called the Newman Building.

Banister gave Ferrie one of his new cards.

GUY BANISTER ASSOCIATES, INC.
CONSULTATIONS ANALYSIS
CONFIDENTIAL, CIVIL & CRIMINAL INVESTIGATIONS
INTERNAL PROTECTION & SURVEYS
PERSONALITY ANALYSIS—NATIONAL COVERAGE
MAgnolia 4532

"What've you been up to, Dave?"

"Just lovin' life."

"No, really."

"Same old stuff. Mice. Masses. Mixed drinks. Mentoring cadets. Moving people on airplanes.

"And Monitoring Cuba. Castro's gone full-on Soviet, right? Russkie agents'll be flowing into America from Havana swifter than Wilma Rudolph. Unnerving."

"Yep. Marcello's unnerved, I can tell you that."

"Not surprising. Now here's something you should like. Marcello's ready to go back and fight for Cuba. And, Dr. Ferrie, know this—the CIA's on the same page."

"Christ. That's fantastic. Give me an assignment!"

"That's why we're here, my friend. That's why we're here. Let's not waste any time. There's a Cuban guy I need you to meet."

\\\\

They walked the two blocks to the Balter Building. Ferrie met Sergio Arcacha Smith there for the first time. Arcacha Smith had another Cuban-looking fellow with him.

"Dave, it's a pleasure." Arcacha Smith's English was excellent, though heavily accented.

"Likewise."

Ferrie knew of Arcacha Smith. Arcacha Smith had made a speech in January to the New Orleans Junior Chamber of Commerce at Lenfant's, a restaurant in Navarre Ferrie frequented. This speech was well-covered in the local press. Ferrie actually remembered some of the things Arcacha Smith was reported to have said. "Cubans will launch an invasion sometime in 1961 to overthrow the regime of Fidel Castro," according to the January 5 *Times-Picayune.* While the actual invasion would not be launched from US territory, "Cuban citizens are being recruited by the front in this country and sent elsewhere to train for the invasion." Six months of fighting were expected to be necessary to achieve victory, Arcacha Smith predicted.

He'd emphasized that Castro can be overthrown by three methods—invasion, internal revolt, and intensive propaganda. "We are trying all three of them," he asserted, "and would like you to help us with the third."

Ferrie was aware of other less bombastic talks and presentations Arcacha Smith had made around town to explain the situation in Cuba. Ferrie in fact had attended a very recent one at the First Methodist Church on Canal Street. Arcacha Smith's topic there was, "What Will Happen in Cuba."

"Welcome to the team," the other Cuban said. Carlos Bringuier. "The last name is tough, I know. Let's just go with 'Carlos.'"

"Carlos is a fighter against Castro *and* he sells clothes. Great combination, *correcto*?" Banister asked.

Bringuier was a young lawyer trained—like Castro—at the University of Havana. His father had been a judge in Cuba until he was threatened by Castro officials and escaped to South America. Bringuier followed suit, fleeing to Guatemala and then Argentina.

After arriving in New Orleans just a month earlier, Bringuier quickly started an anti-Castro newsletter and began interfacing with the FRD, working all the while at Ward's Discount House at Canal and Royal Streets. With an energetic gift for public speaking in multiple languages, Bringuier became known in the Cuban exile community within weeks of his arrival.

In a serious and confident voice, Arcacha Smith said, "It took Castro, Dave, to bring your mafiosos and your government together to work for a good and just common purpose—to take Cuba back. My fellow Cuban patriot Carlos and I are trying to help. We could use your services."

"*Cómo es eso?*"

"The CIA is helping us to set up a training camp in Belle Chasse, at the air station there. We'd be grateful, my new friend, if you could be there. And if you could bring along some cadets."

Banister spoke up, "We're supporting this assignment."

"Then I do too, sir."

"*Gracias acere,*" Arcacha Smith said. "Carlos will meet with you in the next week to give more details."

"I've got a couple of overnights for Eastern over the next five days," Ferrie said. "Then I'm good to go."

||||

On February 18 Ferrie and Bringuier travelled the twelve miles to Belle Chasse, a small city in Plaquemines Parish by the river just as it turns south toward the Gulf after slipping by New Orleans. The French words "Belle Chasse" mean "nice hunt." While the area in and around Belle Chasse indeed had long provided fruitful hunting, the city was in reality named after Joseph Deville Degoutin Bellechasse, the first adjutant general of the Louisiana National Guard, who was accused in 1814 of aiding the British to plot the capture of New Orleans. He avoided arrest, ironically, by fleeing to Cuba.

The site of the Belle Chasse Naval Air Station had hosted an airstrip since the early 1920s when a man named George Hero drained the swampy land there and built a single grassy airstrip. A genuine hero Charles Lindbergh landed on this strip in 1929 during a national tour. The Navy later took over the facility and built three modern airstrips. It was commissioned as an air station in 1957 with new hangars and barracks, along with the runways and a tower, comprising 3,252 acres.

Ferrie and Bringuier were accompanied by twenty cadets, in four borrowed cars. Arcacha Smith met them at the front gate and took them to a remote part of the station.

These men were excited to see what appeared to be about three hundred Cuban fighters. Open crates of all kinds of weapons were lined up, including a large number of crates packed with M1903-A3 bolt-action rifles. There also were dozens and dozens of M1911A1 sidearms.

Several highly trained instructors in unmarked camouflage prepared this cobbled-together band of Cubans and private-citizen Americans for action in Cuba over the next month. Ferrie learned that the instructors were active US Army specialists. *The new JFK administration was coming through.*

Ferrie and Arcacha Smith spent many hours together in Belle Chasse. They developed a strong, almost brotherly bond. And back in the city, they worked together on some of the logistical details of the upcoming invasion, visiting virtually every business concern that had business with Cuba to ask for money and intelligence. One of their largest supporters was Lykes Steamship, which had built its business shipping cattle and lumber to Cuba, a profit center now shut down by Castro. Lykes, which owned a full block along the river on Tchoupitoulas Street, was hell bent on throwing Castro out of Cuba.

At the same time troops were drilling secretly at the Belle Chasse Naval Station, the FRD's Brigade 2506 fighters were being trained in Guatemala, most of them close to the Pacific Ocean near a small city called Retalhuleu. This was a much larger operation than Belle Chasse, fourteen hundred men in all. Arcacha Smith informed the Belle Chasse troops about this larger operation. It was good for them to know they wouldn't be alone in any action they may take.

Toward the end of March, there was a growing air of intensity at Belle Chasse. The troops could feel that something was about to happen.

Ferrie took a three-week vacation from Eastern Air Lines.

Standing apart from the troops on the tarmac, Ferrie asked Arcacha Smith, "What do you hear?"

"Miami tells me the final plans are in place. A war council has been put together to oversee and coordinate an attack. They call it the Cuban Revolutionary Council. My FRD is being absorbed into this new CRC, we'll be getting orders soon."

The CRC was headquartered in unremarkable office space near the Eastern Air Lines headquarters at Miami International Airport, an area familiar to Ferrie. He'd been there several times for mandatory pilot training.

"The CIA funds and largely controls the CRC," Arcacha Smith said. "And it uses the CRC as an intermediary to co-ordinate with the mob." Ferrie and his mob compatriots were energized to see a concerted mission coming together to liberate Cuba for the good of its people and the good of American businesses.

〰

But on April 4, in the midst of the final planning of what became known as the Bay of Pigs invasion, a lightning bolt hit New Orleans.

In 1951 a US Senate committee chaired by Senator Estes Kefauver of Tennessee investigating organized crime had come to New Orleans for hearings. Carlos Marcello appeared but refused to answer questions, taking the Fifth Amendment fifteen times. Angry with Marcello, the committee, having discovered that Marcello was an illegal alien, set the wheels in motion to obtain an order of deportation. That order was issued in late 1953 but never enforced until the Kennedy Administration and the rise to power of Bobby Kennedy, who was determined to address the "enemy within."

RFK had detailed knowledge of Marcello's businesses from his work on the McClellan Committee. Hitting the ground running, the new Attorney General checked with the Immigration and Naturalization Service in mid-March and learned that it had a document certifying that Marcello had been born in Guatemala. Though doubtful that this certificate was legitimate, RFK nevertheless made his move.

Ever since the 1953 deportation order, Marcello was required to report in periodically to an INS probation officer. On this mild Tuesday morning, he dutifully visited the INS offices in the 1926 Masonic Temple Building at St. Charles and Perdido. Without warning or notice, he was arrested, roughly handcuffed, and quickly caravanned out to Moisant Field. He was immediately whisked off to Guatemala City.

Mob leaders were gravely roiled by this act. Phone lines began crackling with shock and anger. Merely ten weeks into their administration, the Kennedys had broken their word to leave the mob alone. Breaking commitments to the mob always had consequences.

CHAPTER 13

Notwithstanding the Kennedys' perfidious and sudden deportation of Marcello, the mob believed it had no choice but to continue to work with the US government on the invasion of Cuba. Getting rid of Castro was its immediate priority.

Several days after Marcello's seizure and deportation, the troops at Belle Chasse Naval Station were transported in stages to Houston and then shipped over to Guatemala to join Brigade 2506. Unbeknownst to Ferrie, additional troops had been training at Abita Springs and Houma and were also being sent to Guatemala.

Neither Ferrie nor Arcacha Smith would accompany their troops. Ferrie instead had been ordered to fly to Key West and await further orders there. Arcacha Smith would be moving over to the CRC headquarters near the Miami International Airport.

Before leaving New Orleans, at the direction of the CRC, Arcacha Smith spoke again to a reporter at the *Times-Picayune*. As reported in the April 11 edition, he said that preparations were almost complete for an anti-Castro Cuban invasion. "We are well-equipped and well-trained. We have been training for more than a year now." The invasion, he asserted, "could begin this afternoon, tomorrow, anytime. We are just waiting for the signal." He *didn't* disclose that the attack signal in fact had already been dispatched.

The CRC and CIA had similar statements made to press outlets in other southern cities that might be picked up in Cuba. They were banking on the invasion generating a public uprising against Castro and wanted the Cuban people to know that help was coming soon. In fact, Arcacha-Smith had disclosed this strategy on a show on WYES-TV, an NET station, called "Working Press" a few months earlier, telling the interviewer that an attack on Cuba will cause "an internal revolt" that "will be most successful."

\\\\

Ferrie flew his Taylorcraft, with several stops, as before, to Key West.

He checked back into the Flagship Motel and Restaurant. His instructions were in his room in a sealed envelope. "Go to Brown Derby. Seven p.m. Look for man with Washington Senators baseball hat."

The man was a CIA covert operative named Robert Morrow. The hat was for the new expansion Washington Senators, dark navy blue, flat-brimmed with an embroidered sans-serif, red "W" bordered in white on the front panel.

Morrow was well-prepared for Ferrie. "I've heard a lot about you. Many say you're the consummate pilot."

"Those people haven't seen many pilots," Ferrie laughed. "But I can hold my own."

"Speaking of pilots, as we sit here today—Saturday, April 15—eight World War II B-26 bombers should be on their way back to Nicaragua from Cuba. Should've bombed the shit out of Castro's little air force. They're all painted like stolen Cuban military planes, supposedly to hide the fact that America is behind this."

"That'll never work. Castro may be evil, but he's not an idiot."

"Of course not. But there'll be some confusion because all the planes are marked with the same registration number. While these birds *are* shitty, they should be able to knock out most of Castro's air force at its three main airports, the two around Havana and the one in Santiago de Cuba."

"Then, tomorrow, you and I are flying over to Cuba," Morrow continued.

"Great. My plane?"

"Nope. My fearless leader General Cabell got us a Twin Beach-Super G with tricycle gear."

"Hmmm . . . Okay, easier to land."

"Since Castro's air defenses should be done in today, we'll be free to buzz around where we want."

"What're we doing?"

"I'll go over the details with you early tomorrow morning, but here's the gist of it. We're heading to a mountaintop in the Camagüeys. There's a tricky landing strip there. We need to plant several radio antennae to help our guys talk to each other. The invasion will start the day after tomorrow."

"Excellent."

"We're then supposed to do a little reconnaissance."

"What of?"

"Castro's building a large facility in a ravine in the Camagüeys jungle. We're going to see what we can see, mainly whether there's any sign of the Russians there. We can then refuel at Baracoa near Guantanamo. Assuming we're still in one piece, we'll come back to the Derby and do some serious drinking—we'll drink like real Conchs."

They chatted over Cuban sandwiches and beers for an hour. A main topic of conversation was the Russian Yuri Gagarin, the first man launched into space, just a few days earlier. He circled the entire Earth. This Soviet accomplishment rattled Americans. Was Communism a stronger system? This stunning achievement made the success of the Bay of Pigs invasion that much more important.

They took off from Key West the next morning. The skies were muddy, they couldn't see any sign of B-26s. Ferrie had no trouble finding the mountain landing strip, though, for rebels had lined it with small smudge pots. The landing was easy, *like landing on the back of a hog,* Ferrie thought to himself. Their mission on the mountaintop was neatly accomplished. Morrow installed the radio equipment. The view from on high, even with the clouds, was stunning.

Ferrie gently lifted the Twin Beach off the short runway. They flew over the small city of Camagüey and headed toward the jungle ravine. Descending into the ravine was tricky. He had to dive deeper than he was comfortable with to get a good look at what might be happening on the ground.

The right wing of the Twin Beach clipped a jocuma tree and the plane began to wobble and shake. The engine sputtered. The two men found themselves descending rapidly into the ravine. A spiritual calm came over Ferrie as he worked the controls. Less calm, Morrow nevertheless was able to look out the windshield as the ground got closer. Being below the cloud cover, visibility was good.

Ferrie steadied the plane and pulled back on the yoke. The plane began to climb. It cleared the ridge—barely—and burst free into the blue yonder.

"What'd you see down there?" Ferrie asked.

"Dozens of people—big ugly eyes staring back at me. Looked like they were building large structures, blocky structures. A few tractors and machines, bulldozers or maybe loaders. Stacks of what appeared to be large shells or small missiles."

"They're building an arsenal."

"I could see the machines had lettering on them, starting with an *M*, and then letters from a different alphabet, looked like Greek. I'm pretty sure I saw a few white guys."

"Russians," Ferrie said.

"Probably."

"Man alive! The Russians aren't just buddying up to Castro, they're arming him. That's gotta be it. The equipment was probably from MTZ, *Minsk Tractor Works*. The lettering was Cyrillic. Russians."

"It's clever they're doing this deep down in the jungle. You can't see them from those high-altitude surveillance planes. Shit. The CRC and the CIA are assuming the Cubans don't have many heavy arms, but—"

"Get some pictures?" Ferrie asked.

"Shit, yeah—even though my life was passing before my eyes." In the cabin behind the cockpit, CIA whiz-kids had installed a custom-built, battery-operated Tektronix spectrum analyzer with a Polaroid camera attachment.

Back on American soil that evening, Morrow radioed his CRC contacts about the Russian presence in Cuba. The invasion early the next day—set to begin around 1:00 a.m. Monday—would face a stronger Cuban army than expected. This information would be passed on to the CIA.

\\\\

At the Brown Derby Monday afternoon, Morrow left Ferrie at the bar to take a long phone call. Rejoining Ferrie, Morrow looked stunned. "Complete shit-failure. Fucking disaster."

"What?"

"It was one big cock-up. The old B-26s did get some targets on Saturday, even though they were incredibly inaccurate and didn't have the fuel to wait out morning fog and clouds. Half of Castro's air force was utterly unaffected. Kennedy was supposed to send a second wave of bombers yesterday, but the fucker cancelled that strike at the last minute—the planes were sitting on the runway ready to take off. He apparently got concerned people were guessing he was behind the invasion, that we'd lied to the UN. Which we did. So, when the troops tried to come ashore this morning, they were sitting ducks. Castro had enough planes left to attack back."

"JFK didn't send in help?"

"That chicken shit. No. An hour of air cover this morning and that was it. Just a little more air power could have made the difference. With hardly any air support, our guys were sitting ducks. It was particularly ugly for some of them 'cause their boats got stuck on reefs. Target practice for Castro."

"Why no real help?"

"My CRC guy said that JFK pussied out because he's afraid of getting into it with Russia. Decided to sacrifice a free Cuba to avoid having Nikita in his face."

"Makes no sense. Fucking point is to keep the Commies away from us. Did he really think the Russkies wouldn't know he was involved? I guess he'd rather spend time locking up good Americans like Mr. Marcello than liberating millions of poor Cubans."

Morrow drained a large shot of Bromista white rum and nodded. "JFK's just making Russia stronger. And, ironically, Uncle Nikita's apparently getting kudos by saying he'll protect the sovereignty of this poor little country from further illegal invasions from the big bad United States."

"Gives him an excuse to move more arms to Cuba. Missiles'll be next."

"Here's the really bad news for you *and* yours truly," Morrow continued. "We gotta go back. Some of our guys got on land and are holed up there, still alive. The CRC knows where they are."

"Holy God. Castro knows where they are too—we won't make it out still breathing."

"The guys are on a beach close to a bumpy landing strip. We're going to the airport tomorrow at noon to get the details."

They didn't stay very late at the Derby. No drinking like a Conch.

Back at the Flagship, Ferrie listened to the radio into the wee hours. At the International Airport the next day, a Hispanic man named Mateo, wearing generic fatigues, gave them the details of their mission. "The beach at Girón," Mateo began. "There's a landing strip there by the sand. A couple of destroyers should be just off the shore by the time you land. They'll get most of the survivors, but you need to get the rest of 'em."

Mateo gave them a detailed map of the Bahia de Cochinos—the Bay of Pigs—which showed Girón and the landing strip.

"We have a Beechcraft Queen," Mateo continued. "More room and sturdier than that Super G. The Queen's laid out so you should be able to get at least fifteen guys in there. I'm sure you can fly that, Señor Ferrie, and land it on the strip. It'll be tricky. I hear you're a pro, though."

"Get your hearing checked."

"The guys on our ships know you may be coming. Just do your best when you get there and then get out as quickly as you can. Castro has a bunch of tanks nearby."

The Beechcraft had a range of fifteen hundred miles, so there was no need to worry about refueling. Ferrie and Morrow sliced over the far western tip of Cuba at Cabo San Antonio. They approached the underbelly of the island and the Bay of Pigs. Clearly visible as they began to descend were two destroyers beginning to move southward away from the beach. Ferrie later learned these were the USS *Murray* and the USS *Eaton*. The ships appeared to have survivors aboard.

Descending farther, Ferrie and Morrow could see a small group of battered men on the jungle side of the beach. They could also see four or five Russian-made T-45 tanks approaching the beach from the hills. The *Murray* and the *Eaton* were clearly trying to get out of the tanks' firing range.

"We gotta try," Morrow said.

"*In nomine Patris, et Filii, et Spiritus Sancti.* Amen."

"Ditto. Amen."

Ferrie cautiously landed the plane on the small strip, burning rubber as the plane skidded up close to the edge of the concrete but with enough room to execute a U-turn.

More than a dozen disoriented freedom fighters ran toward the makeshift runway and climbed aboard the Beechcraft. Ferrie quickly powered the plane down the strip and lifted off. As Ferrie banked the plane and sped out over the water, he heard several loud artillery reports and saw a Cuban-owned World War II British Sea Fury flying toward them from over the mountains. But he and his passengers ascended safely up into the Caribbean skies.

\\\\\

Ferrie took his time flying back to New Orleans after a last night's sleep in his lumpy Flagship Motel bed and a bad morning hangover.

For months after the CRC's crushing defeat at the Bay of Pigs, Castro relentlessly trumpeted his victory, stirring Cubans with speeches on nationalism and the supremacy of Communism. Cuba's first May Day celebration was held a few months later. There were colossal and triumphant festivals around the island.

Back in New Orleans, Ferrie's commitment to the anti-Castro cause only deepened. And, formerly a fan of JFK, he turned sharply against the president, who had abandoned dozens of brave freedom fighters to torture and death. He even began to wonder whether JFK might be a closet Communist, as many southern right-wingers already long believed.

He shared his experiences and feelings with Sergio Arcacha Smith at Mancuso's Restaurant and Bar a few days after returning home. "We're not done with this," Arcacha Smith said. "The CRC lives on—you're still a CRC man, right?"

"Proud of the moniker, my brother."

CHAPTER 14

"Got a new assignment for you, Dave," Banister announced over the phone in late May. "No rest for the weary. You'll now need to point your plane in a different direction."

Ferrie met Banister later that day at Banister's office in the Balter Building. They were to talk about their deported leader, Carlos Marcello.

"Word came in yesterday," Banister reported, "that the Little Man has managed to escape Guatemala and is now in Honduras. And Honduras is more than happy for him to get out of its hair. He's 100 percent free to go. But, for obvious reasons, he can't reenter the US of A through normal means. Immigration would just turn him around and send him back."

"You want me to get him?" Ferrie asked, excited by the prospect.

"That's your next mission, Captain. Tegucigalpa."

"Been there," said Ferrie. "Nice town—'the Home of Nobles.' How'd Marcello get out of Guatemala?"

"Crazy story. I got the lowdown from a Marcello lawyer named Maroun. Marcello had summoned Maroun right away to join him in Guatemala. Maroun does a lot of business down there.

"The Guatemalan government locked Marcello up right away," Banister continued. "But he wasn't in jail for long, though long enough for some government goons to extort money from him. Then, presumably as a reward for his generosity, the authorities released him and put him up in a suite in a fancy hotel.

The Biltmore. It was like a vacation for a while, Maroun told me. Marcello's wife, kids, brothers all came down. They partied, shopped, went to the racetrack."

"Nice. Why would he ever want to leave?"

"Because after about a week, some military guys showed up unannounced and took him away. Fucking schizophrenic President Ydigoras must've been spooked by something, probably worried about an anti-American coup—didn't want to be seen harboring an American outlaw in Guatemala. The goons said he had to go back to the United States and had to do it through El Salvador. He was shuffled onto a plane. Maroun went with him."

"They took him to Honduras instead?" Ferrie asked.

"Nope. Gets more loco. Marcello and Maroun were dropped off in the middle of nowhere, just over the Guatemala-El Salvador border.

"Marcello and Maroun were left in a Salvadoran army camp in the middle of the fucking jungle. These jungle army guys had no idea what to do with two gringos who just seemed to fall from the sky. Rather than help the gringos out, the Salvadorans threw them in a bus and shipped them to the big army barracks in San Salvador."

"Shit. I assume I don't joke with Marcello about this?" Ferrie asked.

"Only at your own risk," Banister said. "The army guys at the barracks locked them up for about a week, interrogated them for a couple of days. Then late one night, Marcello and Maroun were tossed in another army bus and driven, like, six hours to the border with Honduras."

"This sounds like a really bad movie."

"The movie gets worse. The bus went twenty miles or so into the mountains in Honduras. And then Marcello and Maroun were dumped by the side of a road in shit-nowhere."

"Jesus," Ferrie said.

"They had to walk on rutty dirt roads in the mountains for seventeen miles, still in street clothes. Marcello kept his money in his alligator shoes. He was losing it—was crazy pissed."

"I'm surprised the old guy made it," Ferrie said.

"He barely did. Maroun said Marcello collapsed several times but got back up. Broke a rib or two. He apparently put hundreds of Sicilian curses on RFK, including the dreaded 'evil eye.' Marcello told Maroun that if he died, Maroun was to tell Marcello's brothers to kill all the Kennedys. And their wives. And their girlfriends.

"Marcello and Maroun finally made it, somehow, to a dirty Indian village after a couple of days."

"Probably Lencas."

"Whatever they were, they gave our boys something to eat and a place to rest. Marcello and Maroun then hired two Indian teenagers to take them to the nearest airport. There *was* a little airport in the region. However, it was miles down the mountain through underbrush and other shit. They had no choice. The Indians used machetes to clear paths."

"This is hard to believe," Ferrie offered.

"Bananas, right? But totally true. Marcello starts to get worried that the Indians are going to murder them with the machetes to filch their money and clothes, if not just for the fun of it. Why not?"

"Because Lenca Indians have been Catholic since Columbus showed up uninvited," Ferrie lectured. "They love their fellow man."

"Don't think Marcello and Maroun felt much love, so they promised the Indians some extra wampum if they made it to the airport. And your Catholic brethren came through. At the jungle airport, Marcello and Maroun hired a guy to fly them to Tegucigalpa. And there they be."

"Wild. I gotta lot more respect for Marcello now."

"He's been at a hotel in Tegucigalpa for a couple weeks licking his wounds. Maroun is back in Louisiana. He and I agreed we have to smuggle Marcello back into the country in a private plane."

"I'm your guy."

Banister arranged for Ferrie to use a Cessna 172 Skyhawk, which had a longer range than the Stinson and Taylorcraft. Ferrie hopped over to Galveston, refueled, and then flew the long seven hundred miles to the Veracruz, Mexico, airport on the outskirts of that city, in a town called Las Bajadas. After refueling again there, he reached Tegucigalpa.

The airport serving Tegucigalpa, in Toncontin, was one of the most dangerous in the world, sitting smack up against the mountains. Ferrie relished the challenge. He made a textbook landing. He'd been told to taxi to the Pan Am hangar and have the manager call the Hotel Toncontin, which TACA Airlines had built in the 1930s for transiting passengers. Marcello had moved to the Toncontin the day before. He met Ferrie at the Pan Am hangar a half hour later.

Ferrie and Marcello hopped airports back to New Orleans.

The two formed a connection during their many hours together flying home on the Cessna. This was surprising, for the two obviously were very different characters with very different backgrounds. Ferrie was well-educated, having gone to seminary and college and having earned a PhD in philosophy, which was conferred on him in Bari, Italy, in 1959. Ferrie had read extensively. Marcello, on the other hand, was barely literate, having dropped out of school at fourteen. He spoke like a Sicilian day laborer.

But there were common threads between the two. Marcello was a profoundly curious man. He peppered Ferrie with questions on a wide range of subjects. His inquisitiveness and intuition clicked with Ferrie. Each had translated his life's challenges into a craftiness one couldn't learn in books. Marcello was charming and regal. Ferrie was outgoing and engaging. He had a leadership demeanor that Marcello admired. Their bond was strengthened by their mutual hatred of Communism and love of the freedoms America provided. And by their shared apoplectic rage at the Kennedys.

Both Marcello and Ferrie actually enjoyed the rocky ride back to Louisiana, talking nonstop. Ferrie became well accustomed to Marcello's poor English.

Marcello was deeply grateful to Ferrie for getting him out of Central America, which came at real risk to Ferrie. Marcello never forgot Ferrie's brave act and loyalty.

Banister and Gill, along with Marcello's body man Sam Termine, a jovial former state policeman, met Ferrie's airplane at Moisant Field. Exhausted, Ferrie split off and headed home to Airline Park Boulevard. Banister drove Marcello out of Moisant Field through the back, to Veterans Highway, away from any prying eyes. Marcello went into hiding.

Ferrie closely followed the news coverage of Marcello's return. Initially, there was rampant speculation about his whereabouts, probably in New York some reporters guessed. Ferrie didn't know and frankly didn't care. He knew Marcello would land on his feet.

Marcello's litigator, Jack Wasserman, made several court appearances on Marcello's behalf and then struck a deal with the Immigration and Naturalization Service to surrender Marcello in exchange for the INS agreeing not to immediately deport Marcello and not to do so again without due process. After surrendering, Marcello was sent to a detention center in McAllen, Texas. As part of the surrender deal with the INS, Wasserman had worked out a quick release of Marcello from McAllen, subject to Marcello going home and not leaving the parishes of Orleans, Jefferson, or St. Bernard. And subject to a $10,000 surety bond, which was swiftly posted by bondsman Hardy Davis, a frequent customer of the Marcello network.

After just a few days in McAllen, Marcello was released. He flew from Brownsville through Houston to Moisant on Eastern Air Lines, arriving back home in Metairie on the evening of Monday, June 19. The next day, rather than rest, he went to his office at the Town and Country Motel. From four miles away, Ferrie could feel Marcello's heat radiating from 1225 Airline Highway.

Wasserman then turned the tables on RFK. He attacked quickly by filing several legal actions *against* the United States, including one claiming felony kidnapping. RFK wouldn't be giving up, Wasserman knew, but these offensive actions would tie him up for a while.

CHAPTER 15

As the paralyzing sting of the Bay of Pigs debacle began to dissipate in the late spring of 1961, a network of recent Cuban exiles was marshaling in Puerto Rico and Miami to form a new militant anti-Castro group to be called Alpha 66. The CIA, through a slick operative using the benign, fake name Maurice Bishop, was aiding this effort. The CIA's role in this attempt to rebound from the Bay of Pigs and throw a more robust blow at Castro was so sensitive that it wasn't reported to either JFK or RFK, nor for that matter to Director John McCone. "Bishop" reported in a direct line to Director of Plans Richard Helms, who was in charge of the CIA's Castro work.

The CRC, which stayed intact after the Bay of Pigs, supported Alpha 66, though its influence in this arena was waning.

Marcello and his mob colleagues quickly signed on and began assembling and funneling arms to the fledgling Alpha 66, which was putting together a military arm to effectively replace Brigade 2506. Guy Banister was Marcello's point man on this project. At Banister's request Ferrie made three weekend flights to Miami in a Marcello-provided, medium-range de Havilland Dove loaded with arms to support the formation of the group's new military arm.

In undertaking these missions, Ferrie intersected a number of times with the man set to be Alpha 66's military leader, Eloy Gutiérrez-Menoya, a former rebel who'd fought with Castro and been an officer with the troops that captured Havana. Gutiérrez-Menoya had turned quickly on Castro, though, as Castro began governing as a dictator and not as a man of the people. He became a fiery opponent and fled to Miami in a small boat in early 1961, not knowing that the Bay of Pigs operation was in its final planning stages.

Having had his mind diverted by the Honduras adventure, Ferrie's stinging feelings toward Castro and JFK were rekindled and thickened by the electricity he felt from Gutiérrez-Menoya and the new life he saw in the anti-Castro movement. He became gripped with fervor and the urge to do more than shuttle arms to Florida. Bubbling with anger and commitment, and feeling the wakening grip of his underlying impulsive control disorder, he decided he should leverage his innate communication skills and violently speak out. *He could help rally the people*, he knew. *They need a jolt, the wolves have to be kept at bay!*

Ferrie was known by many in New Orleans for his periodic and thought-provoking speeches to various groups about one or more of his array of activities. The speech he now had in mind, though, would be different. It would be strident and aggressive— not a lecture but a call to action. Ferrie wrangled an invitation to address a group called the Military Order of the World Wars, an organization started by John "Black Jack" Pershing after the Great War. His talk before the New Orleans branch, according to a notice circulated in advance, would be on "Cuba: April 1961, Present, Future." He was identified as "Captain D. W. Ferrie, Senior Pilot, Eastern Air Lines." The event was put on the calendar for July 24.

Ferrie warmed up for the Military Order speech by appearing with a Cuban exile named Angel Maruri at a July 19 lunch meeting of the Young Men's Business Club at the Roosevelt Hotel. Maruri had participated in the Bay of Pigs invasion as an officer on one of the five Brigade 2506 cargo ships supporting the attack. The *Caribe*. Ferrie in part translated for Maruri and in part provided a calm version of his upcoming Military Order appearance.

The July 24 meeting was in the Boulevard Room at Lenfant's, a seafood restaurant on Canal Boulevard in the Navarre neighborhood of New Orleans, near the 1911 neo-classical,

Beaux-Arts-style Museum of Art in City Park. Lenfant's had been a New Orleans fixture since 1940, catering to private parties, weddings, Rotary Club meetings. The building, like the Greyhound bus station in Cleveland, was one of the rare examples of Streamline Moderne architecture still in existence in the country. Greeting visitors to Lenfant's was a neon lobster dressed in a tuxedo and standing upright above the entrance with a napkin draped over one claw. The Lenfant's neon lobster was one of the allures of the restaurant—though it seldom served lobster.

John Reininger and his band were entertaining in Lenfant's "Beautiful Cocktail Lounge" that night.

Lenfant's had an unusually large parking lot that was also often used by visitors to the adjacent Greenwood Cemetery. Ferrie—who enjoyed visiting the historic New Orleans cemeteries and their fascinating and ghostly monuments and gravestones—had parked there many times to visit Greenwood. It was an inspirational place for Ferrie, a place he often went when he needed to regain energy. Less crowded than the better known St. Louis and Lafayette cemeteries.

Arcacha Smith accompanied Ferrie to Lenfant's. They arrived early because Ferrie wanted to show Arcacha Smith a part of Greenwood Cemetery that particularly inspired him—a large 1874 Confederate monument. The body of the last man executed for treason in the United States, a New Orleans Confederate hero, had been moved to this monument about the time Ferrie moved to the city.

> Underneath this monument lies the grave of William Bruce Mumford, a New Orleans patriot. A hundred years ago he tried to protect the City from the Union takeover. Before the City had surrendered, some Union troops had planted a federal flag at the old Mint in the French Quarter—they were operating under the orders of Commodore Farragut. Mumford tore it down

and paraded around town with it in shreds. For that, he was hung for treason in front of a huge crowd of citizens, 10,000 at least, at the Mint— at the direction of the arrogant Union General Benjamin Butler.

"I feel Mumford's spirit," Ferrie continued. "We gotta stand up against aggression, against tyranny. The city, the whole fucking country—our very way of life—are all under siege. That's why I'm here."

When the meeting was called to order at 7:00 p.m., seventy members of the Military Order were present, a larger number than usual for these gatherings. Many were in uniform.

There was almost an hour of preliminaries before Ferrie took the microphone, including the invocation by Colonel Lansing L. Mitchell and a discussion of the minutes of the previous meeting. Ferrie was introduced by Rear Admiral T. J. Ryan Jr.

"Thank you for having me, I am truly honored," Ferrie began. "This is a critical time in America's history, and my remarks might be deemed controversial. But I don't want to mince words. I *won't* mince words.

"As you know, my friends, we are now engaged in a great Cold War, testing whether the Soviet Union, conceived in treachery and dedicated to Communism, will conquer our freedoms, will defeat everything we cherish. Communism is an evil system. It rejects God. It rejects the principles of liberty our country was founded on. It rejects ambition. It rejects free trade. Through Uncle Fidel, the Russians and other Commies have taken Cuba—ninety miles from our shores. You can smell him from Key West. Believe me, I know.

"My colleague and Cuban friend Sergio is here with me this evening. He has devoted his life to freeing Cuba from Castro. Stand up, Sergio."

Arcacha Smith stood up to hearty applause from the crowd.

"We elected Senator John F. Kennedy to stop this scourge and defeat Communism and the Soviet Union," Ferrie continued.

"He promised to do so on inauguration day, saying he'd defend freedom in this hour of maximum danger. That hour has come, the bell has rung.

"President Kennedy had an immediate test—to nip Communism in the bud in Cuba and to depose Castro. President Eisenhower, a true American hero, had put together a knock-out invasion. It was well-organized and ready to go by the time Robert Frost read his fucking senile poem and JFK was sworn in. In April the Bay of Pigs operation started. It could've been epic. It wasn't—sabotaged by our president.

"Though I can't speak in detail about this, suffice it to say that I played a small but important role in the operation." Ferrie could hear murmurs in the audience. "I wish I could've done more."

His voice began to rise. Most in the crowd leaned a little forward.

"The Bay of Pigs operation should've taken out Castro. Easily. This, my friends, should've been a piece of cake. But, as you patriots know as well as I do, it was an utter failure. An utter *goddamn* failure! It was an utter failure because of one man, John *Fucking* Kennedy. As the freedom-loving insurgents stormed the beaches at Girón and Larga, JFK decided not to send the promised air cover that was vital—*vital*—for the invasion to work. These brave men, these Cuban freedom fighters, were easy pickings. Like lambs to the slaughter. Hung out to dry by your president. Many were killed.

"JFK double-crossed these selfless men, heroes like you. He has blood on his hands! Bloody hands that have never done an honest day's work!

"Our Cuban brothers either died or were captured—some are being brutally tortured as we sit here this evening. The beaches, *las playas*, were splashed with blood. I saw the blood, my friends. I could smell it. Smells like pennies, I'm serious. Horrible. Castro and his fellow thugs, *and* his Russian comrades, celebrated. They drank mojitos, danced the fucking cha-cha-*cha*, screwed their women—celebrated."

Ferrie began to get red in the face. Veins were bulging in his neck.

"Kennedy is a traitor, none of you can gainsay that. He's committed treason, gentlemen. *Fucking* treason!" he began to bellow. "*Treason! Treason!*" The audience was getting uncomfortable with the tone, though most of them agreed with the message.

"Kennedy is one of *them*. Kennedys, Castros, there's no *goddamn* difference."

Rear Admiral Ryan rose from his seat and moved to the podium to try to get control of Ferrie and bring some decorum to the meeting.

"If this were still a revolutionary country," Ferrie shouted, "people would be chanting, 'To the wall with Kennedy. Kennedy to the wall!'" Ferrie began screaming, "Kennedy should be shot, he should be shot. Blow off his head! Hang 'im like they did Mumford!"

Rear Admiral Ryan grabbed the microphone. "Thank you, Mr. Ferrie. Thank you, sir. But that's enough."

"To the barricades!" Ferrie bellowed as he left the podium. "God bless America!" He and Arcacha Smith marched out of the building.

||||

Marcello and his organization quickly learned of Ferrie's over-the-top anti-JFK tirade. They didn't need him getting this kind of notoriety.

Banister directed Ferrie to lie low for a while. Ferrie came to recognize that he'd overdone it at Lenfant's.

He prayed intensely to Mother Mary for calm and did his best to comply with Banister's direction. He dutifully did his flying for Eastern. He tended to his mice. He ministered to his Catholic flock, celebrating small masses once a week.

In part to keep him busy, Banister assigned Ferrie to a small-time undercover project—a follow-on to Jack Martin's hunt for Communists at New Orleans colleges. Communists were using fringe religious groups, Banister told Ferrie and Martin, to lure vulnerable believers into their clutches. There were shameless and predacious priests and preachers, Commie money in their pockets, willing to brainwash the weak among their followers, persuading them to engage with certain fellow "parishioners" who were in reality undercover Communists. Banister provided Ferrie and Martin a list of organizations to check out.

To kick off this chore, Banister sent Martin and Ferrie to bourbon country, Louisville, Kentucky, to investigate a "bishop" named Carl Stanley who looked phony. Stanley operated under the purported authority of the American Orthodox Catholic Church. There was intelligence that he ran a Communist front. It had to be checked out, Banister believed. The trip to Kentucky served another good purpose—to get Ferrie out of town for a while.

At six feet four, Stanley was an imposing figure. He often dressed like a Greek Orthodox priest, wearing a black cassock with a large iron-cross patch on his left sleeve. This outfit included a black mitre and several large crosses dangling from his neck. His "church name" was Christopher Maria.

Stanley's majestic appearance betrayed a criminal past, as Banister had suspected. He'd first been arrested in Los Angeles on November 22, 1927, for grand theft auto. Arrests followed into the 1930s for a range of bad conduct, including sending obscene material through the mail and assault and battery.

Though he was an American citizen, born in Massachusetts, and though he had lived his entire life in the United States, he joined the Canadian Army during World War II. His American rap sheet would be less apparent to the Canadian Army. Though he never left Canada, the constant prospect of being shipped off to the killing fields changed him. He made a sharp turn toward God after the war.

He boomeranged back and forth between Canada and the United States over the next handful of years, studying religious tracts and attending a kaleidoscope of different church services and meetings. The American Orthodox Catholic Church proved to be an efficient way to gain a titled position, though the church itself was not official. Stanley nevertheless assumed the mantle of a Catholic priest and bishop in that church in the mid-1950s. This wasn't a fraudulent ruse. The army experience had motivated a genuine interest in religion and commitment to leading a better life. He was serious about his church duties. Though his innate nature still caused him to sail close to the law at times, he did his genuine best to be righteous.

After a few days together in Louisville, Ferrie and Martin agreed that Stanley ran a loose operation but was not a Commie. They differed, though, on whether he was a complete phony. To Martin, Stanley's continuing petty crimes suggested he was bogus. But Ferrie connected with him.

He'd actually heard of Bishop Stanley through his Catholic contacts. Though based in Louisville, Stanley had followers in several other areas of the country, including Louisiana. He traveled around, frequently to New Orleans.

Stanley's American Orthodox Catholic Church, an organization founded in the 1920s by followers of "Old Catholicism," had once had canonical status. Its driving theology, like that of Ferrie's, was grounded in the pre-Vatican I world, where local dioceses and priests had meaningful authority, where reasonable flexibility mixed with tradition, and where congregants believed they had a more direct path to God.

Though Stanley's church had lost its Vatican sanction, Ferrie came to believe that it retained sufficient legitimacy, was legitimate *enough*, to conclude that Stanley was an authentic religious leader. Ferrie persuaded Martin to lay off Stanley even though Martin believed Stanley was a crook.

To Martin's amusement, Ferrie began worshipping with Stanley when he was in New Orleans, usually at Ferrie's apartment. He impressed Stanley with his knowledge of traditional Catholicism and his capabilities as a true man of God. Stanley offered him the opportunity to actually earn the vestments he already wore.

||||

In July Stanley ordained Ferrie as a "missionary bishop" in the American Orthodox Catholic Church—"with the Holy Apostolic power to perform all functions appertaining to such Office." There was an official, though small, ceremony. Martin assisted but later told Ferrie the show was "half-assed," he attended "only for the free wine."

Ferrie knew his new status wasn't officially recognized by the Vatican, but he nevertheless felt a holy spirit when he received it. His religious commitment deepened, though not deep enough to change his lifestyle choices, not even the sinful ones. Had he focused resolutely on his new duties as a bishop, his life would've been a safer, more comfortable—and longer—one. But, though religion was always in the calm eye of his personal hurricane, he just couldn't stay away from his hurricane's eye wall and rainbands. New adventures were to come but so were personal losses, criminal acts, and danger.

CHAPTER 16

Ferrie had developed a band of loyal flying followers over the previous year through a new endeavor—providing pilot lessons on his own, outside of the CAP. This band was comprised of former CAP students of Ferrie's and a number of brand new trainees, including a few who'd run away from their homes outside the city. Ferrie worked with these men over the summer of 1961 in what was in effect an informal, non-sanctioned CAP squadron. Not being part of the official CAP organization, Ferrie's squadron—which he called the "Falcons"—had few personal conduct rules.

The training was serious, but there was a lot of off-duty socializing. Ferrie's favorite party stop after a training session was Graci's Lounge on Homedale Avenue in Navarre, not far from Lenfant's and the Greenwood Cemetery. Not infrequently, after beers and cocktails at Graci's, a trainee or two would end the evening at his apartment on Airline Park Boulevard. There, he liked to organize games that, if well-played, would turn sexual. His skill at hypnosis was often on display on these evenings.

Ferrie housed a few of the runaways in this band of merry young men for brief periods of time, including a few who had anxious parents searching New Orleans for them.

On August 8, 1961, he was visited by the police for suspicion of being involved in the disappearance of fifteen-year-old Al Landry, the youngest of Ferrie's Falcons. Landry's parents had learned that their son had been living at Ferrie's apartment off and on. They convinced the police to surprise Ferrie there. On that occasion, luckily for him, Landry was out of town. With

Ferrie denying any and all malfeasance, there was no basis to arrest him.

But when Landry returned to Ferrie's ten days later, the police learned about it and paid another visit. They heard enough from the young man—including that Ferrie had taken him on several short joy jaunts to Mexico—to have Ferrie charged with contributing to the delinquency of a minor. Before long, the New Orleans police located three other cadets who, under questioning, alleged sexual abuse by Ferrie. One was Al Landry's sixteen-year-old brother James. Ferrie was arrested.

The police searched Ferrie's unorthodox and unkempt home. There was ample evidence that he'd had young male roommates—a closet had male underwear too small to fit him, there were scattered tennis shoes, which he didn't wear, jeans with small waistlines. They also found all the oddities that accompanied Ferrie's odd life—priest robes, a chalice, an altar, dozens of pill bottles, medical syringes, microscopes, blood pressure gauges, mice in cages, several maps of Cuba. As the police had already suspected, this was no normal guy.

The *Times-Picayune* reported on the arrest in its August 26 edition. "New Orleans police juvenile bureau officers and Jefferson parish deputies said the 43-year-old airline pilot apparently used alcohol, hypnotism, and the adventure of flying to lure the juveniles—mostly 15- and 16-year-olds—into committing indecent acts."

Anxiety seized Ferrie. He spent hours communing with Mother Mary. But his only worldly hope, he knew, was intervention from Marcello and friends. They could make this all go away with a virtual snap of their fingers. As he thought about it, how his Marcello colleagues dealt with his current crisis would be a test of his value to the organization. They could easily cast him adrift to deal with this disaster alone. He called Banister.

Ferrie passed the test. Marcello troops marched to his rescue.

His case came directly to District Attorney Austin Anderson. As luck would have it, Anderson's former boss was G. Wray Gill, Marcello's principal lawyer. Briefed by Banister, Gill requested that Anderson release Ferrie from custody without bail. And it was done.

Marcello was also briefed by Banister. He directed Gill to make every effort to get Ferrie off. Marcello felt he owed it to Ferrie, who had bravely rescued Marcello from Honduras. He also had some new plans for Ferrie. The "Little Man" couldn't allow Ferrie to be locked up or otherwise distracted.

With Marcello's imprimatur, Gill engaged Jack Wasserman, Marcello's trial lawyer, to represent Ferrie in court. Though based in DC, Wasserman was continuing to spend considerable time in New Orleans working on Marcello's deportation war with RFK.

Wasserman was primarily an immigration lawyer. He once had served as chief counsel of the INS. His legal skills, though, went well beyond just immigration issues. He was a tough and creative litigator. A Harvard Law School graduate. He'd become well-connected in New Orleans through his many years of work for Marcello.

Gill, through Banister, had Sergio Arcacha Smith investigate Ferrie's young male complainants, "spend some time with them." Arcacha Smith—not a trained investigator but a savvy and discreet man—was happy to oblige. He continued to value his friendship with Ferrie, forged in Belle Chasse. And he imagined additional anti-Castro adventures with him.

District Attorney Anderson and his staff tried to investigate the morals allegations against Ferrie, calling witnesses into their offices on Tulane Avenue. Each boy's story, however, had softened. Landry, after a sharp visit with Arcacha Smith, recanted completely.

Wasserman met with Anderson several times to argue the legal weaknesses of the case. He didn't have to mention his relationship with Marcello nor with Anderson's former boss, G. Wray Gill. These facts were well known to Anderson.

As part of his advocacy for Ferrie, Wasserman brought in character witnesses, including a respected St. Charles Parish banker named Herbert Wagner, who'd done business with Ferrie over the years. A priest and several nuns from Loyola's Holy Name Church, where Ferrie had provided volunteer support, visited with Anderson on Ferrie's behalf. Guy Banister, known by Anderson to be a former high-ranking FBI official, took the district attorney to lunch at Antoine's to talk about Ferrie's good qualities.

After considering how this grand lineup of defense witnesses would look compared to the weakening prosecution case, Anderson dropped the serious charges against Ferrie. For the sake of appearances, and with the blessings of Gill and Wasserman, he preserved one lesser charge—indecent behavior with a juvenile, a misdemeanor. This single charge would be tried to a judge early the next year.

Ferrie was pleased that his legal troubles were, for the most part, solved. Even more so, he was gratified that he'd passed the test—he knew now he was squarely a part of Marcello's team.

||||

One morning in early September, Arcacha Smith called and asked Ferrie to meet him at the Sho-Bar that afternoon. The two enthusiastically shook hands and clapped each other's shoulders when they met at the strip club. Ferrie knew about the role Arcacha Smith had played in the morals case.

The Sho-Bar strippers, per usual for daytime, were the "B team."

"I've got one thing to get out of the way first, Dave. My CRC guys in Miami have heard about you frolicking around with young guys and about your run-in with the law. They have sources in New Orleans. They don't like what they're hearing. I know we're in common cause against Cuba, but these guys are strict, by-the-book Catholics, not fancy intellectual ones like you."

"I can assure you, and them, that God is just fine with homosexuals. Shit, *He's* the one who made me this way."

"Don't matter, amigo. Whatever *you* believe, *my* guys see you as a weirdo. I'm getting pressure to drop you from the group. It pains me, man, but I need to do it."

"What about the Houma raid?"

"No change there. We're too deep into those weeds. But after that, while we'll still play together on Marcello stuff, it's *sayonara* to the CRC, I'm sad to say. Sorry, my friend."

"Great. They keep me in the Houma thing—a fucking dangerous job—but I'm otherwise an outcast. I don't know."

"Understood—but I wasn't kidding about the Marcello stuff. I worked it out with Guy. You help us with Houma and then Banister'll have some better Cuba-related stuff for you, well-paid stuff. I'll work with you on some of these things, as needed. And he's promised he'll have other Marcello work for you, non-Cuba work. It'll all be fine. You'll make some real money."

\\\\\

Ferrie confirmed all of this with Banister and then got ready for Houma.

Houma was an hour southwest of New Orleans. The parish seat of Terrebonne Parish, it was known as the Cajun capital of Louisiana. The favorite pastime of Houma's residents, in addition to eating oysters harvested from Lake Boudreaux, was Cajun dancing. The small city had a dozen Cajun dance halls, where traditional jigs were skipped out one foot at a time and more elaborate open-handed and cross-handed dances such as "The Sweetheart" and "The Big Window" were performed. Every Saturday night there was at least one big *fais-dodo*.

Early versions of the Cajun dances dated back to French Acadia. During the French and Indian War, and particularly after what went down on the Plains of Abraham in Quebec in 1759, thousands of French Acadians were forced to flee eastern Canada. Many of these refugees settled in southern Louisiana.

The word *Cajun* was an American corruption of the word *Acadian*.

The accordion-based bands played old favorites like *"Allons á Lafayette," "Hip et Taïaut,"* and *"Jolie Blonde."* The locals invariably stomped their feet when this music played.

Houma's other claim to fame was having a World War II airfield the Navy had used as a blimp station. The blimps were located there so they could easily reach the Gulf of Mexico and float around looking for U-boats. The blimp station was closed in 1947. A municipal airport was now operating on the property. Though the immense timber blimp hangars were long gone, the large grass field where they'd sat and where the blimps lifted off was still there, perpendicular to and on the northwest side of the functioning airport. The old "blimp field" was used primarily to house storage units for air freight companies.

The CRC and Arcacha Smith had hatched a plan to steal the contents of a large wooden shed owned by Schlumberger, an oilfield services company, at the blimp field. Marcello was supportive and allowed Guy Banister to be hired to assist. The Schlumberger shed housed "downhole" seismographic explosive charge cartridges. These devices employed powerful charges of dynamite, which were desperately needed by the groups planning to take Cuba back.

Arcacha Smith and Ferrie devised the details of the raid and led the attack. Seven other anti-Castro adventurers participated, as did a Banister friend and supposed electronics expert named Gordon Novel. Novel's main benefit to the team, however, wasn't electronics expertise. It was his car, a 1959 Lincoln. Some of this band of bandits drove the Lincoln to get to Houma. Amusingly, the others traveled in a CRC-owned laundry truck. Layton Martens, a former CAP student and friend of Ferrie's *and* a CRC volunteer who knew Arcacha Smith, drove the truck. This innocent-looking vehicle was used out of necessity, though it would've been a clever move had it been planned.

The team left Ferrie's apartment at about eight o'clock on Sunday evening, September 17. The airport had shut down for the night and the storage sheds at the blimp field were unguarded. The raid went smoothly, and the team returned to Ferrie's after midnight, stopping once to detonate a charge in giddiness over the success of the mission. The next morning, Banister came by Ferrie's place in a rented Impala station wagon and picked up the cartridges. The dynamite would go to Miami from there.

While Ferrie had been focused on planning and carrying out the Houma raid, news of the sexual allegations against him—even though largely dismissed by the district attorney—was spiraling around the city, fueled by the article in the *Times-Picayune*. Shortly after Houma, this news bit Ferrie hard and sharply, much more painfully than his boot from the CRC. Eastern Air Lines management had learned about the sordid stories in blistering detail. Ferrie suspected that the parents of several of the young men who had bedded down at Ferrie's apartment had directly contacted Eastern to punish him. They'd come to see that they wouldn't get any redress from the local authorities.

Ferrie was summoned to meet with Eastern's manager at Moisant Field, Captain G. E. Grenier. Ferrie was accompanied by Arcacha Smith and a new Marcello-connected attorney named A. J. Graffagnino. Marcello had arranged for Graffagnino to be paid $5,000 for this work. Even though Graffagnino was a government lawyer, an assistant DA, and shouldn't have been arguing a private citizen's case, Marcello believed Eastern would pay more attention to someone in authority. Though concerned about the impropriety of the representation, Graffagnino had no choice but to do this favor for Marcello—he wanted a future in the city.

Notwithstanding the status of the new lawyer, however, the meeting didn't go well. Ferrie was suspended indefinitely from Eastern shortly thereafter.

He was shell-shocked by the removal of this pillar of his life—other than Catholicism, the most important pillar. Flying had kept Ferrie free of serious depression since he was twenty years old, a lifetime gift from his father. Knocked off balance, his tether to reality loosened, which sometimes happened at anxious times like this, he rashly penned a rambling, irrational letter to Eastern's Captain Grenier on October 30, 1961. The letter lumbered on, without direction, for four pages. He complained about having Communist enemies out to get him—they'd even wiretapped his phones. It was these bad people who were behind the spurious allegations, he wrote.

"At this time we don't know the chain-of-command of the Communists at the local level. However, my problems have been traced with certainty to a highly placed local official. Whether Communists within Eastern Air Lines are involved is not known at this time."

Ferrie suggested that evil forces were laboring against him because of his efforts to liberate Cuba. But that work had been "approved of and encouraged by the President of the United States." He attempted to layer this crazy fabrication with an air of intrigue. "No one knows of the composition of this letter, including Mr. Graffagnino." He said he was keeping the only copy of the letter in "a strong box."

Ferrie vowed to Captain Grenier that he'd pursue all "civil suits" possible against Eastern. He did file grievances, which were litigated over the next few years to no avail.

CHAPTER 17

As was the pattern, Ferrie's dive into disorder was short-lived. As 1962 began he rationally saw that he was running out of money. His Eastern salary was gone, at least for the time being, and his old retainer from Marcello's organization had long since terminated. He went to see Banister, who'd promised projects.

Banister had moved to a different office a few blocks from the Balter Building, which was about to be eminent-domained by the city for a new hotel. Banister's new place of business was in a thirty-five-year-old structure at Lafayette and Camp Streets, owned by a largely unsuccessful local businessman named Sam Newman. The Newman Building skirted Lafayette Square, which oddly had a statue of Henry Clay in the middle and one of Benjamin Franklin on the Camp Street side. There was no statue of the Marquis de Lafayette. Why the square was named for the French aristocrat was lost to history, though he did spend a few days in the city in April 1825, staying at the historic Cabildo by the St. Louis Cathedral.

The three-story, granite Newman Building was unique in that it had two addresses and was structured as if it were two different buildings, one significantly larger than the other. Entering from the square, it was 544 Camp, the address for most of the building. The original name of the building was still evident over the entranceway—Stevedores and Longshoremen's Building. Several employee organizations were located at 544 Camp.

The entrance on Lafayette Street provided access solely to the offices of Guy Banister and Associates. The address of Banister's offices was 531 Lafayette.

Following Banister's lead, Arcacha Smith had arranged to move the CRC offices to the Newman Building as well, though these offices were in the main part of the structure. Visitors there, 544 Camp, couldn't access Banister's offices. Instead, they had to immediately ascend stairs to the second floor. By the same token, Banister's guests—which frequently included his friend and Arcacha Smith benefactor Orlando Piedra, a former Batista official—couldn't get upstairs to the offices of the labor groups nor of the CRC.

Banister had introduced Piedra to Marcello. These two men, Banister had heard, thereafter dined alone together on occasion. What they talked about he never knew.

The odd structure of the Newman Building provided a certain level of privacy for Banister's business and visitors. The Lafayette Street entrance had no signage identifying Guy Banister and Associates. Clients could come and go in relative anonymity. The isolated layout provided Banister the flexibility to discreetly store equipment, supplies, and even munitions.

There was a third means of ingress into the Newman Building, the entrance to Mancuso's Restaurant and Bar on the corner of Camp and Lafayette. Jack and Felicie Mancuso's establishment, which had yet another address, 546 Camp, was self-contained. The CRC's new offices were above Mancuso's.

Departing a bus on Poydras, Ferrie walked over to Banister's offices. Banister's secretary, Delphine Roberts, served Ferrie coffee. Delphine whispered in Banister's ear and rubbed his shoulders. She laughed bawdily.

Delphine was a lively, kooky, tough-talking force in the Banister operation, obviously quite close to Banister. She was middle-aged with scattered fake-blonde hair. She didn't need this, or any, job. Delphine was well-to-do—a Daughter of the American Revolution. She could've lived her life as a society woman, hosting teas at her large Second Street house in the

Garden District, close to the Frank G. Strachan house, where Jefferson Davis died in 1889. However, she wasn't remotely the Garden District type of person. She liked living an edgy life, engaging in right-wing protests and running for various offices on extreme platforms. She needed an edgy job, like working in Banister's often clandestine world. And she was smitten with Banister.

"Ray Gill and I do have some work for you," Banister said to Ferrie. "Mainly, some legwork on the deportation crap for Mr. Marcello."

Banister told Ferrie that G. Wray Gill was prepared to hire him as an "investigator and law clerk" to help on Marcello's case. He'd be paid at a rate of $3,600 a year, a financial lifeline.

"Mr. Marcello and Gill have a Cuba thing for you too. They'll explain soon."

Ferrie was thrilled and more than ready to get going. First, though, he had to go through the court trial of the remaining morals charge against him. Paid by Marcello, Jack Wasserman continued as Ferrie's trial attorney. Banister continued to lend a hand.

In February, a week after John Glenn became the first American to orbit the Earth, Jefferson Parish Judge Leo W. McCune acquitted Ferrie of the one remaining charge. The victims' stories had become wishy-washy. The credible character witnesses, including the nuns from Holy Name, came out again for Ferrie. The judge's decision was covered in the February 28 edition of the *Times-Picayune*, which seemed to be warning readers that, though Ferrie "was dismissed from a post as a commander of the Civil Air Patrol about a year ago," he'd more recently "formed his own patrol unit, according to police."

Ferrie had moved from the apartment at 704 Airline Park Boulevard to another small apartment on Atherton Drive in Metairie, four miles closer to the airport. The move was a step sideways. More convenient for his pilot activities, the new quarters, however, didn't provide sufficient room for all of his extra-curricular activities, particularly his space-consuming religious and scientific work. Nor was there room to throw a decent party, or "get-togethers," as Ferrie liked to call them.

But now, with the promised influx of new funds, Ferrie began looking around for a nicer, larger place.

Banister told him about a larger apartment available in a house on Louisiana Avenue Parkway, on the same street as the "safe house" Ferrie and Martin had used to interrogate student Commies a few years before. Marcello had kept the "safe house" after that project had run its course, using it for a variety of purposes, including as a hideaway for colleagues on the run.

This larger apartment was in a distinctive house—3330 Louisiana Avenue Parkway—defined by a narrow, two-story window topped by a circular window. Taken together, these two windows formed a large letter "I."

Ferrie was able to get this new home surprisingly easily. He moved in in March.

The new apartment was on the second floor. It had a screened-in porch and nice appointments but, like his other apartments, it soon became cluttered with old furniture and lamps, tattered rugs, his old out-of-tune piano and ratty piano bench, cages and lab equipment, religious paraphernalia, and a makeshift altar. Numerous books were quickly scattered about the space. And cigarette butts.

Louisiana Avenue Parkway was a quiet enclave situated between South Broad and South Claiborne, surrounded by poorer neighborhoods. It was in the Broadmoor neighborhood of New Orleans, part of the broader Carrollton area of the city. The neighborhood, a swamp in the early twentieth century, was subject to frequent flooding. It wasn't far from the Garden District and was closer to the French Quarter than Ferrie's previous apartments in Metairie. The location suited him. Convenient. Private.

Shortly after he'd completed his move, Ferrie was summoned to meet with G. Wray Gill at the Pere Marquette. It was early April 1962. He hustled the three miles over to Baronne and Common.

"Take a seat," Gill said as he shut his office door. "Let me finish a few master strokes on the appeal papers on that perjury case you've helped out with for Marion James Johnson."

After ten minutes, Gill got down to new business. "What you're soon going to hear isn't to go anywhere outside your weirdly wired brain," Gill continued. "If you leak any of this information, in a drunken stupor or however, you can kiss your tiny hairless testicles goodbye. You'll also be kissing some serious cash away."

"I'm all ears." Gill had gotten Ferrie's attention.

"Not here. We're going to go see the Little Man. This is that important."

Gill drove them out Tulane Avenue to 1225 Airline Highway. They went out back to Marcello's office. Marcello hugged Ferrie Sicilian-style—he never forgot the rescue mission to Honduras.

Marcello spoke. "Ferrie—my friends from around dis country have decided we have-ta hit Castro. We have-ta, Ferrie. No more hav-azzed invasions.

"Dis is not just about me and my friends and our casinos. You get it, Ferrie? It's about dis town. Nor-leens does huge dollars of bidness with Cuba. Dat Commie bastard don't believe in bidness. He's cuttin' our dicks off. You get it, Ferrie?"

"This is tricky," Gill chimed in. "We can't have Castro murdered in a way that looks like a mob hit. We'd have a world of hurt. We have to get him in a way that looks like he wasn't murdered but died naturally."

"Dat's where you come in, Ferrie," Marcello said.

"But first know that the Kennedys purportedly have authorized the CIA to work on a plan to kill Castro," Gill said.

"They're showing some balls?" Ferrie asked.

"They're under pressure from the Cubans in Florida and the right wingers in Texas and other southern states. They're freaked about the 1964 election, so they're leaking out to certain groups that they're going after Castro."

"How good is our information about what the Kennedys are willing to do? Is it reliable?" Ferrie asked.

"We know hundred puh-cint what they're sayin', Ferrie," Marcello said. "One of my pot-ners is humpin' the same *puttana* Kennedy's humpin'. The slut gets all kinds of info from Kennedy and passes it on to us."

"She's a great middleman—actually a middle-woman." Gill smiled.

"Extraordinary," Ferrie offered.

"What we just told you's top secret, of course," Gill said.

"Of course."

"God bless the Kennedys if they're serious about actually getting this done," Gill said. "But we think it's just talk, tough talk for political reasons. In any event, we know we'd be more effective. They're amateurs."

Ferrie quietly waited for more from Gill.

"What I'm about to tell you now is even more top secret, over-the-top top secret," Gill said. "We'd have to eliminate you if you even dreamed about what I'm about to tell you. Okay?"

"Go."

Marcello fingered an unlit cigar and nodded to Gill to keep talking. "You know Dr. Alton Ochsner?"

"Well, sure, everybody knows who he is. I met him once a few years ago."

"You may not know, but we have a very tight relationship with him," Gill said. "We do a lot of favors for each other. And he's a big-time anti-Commie."

In 1961 Alton Ochsner formed a group called the Information Council of the Americas. INCA's main purpose was to prevent Communist revolutions in Latin America. Ochsner had powerful associates funding the organization, including Texas oil man Clint Murchison and Richard Nixon's friend Patrick Frawley. Members of INCA included Edgar Stern, owner of New Orleans's main TV station, and Eustis Reily of the Reily Coffee Company.

Dr. Ochsner had talked to the *New Orleans States-Item* about INCA. "We must spread the warning of the creeping sickness of Communism or Central and South America will be exposed to the same sickness as Cuba." INCA colleagues of the doctor told the *Times-Picayune* the group was comprised of "hemispheric patriots."

"I know he's a Commie-hater. But what could *he* possibly do to help on Castro?" Ferrie asked.

"He's working on a cancer-causing bioweapon, Dave," Gill announced.

Ferrie was speechless. The room was silent, except for the sounds of breathing, for a full minute.

Gill then picked up the conversation. "You know about Ochsner's commitment to cure cancer. We asked him, as a patriot, to turn that around, to figure out a way to *give* Castro cancer. If he can figure out how to do that, it would be much more effective than exploding cigars or seashells, poisonous pens—or whatever gimmicks the Kennedys and their amateur spooks are working on.

"He agreed, of course," Gill continued. "He's put a hot-shot cancer doctor on the job. Surprisingly, the doctor is a lady. Frankly, I didn't even know there were hot-shot lady doctors."

"You're just ignorant, Ray. Apgar, Sabin, Eddy, Stewart," Ferrie said.

"In any event, her name is Mary Sherman. She worships Dr. Ochsner and shares his views on Castro."

Dr. Sherman had become one of the most prominent female doctors in the country. After a meteoric start to her career in Chicago, Dr. Sherman was enticed by Dr. Ochsner in 1952 to join the Ochsner Clinic Foundation as director of the bone pathology laboratory. Through the mid-1950s, Dr. Sherman blossomed and spread her wings to the Tulane Medical School and the Medical Center of Louisiana at New Orleans. Her growing specialty was cancer research.

"That name rings a bell," Ferrie said to Gill, scratching his chin. "Let me think." He paused. Then, the right neuron passed through a synapse in his brain and hit the target. "I got it. I've actually met her—at the Crippled Hospital at Christmas a few years ago. Nice lady. Elegant."

Ferrie remembered that Dr. Sherman—Dr. Mary as her colleagues called her—had been running various experiments to understand better the role that viruses played in causing cancers so that vaccines could be developed to neutralize the viruses and prevent the cancers.

"And what does this cancer project have to do with me?" Ferrie asked.

"Ferrie," Marcello answered, "I told Alton I need one of my guys in on dis work. You da guy, *se*? Hey, you goin' ta like it. You homos like ta work wid da ladies, right?"

"Yes, sir. But I gotta say that my religion isn't big on killing people," Ferrie said.

"Doesn't the Bible talk about 'an eye for an eye?'" Gill asked. "Exodus 21. Right? Isn't that what we have here?"

"Well, impressive you've read Exodus, but that's a really confusing passage. Can you give me a night to think it over, check with my spirits?"

"Talk to the spirits, go crazy," Gill said. "And don't forget to tell them there's money in this for you."

"My god tells me that money isn't everything."

"Ferrie, we got da same god and mine luv da moolah," Marcello responded. "You gotta tok to 'im *ancora*. Go hava drink with Ray."

Gill ushered Ferrie out to his car in the Town and Country Motel parking lot. They drove back to the Pere Marquette, parked there, and walked across Baronne to the Roosevelt Hotel for a drink.

The Roosevelt Hotel was replete with pictures of Huey P. Long. Long, the "Kingfish," had used the hotel as his New Orleans home when he was governor in the late 1920s and early 1930s. He'd built the Airline Highway—home now to the Town and Country Motel—so he could get to New Orleans and the Roosevelt Hotel more quickly from Baton Rouge. Unlike New Orleans, Baton Rouge had few amusements to offer Long. As it turned out, Huey Long should've spent more time in New

Orleans, for he was gunned down in Baton Rouge one day after announcing his candidacy for the presidency in 1935.

Gill frequented the Sazerac Bar at the Roosevelt—not because he liked the rye whiskey-based Sazerac, though. He always eschewed the bar's signature drink and ordered Huey Long's favorite, the Ramos Gin Fizz.

A bartender named Henry Charles Ramos, "Carl" to his friends and customers, invented this landmark drink in 1888 while managing a bar called the Imperial Cabinet Saloon at the corner of Gravier and Carondelet Streets. At that time Ramos called the drink "The One and Only One." Largely because of the success of that single drink, Carl Ramos and his brother were able to open their own establishment, the Stag, an elegant saloon a few doors east on Gravier, across from the side entrance to what was then the St. Charles Hotel, later the Sheraton-Charles. The Stag was decorated with a mahogany bar, a grandfather clock, and a two chandeliers.

A temperate and fastidious gentleman, Ramos didn't drink, nor did he condone drunkenness. He closed his bar every night at eight o'clock. At his bars, drinks were an art form to be enjoyed slowly, not used to intoxicate.

The recipe for the Ramos Gin Fizz was a closely held secret until shortly before Mr. Ramos's death in 1928, when its main ingredients were revealed—sweet gin, the white of one egg, two tablespoons of cream, powdered sugar, lime and lemon juice, seltzer water, and three or four drops of orange flower water. Making a good Ramos Gin Fizz takes experience and flair. And, before being poured into its glass, the concoction had to be shaken sternly for at least several minutes—twelve by Ramos's standards. Even an experienced bartender can't produce a good Ramos Gin Fizz on the first or second try.

Ferrie followed Gill's lead and ordered a Ramos Gin Fizz as well.

"This whole project really feels so wrong to me, Ray. Don't you think?"

"Seems okay to me. But it's America. Do what you want."

"I have no free will here, right?"

"You Catholics don't really believe in free will, do you?"

"Depends who you ask."

"Dave, you're just looking at this the wrong way. Dr. Sherman's one of the best cancer doctors in the country. She had the same reservations as you, believe me, but realized that the potential benefits of this project outweigh the moral dilemma. Not only could it take care of Castro, she believes that, in trying to figure out how to cause cancer, you're likely to figure out how to cure it."

"Okay, shit. Fill me in a little more."

"Dr. Ochsner, as you gathered, is a big-time right-winger and is big-time close with Marcello."

"I saw them together at the Sho-Bar a few years ago. With Santo Trafficante."

"That's not a rare occurrence, by the way.

"Marcello, Ochsner, and I were kicking around ways to get Castro," Gill continued. "Ochsner was kinda joking, I think, when he mentioned this cancer idea—he'd already been doing some work on viruses and whether they can cause cancer. Marcello, though, jumped on the idea.

"Ochsner insisted that, if this went forward, his own hands had to be clean, he had to have deniability. So, he assigned Mary Sherman to manage this. She'll keep him informed but generally keep him out of the picture."

"When I met her at the toys for sick kids thing at the Crippled Hospital," Ferrie said, "we chatted for some time about cancer and mice and some of the stuff she was doing. By the way, people that know her call her Dr. Mary."

"Sherman—Dr. Mary—is going to give you your marching orders soon. Hard to believe, but I'm told much of the work will be at your messy place, not at the clinic on Prytania or the one they're building by the hospital. They don't want hundreds of mice running around those places. People might start asking questions."

"I don't want hundreds of mice running around my apartment either," Ferrie said.

"You won't. Dr. Mary'll explain."

"One other thing. Also top secret. There's some space-age device the government owns that supposedly will speed this project up. It shoots magic rays or something. I can't remember what it's called. Has 'particle' in the name, I think."

"Shit, Guy, a linear particle accelerator? There's actually one of those in New Orleans?"

"Yeah, that's what they call it. Only a few people know about it. It's supposed to be like something out of the future."

"You don't know the half of it, Ray. It's real Robert Heinlein stuff. I've read a lot about the technology."

"I don't *want* to know much about it. All I know is that Dr. Ochsner helped buy it and get it here. It's at the Public Health facility. You know, on State Street near that hospital for cripples where you met Dr. Mary."

"Like most things, I must say, *I* know a lot about that place. Used to be a Marine Hospital in the thirties. It's built on an old slave plantation brickyard. The plantation was owned by the first mayor of New Orleans. It stretched twenty arpents along the river and—"

"Enough, Captain!"

"Does Dr. Mary know about the accelerator?"

"I assume so. What I do know for sure is that the CIA said we could use it. There aren't many of these things, I'm told. There's one around London, I think."

"The CIA's in on this project?"

"No, no. They just think Ochsner's using it for his regular research."

Though tense, Ferrie had enjoyed the Roosevelt Hotel. He suggested to Gill that the meeting with Dr. Mary occur there.

CHAPTER 18

Ferrie and Dr. Mary met in the lobby of the Roosevelt two days later. They didn't go downstairs to the Sazerac Bar, though. Instead, she directed Ferrie to a table at the casual but classy Fountain Lounge in the lobby.

Turning her cancer research upside down to look for a way to *cause* cancer, not cure it, had been a jarring assignment for Dr. Mary. A blunt violation of her Hippocratic Oath. After being given time to think it over, she'd told Dr. Ochsner she was prepared to do it—for use solely on Fidel Castro. Preserving America and its values was worth this pact with the Devil, she'd concluded. Though not an activist, Dr. Mary was an intense anti-Communist.

When she'd learned from Dr. Ochsner that he had been asked by some of his business colleagues—code words, she knew, for Marcello's organization—to find a role for a man named David Ferrie, she remembered the name. His seriousness and knowledge of cancer and viruses, not to mention his unusual appearance, had quickly come back to her. Christmastime 1959. The vigor with which he pursued his scientific work *had* impressed Dr. Mary. However, she was skeptical of having him, an amateur after all, on this serious project. Dr. Ochsner nevertheless demanded this favor. She knew she had no choice. She'd make the best of it.

The Roosevelt Hotel was buzzing more than usual this particular day because Frank Sinatra was appearing that night in the Blue Room before the start of his charity tour of Asia and Europe to raise money for orphans. His friend President Kennedy had requested that Sinatra make this charity trip.

"Good to see you again," Dr. Mary said.

"Likewise. I remember very well our visit at the Crippled Hospital Christmas 1959."

Dr. Mary was about fifty years old. Serious and stylish. Attractive. She had a firm and confident voice.

"Ray has given you an introduction to this project, I know. I understand you're on board?"

"Yes, ma'am."

"I just want to give you an outline today and then would appreciate it if you could meet me tomorrow at the clinic's lab on Prytania Street in Touro. Okay?"

"Yes, ma'am."

"Are you still doing your own cancer work, Dave?"

"Yes. Probably not very well, but I'm trying."

"Splendid. How do you find time? I've heard about some of your other activities—flying, masses, PhD."

"I've given up sleep!"

"You're a real, what's the word? *Polymath*."

"Hardly. I've got a lot of flaws. I *am* good at juggling things, Dr. Sherman."

"Good. Though what we might need is a medicine man. And call me what most of my friends call me—Dr. Mary.

"Here are the broad strokes of the project. We're going to inject healthy mice with a cancer-causing virus found in some monkeys—the SV-40."

"Of course. Sweet and Hilleman."

"Bingo. We'll then try to isolate the most dangerous cancers the viruses cause and reinject them in other healthy mice. These cancers will be in a solution consisting of the pulverized tumor, bovine serum—which is basically centrifuged blood from calves or adult cows—and a glycol ether, which'll serve as a preservative. We then will take the tumors that grow from that step and run them through the process again. And on and on. Through multiple cycles, we hope to produce some super-powerful, rapidly developing cancers. Along the way, we'll zap the best stuff with radiation."

"Wow. Fantastic science, though I'm not sure Jesus'll be too wild about it."

"He'll see a good and just motivation."

"I'll need to do some serious praying about this."

"This is going to happen in a circle of different facilities. Your home lab on Louisiana Avenue Parkway will be one of the key ones."

"Mr. Gill told me that. Calling it a lab is a bit of a stretch."

"To be honest with you, I wasn't wild about this idea, but Mr. Gill and his bosses apparently insisted on it. I guess because there'd be less of a chance that information on the project would leak. It *is* true that no one's going to be looking for a criminal bioweapon project at your apartment. And Louisiana Avenue Parkway's a pretty isolated little street surrounded by rough neighborhoods—not a lot of people passing through on it.

"So, with that in mind, we'll need to limit access to your place for a while."

"I sometimes have friends staying with me, but I'll make sure nobody's there once we start up."

"Good. We can probably figure out a way for you to have folks over on the weekends, perhaps lock away any new equipment we bring over."

Ferrie smiled to himself. He didn't want to completely interrupt his private-time social life. Or his periodic, larger "get-togethers."

Dr. Mary continued. "The plan would be to start the cycles at your apartment. Cycle by cycle, I'll take the worst of the worst of the tumors from your place over to a real lab and inject them in the kidneys of monkeys."

"That's how the polio vaccines were done, right?" Ferrie said.

"Yep, good. It wasn't known back then that the kidneys of certain monkeys contain the SV-40. These kidneys thus work well for what we're doing—they can regenerate stronger cancers. From there, I'll take the uber-cancers produced by the monkeys over to a special device that will blast them with radiation. That should cause mutations in some of them that will produce a super-uber-version. And, *ta-da*, we should get a solution that will cause a galloping cancer in humans."

Ferrie was momentarily speechless. "Ma'am, I have a million questions."

"That's all too general, I know. I'll go into more detail on this process at the clinic. What you need to know now is that we'll have four locations for most of the work, with your out-of-the-way abode being the anchor location."

"The other places?"

"One is the lab at the clinic on Prytania, which will be moved next year to the new clinic facility by the Foundation Hospital on Jefferson Highway. And, because of the secrecy of this project, we'll also use my apartment on St. Charles. I have equipment there."

"I'm not sure I'm qualified to be at the center of this."

"Frankly, you're not, you'll need some expert help. I have a colleague Carolyn Talley who has agreed to work with you. She's a doctor specializing in diseases of the blood, works mainly at Tulane Medical. Trustworthy."

"I'd freak out doing this without a real doctor."

"She's the best. And a real sweetheart. You can call her Dr. Carolyn. It helps that she and I are quite close.

"But let's be clear. Dr. Carolyn is not going to have the full picture. She won't have the Castro part. She'll be told this is work to better understand cancer. I'm too fond of the girl to get her involved in the bigger picture."

"Got it, ma'am."

"The last piece to make this work—the fourth place—is really the starting place, a location where we can keep the live mice before they're injected. There could be a thousand at a time."

"Close by?"

"Just a little down the block and across the street."

"Oh, I get it. The house at 3225?"

"Yep. I'm told there's no coincidence you were able to get your apartment on Louisiana Avenue Parkway so easily. This other place was already lined up."

"Finding my place *was* too easy! I know that other house well from years ago. 'Twas another project."

"I don't want to know about other projects! I have enough secrets in my little head."

"Kind of funny that the only residents of the house will be mice. Ha!"

"Like where Mickey Mouse lives. Mouseville."

"Bet you didn't know this," Ferrie offered. "Mickey's hometown was first named by Italians—*Topolinia.*"

"Has a nice ring to it," Dr. Mary said. "Topolinia. *Divertimento.*"

"What can you tell me about the last step? The radiation?"

"Right. We actually have *five* locations for this little adventure. The last being a kinda creepy old brick building.

"You won't ever go to this spot nor, obviously, will Dr. Carolyn. The radiation piece is very hush-hush and, frankly, dangerous. If you don't know what you're doing, you can get seriously burned. Even killed. So I'll own that step. I *can* tell you the radiation will come from a machine over at the US Public Health complex."

"I'll spare you my history lecture on that place."

"Merci. It's housed in the Infectious Disease Laboratory there. Behind the domed building. Sounds like you know the property, it *is* a creepy building, right?"

"Yep. Fitting for a linear particle accelerator."

"Guy told you. My, Mr. Loose Lips. It's obviously top secret that we're using the accelerator for this project. I hope it goes without saying—leaking any information about this entire project will probably get us both killed."

"Gotcha, ma'am. Can you tell me anything about the machine and this last step?"

Dr. Mary made sure no one was close enough to listen in. "Just a little. These machines are incredible. They look like space weapons. The one here in New Orleans is so large it has to be housed in a three-story structure—the old infectious disease building fitted the bill. Basically, a radioactive beam is shot at incredible speed through a long vacuum tube. The beam strikes a metal structure near the bottom of the tube that splits the beam into four beams and shoots them into four containers. The containers hold the targets. In our case, the targets will be the mashed-up viral tumors from the mice."

"I know these accelerators are few and far between. How did we get this one, ma'am?"

"Dr. Ochsner pushed hard to get this machine. In fact, he had the pull to get it paid for up front in cash. Ten million dollars."

"Ten million dollars?" Ferrie asked.

"He developed a desperate need to work on a specific project using that equipment."

"Trying to cure lung cancer?"

"Trying to fix the polio vaccine."

\\\\\

Before 1955 the country had been in a state of alarm over polio since the epidemic of 1916, which killed six thousand people. The alarm was fueled over the years by the growing public recognition that FDR had polio. It was a frightening health issue. Tens of thousands of people in the country were struck with this disease every year, most of them children. Many kids were placed in horrifying, casket-like ventilators called iron lungs. Shocking pictures of rows of kids in iron lungs were ubiquitous.

Virologists worked frantically when resources freed up after World War II to develop a vaccine.

Dr. Jonas Salk, a son of Ashkenazi Jewish immigrants and an up-and-coming medical researcher, was asked by a group set up by FDR, the National Foundation for Infantile Paralysis, to undertake a project to better understand polio and to work on a vaccine. Dr. Salk worked out of a lab at the University of Pittsburgh School of Medicine. Some of the better known medical schools hadn't had a place for him because they'd exceeded their quotas of Jewish doctors.

By 1955 Dr. Salk had developed a vaccine that contained a version of the polio virus grown in the kidneys of rhesus macques, a type of "Old World" monkey. He took these viruses and "killed" them, using a drug called formalin. This approach, to pump "killed" viruses into patients, was approved by industry experts as sound. It was announced with much fanfare.

As the vaccine was being prepared for mass deployment, Dr. Salk and the six laboratories set to manufacture the vaccine took what they thought was a necessary but pro forma step of having the National Institutes of Health certify that the vaccine was safe. The NIH researcher assigned to the testing was Dr. Bernice Eddy, a pioneering female PhD virologist and epidemiologist. She was supported by another accomplished female PhD Dr. Sarah Stewart. They injected hamsters and monkeys with the vaccine.

The two doctors were shocked by what happened. With certain batches of the vaccine, numerous injected monkeys quickly died from polio or became severely crippled. Many doses in these batches, they discovered, though supposedly containing the "killed" polio virus, actually contained a "live" version of the virus.

Even more shocking, Drs. Eddy and Stewart found that *all* the doses of Dr. Salk's polio vaccine, which carried viruses grown in monkey kidneys, contained a cancer-causing polyomavirus—the yet-to-be-identified SV-40. They observed that this polyomavirus frequently caused sarcoma and ependymomas in hamsters.

With Salk's laboratories starting to churn out the vaccine, and given rising public excitement, the conclusion that the Salk vaccine could be lethal, however, was kept under wraps, treated like a state secret.

Dr. Salk was unconvinced by the findings of Drs. Eddy and Stewart. Also unconvinced was Dr. Alton Ochsner. Dr. Ochsner was a long-time acquaintance of Dr. Salk's. He also was part owner of Cutter Laboratories in Berkeley, California, one of the six labs that was beginning to mass-produce the vaccine.

Dr. Ochsner set out to demonstrate to the world that the vaccine was safe. In an auditorium filled with the medical staff of Tulane University, he took the dramatic step of inoculating his two grandchildren. This was a tragic mistake. His thirty-month-old grandson, Davey, died of polio eight days later at the Ochsner Hospital. His granddaughter, Mary, also contracted polio but lived. Naturally, Dr. Ochsner was shattered.

In what became known as the "Cutter Incident," Dr. Ochsner's Cutter Labs had already distributed two hundred thousand doses of the vaccine, mainly to schoolchildren, that erroneously contained live strains of the polio virus. Forty thousand recipients developed various types of polio. Two hundred children were severely paralyzed and ten children died, the first being a young girl named Susan Pierce, who'd received the vaccine on April 18, 1955. Toddler Davey died from a Cutter vaccine sixteen days later.

The original Salk vaccine was scrapped. Working with the US Public Health Service, Salk revised the vaccine and the procedures for producing it. The new version was released to the public, and, though improved, it still periodically produced a unit with a dangerous live strain. More important, the new vaccine still contained the SV-40 virus. Even the alternative being worked on by Salk's chief rival, Dr. Albert Sabin, also a Polish Ashkenazi Jew, included the SV-40. Sabin's version, which was designed to be taken orally, was being tested in Russia at the time, but later would become the primary vaccine administered in the United States.

||||

"Long story short," Dr. Mary explained, "Dr. Ochsner was desperate to make amends for what he'd done to his grandchildren. Even though the live-virus problem in the Salk vaccine that killed Davey and ruined Mary's life had been largely eliminated, he knew about the SV-40 issue and decided to work on that. Thus, the linear particle accelerator.

"Dr. Ochsner's plan was to use the machine to fire radiation at mouse tumors caused by the monkey virus in the Salk and Sabin vaccines. These tumors, of course, still contained the SV-40. The idea was to produce mutations in the virus that would weaken or eliminate it. Then, the weakened virus would be injected back into monkey kidneys. Those kidneys would be used to produce a polio vaccine with a greatly weakened SV-40. And the rest would be history—a safer vaccine."

"What happened?" Ferrie asked.

"The radiation produced even *more* potent SV-40 viruses—more lethal and faster-acting."

"The machine creates a mutation that makes viruses stronger!" Ferrie exclaimed. "Ah, I see. That's why you're going to use it."

"You got it."

Dr. Mary had enjoyed her talk with Ferrie and now believed Ferrie's role in the project could work. He was clearly bright and committed. And deferential to her.

Ferrie needed to pray about participating in the Dr. Mary project, though Gill had left little doubt that the decision had already been made for him. To clear his head, he returned later that night to the Roosevelt Hotel to see Frank Sinatra in the Blue Room. He'd been there once before to see Ted "Is Everybody Happy" Lewis and his orchestra play "Me and My Shadow" and other Blue Room favorites. Sinatra, though, was in a whole different league. He was the coolest guy Ferrie had ever seen. The standout of the night was his swinging version of "Too Marvelous for Words," punctuated by Harry Klee's biting saxophone.

Not surprisingly, Marcello was parked at a front VIP table. Jack Wasserman was with him. Also with him was Santo Trafficante. Dr. Ochsner—whose godly aura had dimmed for Ferrie after learning of what he'd done to his grandchildren—rounded out the table of four. When the show was over, Marcello and his entourage went backstage.

CHAPTER 19

Ferrie's collaboration with Dr. Mary started slowly. She got busier than expected in mid-1962 helping to plan the logistics of setting up the new Ochsner Clinic, which was to be fully up and running, with Prytania shut down, by March 1963. These new facilities would be much more modern than Prytania, with cutting-edge equipment—good news for Ferrie's new assignment. The bad news for him and his wallet was that Dr. Mary's Castro project was temporarily back-burnered.

With time on his hands in the late summer and early fall of 1962, Ferrie, once again, solicited new projects from Banister.

Though focused on New Orleans, Marcello also controlled important swaths of Texas—primarily Dallas through the local mob chieftain, Joseph Civello. Banister regularly was called on to direct Marcello assignments in the Lone Star State.

Marcello had known Joseph Francis Civello for many years. Both were raised in Louisiana as part of Sicilian families. They entered the mob as young men at about the same time and became close.

Marcello rose more quickly than Civello through the ranks of the New Orleans organization. When Marcello became boss, Civello was assigned to be Marcello's lieutenant. Marcello sent him to Dallas. Civello succeeded long-time Dallas strongman Joseph Piranio. The mob had been active in Dallas since the early 1920s through the Piranio family.

Civello was effective. He increased the mob's presence in Dallas threefold. While Marcello oversaw Civello, he gave him a long leash.

Civello's main aide-de-camp in Dallas was a tough but genial man named Joseph Campisi. Campisi and his family had a generations-long talent for rackets—as well as for making pizza. Campisi's operations were headquartered at his popular Italian restaurant, the Egyptian Lounge.

Ferrie met with Banister in his office in the Newman Building.

"Good timing," Banister said. "I got something for you. You still have your Stinson?"

"Yes, sir. Out at Moisant."

"This requires travel to Dallas, maybe several trips."

"I flew a Silver Falcon there a million times for Eastern."

"Marcello and Gill have a guy, Jack Rubenstein, or Ruby, who runs some businesses for us there—strip clubs, other things. You know the guy, right?"

"Yeah. The Cuba trips—Key West."

"Ruby's a useful hoodlum for Marcello and Civello. He's a decent club manager but, more important, he has unbelievably good connections in Dallas, particularly with the cops. He works the cops constantly, keeps them happy in lots of different ways. In turn, they don't bother him much. He gets a lot of leeway to run a pretty good drugs and hooker operation along with his clubs."

"Yeah, he bragged a lot about that at the A&B, his favorite restaurant in Key West."

"The bragging's justified. The guy's always networking. Shit, he goes to every game at the Cotton Bowl just to find important people to schmooze. And he doesn't know goddamn shit about football."

"Sounds like I'll get to see him again."

"Marcello's getting a little worried about Ruby. He's letting some things slip. He's missing deadlines and his financial numbers aren't growing. He sometimes sounds disoriented on the phone. Or just off. And we're getting some reports, mainly secondhand from strippers and other employees, that he sometimes gets violent. There've been complaints to the unions."

"And I do what?"

"We need some objective and trustworthy eyes on Ruby. Civello and Campisi are too close to him. They also have a dog in the fight 'cause criticism of Ruby might reflect on their leadership. Marcello specifically asked for you to do this. He likes you, Dave."

"Sure beats the alternative."

"Ruby's main place of business is called the Carousel Club," Banister continued. "It's a pretty shitty burlesque club, across from the Adolphus Hotel on Commerce Street. Has a 'Bar-B-Q' sign in the window—it's not exactly fucking *Le Crazy Horse de Paris*. Carousel gets good business, though, because of its location and the freedom the cops often give the strippers. In fact, a lot of cops hang out there.

"Ruby also manages some girls who work out on the streets. And he operates a Fort Worth tits-and-music place called the Skyliner."

"Busy guy."

"We have two other Jews there that do similar things. Brothers. Abe Weinstein runs the Colony Club, which is a nicer joint a door or two away from the Carousel, and Barney Weinstein runs the Theatre Lounge around the corner. These guys are 100 percent reliable but not as well connected as Ruby. They're not thugs. We usually just let them quietly run their clubs and print money for us. On the other hand, Ruby has a thugly side to him—he grew up among mobsters. We use him for special projects."

"Yeah. I've seen him in action on one of your special projects. So tell me more about what I do."

"Get over to Dallas in a few weeks. Go right to the Carousel when you get there. Ruby'll remember you. You're a pretty memorable guy. Just tell him you're in town for a few days working for us, getting an update on operations. Tell him you've been asked to spend some time with him and his businesses. Then, get a sense for how the guy's doing. Does he seem stable? Seem okay, or is he going mental? Pick up anything you can. Give me regular reports over the phone and then a full report when you get back. If you feel you need to go back two or three times, do it."

"I'll need some *dineros*," Ferrie noted. "Am kinda broke without Eastern."

"Sure. We'll cover your fuel and hotels, of course. Plus $3,000 for a decent report. And we'll throw in some dollar bills for the strippers' thigh garters and G-strings."

"Not really my style, but I'll buy some drinks with the bills."

\\\\

On a Thursday evening in mid-October, Ferrie landed at Dallas's Red Bird Airport in his Stinson and swung by the Carousel Club, which Civello had helped Ruby acquire in late 1959 when it was called the Sovereign. Ferrie and Ruby reconnected there briefly and made a lunch date for the next day.

Lunch was at Joseph Campisi's Egyptian Lounge.

The word *Egyptian* in the neon sign adorning Campisi's Italian restaurant puzzled first-time customers.

When the Campisi family moved its previous restaurant to the current location on Mockingbird Lane in northeast Dallas in 1950, it replaced a longtime bar and nightclub called the Egyptian Lounge. Not as wealthy then as they later became, the Campisis spent much of their savings on renovations to the kitchen and interior. They had little money left for a custom-made, neon *"Campisi's Restaurant"* sign. While they were able to secure an off-the-shelf *"Restaurant"* sign, and adhered "**CAMPISI'S**" decals to the windows, the decorative neon *"Egyptian"* stayed. With "Egyptian" still in the main title, regulars stuck with "Lounge," which had the benefit of familiarity and sounded snappier than "Restaurant."

Campisi greeted Ruby warmly and gave Ferrie a hug of welcome. The hostess led Ruby and Ferrie to a table near the back. As with all the other tables, this one had a red-and-white checkered tablecloth.

"Seeing you last night, man," Ruby said, "it all came back to me—Key West, the Flagship, the Brown Derby, La Plata, Castro. Didn't work out too well, did it?"

"Nope. We're not done with Cuba yet, though. New plans are in the works."

"Well, good fucking luck with that. Whatcha doing in town?"

"I'm now on the company payroll, doing a lot of projects for Gill and Banister. Marcello, they tell me, is getting more organized with his businesses. They asked me to do a status check on his Texas stuff."

Ruby gave Ferrie his card for the Carousel Club. *"Offering Sophisticated, Risque, Provocative, Delightful Entertainment— Your Host-Jack Ruby."*

"Anything more to your visit? Be honest with me." Ruby was paranoid by nature. His four right fingertips were tip-tapping his knee rapidly, seemingly beyond Ruby's control.

"Not that I know of. You're the main guy here so I'm starting with you. It's a two-way street, Jack. Tell me what you need from the guys in New Orleans. And tell me if I need to talk to the guys at the Exchange Bank if you need more cash flow."

"Those tight-sphinctered jackasses at the Exchange are Christ-slow getting me my money. May need some help there."

"Give me the details later. When I'm done with you, I'll do the rounds with Abe and Barney, and then do a courtesy call on Civello. Marcello has a gift for him."

"I do have a big favor to ask of Marcello. There's a girl at the Sho-Bar. Jada. I'm sure you know her. I really need her here. All the Carousel needs to move to the next level is some big-league talent. Jada's big time."

Jada was a flashy stripper with swirling copper-red hair who drew big crowds in the French Quarter. She was young though not too young—twenty-six. Had experience. Ferrie himself had felt her radiating pheromones at the 500 Club four years earlier, the night he'd first met Marcello. She'd since moved to the Sho-Bar.

Ruby had a good stable of strippers but had trouble compet-
ing with the Colony Club's huge draw Candy Barr. Candy Barr,
who occasionally traveled to the Big Easy to perform at the
Sho-Bar, was an elite, creative entertainer. She was well-known
even outside of Texas. She was so good that Hollywood had hired
Candy to train the actress Joan Collins for her role as an exotic
dancer in the 1960 movie *Seven Thieves*. Barr's trademark cos-
tume consisted of a ten-gallon hat, pasties, "scanty panties," a
pair of six-shooters, and cowboy boots. She was sweet-looking
though, at bottom, an old-fashioned "bump-and-grind" girl.

A show horse like Jada could elevate the Carousel into the
Colony Club's league, Ruby emphasized to Ferrie.

"Jada's a favorite of some of Marcello's guys. And One-eyed
Pete's not going to like it."

"He's a nebbish," Ruby responded.

"Don't matter. Let me see what I can do," Ferrie said. "Sounds
like a good business move for you."

"My favorite business—turning tits and ass into money."

"Seems to work."

"It's as old as recorded time."

"I guess. Are you good for a few questions?"

"As our host Mr. Campisi would say, *sì*."

"I get it that your main operation in downtown Dallas is the
Carousel Club. Beyond that, how many street prostitutes are
you working with?"

"That shifts around. Usually around twenty-five. I've got
the classy girls in the hotels. They do particularly well at the
Adolphus. And sometimes the big oil guys like Murchison
and Hunt pay for them to go out to their ranches. *That's* good
business.

"The rougher gals, the cheaper ones, are working outside,
many on Commerce Street. That business is pretty good too.
This city is full of right-wing nuts and evangelicals who seem
to love hookers as much as they love their wives and the Baby
Jesus."

"And in Fort Worth," Ferrie said, "you run the Skyliner, right? You keep a good eye on that?"

"I'm out at the Skyliner several days a week. It's mainly a music place, though they have strippers on Friday and Saturday nights. I book the strippers. The guy who runs the place on a daily basis and books the music is a Fort Worth club guy named Levens. Seems to do a good job, but I need to go over the books pretty carefully. And sometimes I help him out with other acts—he likes my ventriloquist, Demar. That guy is fricking unbelievable, by the way. You'll see him."

"I'd like to go to the Skyliner."

"Tomorrow? That work for you?"

"Sure," Ferrie responded.

"To be complete about my vast empire, I've still got the Vegas Club as well. It's more of a suburban club, up in Highland Park. Oak Lawn and Lemmon. Not very big. And you guys don't pay much attention to it. My beautiful sister Eva runs it most of the time."

Ferrie nodded and changed the subject. "Got it. And you, how're you doing? Health okay?"

"I'm in good shape." Ruby had Ferrie feel his biceps. Although Ruby led a nightclubbing life, he actually *was* in pretty good shape. He liked to lift weights.

"Family okay?"

"I'm a plain man," Ruby said. "I work hard, I live simple. I got a roommate, George, to save money. I love my country and freedom. And I'm a proud Jew. Beyond that, I really only care about two things. My sister Eva is number one. She's a little fragile, but she's a shining light in this dark world. Other than my mother—God rest her soul—Eva's always been my rock. I couldn't live without her."

"And the second thing?"

"I got a little dachshund named Sheba—you know, from the Queen of Sheba. It's in the Bible."

"She screwed Solomon, right?"

"Wrong, dummy. She was Goddess, Queen of Egypt and Ethiopia. My dog is a queen too, Dave. She's my other rock." Ruby spoke about Sheba for five minutes. "Sheba keeps me sane. This may sound fucked-up, Dave—she's like a wife to me. My soulmate."

That is *fucked up*, Ferrie thought.

The next day, a Saturday, they met for breakfast at Norma's Cafe in Oak Cliff, near Ruby's apartment. Ruby then drove Ferrie out to Jacksboro Highway in Fort Worth. The Skyliner was in the middle of a section of the Highway that looked like the Old West meeting the twentieth century. The Skyliner sign out front had flashing neon arrows pointing to the club.

The three-and-a-half-mile stretch of the Jacksboro Highway between Tiffin Hall's Mexican Inn and the Skyline Drive Motel was known as "Thunder Road." Thunder Road was a neighborhood of gamblers, gangsters, grifters, and girls. Drug peddlers. Drug addicts. It fell under the national spotlight briefly in 1950 when an ex-con high-roller and drug dealer named Nelson Harris, whose world centered around businesses on Jacksboro Highway, was blown to hell one day by a nitroglycerin bomb when he started his car in front of his apartment on Wingate Street. His pregnant wife Juanita was killed as well. Newspapers around the country published pictures of Harris's body being pulled from his car.

"What do you think?" Ruby asked as they got out of the car in front of the Skyliner.

"It's huge."

"Yeah. It's *too* big. I think they used to call it the Skyliner Ballroom, but that makes it sound more like a place where a bunch of crackers do the fucking Texas Two-Step, not a place to hear rock 'n' roll and ogle strippers. I shortened it to just 'Skyliner.'"

"Texas Two-Step?" Ferrie asked.

"It's like the redneck *Horah*, pardner."

"What's that across the street?" There was a large, virtually windowless, warehouse-looking building with a small inconspicuous sign that read, "The Four Deuces."

"Was a major gambling club back in the 1940s and '50s," Ruby said. "The Four Deuces. It still limps along. However, it's way past its prime. We still get some customers later at night from the place, though, when our strippers come on after the other acts."

Pointing north up the highway, Ruby said, "That's the Rocket Club. They have an orchestra most nights and, on weekends, some pretty good strippers. Trudine, 'the Quiver Queen,' is my favorite. Fucking clever name. The Rocket's the main competition out here."

Ruby and Ferrie walked across the sticky floor of the cavernous main room at the Skyliner and went through a side door to an office. Jimmy Levens sat at a desk with a large calculator, clacking fingertip-sized keys as paper rolled out of the machine and onto the desk.

"How they hanging, Jimmy?" Ruby asked.

"Low and blue—ready to blow. Who's your friend?"

"Dave Ferrie. A Marcello guy. He's going to examine us for the Little Man."

"Swell. Just hope he's not a proctologist."

Ruby and Levens sat together for several hours going over ledgers, invoices, bills. Ferrie observed them for a while and then took in the club. The Skyliner wasn't fancy or glitzy. Was better suited for workaday cowboys than moneyed oilmen.

Musicians started to arrive with equipment and instruments. A band called Levon and the Hawks was playing that night. They'd do two sets and then the real entertainment would come out. Jimmy Levens himself would be the master of ceremonies.

Ferrie wanted to get another look at this cowboy highway, "Thunder Road." He went back outside.

There was a surreal warren of establishments up and down Thunder Road, each with some gimmicky structure or sign to catch the eye. The rival Rocket Club had a bright neon comet with streaming tails. Williams Ranch Steak House had a large windmill. The Avalon Motel, a real water tower. The Inez 50-50 Club, a giant martini glass. Massey's Club 21, "Massey's" and "Dancing" written in huge cursive letters. Vivian Courtney's Restaurant was topped with a towering *V* that could be seen for two miles. The Caravan Inn had four fake eight-foot palm trees sprouting up from its main sign. A giant steer, staring up at an airplane in the sky, painted on the back of the Cowtown Drive-in's screen. The Skyliner's flashing arrows.

This landscape looked like a gargantuan, wondrous work of folk art to Ferrie.

He reentered Ruby's club.

The band began playing even though, save for two couples, the club was empty. Levens had hired a one-armed "go-go" dancer to work early in the evenings to get people to dance. She got the couples up. The dancing was desultory, but the two guys were in belligerent moods. A fight broke out on the bare dance floor. *It's going to be a long night*, Ferrie mused.

It was too bad for Levon and the Hawks that there were so few people in the club. They were tight, even though the skinny piano player seemed a little drunk. They played a hard-driving rockabilly, with songs like "My Girl Is Red Hot" and "Hey Boba Lou." They finished with a raucous "Who Do You Love" backed by a thumping drum, a rolling organ, and a wailing 1950s Fender Stratocaster. The audience grew by the second set and was shouting along with the band: *"Who do you love?"*

In the hour it took to break down the band's equipment, the Skyliner started to fill up in anticipation of the main show. Smoke billowed up toward the ceiling from hundreds of Marlboro, Kent, Camel, and L&M cigarettes being fired up by the expanding crowd. The house band, led by Billy Todd, took the stage. Billy started a drum beat. Sherry Lynn, the opening act, glided out onto the stage, wearing long white sleeves that elegantly stretched well past her elbows. She had big hair swept into a wave across the left side of her head. Sherry had practiced her craft for a decade and was a mentor to the other girls. One of her protégés Tammi True had become the main act.

Tammi followed Shari, taking the stage to hoots and hollers. She was edgier and more playful than Sherry. She removed her cape and teasingly flipped off her few other pieces of clothing one by one until she stood on the stage in her sparkly G-string.

Tarrant and Dallas county law, like in Orleans Parish, prohibited pure toplessness, so she also had a very small, glittery pasty over each areola. Ferrie liked this colorful Texas way of complying with the local public decency laws. In New Orleans, the strippers instead used inelegant clear adhesives, commonly referred to there as "nipple tape." Though these rectangular strips covered less territory than pasties did, to the delight of many patrons, they lacked the sinful glamour of the cowboy approach.

Tammi had several trademark moves. One was to turn her back to the crowd, bend over, and look through her legs, asking, "Can you see the whole show?" Her pièce de résistance, though, was a unique trick requiring uncommon dexterity. She put a small cowboy hat on her right breast. She then spun the hat clockwise and flipped it over to her left breast—completely hands-free. After spinning the hat counterclockwise on her left breast, she flipped it back to the right breast. This dependable crowd pleaser was the climax of her act.

"Thank you from the bottom of my bottom," Tammi said in closing.

CHAPTER 20

Back in Dallas, though the Carousel Club was open seven days a week, Ferrie decided to take the next day, Sunday, off from his Ruby-monitoring. In the morning, needing to nourish his spiritual side, Ferrie took a cab up Preston Road to Christ the King Catholic Church in University Park. The mass wasn't conservative enough for Ferrie, though nourishing nonetheless.

After church Ferrie set out to take in the sights of Dallas. It didn't take him long, though, to realize that there weren't many. He did go over to Fair Park and visit several of the Art Deco buildings, including the Dallas Museum of Fine Arts. Seeing the Cotton Bowl in Fair Park reminded him of a banter he'd had with Jack Martin five years earlier about LSU quarterback Y. A. Tittle. Later he wanted to soak in downtown Dallas nightlife. Dallas indeed was a city of contrasts, as Ruby had suggested. On the one hand, it was sharply conservative and old-time religious. Wealthy right-wing white men—H. L. Hunt, Clint Murchison, David "Dry Hole" Byrd, Perry Bass—wielded more power here than the mayor and city council. The dangerously fascist General Edwin Walker made Dallas his home. Right before Ferrie's visit to the city, Walker had gone on local radio and TV to publicly rail about the "anti-Christ Supreme Court" and call for resistance to the federal government. *"It's now or never!"* Anti-government evangelist Billy Hargis's biggest radio audience was in Dallas.

On the other hand, when the sun set, Dallas was a vibrant city of fun and sin. There were burlesque clubs right in the center of the city on Commerce and Jackson Streets, including the

Carousel and the places owned by the Weinstein brothers. And there was Donnie Voorhis's Montmartre Club on Browder Street. The big hotels also had lusty good-time shows. The Adolphus itself, the queen of Dallas hotels, had *Bottoms Up*, a sexy musical comedy revue with a live orchestra. The Statler Hilton had edgy entertainment in its Empire Room.

Ferrie attended the Sunday-night *Bottoms Up* show at the Adolphus. The star of the show, which featured a dozen cross-dressers, was a transvestite named Breck Wall. He was humorous, and the "girls" were pretty. Ferrie got a late-night bite at the Copper Cow nearby, recommended by Ruby. Ferrie then went back to his hotel out on the Stemmons Freeway, the large three-hundred-room Cabana Hotel. The Cabana was a relatively new mobster-controlled property. Banister had set him up there. Ferrie had a cognac in the Bon Vivant Room, where the waitresses were called "goddesses." His goddess wore a name tag reading "Jo Raquel." Ferrie then went to bed.

Monday and Tuesday were dreary, sprinkly days in Dallas. Ferrie stayed dry inside the Carousel. Monday morning, he and Ruby went through the early financial returns from Sunday, not a busy day for strip clubs. But the results weren't bad. Some customers liked to leaven a church day with some entertainment.

Ruby reviewed the plans for that Monday evening with Ferrie. The show would start at nine o'clock. The normal schedule consisted of a singer, a ventriloquist-ESP-mentalist, strippers, and a comedian to finish up. The comedian—Wally Weston—also would be the emcee for the night. Weston was married to one of the club's strippers Shari Angel, who was also on that evening's bill. Over the course of the night, there would be five strippers on three runways.

Ruby took Ferrie to lunch at Lucas's B&B Restaurant— *Quality Foods Since 1911*—on Oak Lawn Avenue next to the Vegas Club and across from Lucky's Cafe. Ruby was greeted warmly by Pete, the owner. They were joined by Ruby's friend and "financial advisor" Ralph Paul. Paul dated stripper Tammi True.

Ferrie had been briefed on Ralph Paul. On paper, Paul was the owner of a small restaurant called the Bull-Pen Drive-In. His off-paper job, though, was as a money-mover for the mob. The money he funneled to Ruby came from Joseph Campisi, at Marcello's direction. The money helped Ruby operate the Carousel and his other clubs. Cleaner money for Ruby was kept at the Exchange Bank.

In the afternoon Ruby employees, mainly strippers, stopped by the Carousel, including some that weren't working that night. Ferrie overheard a few complaints in the club about not getting paid on time. There also were claims that Ruby occasionally brought in amateur strippers to save money. Several strippers talked about getting the labor union more involved. But, for the most part, the small crowd of Carousel workers hanging around the club were there to socialize, go over schedules, or pick up money. Notwithstanding scattered griping, they seemed generally content.

Ferrie sought out a stripper named Penny Dollar. He'd heard that she'd had problems with Ruby. Penny, who actually was a married woman named Patricia Kohs, wasn't happy about slow payments and the way Ruby treated other strippers, firing them more than once without notice.

She also thought that Ruby was impulsively violent. She'd seen Ruby throw a man down the stairs to the street, pounce on him, and slam his head repeatedly into the sidewalk. On that occasion, Ruby had got up and, strangely—with a look of confusion—said, "Did I do this? Did I do this?"

Ferrie heard other stories. Ruby had sucker-punched a guy who was arguing with his date. He'd struck a cabdriver who came in complaining about a customer who didn't pay his fare. Ruby was witnessed at a party stripping naked and rolling around the floor *au naturel*. Ferrie took notes.

Patrons started filing in shortly after nine. Wally Weston came out to start the show and welcome the crowd.

The program started with a special appearance by a co-median named Gene Tracy, nicknamed "Mr. Truck Stop."

Chubby-cheeked and dressed like he'd slept in his suit, Tracy shouted dirty jokes in rapid fire, with Ruby's bandleader and drummer Bill Willis tapping a beat matching the fast pace of the jokes.

"I was at the drug store in this big goddamn truck stop. A driver for the Pilot Truck Lines came in, walked up to the clerk behind the cigar stand. He said, 'I want to buy a pack of rubbers.' The clerk said, 'Okay, what kind do you want? Do you want the old-fashioned three in a pack, or do you want the new party pack?' The Pilot trucker said, '*Party* pack? What the hell's a *party* pack?' Clerk said, 'Well, they come a gross to a box, 144 to the box. And they're multi-colored. They're gray, purple, green, blue, red, orange—you know, adds a little festive note to your orgy.' Trucker said, 'Well I believe I'll try the party pack.' He came back in about seven months, said, 'I want to buy a maternity brassiere.' The clerk said, 'Yes, sir. What bust?' The Pilot truck driver said, 'The *blue* one.'"

Ferrie was amused by Gene Tracy and bought an LP from him. Tracy had set up a table in the back of the Carousel with a stack of records. Tracy signed the back of Ferrie's LP— *"Dave, you're an ice cream eating motherfucker."* This peculiar note referred to the punchline of one of Tracy's more sexually explicit jokes.

The singer Paul Salos followed. Ruby earlier had told Ferrie, chuckling, that Salos would sing the entire Hank Williams song-book. "Whether you like it or not." Salos was backed by Bill Willis's band.

Bill Demar was next. Demar's routine, in addition to ventriloquism, included memory tricks. One of his fan favorites was to ask ten patrons to give him two words each. At intervals, during the remainder of the show, he'd come back to each one of these ten patrons and remember what their two words were. Shari Angel, "the Heavenly Body," followed Demar.

Ester Ann Nash, the waitress, and Wanda Killam, the cig-arette girl, were snaking their way among the patrons. Nancy

Perrin was behind the bar, steadily pouring cheap beer and wine for patrons—Ruby's license didn't allow hard liquor.

There were several private rooms where "champagne girls" would serve patrons looking for a more personal experience. Champagne was the fanciest drink Ruby was legally allowed to sell. And he could easily sell dirt-cheap champagne, wrapped in a towel covering the label, to aroused patrons behind closed doors for nine times the cost. Ruby's regulars, Ferrie was told, agreed that the best champagne girl at the club was a particularly inventive gal known as Dallas Alice. A nervous young mother with spaniel eyes named Diana Hunter, though, was Ruby's favorite champagne girl. Often wearing his heart on his sleeve, Ruby felt sorry for Hunter, who had been abandoned by the father of her four children. "Sometimes I let Diana dance, she needs the money," Ruby told Ferrie. "Even though she has banana tits, the guys seem to like her act—Diana the Huntress. Does a kind of Greek ballet, a hunting scene with a topless victory dance. Pretty highfalutin."

Ruby joined Ferrie in the back of the club. Ralph Paul was there too, as he usually was. Also present was Ruby's roommate, George Senator, a dandy-looking middle-aged man wearing black, horn-rimmed glasses. Senator was a salesman, Ruby had told Ferrie, though he sometimes did odd jobs for the Carousel. Ruby had been running around nervously, making sure everything went smoothly and schmoozing customers. He appeared to be on uppers. There were beads of sweat on his forehead.

Some of the cops in the club periodically went back to Ruby's office with him and came out with brown bags. Ferrie could hear the clanking of bottles coming from inside the bags.

Ruby returned. "Dave, you may not notice, but about a tenth of this crowd is made up of Dallas police and detectives. My advantage over the other Jew clubs is that I'm in deep with the cops."

"I've heard."

One of Ruby's best cop contacts was Sergeant Patrick Dean, who also had a close relationship with Civello and other Dallas mobsters. Sergeant Dean oversaw security in the Dallas police station. Even more useful, Ruby was tight with Captain Will Fritz, the department's lead investigator. Fritz had been with the Dallas police so long that he'd been part of the posse that hunted Bonnie and Clyde.

Ruby had taken high-ranking Dallas policemen on pleasure trips over the years, including gambling trips to the old and magnificent Arlington and Majestic Hotels in Hot Springs, Arkansas.

"I get some of my strippers to date cops. Kathy Kay—one of my best—is dating a cop named Olsen now."

"They get free liquor in brown bags?"

"Sometimes. They know there's 'private stock' back in my office, they're free to draw from that. And they always get free beer and wine on the floor. Sometimes a cop'll also want a hooker. I try to keep that to a minimum, but for the key guys I'll set them up with one of the expensive hotel girls at a reduced rate.

"I also bring stuff to their offices—sandwiches, booze, cigarettes. I can waltz into those offices about any time I want."

Ruby pointed out one of the cops. "See the guy by the stage with the black hair and Hawaiian shirt? Cigarette stuck to his lip. His name is Tippit. A farm boy in the big city. He still can't believe we have nearly naked women on display in this town. His full name is J. D. Tippit, though the girls call him 'H. D.' Tippit because he's so fucking cheap—stands for 'He Don't Tipp-it.' J. D.'s gotten some private time with a girl or two, particularly a little redhead I got named Joy."

"I assume the cops do *you* some favors."

"Of course. Breaks on alcohol violations, some free security when we have troublemakers, permission to fully expose nipples on certain special occasions, that kind of thing. They sometimes get my girls out of jail and even fix their traffic tickets."

Ferrie slipped out at one point to check out the Colony Club. Abe Weinstein's place *was* a step up from the Carousel. There was palpable electricity when Candy Barr came out on the stage. That night, rather than her signature cowgirl act, she was performing as a Society Debutante—all sweetness and light in a demure evening gown. She began facing the crowd, arms akimbo. She pageant-walked in a circle. But then the gown dropped in a swoosh to the floor and pastied breasts popped into view, seemingly defying gravity. She began making hootchy-kootchy gyrations. Society Debutante had suddenly turned into Naughty Rich Girl. The crowd was roused. Ferrie could see why Ruby felt he needed a star like Jada to compete.

After most shows Ruby liked to go the Deluxe Diner nearby on South Ervay Street. Ferrie joined Ruby that night, along with Ralph Paul. Done with club business for the day, they talked about Kennedy and Cuba. Kennedy had just negotiated to get the Russians to take their missiles out of Cuba.

"But if he hadn't fucked up the Bay of Pigs," Ruby angrily claimed, "or if he'd kept pressing to get rid of Castro, the Russians wouldn't have been there in the first place."

"Another fucking Neville Chamberlain," Paul said.

Ruby quickly called it a night. He said he had to check on his sister and his dog.

))))

The next night went about the same at the club, with one difference.

At the right corner of the stage was a clean-cut, serious-looking young man in a short-sleeved white shirt. Ferrie recognized him. Lee Oswald. The last time Ferrie had seen Oswald was through a gush of blood streaming down his face from his temple after Oswald pummeled him.

"Jack, you know that guy in the Mormon shirt?" Ferrie asked.

"He's been coming in a lot the last week or so. I keep an eye on him because he has a temper—I don't tolerate *characters* in my club. And he just seems odd. He'll sit there quietly with that cold stare, sipping slowly on a beer. Every now and then, though, he'll get pissed about something minor. Last week, Dallas Alice brushed by him and accidentally knocked a beer out of his hand. She apologized profusely. That skinny prick stood up and started screaming at her anyway, finger in her face. I thought he was going to punch her, but he didn't."

"I used to try to teach him how to fly. What's he doing in Dallas, do you know?"

"I sat with him for a bit after that Dallas Alice incident to calm him down. We chatted. He's been in Russia, of all places. Said he saw how fucked up Communism actually was and high-tailed it back to America. He's looking for a job and staying at the YMCA, which is close by, over on North Ervay, easy for him to get here. Fucker's staying there even though he brought a wife and baby girl back with him from Russia. Weird."

"The kid was kinda queer when I knew him."

"He's gotta big thing for Kathy Kay. Sometimes, I send her over to sit with him, even bump and grind him a little. Seems to loosen him up a bit, though he never seems to get too aroused."

Demar used Oswald in his memory trick that night. Oswald was noticeably reluctant to be in the limelight, but he complied.

"Jack, you should know that the kid's uncle's in tight with Marcello's inner circle. Give him a free beer every now and then."

"You gonna go over and say hello?"

"No siree Bob. We didn't part on the best of terms last time I saw him."

Ferrie and Ruby forewent the usual visit to the Deluxe after closing and got a few drinks at the Sip and Nip on Commerce— Old Taylor for Ferrie, iced tea for Ruby. Ferrie then went back to the Cabana.

He cabbed to Red Bird Airport early the next morning and flew back to Moisant Field. Notes in hand, he met with Gill and Banister that afternoon at the Town and Country to give his report.

"Here are the key points, guys. First, the businesses look pretty good. Ruby is anal and very competitive with the other Jews. The guys around him seem pretty solid—Levens, Paul. Most important, he really does seem to have the Dallas cops in his back pocket. Ruby's been damn successful in saddling up with the police and gaining access to most of the department."

"That's his main reason for being," Gill said. "How's he holding up?"

"He's tightly wound, that's for sure. He appeared to be on uppers, speed, bennies, something during peak hours. And I heard from several sources that he sometimes does some bizarre things—stripped bareass once at a party. And occasionally throws a temper tantrum. Has punched a few guys, nothing real serious. Not yet anyway."

"We'll need to send you back every now and then," Gill asked.

"Ruby does have a big business ask of us," Ferrie said. "He says he needs a star stripper at the Carousel to go up against the Colony. He wants Jada."

"Jada? Marcello won't like that," Banister said.

"He's actually got a point," Ferrie said. "That Weinstein club next door has better talent. Their marquee stripper is damn good."

"I'll talk to Marcello," Gill offered.

"Finally, gentlemen, an observation," Ferrie said. "Even more so than the clubs, Ruby's life completely revolves around his sister Eva and his fucking dog. Sad.

"If you ever wanted to get Ruby to do something that he really doesn't want to do," Ferrie finished up, "just threaten the lives of the sister or the dog, or both. I think he'd happily kiss his own ass goodbye to save either of them."

CHAPTER 21

In late November 1962, Dr. Mary invited Ferrie to her apartment, which was on St. Charles, between Harmony and Eighth Streets, near the Garden District. Her apartment complex was called either the "Patio" or the "Patios"—it was hard to tell the precise name from the odd sign out front. "The" was in small letters on the upper left corner of the sign. Then in large letters was the word *PATIO,* and in the upper right was a tiny "s." Passersby on streetcars argued about the name. Was it singular or plural?

Regardless, each apartment had a patio with a view of the inner courtyard. The complex was upscale and neat. Not surprisingly, Dr. Mary's home—apartment J—was classy. It had fine art, oriental rugs, a library with an array of sophisticated books, antique furniture. In addition to being a world-class doctor, Dr. Mary had taste. The splendor of these surroundings, a characteristic wholly missing from his own home surroundings, cheered Ferrie.

"Good to see you, Dave. I have tea and oranges for you. Pretty fancy, right? The oranges came all the way from China."

"I'm not used to living high on the hog like this, ma'am."

"This high-on-the-hog treatment's going to come with some work talk. The new Jefferson Highway facility, with a super-modern lab and fancy equipment, will be up and running by the first part of next year. We should be able to hit the ground running then."

"I'll be ready to roll, ma'am."

"Magnificent. Can you come to Prytania for an hour or so the last three Fridays of January for some training and planning? We'll have the Prytania space for a while yet."

"Yes, of course."

The Friday meetings at Prytania were keenly interesting to Ferrie and helped divert his mind from an upcoming hearing on the grievance he filed over his suspension from Eastern. He met Dr. Carolyn Talley for the first time and found her to be a friendly intellectual like Dr. Mary, but clearly a freer spirit. She was Irish, descended from a local Irish family who had members killed while building the New Basin Canal. Dr. Carolyn grew up in what was a neighborly though irregular area by the river west of the Lower Garden District called the Irish Channel, where most of the Irishmen working on the New Basin Channel had lived.

Dr. Carolyn and Dr. Mary indeed seemed to be close. Dr. Carolyn called her Mare, an Irish nickname for Mary.

\\\\

Gill and Ferrie flew to Miami for a hearing on his firing, held February 18 at the Administration Building by the airport. The hearing was a bust. Gill and Ferrie took the position that the hearing was unfair because Eastern hadn't provided any specifics on the reasons for the firing and the issues in the proceeding. Eastern in turn said it was still investigating and the hearing was to get Ferrie's side of the story. Its lawyer, William Bell, rejected the claim of unfairness. "This is not a hearing where charges are being preferred. . . . [W]e don't know until we can determine the facts." There was an impasse. Ferrie refused to testify. The hearing was terminated.

With no defense presented by Ferrie, the Eastern decision maker later ruled against Ferrie. His suspension was made permanent. Gill immediately lodged additional grievances.

\\\\

After returning from Miami, disappointed by the events in Miami, Ferrie was eager to turn his attention to the start-up of the Dr. Mary project. In early March, he helped oversee the transfer of dozens of laboratory mice, cages, and equipment from Prytania to Topolinia. Dr. Mary and Dr. Carolyn met him that day at Topolinia after the mice were in place. A young Hispanic nurse named Julia was with them.

"Fantastic job, Dave," Dr. Carolyn said. She introduced Ferrie to Julia, who'd worked as an orderly at the Tulane Medical School and would be assisting on the project. She'd been told the same thing as Dr. Carolyn, that this was a project to find a cure for cancer. She and Dr. Carolyn were not "in the tent" on the kill-Castro project.

"Carolyn will be with you three days a week. Those will be the main working days—Tuesday, Wednesday, and Thursday. That good for you?" Dr. Mary asked Ferrie.

"Good with me, ladies."

This project was grounded in the landmark work done in the 1950s by Drs. Eddy and Stewart, the researchers who found the deadly flaws in Dr. Salk's polio vaccine. They were pioneers in researching the connection between viruses and cancer. Dr. Mary was a personal friend of Sarah Stewart's—they'd studied and socialized together at the University of Chicago for three years.

Sarah Elizabeth Stewart was born in Mexico to a Mexican mother and American father. The family moved to the United States when she was five years old. She earned a BA and masters from prominent universities in New Mexico and Massachusetts and then a PhD in microbiology from the University of Chicago while simultaneously working at NIH. She went on to be the first woman to earn an MD from Georgetown Medical School.

Her work with Dr. Eddy at NIH included the significant discovery of the cancer-causing viral agent in a type of mouse tumor. This virus was named for Drs. Eddy and Stewart—the *SE polyoma*. Dr. Stewart was the first person to successfully demonstrate that viruses causing cancer could be spread from animal to animal.

Ferrie had read several late-1950s articles on the SE polyoma in scientific journals, including in the prestigious *Journal
of the National Cancer Institute,* at the Tulane library. He was
quite familiar with Dr. Stewart's work.

Both Ferrie and Dr. Mary had a copy of an unpublished
though generally available paper Dr. Stewart had written outlining her methodology for analyzing the connection between
viruses and cancer. This paper and the methodology described
in it served as a building block for Dr. Mary's project.

Dr. Stewart's paper began with the hypothesis that "[c]an-
cer seems to be caused by a virus." She then laid out, step by
step, the methodology she'd used to test this hypothesis. In her
experiments, "extracts were made from the malignant tumors"
and "were then injected into other animals. A variety of malig-
nancies appeared: leukemia, chorioepithelioma (cancer of the
uterus) among them."

Dr. Mary and her small team would need to build on Dr.
Stewart's work to produce increasingly strong viruses that in
turn would produce more and more malignant tumors. They also
would need to take her teachings on developing a vaccine to *cure*
cancer and use those teachings to develop a way to *cause* cancer.

"Okay, guys." Dr. Mary said. "For the first day, tomorrow,
we're going to start right up here at 3225—Topolinia. All four of
us should arrive at nine o'clock sharp. These mice were exposed
at Prytania a few weeks ago to carcinogens, including methylcholanthrene, a chemical carcinogen—a hydrocarbon—used
by Dr. Stewart to boost the effects of cancer-causing viruses.
Future mice similarly will be exposed at the Jefferson Highway
lab before they're sent to Topolinia."

"Who'll be taking care of the mice in this mouse town?"
Ferrie asked.

"We have two guys, Eduardo and Sandalio, both also Cuban
exiles, who will take care of this menagerie on a day-to-day basis
and otherwise be available for odd jobs. They helped with the
mice at Prytania and have been told this is a continuation of an
old research project.

"Tomorrow," Dr. Mary continued, "we'll start with about a hundred of the mice and assign each mouse a number. We'll segregate out the abnormally heavy ones. These should be the ones that have developed tumors after being exposed. We'll then have them taken over to Dave's."

"The David W. Ferrie Laboratory and Flophouse."

"Can hardly wait to see it," Dr. Carolyn said.

Dr. Mary turned to Julia. "Once we get going, it'll be your job to go to Topolinia in the morning, assign the numbers to the mice, weigh them, and then take trays of them, with the heavy ones separated out, to the Ferrie lab. Eduardo and Sandalio can help you with the delivery. Then you'll stay at Dave's and help until more mice are needed. Don't worry, we won't overwork you."

"*Gracias, señora.*"

The four of them walked up the Parkway, crossed the street to Ferrie's apartment, and walked up the stairs. Surveying the inside of the apartment, Dr. Mary thought how amazing it was that a potentially history-altering project could be anchored in such a scruffy and disheveled place, a place that really wasn't nice enough to be called a flophouse. Ferrie's Louisiana Avenue Parkway apartment looked much like his other apartments—the Salvation Army-quality furniture, the ratty rugs, the church altar, the priest robes, the piano with an old typewriter sitting on it. Cigarette smells.

Unlike Ferrie's other apartments, though, this one had an American flag in the corner. *Some inspiration for us,* Dr. Mary thought.

The "lab" part of the apartment naturally was of particular interest to Dr. Mary. It was in and about the kitchen. Ferrie had a blender, a few test tubes, and two beakers sitting beside a microscope. There was a relatively small piece of equipment that looked like some kind of kitchen appliance but was actually a centrifuge. "That could be useful," Dr. Mary said to the group. The cages in the apartment were empty. The pale blue Frigidaire refrigerator would store the mouse tumors.

"Nice place, Dave." Dr. Mary smiled.

"Hey, it's home."

"Play piano?" Dr. Carolyn asked.

"They call me Liberace!"

"Here's where we'll be getting down to business," Dr. Mary began. "Let's go over the steps again. Kill the heavy mice that appear to have tumors. Then extract any tumors and examine them under microscopes. Extract the pieces of the tumors that look the most active. Grind them up in a blender with the bovine serum and some of the glycol, mixing in a small piece of tissue from monkey kidneys containing the SV-40 virus. Put the blended concoction, carefully, in test tubes for transport to my apartment. Julia, that's where you'll come in most days."

"Remind me about the bovine serum," Ferrie asked.

"It's centrifuged blood mainly from calves. Serves as kind of a nutrient broth for the virus. The glycol's a preservative. We'll have supplies of this stuff delivered over in the morning along with the monkey tissues. And some new equipment."

"You don't like my equipment?"

"Needs a bit of an upgrade, my friend."

"A bit?" Dr. Carolyn asked. "How about two bits?"

"All right, folks. Before Julia takes the test tubes over to my apartment at the end of the day, call me at home or at the clinic lab."

"I'll write down the phone numbers," Dr. Carolyn said. She knew Dr. Mary's home and work numbers by heart.

"That'll be one cycle," Dr. Mary said. "I'll do further analysis of the tumor cocktail at my place or at the clinic. Then I can use some special equipment in one of the Public Health buildings to refine the work."

The linear particle accelerator, Ferrie knew.

"I'll try to develop the most aggressive tumor cocktails I can with that machine. These'll be mixed in with larger volumes of bovine serum, juiced up with some methylcholanthrene, and then injected into new mice. Those mice'll be shipped to Topolinia and we'll start all over again."

On the first working day of the Dr. Mary project, Ferrie and Dr. Carolyn identified four promising tumors. Ferrie sent Julia home early. He wanted to deliver the four tumor tubes to Dr. Mary.

As before, Ferrie was buoyed by the beauty of Dr. Mary's apartment. On this day, she had mercury glass votives with lit candles placed smartly about the apartment.

She invited him to have a ten-year-old scotch this time. They talked for several hours about a broad sweep of things beyond mice. She enjoyed his wide-ranging knowledge and curiosity.

Dr. Mary's late husband, Thomas Sherman, a cerebral classmate in her master's program at the University of Illinois, committed suicide in 1947. She'd been close to him but couldn't control his depression and alcoholism. Never recovering from the loss of Thomas, Dr. Mary carried a deep though hidden sadness the rest of her life—just inches beneath her glossy veneer.

In spite of her invisible melancholia, Dr. Mary had an active social life. One, though, that didn't involve romantic relationships with men. The scars left by the suicide hadn't healed. Her free time was largely spent with acquaintances who were intellectuals and artists. And with female friends. Ferrie wasn't her typical companion, but, as she spent more and more time with him, she came to look forward to his company. He was well-read and curious. And as a homosexual, there was no potential for sexual undercurrents or risks.

Ferrie, in turn, enjoyed being around someone of her intellect. He had many friends but no one on the brainy and urbane level of Dr. Mary.

The mouse operation churned along well through its start-up period. Dr. Mary grew increasingly confident in Ferrie's competence and industry.

||||

One day in late March, Dr. Mary invited Ferrie to accompany her to the opera, with dinner beforehand with Dr. Carolyn and another friend.

He dressed well, put on a newly bought, neat brown wig, straightened out new fake eyebrows, and met Dr. Mary at Broussard's in the historic 1834 Borrello Mansion on Conti Street. Dr. Carolyn was already there, as was a third woman, an attractive, polished lady named Ida Kohlmeyer, a prominent abstract painter. Dr. Mary said hello to two well-known local writers at a nearby table, a playwright named Christopher S. Blake and a novelist Max White. Ferrie saw firsthand how well acquainted Dr. Mary was with the city's artistic upper crust.

Ferrie had thought about Broussard's Creole turtle soup all day. It did *not* disappoint. The cubed turtle meat, defying science, carried multiple flavors within it.

After dinner a car was waiting to take them the seven blocks to the Municipal Auditorium on the edge of the French Quarter. The St. Peter Street side of the auditorium had a concert hall well-suited for operas. The opera that night was *Faust*.

Ferrie was engrossed by the Gounod opera, floridly put on by the New Orleans Opera House Association. The ending was fantastic. On the night of Walpurgis, Faust's lover Marguerite, imprisoned for killing her child, flees the entreaties of the demon Méphistophélès by ascending dramatically into heaven. Stunning.

The company he was with was better than the riff-raff he usually hung out with. Not that Ferrie minded riff-raff. After he and Dr. Mary parted ways at the Municipal Auditorium, he went back into the Quarter to try to find some of his riff-raff friends. He walked down St. Anne Street to Royal, turned right and trekked to the Lomalinda to see if Dutz Murret was there. He was.

It had been a while since they had seen each other. Dutz was happy to see him. He was impressed with how "normal" Ferrie looked that night—all spiffed up for the opera, Ferrie was almost handsome.

They caught up on all the local gossip and the work Dutz was doing for Marcello. Ferrie eventually ran out of steam, slapped Dutz on the shoulder, and said, *"Adios, mi amigo."*

"Hey, one more thing, Dave," Dutz said. "You remember my nephew? You know, you helped him learn to fly and got him away from hanging out around Exchange Place?"

"Lee Oswald?"

"He's been around the world since then. Got married to a good-looking Russian gal. He's back in the country."

"Great," Ferrie said coolly.

"He's coming to New Orleans in a couple of weeks to look for work. He's had some trouble holding a job in Dallas. Recently got fired from a good job at a photographic firm. I'm afraid he has a bit of fuck-up in him. Or maybe an attention-span problem, I don't know. Coming home to New Orleans might help focus Lee.

"I'm sure he'd like to see you. I expect he'd like to reminisce about old times."

"Nah . . . He'll probably just wanna see his old friends."

"He specifically mentioned he wanted to see you, Dave."

Ferrie said good night to Dutz.

Fuck me, Ferrie thought. *Fuck me.*

CHAPTER 22

I t had been just over three years since Judy Campbell met JFK and Sam Giancana. She'd spent intimate time with each off and on during those three years. She'd also served as a courier between them, though she was blind to the contents of the parcels she ferried back and forth.

This ping-ponging was taking a toll. Judy was stressed and tired, ready to end the double dating. There was nobody she could talk to about her unbelievable situation. Not her older sister, who was quietly raising a family in Southern California after spending some time as an actress. Uncle Armand was completely focused on his Florida fish restaurants—she hadn't seen him in two years. There were no bosom buddies to confide in.

Judy had decided she needed to focus on one man, the man she loved, JFK. This in spite of the great kindnesses Giancana had shown her, the greatest one being his recent favor to get her quick access to an important though illegal medical procedure at Chicago's Grant Hospital. *God bless him.* But she had to stake her future on JFK.

On the last Thursday morning of March 1963, she was ready to make the break from Giancana.

Though Sam Giancana's house was average-looking from the outside, his bedroom was stunning. The bed was bigger than any bed she'd ever seen. That morning, she slipped naked and glistening from under the sheets and put on her sheer nightgown. She tiptoed to the lush, spa-like bathroom—French bidet and all—and sat for a while on a Victorian-era chaise longue in a connected morning-room.

Giancana's last communication to JFK was an angry one. JFK and RFK, contrary to promises made in 1960, were not going easy on the mob. Quite the opposite. It wasn't just the relentless pursuit of Giancana's colleague Marcello. They were chasing after other mob kingpins, particularly the Teamsters' slick, flat-topped president Jimmy Hoffa. And Giancana was now in RFK's crosshairs, he'd heard.

The Bay of Pigs failure also weighed on the relationship between Giancana and JFK. Castro was still in power and the casinos were still shuttered. In Giancana's view, the so-called Cuban missile crisis the previous October had only made Russia and Cuba stronger. Khrushchev had played JFK. He never would've used the missiles. JFK fell for it and gave Khrushchev a big victory by not only agreeing to remove American missiles from southern Italy and Turkey but by also privately promising not to invade Cuba again. The mob had easily learned about this secret agreement. *Was the earlier-leaked Kennedy-CIA "plan" to kill Castro just a PR stunt to keep the exiles and us happy,* Giancana wondered.

Giancana was slowly waking. He propped himself up on his elbows when Judy returned to the bedroom and smiled at her. "What do you got for me, Judy?"

"Here." Judy reached into her satchel and pulled out an unmarked brown manila envelope.

Giancana read what JFK had written: *"Can't change course on you guys until after election. Need Bobby, need him energized. Things will change thereafter. And on Cuba. Promise. Jack."*

"Fuck," Giancana blurted out. "Son of a bitch is stringing us along. Goddamn Kennedys—you can't believe nothing they say. Their word's shit."

"I don't know anything about that. We need to talk, though."

"Gimme a second." Giancana went into the bathroom and splashed water on his face. He returned to Judy.

"Okay. What is it?"

Judy grew tearful. "I'm not in good shape. I can't sleep. I got anxiety. Shit, I think my hair's falling out." She began to cry in earnest.

"Doll, what's wrong?" Giancana tried to hug her. She brushed him off. "How about a morning eye-opener?"

"I don't need a damn drink. Look, you know I love you. But, Sam, I love him more. I can't help it. I can't keep going back and forth between you and him. The strain is . . ." She began trembling. "The strain's killing me."

"Calm down, it'll be fine. It's okay, babe. We're all under stress, believe me. How about that drink?"

Giancana had fallen in love with Judy. He indeed had been hit by the "thunderbolt" the day he met her at the Fontainebleau Hotel in 1960. The "thunderbolt" was a revered and well-recognized phenomenon in Sicily—an immediate and electric obsessive love at first sight. When a woman generated a "thunderbolt" reaction in a man, the man, at least a Sicilian man, knew the woman would haunt him every day of his life if he didn't possess her. It was inerasable.

Blowing her nose, Judy repeated, "I love him. I'm sorry. I'm so sorry. Can't help it."

Giancana hadn't seen this coming. He was momentarily speechless. He quickly gathered himself. *This can't be. After all I've done for her.*

"C'mon, baby. Let's get some breakfast. We can talk about it. Please."

"No. No. I think it's best just to cut the cord. Best for both of us."

Giancana stared up at the high ceiling. "*Merda.* You really think JFK's ever going to see you as anything other than an occasional good fuck? He'll never get rid of Jackie. He needs her class, even if she *is* a goddamn ice queen. *Un magera.*"

"Well, maybe yes, maybe no. He really doesn't have much of a relationship with that woman. And she's not always around. She slips off to Greece or the Amalfi Coast when she can get away with it to play around. She's bored in the White House, though she's stuck there now for a while—she's preggers."

"There's a lot of that going around. You ain't going to see him until she pops the kid out, you know."

"Jack says if he loses next year, he'll divorce Jackie and we'll be together. It may be bullshit, but who knows? I'm going to see."

"It *is* bullshit. Pure bullshit. And *you* know it. Listen, honey, if it wasn't for me, your boyfriend wouldn't even be in the White House."

Judy got dressed, pecked Giancana on the cheek, and left. She'd called a cab from a phone in the bathroom. Giancana's caretaker Joe DiPersio carried her bag out to the cab.

DiPersio could see that Giancana was upset.

JFK was nervous about the 1964 election, Giancana knew. The South was turning on him because of his failures with Cuba. And his moves toward civil rights. JFK would've been even more concerned had he known what Giancana knew, that LBJ—who was sick of the Kennedys and just wanted to get back into the Senate when his old seat was up in 1966—was working against him behind his back.

Giancana didn't doubt that JFK would be coming back to the mob for help before the election on the promise that he'd pay them back during his second administration. *Not this time*, Giancana swore. He was sure the other mob bosses would agree with him. It was time to be men—JFK should pay a serious price for his betrayals.

Giancana was crestfallen, he tried to shake off his emotions. *You can't be emotional in his business.* He called Marcello.

"You know I'd put it to Kennedy that he had to stop shitting on us."

"Am guessin'—stiffed us, yes?"

"*Se.* He's going to keep shitting on us. We've been betrayed, Carlos. You know that better than anyone with all the craziness you've been put through. Enough is enough, my brother."

Marcello could hear more emotion than usual in Giancana's voice. *Rage*. This sounded serious. Marcello told Giancana he'd come up and see him in person.

\|\|\|

Ferrie flew Marcello and his bodyguard Sam Termine up the Mississippi to Chicago's Midway Airport, dropped him off, and headed home. Marcello was driven straightaway to Giancana's home on South Wenonah Avenue in Oak Park, not far from the airport.

"Carlos, the bastard's jerking us around—says he'll relax on us and turn back to Cuba after the next election. But you can't believe him, right?"

"Nah, he a fibber. Udder den pussy, he only care for power."

"Sounds a little like Roselli, am I right?" Giancana gave a sad smirk.

"*Esatto!* Johnny's a player, *tu* got dat right."

"My gal Judy has broken with us. She says she's in love with Kennedy. She came here a few days ago. We screwed and then she says she's done with me—and done with being a messenger. I think the bastard's messed with her mind."

Though uneducated, Marcello had an extraordinary ability to read people. Giancana was deeply hurt. Capsized. His heart was shattered, Marcello could tell. Sicilian men, at bottom, were lovers. Lovers, though still tough men. They were inherently prone to revenge when people intruded on their love lives.

"*Cu duna pi primo, duna a'ncarzari, cu duna d'appressu duna cu tuttu u versu.*" This old Sicilian proverb came into Marcello's head. "Those who cause harm first, can expect greater harm in return."

"*Minchia buttana,* Sam. Forget her. We need ta focus on wad we do about dat tit-licker in da White House."

"I say blow his tit-licking head off! When can we have a meeting, get our brothers together? We can't just keep sitting on our asses."

"Agree, my friend."

"They're still after you, right?" Giancana knew the answer.

"Shit. RFK's got J. Edgar lookin' in my trash. I got Frank to call RFK to get 'im to back da fuck off. No luck"

"If Sinatra can't stop them, we're screwed. Though I think Frank's losing his sway with the Kennedys."

"We need to get ta-gedder wid Louie Santos and Johnny and figger it out. I don't need a-nudder holiday in fuckin' Guatemala."

"Let's use your poor excuse for a fishing camp down there on the Gulf for a pow-wow. I hate that place—goddamn mosquitos—but it's safe. Protected. I'll check with Trafficante and Roselli. Gotta do it in the next couple of weeks."

"*Sono d'accordo.*"

Marcello decided to take the train back to New Orleans. He needed some time to think, and he loved the train. He could relax without people all over him. It was just him and Termine. The train wasn't crowded.

The Illinois Central's *City of New Orleans* left Chicago's Central Station in the morning and took over sixteen hours to travel the 921 miles to New Orleans's contemporary Union Passenger Station in mid-city. It traveled down the flat Mississippi River basin, rolling through Kankakee, Centralia, Carbondale, Memphis, Winona, Jackson, Hammond. At some places the cows were so close to the train Marcello could hear them lowing.

The word *lowing* actually popped into Marcello's head. He didn't have an extensive English vocabulary but had learned that word from a Christmas carol, "Away in a Manger." Marcello led a rough business life but, like most Sicilians, he wasn't only a lover but, in his own way, deeply religious. He revered Christmas and had memorized hundreds of carols. *Lowing* always sounded classier than *mooing*, which seemed to him like a children's word.

He was worried that Giancana was blinded by his Sicilian instinct for revenge. As Marcello thought about things, though, feeling the soothing rhythm of the rails, he came to agree with Giancana that it was time for the mob leaders to address the Kennedy problem.

Crazy, Marcello thought, *but it may have taken Giancana's broken heart to motivate the mob to turn the page on the Kennedys.*

CHAPTER 23

Banister summoned Ferrie to the Town and Country Motel on a spectacular mid-April day. Thousands of Louisiana redbuds and Indian azaleas were in bloom. The fresh fragrance of wisteria mixed with the smells of sweet olive was in the air. But inside the motel office, the mood was gray and serious.

"You'll be taking a short break from Dr. Mary," Gill said. "Marcello has an urgent matter he needs our help with."

"Fire away."

"Marcello and his peers from Chicago, LA, and Tampa are having a summit meeting at the Camp," Gill said. "We need to be there. Me, you, Guy."

"When?"

"Friday. First, though, you gotta fly over to Tampa and get Mr. Trafficante. Marcello can get you a Cessna 310. It'll make it straight across the Gulf to Tampa. Pick up Trafficante and his guy and bring them back to Moisant. You three will then be driven right away down to Grand Isle from the airport."

\\\\

Ferrie landed at Tampa International Airport two mornings later. He waited for Trafficante near the old Drew Terminal. Ferrie had met Trafficante a few times during his stay years earlier in Tampa.

Trafficante's power went beyond Tampa. He had pieces of the east coast of Florida, sharing control with Meyer Lansky.

Along with Lansky, he had also been in charge of managing the mob's businesses in Cuba under Batista. More than anyone, Trafficante desperately wanted to get rid of Castro and get back to the good old days.

An hour late, Trafficante arrived with a small entourage. He warmly shook Ferrie's hand. "Very good to see you again, Mr. Ferrie." His chief aide had reminded him of Ferrie's work for the Tampa mob in the fifties.

Trafficante was a gentleman. He apologized for being late. "Something came up during my breakfast at the Columbia. Remember my restaurant?"

The Columbia Restaurant, controlled by Trafficante, was an Ybor City landmark, a few miles from Tampa's city center. It was the oldest restaurant in Florida and one of the largest Hispanic-food restaurants in the world. Ferrie knew the restaurant and the surrounding neighborhood of Ybor City well.

Though not open to mere mortals for breakfast, the Columbia was always available to Trafficante. The staff of the Columbia had whipped up *huevos habaneros* for him that morning.

The flight back across the Gulf to New Orleans was uneventful. Ferrie, Trafficante, and Trafficante's colleague arrived at Moisant Field around noon. A driver in an unassuming Buick Riviera was waiting. The drive to the Grand Isle camp took two hours.

Grand Isle is a barrier island on the Gulf of Mexico, a hundred miles due south of New Orleans. A popular beach and fishing location. From New Orleans, travelers to Grand Isle had to drive down US 90 and then left on Louisiana Route 1, which trailed along beside Bayou Lafourche through the parishes of Ascension, Assumption, and Lafourche on what was known as "the longest main street in the world." This stretch of Route 1 passed through the plucky little towns of Cut-Off, Galliano, and Leeville. Colorful boats with colorful names sat on the bayou just yards from the road. There were swing, lift, or pontoon bridge crossings every five or six miles. In some areas, sugarcane fields bordered the other side.

"This is kinda pretty," Trafficante said pleasantly.

It was a ritual for Marcello and, frankly, anybody heading down to Grand Isle to stop at the Hubba-Hubba Restaurant and Bar in Galliano. This was a last-resort stop before the road left civilization and was swallowed up by the rivers, lakes, and small islands leading to Grand Isle.

The Hubba-Hubba was established in 1947 by Manuel Toups, widely known as the Cajun Ambassador of South Lafourche. Toups had been visited by everybody of note in Louisiana in the twentieth century, including Huey and Earl Long, New Orleans Congressman Hale Boggs, Louis Armstrong, the Prima brothers, and, of course, Carlos Marcello. Ferrie picked up pimento cheese sandwiches and Nehi grape sodas at the Hubba-Hubba, paying into an open cash register. Toups operated the Hubba-Hubba on the honor system, which invariably was adhered to by his patrons, rich and poor, black and white.

Continuing south the Buick Riviera passed through Leeville and then over the South Louisiana Canal several times, over Bayou Moreau, and across the causeway to Grand Isle, finally pulling up to the Camp. "*Bellissimo,*" Trafficante said to his car companions.

Marcello's beach compound was anchored by a nondescript wooden home by Route 1 on the Gulf of Mexico side of Grand Isle, just yards from the beach. The home was thirty years old. While others referred to it as the "Camp," Marcello called it the "Tide."

It was hard to imagine a more secure place for this meeting. Given the topography, there was only one road in and out of the island. It was easy to have several of Marcello's men patrolling around the causeway and even up to the town of Golden Meadow, the gateway to Grand Isle, monitoring comings and goings. For a generous annual stipend, Manuel Toups also kept an eye on things for Marcello. Toups would call the Camp when Marcello was there if he saw any suspicious folks passing south toward Grand Isle—particularly clean-cut guys who could be law enforcement. Even these guys would stop at the Hubba-Hubba.

Ferrie, Trafficante, and Trafficante's aide were the last to arrive. Trafficante and Marcello man-hugged and talked briefly in words Ferrie couldn't understand, except for Marcello's loud greeting—"Louie Santos!"

Gill and Banister were already there. Ferrie recognized Sam Giancana. He looked somber and focused. He was speaking with a man Ferrie didn't recognize but who clearly was a peer of Marcello and Giancana's. Gill introduced the man to Ferrie. "Meet Johnny Roselli."

Roselli was a handsome, cheerful-looking man wearing a turtleneck and sunglasses. "Hey, buddy. Ray's told me good things about you. Nice hair, by the way." Roselli grinned.

The private meetings began right away and continued for two days. For most of that time, Marcello, Giancana, Trafficante, and Roselli were locked away in a room upstairs looking out over the Gulf of Mexico and Marcello's boats. They came out for meals with the others, and there was some group drinking in the evening, though nothing crazy. It was a serious atmosphere.

The meetings broke up on the third morning, after a call with the Gambinos in New York, Gill told Ferrie. The various groups left in shifts to avoid attracting the attention a convoy of cars tended to attract.

From Moisant Field Ferrie flew Trafficante and his colleague in the Cessna back to Tampa. He declined Trafficante's invitation for a late lunch at the Columbia, refueled the plane, and flew back to the Big Easy. While Ferrie was flying back and forth to Tampa, Gill and Banister were getting briefed on the Grand Isle meetings by Marcello at the Town and Country.

Ferrie met Gill and Banister at the Pere Marquette the next morning.

"What came out of our camping trip?" Ferrie asked.

"Hold your horses on that for now," Gill said. "Guy and I need to spend some time gathering more intelligence on a few things and thinking about next steps. This is very serious stuff, my friend. We'll need you, but just give us some time.

"For now, though, you have two assignments on other things," Gill continued. "The fun never stops.

"First, go back to the Dr. Mary project. She believes progress is being made."

"Dr. Carolyn's been filling me in."

"Second," Gill said. "Guy and I need some serious time from you on this RFK court case. We appealed our case up the court chain. The appeals court in DC has now shot us down."

Circuit Court Judge George Thomas Washington had written the opinion for the court. "Since 1955 numerous efforts have been made by the Government to effect Marcello's deportation. Roadblocks have been placed in its path by litigation brought by Marcello, as well as refusals by other countries to accept him." The appeals court issued an order removing the "roadblocks."

RFK was determined to take Marcello to trial. He was already seeking a deposition, Gill reported. "That little shit is like the last leaf clinging to a tree in December. He won't let go."

Ferrie took the Claiborne Avenue bus to Napoleon Avenue and trudged the rest of the way home. He immediately pitched in with Dr. Carolyn and Julia, who were toiling away in Ferrie's lab. Two cages of large mice were awaiting their fate. Ferrie and Dr. Carolyn began their work to determine that fate. At the end of the day, Ferrie excused Julia, packed up the day's best results in his satchel, and headed over to St. Charles Avenue and Dr. Mary's apartment.

"Look who's back," Dr. Mary said.

As was her custom, she laid out afternoon tea. She updated Ferrie on the project.

||||

Ferrie was feeling stressed as he headed home from Dr. Mary's. He had a bad feeling about the results of the Grand Isle meetings—he'd probably be called on to do something big and dangerous. He was ready for a night in the Quarter with friends. Driving the 1961 blue Mercury Comet station wagon he'd just bought from Delta Mercury Company, he rounded up friends Al Beauboeuf and Melvin Coffey.

They started their evening at an oyster bar called Felix's, which locals pronounced "Fay-lix's." Al had lobbied for the Acme Oyster House, Felix's main rival situated almost directly across Iberville, which locals pronounced "Abba-ville." Al was outvoted.

Ferrie noticed Sam Saia sitting in the corner leafing through an obviously well-used notebook.

Al and Melvin split char-grilled oysters. Ferrie ordered the crawfish étouffée. They shared red beans and rice with andouille sausage. Pecan pie for dessert. This was a good start to the evening.

Bourbon Street was in spitting distance. Stomachs full, they hooked a right on Bourbon and headed up that never-disappointing strip.

First stop was the Sho-Bar. The magnificent Lilli St. Cyr, "the Anatomic Bomb," was dancing that evening. Lilli was a former professional showgirl and Hollywood actress—she'd appeared in the same 1955 movie, *Son of Sinbad,* in which Kalantan, "the Heavenly Body," performed an exotic Afro-Cuban dance.

Lilli prided herself on delivering a high-brow act. As with all the best strippers, she always had a theme. And she always used props, often a bathtub. But this night there was no tub. Instead, she was doing her famous "Flying G." After a long and seductive dance around the stage, a male stagehand dressed only in a Tarzan-like loin cloth came out and attached a small fishing rod to the back of her G-string. As the lights dimmed lower and lower, he ripped off Lilli's G-string and flung it into the crowd. A scrum of guys scuffled for the prize.

Ferrie and the boys exited. Al was flushed. He announced, "I'm so horny, even the goddamn crack of dawn better be careful around me. I'm as hard as Chinese algebra."

"Grow up, asshole," Ferrie said. "Idiotic tropes."

They turned right and walked farther up Bourbon, passing the building that had housed the recently-closed American

Brewing Company. Eight scruffy teenagers sitting on the sidewalk at Conti and Bourbon were circulating a pack of Pall Malls and a guitar. One bearded young beatnik began singing, "If I had a hammer, I'd hammer in the morning, I'd hammer in the evening, all over this world."

Melvin couldn't hold himself back. "Hey, jerk-offs. There're tons of stores on Canal—Krauss Department, Maison Blanche, Godchaux's. Just go buy a fucking hammer. Go crazy with it."

Ferrie pulled Melvin away, chuckling. They and Al crossed Conti and continued on Bourbon toward St. Louis Street. Melvin said, "Why the fuck do they want to hammer things all day, I don't get it."

"Don't strain your brain, my friend. Think metaphor. Focus on our next entertainment opportunity."

The three friends crossed Bourbon to the other premier strip club in the Quarter, the 500 Club. The 500 Club had two superstar attractions that night, so there was a long line to get in. However, Ferrie caught the eye of owner Leon Prima, who was manning the door. He let Ferrie and his friends bust the line.

The opening act in Prima's club that night was Linda Brigette, "the Cupid Doll." She was short, under five feet, but had boobs the size and shape of rugby balls. And towering platinum hair. Her specialty was dancing in a large champagne glass while "eating" fire from a short torch. She'd learned the fire trick from a performer at the Louisiana State Fair, the key being breath control to extinguish the flame. Not long before, "the Cupid Doll" had been convicted of lewd dancing. The DA, Jim Garrison, though, got her freed when he was reminded that she worked, at least indirectly, for Marcello.

The other feature act was the stunningly creative Lilly Christine, "the Cat Girl." With her shock of blonde hair, she prowled around the stage on all fours like a feline and then went into her "Voodoo dance." The hypnotic beat of jungle drums energized the crowd.

With top-drawer acts at the Sho-Bar and the 500 Club, Al, Melvin, and Ferrie had hit the quiniela.

For a change of pace, they walked the thirty feet across St. Louis to Al Hirt's new place on Bourbon. Hirt, who'd become renowned around the country as a jazz trumpeter, had shaken up Bourbon Street the year before by taking over Dan's Pier 600 and renaming it, simply, "Al Hirt." Former owner Dan Levy, deferring to the now famous Hirt, willingly moved his club to 600 Bourbon.

Hirt revamped the facility to feature a stage in the round. He'd gotten Paul Ferrara—who'd played drums on Louis Prima's "Sing, Sing, Sing" and had created the distinctive jazz mambo-drumbeat opening to Prima and Keely Smith's "That Old Black Magic"—to anchor the backing band at the club.

Hirt's trumpet was flying through what sounded like a jazzy version of Rimsky-Korsakov's "Flight of the Bumblebee" as they entered the club. The crowd was wowed. Hirt and his band then went into his new version of "Sleepy Time Down South."

No other city in the world produced the unique and remarkable music New Orleans did. Jazz, Dixieland, ragtime, zydeco, Cajun. Blues music descended from antebellum "ring shouts" performed by blacks at Place Congo in Tremé. Brassy and percussive street and parade music dating back to soldiers' rituals during the War of 1812 and supercharged by Caribbean and African Voodoo beats later that century. These soundtracks blossomed from the *sui generis* mixing bowl of peoples who found their way to this fertile land hugging the Mississippi. French, Spanish, Sicilian, Haitian. Freemen and fugitive slave. West African, particularly immigrants from the Senegambia region and Benin.

This open city welcomed Acadian refugees deported by the British and Irish fleeing famine and looking for work. You could still hear hints of Acadian and Irish accents in the voices of modern day New Orleanians.

Jazz—the greatest of Big Easy creations, named after a local slang term meaning "energy" or "vitality"—grew out of black communities in the city, particularly from sounds backing plantation cakewalks and spirituals but also drew on syncopated music written to support French quadrilles and on whistling Irish folk tunes for jigs and reels. The jingle-jangle of Sicilian tambourines and *cupa cupas* played a role. Spanish-Cuban melodies for habaneras, too, were ancestors of jazz—Jelly Roll Morton told the Library of Congress in 1938 that "if you can't manage to put tinges of Spanish in your tunes, you will never be able to get the right seasoning, I call it, for jazz."

This melting pot of cultures was largely isolated from the rest of America, except for trade that flowed in and out of the port, for two centuries. In 1820, five years after Andrew Jackson's unnecessary Battle of New Orleans, while New Orleans was the fifth largest city in the United States with 27,176 residents, the closest city with a population of at least 3,000 was Savannah, 642 miles away. Because of its exotic and remote nature, New Orleans attracted adventurous and independent people, people looking to live without all the rules and regulations extant in their home countries or states. Pioneers, rogues, pirates. City dwellers and farmers taking a chance on having a new, more sparkling life.

In addition to music, this broth of disparate cultures and seclusion produced distinctive fine and street art, dance, and sculpture. Since the time of George Washington, while still a Spanish colony, New Orleans promoted and put its own stamp on opera. In the 1800s New Orleans was the opera capital of North America. The French Opera House, with its great elliptical auditorium, graced the corner of Toulouse and Bourbon Streets from 1859 to 1919. The blaze that brought it down, according to the December 5, 1919, edition of the *Times-Picayune*, "was more splendid and more terrible than Walpurgis Night, that long-famous brocken of the opera 'Faust.'"

For generations, the souls of New Orleanians have been infused with joy and kindness but also with an innate drive to find different and often mischievous ways to amuse themselves. They have produced the most interesting city in the United States. On occasion, however, the New Orleans heartbeat creates individuals whose quirks swamp their ability to make reasonable and rational decisions. Odd characters and misadventures have seasoned the history of the city.

Departing Al Hirt's club, the three revelers stumbled down St. Louis to Royal Street. "I'd like to finish up at the Lomalinda," Ferrie announced. "Play a few rounds of cards. Al, you know Dutz Murret. He runs the place."

Ferrie immediately saw Dutz when he entered the Lomalinda. The three of them took a table and Dutz approached. Another man was with him—nephew Lee Harvey Oswald.

CHAPTER 24

U pon encountering Ferrie, Oswald paused and began to reflect recognition. He quickly flushed. Ferrie straightened and braced himself as Oswald took a step toward him. Dutz could see the impending confrontation and grabbed Oswald's arm.

"Lee, you remember Dave Ferrie."

Oswald, of course, remembered Ferrie. He was beginning to boil over.

Ferrie spoke up first. "Lee. It's been a long time."

Oswald bearded Ferrie. "You freak. Goddamn homo. I remember what you did. Asshole clown." Oswald took another step toward Ferrie. Dutz intensified his grip on Oswald's arm and prised a glass out of Oswald's hand.

Ferrie stepped back. Looking at Dutz, he said, "Lee and I ended our CAP relationship on a bit of a bad note. It was my fault."

Dutz corralled both of Oswald's arms as he tried again to step forward.

Ferrie said to Oswald, "You're right. I was an asshole. I know that and I'm sorry, man. But, believe me, there's been a lot of water under the bridge since then. I was going through some bad shit. That's over. I'm working with Dutz now for Mr. Marcello. Dutz'll tell you."

Dutz pulled Oswald aside. "I don't care if Dave treated you tough back then. Since you left, he's become one of Marcello's favorites. He helped save Marcello's ass after RFK threw him out of the country. And Dave actually went to Cuba, several times, working against Castro, doing really dangerous stuff."

"So what?" Oswald responded. He was too embarrassed to mention Ferrie's sexual advance eight years back. Dutz wouldn't believe him and might assume he'd sent some kind of subliminal gay signal. "Once a weirdo, always a weirdo. Get him out of my face."

"Listen to me," Dutz whispered to Oswald. "He's now involved with some powerful people. You can't piss him off. You could use him on your side."

Oswald went out on Royal Street for a few minutes to calm down. He came back stone-faced and sat down with Dutz on a bench on one side of a long table. Ferrie, Al, and Melvin were on the other side.

"Dutz has filled me in on what you've been doing the last five, six years—Marines, Japan, Russia," Ferrie said to Oswald. "Sounds monumental. Tell me about it."

"Nothing to tell, really. I'm goin' to get another beer."

Oswald went to the bar, pounded his fist several times on the counter, and ordered a Falstaff. He'd met alcohol in Japan.

Dutz gently suggested that Al and Melvin go play some *vingt et un* or one of the other games at the Lomalinda.

He then leaned over to Ferrie. "I've told some of the Marcello guys, including Sam Termine, the boss's bodyguard, that Lee could actually be of great value to us. Termine's a friend and, by the way, used to hang out with Lee's nut-bag mother.

"Here's the deal. Lee got in the Marines, got trained up on guns and on other shit Marines learn. In Japan he worked around spy planes. He could be a real asset, Dave."

"Why Russia?"

"Part of it was that he was just bored and was looking to shake his life up. But he also really was flirting with Communism— was Russia the paradise of the world, as Commies say? He got over there and was sorely disappointed. I'll tell you more about that later."

"You don't think he's a real Commie, do you? Or maybe even a double agent?"

"C'mon. The Russkies wouldn't trust him to be a double agent, particularly six thousand miles away from KGB headquarters. With no supervision. Would you?" Dutz smiled.

"Uhhh . . . no."

"I think they were just happy to get rid of him. He didn't end up complying with their concept of a good comrade.

"As I said, he did kinda go Commie for a while," Dutz continued. "He read all their crap. He told me a lot of it sounded good on paper, but he saw that it sucked in practice. The Commie theories weren't used to help the common folk. They were used mainly to make the Commie bosses rich and powerful. I guess no matter what philosophers come up with, human nature is what it is.

"The government got full employment by refusing to automate, Lee told me. It was like being in the nineteenth century. He's not a Commie fan now, to say the least. He's been bitching night and day about Russia *and* about Castro."

"Must've matured, at least a little."

"Not completely. He told me he shot a bullet through the window of the house where that Neanderthal right-wing loon General Walker lives in Dallas a few weeks ago. Walker was just sitting there at his desk working. Bullet whizzed over his head."

"He doesn't like right-wingers either?"

"He basically just thought Walker was a dumb fuck. He said he was only trying to scare the asshole. Shows he has some big balls, though, right?"

"Big balls can come in handy."

"You *know* Lee's a strange guy. And he's full of himself. I can tell you, though, that he's intense and determined. Fearless. He wants to be somebody. With some smart direction, I think he'll do almost anything."

"When I knew him years ago," Ferrie said, "he seemed like kind of a smug know-it-all, like a young Barney Fife but with no humor. And, like Barney, he imagined he could be an important person. Delusions of grandeur. But, *un*like Barney, he had a severe edge and seemed to actually believe he could be important."

"A severe edge ain't all bad in our business. Maybe you can be his Sheriff Andy and keep an eye on him."

"As you can tell, he's not real happy with me."

"I'm sure whatever happened wasn't your fault, he's just a little touchy. He'll come around."

"Well, maybe, but I'm not giving up my guns like Sheriff Andy did."

"Just don't wear a tie.

"Do me a favor," Dutz continued. "When Lee gets back, get brainy with him. Get him talking about Marx or shit like that. He'll warm up to you, I promise."

"Doubt it. But I'll try."

Oswald returned with his Falstaff half gone. The beer appeared to be smoothing out his edges.

"Hey, Lee," Ferrie said. "Can I ask you some things about your time in the Soviet Union?"

"I'd rather you not."

"What's the real deal with religion over there in Russia? I'm sure you know better than me what Marx said. 'Religion is the impotence of the human mind to deal with circumstances it can't understand.' Marx believed that abolishing religion is necessary to make people happy?"

Still grumbling a bit, Oswald said, "Yeah. And Lenin called religion a kind of spiritual booze. Lenin was a prohibitionist, you know. Calling religion booze was a fucking serious thing for Lenin to say."

"Didn't know that. Funny that Marx, and Engels for that matter, were raging drunks," Ferrie noted.

"Yep. Look at what they accomplished while drunk half the time. They first got to really know each other during a ten-day beer binge. Crazy, huh?" Oswald asked.

Ferrie began to engage with Oswald. "Nuts. But it seemed Lenin was a little more flexible on religion than Marx, right?

He allowed religious people and even priests into his Workers' Party."

A student of Eastern Orthodox Christianity, Ferrie was genuinely interested in the role religion played in the USSR.

"When I was in Minsk," Oswald said, "I saw many old churches that had been shut down by the Soviets. Mainly Eastern Orthodox churches. There *was* one Catholic church from, like, 1700. The Virgin Mary Cathedral. After World War II, the Soviets just fucking blew away its bell towers. For no reason. Not that I really care. I'm not a fan of the Catholics.

"Even though I don't believe in God," Oswald continued, "I've never understood why Marx and then the Soviets wanted to get rid of religion. What's the harm in letting people get some comfort in believing unbelievable things that might make their miserable lives more tolerable, if that's what it does for them? They'd be more peaceful, more secure—just what Marx wanted."

"I've always wondered about that too. What's the harm? But from my view—and I *am* a religious man, by the way—I think it's worse than that. By not allowing religion, they're shooting themselves in the foot. Or more likely, in the heart. Mark the words of the Lord from Psalm 127—'except the Lord keep the city, the watchman waketh *but* in vain.'"

"Makes no sense but does have a certain ring to it."

"How about this one. When the inevitable day of ruination comes for the Commies, they'll say, like Nabokov did in *Lolita*, 'how I misinterpreted the designations of doom.'"

"I *really* don't get that one," Oswald said, "but I will say that *Lolita* is a much better book than the Bible—though the Bible has more sex."

Ferrie couldn't let Oswald's view on Catholics go. "What's your beef with Catholics?" Ferrie asked.

"Catholicism is different from the other religions. I don't even think it *is* a religion per se. It's a powerful political organization that's looking to subvert all nations to its will and domination. George Orwell's *1984* had it right. That book's really about Catholics taking over the world. You know that?"

Dutz brought them two beers. Dixie beers this time. "Best beer on the planet," he said. Ferrie lit a cigarette.

"Orwell's a much longer discussion," he said.

"How about guns?" Oswald asked. "I remember you like guns."

"I don't like them. They're just a necessary evil."

"You seemed to like them the first time we met. Had some nice ones."

"What's your point about guns?" Ferrie asked.

"It's actually one of the many things I didn't like about Russia. Regular folks can't get handguns or rifles, except for a few types of shitty hunting rifles if you got the money. Russia bans most guns. In America, we have a right to guns."

"Not really," Ferrie said.

"It's in the Constitution. You should read it sometime."

"You talking about the Second Amendment?" Ferrie asked.

"I don't know the goddamn number, but there's a right to have guns in there somewhere."

"It may seem that way since every chucklehead down here has a gun. It just ain't the case, I'm sorry to say."

Ferrie went into lecture mode.

"The Second Amendment does provide a 'right to keep and bear arms.' However, that's only if you're using the 'arms' in a state 'militia'—'a well regulated militia.' The fact of the matter is there really *aren't* any state militias any more. This provision is really a dead letter. It means nothing. *Nada. Rien.*"

"What the hell's a militia?"

"Here's a little history lesson, my friend. Get out your quill pen. When we fought the Brits in the Revolutionary War, there was no United States of America and no US Army. Each state, in effect, had its own army. These were called militias. The state militias worked together, agreeing to be led by a small team of generals, mainly George Fuckin' Washington himself."

"Fascinating," Oswald said sarcastically. "I would've loved being a militia guy," he added, seriously. "Maybe I'll start my own now. People'd hear about that."

"After the war, and after trying a weak-ass 'confederation,' James Madison Jr., his Creole friend Alexander Hamilton, and a few other big-wigs—all actually wearing wigs, by the way, though none of them had wigs as hip as mine—wrote the Constitution, creating a much stronger, centralized government. *The* United States. Some of the states were freaked out by that. Shit, they'd fought the Brits so they didn't have to bow down anymore to a big government. In order to get all the states to agree to a central government with some power, the old US of A, Madison had to tack on some written amendments to make sure this new government didn't fuck over the 'unalienable rights' Tom Jefferson wrote about but didn't define—and to protect the states from tyranny!"

"This is getting tedious." Oswald, though, was actually listening.

"Hang in there, young Lee. A number of the states were worried that the new federal government would create a standing federal army and then try to get rid of the militias. The Second Amendment was put in there to prevent the Feds from getting rid of the militias."

"I'm losing you, Professor."

"I'll buy you another beer if you stay with me. And a whole case if you read some *Federalist 46* and another case if you also do *Federalist 29*."

"One beer's enough for now. Thanks for the offer."

"The only way to really get rid of the militias, when you think of it, was to take their weapons away. The Second Amendment says the Feds can't do that. In other words, citizens would have a right to keep weapons to use in the militia—a 'well regulated' militia. That's why they used the terms 'bear arms.' At that time, 'bear arms' was commonly used in the context of military or 'militia' action. The term was never used to refer to an individual's right to a gun for personal defense or hunting—or murdering somebody you don't happen to like."

"You're killing *me*."

"For example, Rhode Island required that men between the ages of sixteen and fifty 'bear arms' in the state militia."

"Holy Ghost. Take me."

Ferrie continued to jabber. "The Founders could have said 'guns,' but that never would've occurred to them. In fact, at the time, there were numerous restrictions on guns all over the place. They said 'arms' instead."

"Enough! That was riveting, but I really am about to lose it." Ferrie's diversion into the guns thicket seemed to be working to take Oswald's mind off his teenage encounter with Ferrie.

"Lee, there were more laws regulating guns in December 1791 than there are now."

"Please stop."

"Many towns even had the authority to confiscate guns for the good of the community. It was illegal in Boston to keep a loaded gun in the home. Pennsylvania banned shooting a gun within any city limit. And, shit, in the nineteenth century, in fucking Dodge City, Kansas, even with dangerous outlaws everywhere you looked, you couldn't have a gun within the city limits. There was a huge wooden billboard—'The Carrying of Firearms Strictly Prohibited.' Wyatt Earp would shoot you in the nuts if you brought guns into the Long Branch or the China Doll."

"Fuck James Madison Jr. and Dodge City. This is 1963—any judge in the land, even the candy-ass Supremes, would say we can have our guns."

"Maybe. Would certainly happen if the judge were Sicilian! Every Sicilian I know, including all of Mr. Marcello's family, believes from birth that he has a right to any gun he wants."

"What I know is that I can get as many guns as *I* want without even leaving my house. Can just give the mailman an envelope with a check inside and a stamp on the outside. And they're cheap. Particularly the old guns. Real cheap. A few days later, the mailman comes back with guns. I can then 'bear' them. I've done this, got a couple in the last year."

"And you're not exactly well regulated."

"I'm not even poorly regulated," Oswald admitted with a rare grin.

"I confess it's a crazy country. But let freedom ring!"

"I'll drink to that. Why don't you get me that beer you promised," Oswald demanded.

Ferrie didn't like Falstaffs—too bitter—so he got a Jax for himself and a Falstaff for Oswald. He gently placed them on the table. Oswald said nothing. He didn't even acknowledge Ferrie's return. He was staring intensely into space, smirking. Apparently in another world, probably thinking about how he'd change this one.

CHAPTER 25

It was a rare Saturday night that Sam Giancana was home alone in his study. He was thinking about Judy. After a couple glasses of his prized 1944 Gélas Armagnac, Giancana picked up the phone. He dialed Judy's apartment on North Flores Avenue near Sunset Boulevard in Los Angeles. There was no answer, so he called the Mayflower Hotel in Washington, DC. He knew that's where Judy stayed when she was visiting Kennedy.

The front desk rang Judy's room. She picked up. Giancana drew in a deep breath. He nervously said hello.

"Sam, hey. How are you?"

Giancana's speech was a little slurred. "I was thinking about you, Judy. I just needed to hear your voice and see if you're okay. You okay, baby?"

"I'm fine. Fine. And you?"

"Good. Busy. Can you gimme a few minutes? I've got a few things to say."

"Hon, I appreciate your call. I really do. I just don't have any time now." She was about to get a visit from the president. She was dressed in a little black dress from Givenchy, like the one Audrey Hepburn wore in *Breakfast at Tiffany's*. Her hair was freshly curled and shining. She was nervous.

"He's coming over to the Mayflower?"

"I just got the heads-up that he's left the White House. He'll be here any moment. It's kind of funny, he leaves the White House lying down in the back of a big black car. The reporters don't even turn their heads, don't even notice." She chuckled.

"I miss you."

"I really gotta go."

"Sure. Can we talk soon?"

"I don't know. We'll see."

"Okay. Do me a favor. Tell the president this—'*Rath De' Ort!*'"

"You sound like a Martian."

"He'll understand. It's Irish for '*The grace of God be with you.*'"

"Ah, that's sweet, Sam. So you don't hate him anymore?"

"Hey, doll, I didn't say that! But we all need the grace of God. These are dangerous times for our country. He'll need God's grace more than the rest of us."

"I worry about him."

"I have no doubt you help him relax."

"I'm trying my best. Take care, Sam. *Ciao.*"

She hung up. Giancana downed the rest of his Armagnac in one swallow.

CHAPTER 26

By early June Gill and Banister were ready for the promised meeting with Ferrie to discuss the decisions made at the Grand Isle meetings and a going-forward strategy. Because this discussion would be sensitive, and because multiple hours of uninterrupted focus were needed, the meeting would not be held at the Pere Marquette Building or the Town and Country Motel. This would be an all-day meeting at Marcello's Churchill Farms.

Churchill Farms comprised sixty-five hundred acres of partially drained swampland hugging US 90, directly across the Mississippi River from Harahan. In the middle of this expanse of land was a modest farmhouse. Marcello and several associates had owned the property since 1950. Marcello frequently held summit meetings there with local business associates and with various members of the mob leadership. Out-of-towners were able to fly into a private runway on the property. Ferrie had flown powerful people to Churchill Farms.

Ferrie met Gill and Banister at the Town and Country to make the trip together. Surprisingly, Sergio Arcacha Smith was there as well. Ferrie was happy to see his old friend and fellow Commie-fighter.

"Sergio is going to be on the team for this project, Dave." Gill said.

"Good to see you, *mi hermano*," Ferrie said. "Cómo estás?"

"Excellent. Just got political asylum from your president."

"*Felicitaciones!* I got some issues with these United States, as you know. But we always help people in trouble—white, black, brown, Haitian, Muslim, Cuban, German, Yugo-fucking-slavian, don't matter. Your tired, your poor. Like the good people fleeing Castro. So, Sergio, you're welcome!"

"I'm tearing up, Brother," Arcacha-Smith said, pretending to wipe his eyes.

Arcacha Smith had left New Orleans seven months previously. He was fired in January 1962 from the anti-Castro CRC, supposedly for mismanagement. He told Ferrie that he actually was let go because of personal friction with Antonio de Varona. Varona had become jealous of Arcacha Smith's rising profile in the CRC. And it didn't help that Bringuier had turned on him as well, for similar reasons. For the ensuing nine months, Arcacha Smith worked with a fund-raising group called the Crusade to Free Cuba Committee with local hotel magnate William Monteleone and a flashy public relations man named Ronnie Caire. Caire had made a small fortune in commercial PR by having the nationwide S&H Green Stamps account.

What Ferrie didn't know was that Arcacha Smith was being groomed for some time to be a key asset in the Marcello network. After the falling out with the CRC, Gill and Banister orchestrated a transition period for Arcacha Smith, working with Monteleone and Caire, and then the move out of New Orleans.

The four men climbed into Gill's new 390-horsepower Cadillac DeVille and headed east to US 90 and then south over the Huey Long Bridge. Three-and-a-half miles past Bridge City, they made a left on Lapalco Boulevard and entered Churchill Farms on a bumpy dirt road that took them deep into the property. They were surrounded by bald cypress trees, wreathed with Spanish moss, tupelo and red maple trees, and dozens of marsh shrubs, mainly buttonbush and swamp rose. The farm structure itself was basic and unimpressive, though its cypress beams and Dombourian oriental rugs lent it a certain marshland class.

They fixed drinks and settled in the back room, looking south toward Lake Cataouatche, the best bass fishing lake in the state.

After one round of drinks and some chit-chat, Gill stood up, solemn and determined. "Gentlemen, I'm going to start with the headline from the Grand Isle meetings, and then we'll talk details."

Gill drew in a breath. He looked deeply into the eyes of each of Ferrie and Arcacha Smith. "The bosses have made the irrevocable decision to hit JFK. Take him out."

Not completely surprised, Ferrie nonetheless raised a fake eyebrow. Arcacha Smith lowered his head. A ticking clock was the only sound in the room for a full minute. Tick. Tick. Tick. Tick.

Then the deep guttural croaks of a double-crested cormorant could be heard from out in the marsh. And a gust of wind whispered through the bald cypress and tupelo trees.

Gill continued. "Marcello wants each of us on this project. Obviously, though, this could be a horribly dangerous, possibly deadly, project. I'll stop here for now. Dave and Sergio—if you don't want to be part of this, Marcello understands. You can leave now, no repercussions. No worries."

The solemnity of the occasion briefly overcame Ferrie, but he knew after a few quiet moments of reflection that he'd be in. Though he'd been favorable to JFK at the beginning of his administration, and pleased a Catholic had been elected president, things had turned quickly. JFK had blown the Bay of Pigs invasion. Intentionally, Ferrie believed. JFK had caved to the Russians after their Cuba missile stunt. He'd broken his word to the mob—instead of laying off it, he was attacking. Replacing JFK with LBJ—an old friend of the mob, a dyed-in-the-wool anti-Communist, and a conservative constitutionalist—would better secure the country, would free Cuba, and would allow the mob to do its work, which on balance served the public good, Ferrie believed.

Grasping the good getting rid of JFK could bring the country, Ferrie decided to push off until later how he'd rationalize being a participant in a murder to God.

Ferrie told Gill he was on board. Arcacha Smith, a true soldier in the war against Castro, agreed as well, tensely energized by the prospect of being on this potentially historic team.

Gill refilled the group's drinks.

"We'll need to get JFK when he's out of Washington," Gill explained. "There's too much security in DC. We have learned that he's going to make some early campaign trips before the holiday season starts. These won't actually be billed as campaign trips, but that's what they'll be. That's good for us. Security won't be as tight because JFK'll want to be seen by as many people as possible. He'll want to show off his pretty face."

"Seems too early to start campaigning for 1964," Ferrie said.

"He's anxious to get going, we're told. He knows the 1960 vote was basically a tie, maybe even a loss for him in reality. Take Illinois. Remember, he only won there because of Giancana—and even then he just won by a short and curly. What he's most worried about, though, is the South. He took a bunch of southern states in 1960, including this one. And Texas, with some help from us and LBJ. The South, though, is looking more problematic this time around."

"Do we have detail on the trips?" Arcacha Smith asked.

"No detail yet, but the outline is pretty clear. LBJ told the *Dallas Times Herald* in April that JFK would be coming to Dallas and other Texas cities before the end of 1963. We hear that JFK, LBJ, and Governor Connally discussed and confirmed that trip recently in a meeting in El Paso."

"An early Texas trip would make sense," Arcacha Smith said. "The Texas Democratic party's a mess."

"Yep," Gill replied. "And we hear LBJ's stirring things up there to make it even messier. He's done with the vice presidency and the elitist Kennedys. He despises Bobby and, frankly, would rather lose next year.

"JFK'll also want to go early to Florida," Gill continued. "He lost Florida in 1960 but just barely. No surprise, the Castro issue is a big problem for him in South Florida, particularly Miami. He's gotta start early on Miami. And Tampa's always tough for a Democrat—lots of Midwestern righties there and Cubans too. He appears to think he has a shot there, though, because of all the military folks in that area who might go for their president, particularly those who thought he did well with Russia on the Cuba missiles. So, there'll definitely be a trip to Tampa and Miami before the end of the year. He'll do Chicago as well, of course. He knows he can't rely on Giancana to win it for him this time around. And maybe even California. You might've forgotten that JFK actually *lost* California. He may need it this time."

Ferrie listened intently to Gill's analysis.

"We're going to have four planning teams," Gill continued. "The four of us'll work under Marcello to focus on Texas. Giancana's got Chicago. Trafficante—Florida. Roselli will plan for a possible West Coast swing."

"JFK's not coming here?" Arcacha Smith asked.

"We doubt it. He was in New Orleans just last year to speak at the opening of the dock terminal. In any event, he won Louisiana in 1960 with Governor Earl's help, and we don't believe he's worried about it for 1964. Our yodeling Governor Jimmie seems to like JFK."

"Where's JFK going in Texas?" Ferrie asked.

"We'll focus on Dallas—he'll certainly go there. He also'll go to Houston. Obviously, the big money's in Dallas and Houston. Dallas'll be an easier hit. Houston's such a messy sprawl of a city that it would be much harder to figure out how to get him. Dallas has a more compact downtown. It provides an obvious parade route."

"San Antonio?" Arcacha Smith asked.

"He'll probably do San Antonio. That wouldn't be a bad choice for us—it's smaller, and there would be some good spots for a hit," Gill said.

"Right in front of the Alamo on Crockett Street—'Remember the Alamo' would take on a whole new meaning!" Ferrie edgily joked.

"Fun," Gill said sarcastically. "But it won't happen in San Antonio. San Antonio's not part of Marcello's territory—we don't have resources there. In any event, JFK's not likely to spend much time in San Antonio, if he goes at all. It's got a lot of people, for sure, though not quite as many as Houston and Dallas. But it doesn't have the big bucks the other places have."

Gill moved on to an essential part of the plan. "The hit *cannot* appear to be a mob job. We'd win the battle but lose the war."

"Right," Ferrie said. "Damn challenging though."

"At Grand Isle," Gill continued, "Trafficante came up with the way to do this—make it look like a senseless murder by a lone nut. Some angry or socially retarded guy who's got a political axe to grind or just wants his name in the history books."

"*Really* damn challenging," Ferrie said.

"Well, that's the assignment," Gill said. "This might be obvious, but it'll require a *second* shooter. Someone who won't miss and won't get caught. We can't rely on the nut actually killing JFK."

"Marcello agrees with Trafficante?" Ferrie asked.

"He likes the overall approach and agrees we'll need a second shooter. He wants us to start looking for candidates for our loner patsy—he's already identified our second shooter. Sergio, my friend, that's why you're here."

"Oh, shit," Arcacha Smith blurted out. The room got silent again except for the clock ticking.

After thirty seconds, Gill continued, looking at Arcacha Smith. "Marcello believes you're the guy."

"Oh, shit," Arcacha Smith repeated.

"While that sinks in, I'm going to give some background on you that Dave may not know."

Gill began. "Sergio had the bad luck of turning eighteen just as World War II was about to start for the United States. Many don't know that Cuba was a good ally of ours in that war. Batista, a military man, had just taken over for the first time. Sergio joined the Cuban military and served for three years. He was trained as a sharpshooter, though he was already a good shot after spending time in military school. He never shipped over to Europe, but he worked hard at home, where there was concern about German spies and U-boats hiding out in Cuban waters.

"We got to know Sergio in 1960 when he came to New Orleans to run the FRD," Gill continued. "Marcello had him checked out and was impressed—the investigators reported on his gun skills and also believed that he had developed a kinda hardened savviness during the 1950s when he lived overseas much of the time. And all of these talents were hidden inside his fancy-looking, intellectual exterior.

"Dave, you've worked with Sergio on training and the raid. You know he's a tough guy, right?"

"He's my hero." Ferrie tried to break the tension.

"Marcello saw great value in Sergio from the beginning. After Belle Chasse and Houma, his idea was to keep Sergio in our back pocket to use for big jobs as they came along."

"Is flattery working on you?" Banister asked Arcacha Smith, who shut his eyes for a full five seconds and then looked over at Ferrie nervously.

Banister picked up the story. "When the CRC thing broke down for Sergio, Marcello decided to move him out of New Orleans and set him up in a regular life away from the mob world. Sergio was happy to oblige—he wasn't getting along too well with the less sophisticated anti-Castro crowd in New Orleans anyway, right Sergio?"

"Bringuier had become a pious asshole."

"The fund-raising work in New Orleans with Caire and Monteleone allowed Sergio an opportunity to meet more folks in the Cuban exile community. Thanks go to Orlando Piedra for providing Sergio some funding for household expenses during that period. After Caire and Monteleone, we bounced Sergio and his family around a few places—Miami, Tampa. Marcello then decided to plant him in Houston several months ago. Sergio was given a job selling air conditioners. And working as an assistant manager at a hotel. Quiet stuff. The idea was to groom him under the radar and then use him eventually to do special undercover projects."

Until the call to come to Churchill Farms, Arcacha Smith was beginning to live the American Dream. Solid jobs. House in the suburbs. His wife Shelia and their kids were comfortable and well-settled for the first time in years.

"Bottom line," Gill finished up, "Sergio is the natural choice to ensure a kill shot on JFK if this thing happens in Texas. And he looks more like a snooty sommelier than an assassin. You have a problem with this, Sergio?"

"When you gave us all a chance to back out of the project a little bit ago, you didn't mention the minor detail about me being a political assassin," Arcacha Smith said.

"It's a free country, Sergio. You still have that chance."

"I just thought I'd point out that little bit of earlier missing info," Arcacha Smith said, his accented English still shaky. "Just for the record. But you know I'm good to go. It would be an honor. I'll do it, if necessary, for Cuba. For my country."

"My fucking head's spinning," Ferrie said. "I think we need me to say a mass or at least a blessing."

"Some other time," Gill said. "I think that's enough for now. Chew all of this over, we've got some time to work on a plan. *You* guys are coming up with the plan, by the way. Marcello's expecting a winner. Let's reconvene down here at Churchill in a few weeks."

"All right, men," Banister said. "Meet at my office the day after tomorrow at ten. Come with some ideas."

"This, obviously, is as confidential as you can possibly imagine," Gill said. "The tent on this is very small. Don't even talk amongst yourselves about this except at Guy's office or mine. Jack Martin is not in the tent. Dave, the doctors you're working with aren't in the tent either. And that includes Ochsner. A few of Marcello's lieutenants know, that's it."

"By the way," Gill continued, "Sam Giancana has code-named this project the 'JFK Affair.' It's a little inside joke for him."

"Funny guy," Ferrie said.

"Now, *bons amis*." Gill smiled. "Our appreciative host Mr. Marcello has had Frank Moran send over a couple of jugs of

Commander's Palace turtle soup and a big pot of that garlic shrimp they make with the sausage, red beans, corn, tomatoes. We just need to heat this stuff up. We can get a few more drinks before we eat."

"*Ga lee*," Banister, a native coonass, called out in Cajun.

Still kind of knocked out by the last couple of hours, Ferrie took Gill aside.

"Jeez, Ray." Ferrie was antsy. "This is scary stuff. Righteous but scary."

Ferrie paused, staring sharply at Gill.

"I know this sounds crazy," he whispered. "But I think I have our lone-nut shooter."

CHAPTER 27

As summer engulfed New Orleans in 1963, great strides were being made in Dr. Mary's project. Dr. Mary, Dr. Carolyn, Ferrie, and Julia had proven to be a good team. The ultimate goal of the project, however, hadn't yet been reached.

The better tumors were being run through the linear particle accelerator, and then the best results were separated out, treated further, and run through the accelerator for a second time. The cream of this crop was spiked with methylcholanthrene and injected in Asian red-faced rhesus macaques. The injections sickened some of the animals but were never fatal.

Dr. Mary was making increasingly regular visits to Ferrie's apartment lab. After one long day at Louisiana Avenue Parkway, and after Julia had left for the day, Dr. Mary asked Ferrie and Dr. Carolyn to join her for dinner. She picked an upscale yet casual establishment—Pascal's Manale on Napoleon Avenue. It was a half-hour walk.

New Orleans in the summer months is more than hot. The air is so thick and soupy that just walking is difficult, like taking each step against an invisible curtain. The walk to the restaurant felt to Ferrie like it was in slow motion. They were sticky and hungry by the time they got there.

The calamari and Pascal's renowned BBQ shrimp, however, were worth the steam-bath trek. And many locals believed that, notwithstanding the better-known Felix's and Acme oyster restaurants, Pascal's Manale had the best raw oysters in the city. The late Pascal Radosta's brother Jake, who was then running the restaurant, greeted Dr. Mary, a frequent customer.

Jake took them back to a private room. The group ordered drinks.

"Folks," Dr. Mary declared, "we are making remarkable progress across the board. Vicious tumors are being produced. They are fast-moving. I wanted to thank you from the bottom of my heart for your efforts. Lady and gentleman, let's have a toast."

They each raised their glasses. *"Salud, dinero y amor."* Dr. Mary smiled. Ferrie and Dr. Carolyn repeated in unison, *"Salud, dinero y amor."*

"Okay," she continued. "We have some business to get out of the way. Important business."

"So, that's why you invited us!" Ferrie said. "More work!"

"Only partially. Look, the powers that be are starting to amp up the pressure on us to get to a workable product—a killer product—ASAP. That's not unexpected, guys. And we can get it done. However, we need to discuss two serious issues," Dr. Mary said.

"Give us the most serious one first," Dr. Carolyn said.

"That's a tough choice—let's start with this. As you know, we haven't actually caused a monkey to die of cancer. We've come close but not close enough. The bosses are getting impatient. Their strong, let's say, *suggestion* is to go ahead and inject a human anyway. See what happens. They think the monkeys might be the problem."

"Whoa, what?" Ferrie was taken aback.

"Dave, you know we have to try it on a human at some point." Dr. Mary said this in a virtual whisper.

"But . . . God almighty," Ferrie whispered back. "We're not ready. We have no idea what would happen to the person. A fast painless death? A slow agonizing death? Years of pain and suffering? And how would we know which version of the product to inject? Tell me if I'm wrong—we have fifteen, maybe twenty concoctions that produce some results. However, we don't really know which one is the best."

"All true. If we acted now, we'd need to try a number of them—on multiple humans."

"Oh, Holy Christ. Can't you buy more time?"

"You gotta, Mare," Dr. Carolyn pleaded. "We're shooting in the dark right now."

"The big guys aren't going to be real keen on letting the perfect be the enemy of the good. But let me see if I can push them off a couple of months, at least until the end of August. Many of them will be cooling their wrinkly asses in Martha's Vineyard or Newport until then anyway."

"Just try," Ferrie begged.

"Look. I'm working on an idea for getting around the problem. I'll talk to Alton—Dr. Ochsner. I probably *can* get us the rest of the summer. Then, though, my friends, we're going to have to shoot somebody up with whatever we have." Dr. Mary looked around the table.

"*Merci*, ma'am. Okay, next issue!" Ferrie blurted out to put an end to that subject.

"This one will require some immediate alterations in how we work. We've had four or five occasions when our *injected* Asian monkeys have been kept in the same cages as our *control* Asian monkeys—and the *control* monkeys have developed the same cancers as the *injected* monkeys."

"Mare! These cancers are *contagious*?" Dr. Carolyn exclaimed.

"Well, that's the fear. Not sure how else to explain it," Dr. Mary replied.

"Jesus H.," Ferrie burbled. "We're getting infected?"

"I'm sure we're all okay now—we'd probably be showing some signs otherwise. To be prudent, though, we need to make some changes in how we handle the tumors. That starts tomorrow."

\\\\\\

Back home after the dinner at Pascal's, Ferrie began to panic. Potentially killing a human was enough to shake Ferrie up. But being personally infected with cancer put him over the edge. Since he was a kid, Ferrie felt he had cancerous cells running around his body. He just sensed it. Now, it seemed, these cells could be activated by exposure to the mouse tumors. He feared cancer more than anything else.

He couldn't sleep that night. He prayed to Mother Mary. He lay on his bed with his rosaries wrapped tightly around his right hand and his wooden crucifix in his left hand. He'd placed chaplets, prayer cards, and scapulars, everything he had in his Catholic bag, in his bed. A lit candle burned away five inches of wax during the course of the night.

Exhausted, he wearily greeted Dr. Mary, Dr. Carolyn, and Julia in the morning. He controlled his nerves by focusing on the changes to his lab Dr. Mary had referred to the night before. Ferrie and Dr. Carolyn, with Dr. Mary's guidance and support, upgraded the apartment lab and tightened their procedures. Extra precautions were taken to have a sanitary environment, with frequent cleanings with disinfectants. The team, including Julia, added surgical masks to the other gear they wore.

A bigger change came in the form of an unusual-looking chamber Dr. Mary brought with her. It was a three-foot-wide clear box with two openings on each side, a left or right plastic glove hermetically attached to each opening. Dr. Carolyn had brought an air pump, which Dr. Mary hooked into an aperture on the side of the chamber.

"From now on," Dr. Mary said, "we'll be cutting the tumors out of the mice inside this isolation chamber."

The box was air-sealed. Pure oxygen would be pumped in. After cutting open the mice and removing the tumors in the chamber, the tumors would then be wrapped in a clear covering before being removed through the air tank aperture. The tumors would be examined under a microscope, through the clear covering. After notes were taken, the tumors, still wrapped, would be transported to Dr. Mary's apartment.

These precautions mitigated Ferrie's hypochondria a few degrees, but, at the end of the first day using the air-sealed box, he was still riddled with anxiety. And knowing that the time was probably coming to try to kill an innocent human tore at him. Though exhausted, he downed a bourbon at home after the women left. He called Al Beauboeuf and then trolleyed to the Quarter. Going to the Quarter was Ferrie's release. They met at Felix's.

\\\\

Banister had told Ferrie that Jack Ruby was in town. Ferrie knew that Ruby was fixated on getting the lush stripper Jada—who was now stripping at the Sho-Bar—to move to Dallas and perform at the Carousel Club.

Al and Ferrie slurped down a half-dozen raw Gulf oysters on half shells at Felix's, washing them down with a couple of Felix's proprietary "Iberville" Hurricanes. Dodging drunks, buskers and tourists, they then walked the block and a half to the Sho-Bar to see if Ruby was there.

Ferrie also thought it would be fun to see Jada perform that particular night. She'd been arrested for public indecency just a few days before. The arrest was "for what police called an obscene dance," according the *New Orleans States-Item*. Ferrie had heard she'd provided a glimpse of her bristly, russet bush while fiddling with her G-string. Unfortunately, there were two cops in the crowd. The manager, Bob Oudibert, was also arrested for "permitting a lewd dance," the paper said. The Sho-Bar had been closed for two nights by order of the New Orleans Police Department.

Tonight was the grand reopening. Jada was going back to work.

The comedian Lenny Gale was on the stage as Ferrie and Al took seats at the long wooden bar and ordered Jax beers. Though the club was smoky and dark, Ferrie could still recognize a few of Marcello's lieutenants close to the stage, including bodyguard Sam Termine. He also recognized David Snyder, one of the main reporters for the *New Orleans States-Item* and its sister paper the *Times-Picayune*. Ferrie had dealt with Snyder over the years. Ferrie gave him a faux salute.

Snyder was sitting with Pershing Gervais, DA Jim Garrison's lead investigator and old friend. Ferrie had contacts with Gervais off and on in the 1950s, when Gervais was a corrupt New Orleans cop. Gervais was a colorful but hot-tempered character.

Lenny Gale clicked through his final joke: "A lady walked into a bar with a duck under her arm. The bartender said, 'Hey, you can't bring that pig in here.' The lady said, 'That's not a pig; that's a duck.' The bartender replied, 'I was talking to the duck.'"

There were some groans and catcalls. Long-time Sho-Bar drummer extraordinaire and former Fats Domino drummer Smokey Johnson, a native of Tremé, banged his snare drum twice.

Oudibert was also the master of ceremonies. As Oudibert began to approach the stage, Ruby came out from the back room where the girls gave private dances. *He must've been auditioning a girl*, Ferrie thought. Ruby had no carnal interest in a private dance.

Ferrie caught Ruby's eye. Ruby joined Ferrie and Al.

"Dave, my Jesus-loving brother. I got her. *Jada*. She's the new main act at the Carousel Club. Thank your Christ the King! And thank his mother. Ha! Drinks on me!"

"Cheers! Did Marcello help?"

"I assume so. Marcello knows it'll help me, and him, in Dallas. I'm told he bought off One-eyed Pete and then had to soothe Oudibert. I'm sure that took some doing because Oudibert's fucking Jada."

"Lucky bastard," Al said.

Ruby continued. "Marcello had the cops arrest her to make her leaving town more, uh, attractive, shall we say—to both Pete and to her."

"Well, for old times' sake, I hope she shows a little red carpet tonight," Al said. "Or at least makes sure that some nipple tape falls off."

"Doubt it," Ruby said. "Not now. Too many luminaries here. She'll have a little more room to be creative in Dallas. The Dallas cops are more loosey-goosey on that shit, particularly at my club. They'll allow an occasional gander at her minge."

Jada swooshed out of the dressing room through the deep burgundy curtain on to the stage. The crowd whooped and gave her a standing ovation.

This night she wore a white tulle and gilt evening gown. And knee-high black boots. She whipped off her G-string in the middle of her act and whirled it around her head, deftly not showing anything inappropriate. She playfully threw extra G-strings she had in the pocket of her gown at Oudibert and Smokey Johnson. The room was charged as she started to shimmy while pressed up against the stage's mirrored rear wall, her back to the crowd. Jada was on her game that night. One of her trademarks, a purring orgasmic hum emanating up from her throat, was hypnotizing the crowd. She was, as many a fan had said, an "animal" on stage.

Ferrie could sense endorphins and adrenaline pumping throughout the room. Even he felt electric vestigial heterosexual tingles. "She's good," Ferrie whispered to Ruby.

CHAPTER 28

Ferrie finished the evening with a swing by the Lomalinda. Prolonging the evening would help keep his mind off of things he'd rather not think about. Cancer. Murder. Castro. *JFK*.

Ruby said he'd meet Ferrie there. First, though, Ruby had wanted to swing by the Old French Opera House at 601 Bourbon—a second-rate girls and music club—and visit briefly with its owner, Frank Caracci, a friend and Marcello associate. Caracci also had a piece of the 500 Club and was a well-known figure in the French Quarter.

Al cashed it in and went home.

Ferrie walked by Felix's and down a block to the Lomalinda. As expected, Dutz Murret was there working the crowd and keeping an eye on the tables. Ferrie picked up two Dixies and sat at a wooden table. Dutz joined him.

Ferrie asked about Lee Oswald.

"He was doing some odd jobs for Sam Saia at Felix's—Sam runs a handbook out of the back room there—but I just helped get Lee a real job a few weeks ago at Reily Coffee," Dutz responded. "One of the main VPs there, a guy named Bill Monaghan, is plugged in with Marcello. Monaghan's tight with Banister too and, by the way, also with Ochsner. Bill comes in here from time to time. We can often get people jobs at Reily."

The William B. Reily Company had been in operation since 1902. It sold ground coffee under the brand name Luzianne. Its popular chicory coffee came in cans with a picture of an Aunt

Jemima-like black lady, scarf around her head, pouring coffee into a cup. Each can contained a "Red Scissors" savings coupon.

Reily was a successful business. And like any successful New Orleans business, it showed respect to Marcello and his organization.

"Lee's working as a maintenance man there, greasing and oiling the machinery for a buck fifty an hour," Dutz continued. "And since my Lillian was ready to get him out of our house—as you know, Dave, he isn't always the most pleasant person to be around—we helped him get a cheap place to live, a narrow little house on Magazine, just west of the Irish Channel and Touro, close to Crone's Bar. No bigger than an average-sized apartment. Sixty-five bucks a month."

"Probably a shotgun house," Ferrie said.

"A what?"

"Jeez, bone up on your history. The shotgun house is part of the fabric of New Orleans. This is coonass CK."

"News to me."

Another lecture from Ferrie. "Haitian refugees brought this structure with them when they settled here after the slave rebellion 164 years ago."

"Okay," Dutz said.

Ruby had arrived in the middle of the lecture. "Who the fuck cares?" Ruby asked.

"A lot of them were built in Creole neighborhoods here," Ferrie continued. "You know why they call them shotgun houses?"

"Sure I do, but prove to me that *you* know," Dutz said.

"That's believable," Ferrie responded sarcastically. "These are narrow, rectangular houses, okay? People used to say that you could shoot bird shot through an open front door and it'd exit an open back door without hitting a wall—shotgun houses."

"I can hardly wait to tell Lee."

Ruby was resting his head on the table.

"What's Lee's game plan now?" Ferrie asked.

"Hard to tell. The pregnant Russian wife's just arrived with their baby to check out New Orleans. I don't think they'll be here for long, though. Lee and the wife don't actually appear to get along too well. He thinks the wife'll want to go back to Dallas after a little while."

"Dallas over New Orleans?" Ferrie asked incredulously. "Looney-tunes."

"She has a close lady friend in Irving, just outside of Dallas. And, surprisingly, there're a bunch of Russian exiles in Dallas that she hangs out with. She likes Dallas. Lee'd probably follow her back there, at least at some point. She can be a pain in the ass, but I think he actually loves her—clearly loves the little girl and appears to be happy there's one in the oven. And he knows she'll cheat on him if he's not around. That drives him crazy. Her internal sex engine apparently runs pretty hot, unlike Lee's. He won't leave her alone too long."

"Have you talked to Marcello about getting Oswald into the organization?"

"I talked to Banister about him," Dutz replied. "He's intrigued. He's having lunch with him on Monday."

Ruby finally came back to life. "Banister's wasting his time. The guy's just a white-trash weirdo."

"Not completely true, Jack," Dutz said. "He's a former Marine. Well-trained. He learned to sharpshoot, and he worked on some sensitive military stuff in Japan. U2s. He could be an asset.

"Lee then became a Communist, renounced his US citizenship, and defected to Russia. He's back now and's flipped 180 degrees, he's *repulsed* by the Commies. The outside world, though, won't know what to think about him—he can appear to be a mystery man. Commie? Anti-Commie? Spy? He's a unique resource, Jack."

"He a *putz*," Ruby said brusquely.

"Whatever that is," Ferrie said.

"A fuckin' dick," Ruby responded.

"Well, hard to argue with *that*," Ferrie said. "I'll see Banister the morning before his lunch, give him more detail about Oswald."

\\\\\\

Ferrie and Banister chatted at the Newman Building Monday morning. Ferrie described his basic take on Oswald. A bright but forever flawed young man, damaged by a rough upbringing. He'd emerged from adolescence with an urge to make a name for himself. And it really didn't matter much to him how this happened. He just wants "to be somebody." Maybe make a name for himself. He'd surely be willing to undertake criminal acts and, in the right circumstance, might even commit violence—after all, he sniped at General Walker.

Banister and Oswald were slated to lunch two hundred feet away at Mancuso's, but Banister had offered to walk the half-block to Reily's to greet Oswald and walk back with him to the restaurant. This offer wasn't entirely selfless. Banister occasionally got some paying work from the Reily business folks and their patriarch, Eustis Reily. Eustis Reily was a Marcello guy. A rabid anti-Communist, he was an active member of the right-wing group started by Dr. Ochsner—INCA, the Information Council of the Americas. He was a hemispheric patriot.

Banister had given Monaghan a heads-up that he was coming to meet with Oswald. He went straight to Monaghan's office. They chatted briefly about another matter. Monaghan then buzzed for Oswald.

"Remember, lunch around here is only a half hour," Monaghan said to Banister and Oswald.

"Lee needs some extra lunch time today," Banister said.

"Just for you, Guy, I can do forty-five minutes."

"You're a benevolent and wise ruler of the land, my liege." Banister bowed.

Banister addressed Oswald. "Honored to meet you."

They took a booth at Mancuso's, ordered lunch, and had a lively forty-minute conversation. Banister walked Oswald back to Reily's and then returned to the Newman Building and re-joined Ferrie.

"So?" Ferrie asked.

"I dealt with a lot of guys like that when I was in the FBI, they make good informants or plants. He's a pseudo-intellectual, committed to fighting for a cause, though not really sure what the cause is. He was for the Commies, now he's against the Commies. And the guy's obviously socially challenged. He just stares at you half the time. His main goal seems to be to avoid being seen as a loser. He has the classic profile the FBI loves. Manipulable. Pliant. Sucker. A gull. Someone you can get to do things others won't."

"Exactly, exactly," Ferrie said.

"We can probably find good uses for him. Here's an idea I was thinking about while I was walking back from Reily. Get him known in town as a Commie. It'll be pretty believable given his Russian adventure. We could maybe write a pro-Castro column for him for the *Times-Picayune*. Or, better yet, stage some kind of lefty demonstration that he leads. Have him piss people off—try to get him in the news."

"And then?"

"We keep him in our back pocket for possible projects, like infiltrating Commie or pro-Castro groups. Jack Martin could help. Or something bigger might come along."

"When we met out at Churchill Farms on the 'JFK Affair,' the first guy I thought of for the lone shooter was Oswald," Ferrie blurted out.

Banister paused to let that sink in. "Yeah . . ." A further pause. "Hmmm . . . Could be."

"He fits the profile like a Siamese twin."

"I can see it. The pro-Castro shtick could work nicely with that. Let me think that one over—and talk to Marcello. Irregardless, this guy does appear to be a unique asset."

"Even with your idiot grammar, I agree."

"I'm having lunch with Oswald again the day after tomorrow. Meet me here before that lunch and let's kick around some ideas."

||||

The next day was a mouse day for Ferrie. Dr. Carolyn arrived mid-morning with Julia and several cages of mice, many with large, visible tumors.

"Jesus." Ferrie was amazed at the sight.

He and Dr. Carolyn worked for five hours killing mice, removing tumors, preparing them in the new airtight chamber. Julia removed the dead mice and kept the work area spick-and-span. They finished up a little early to allow Ferrie time to get ready for one of his scheduled masses. Julia took the tubes containing promising tumors over to Dr. Mary's.

Ten members of Ferrie's flock arrived at five o'clock. He planned to speak briefly about the current Vatican II proceedings, which had just started at Saint Peter's Basilica "to reformulate" Catholic doctrine "in contemporary terms." Would it find the pope now to be fallible? This was unlikely, too much to ask. But there was a betting chance that the Second Vatican Council would adopt Ferrie's approach of conducting masses in the vernacular and allowing priests to face his congregation. Like Ferrie, the bishops should understand that these tweaks in the mass produce a better connection with the flock.

This day Ferrie read a shorthand version of the 1570 Roman Missal of Pope Pius V, though just the "Instruction" from the *Mass of the Catechumens*, which was the easiest and most relatable part of the Roman Missal. The "Instruction" ended with the small congregation reciting the Nicene Creed, genuflecting, and then receiving the Eucharist. Ferrie swung his small thurible with burning incense—three double swings, a step reserved for the Most Blessed Sacrament.

He kissed his wooden crucifix, the mass ended, and the parishioners left. Ferrie immediately sat at his kitchen table, still dressed in his robe and black biretta, and said a prayer for himself, asking for protection against cancer and for forgiveness of his sins, both past and present. He then began working on a public-relations plan for Oswald. At the same time, he called Jack Martin, reaching him before the man's nightly venture into the Quarter.

"Jack, it's Dave. Let me pick your brain for a second."

"What's left of it," Martin grumbled.

"If we wanted to get somebody publicly known as a pro-Castro guy, what groups would he join? What are the best Commie-Castro groups in New Orleans?"

"The best one doesn't have a branch in New Orleans. There *are* groups here but none that has much of a profile. The better-known ones, like the July 26th Club of Miami, have probably been scared away by all the people down here who would hang Castro in Jackson Square."

"Name of group?"

"Real plain vanilla—the Fair Play for Cuba Committee. They have some well-known lefty writers helping them, like Mailer, Capote, Baldwin. As you might expect, they're out of New York City."

"What genius came up with that idiotic name?" Ferrie said.

"Yeah, Jesus. It sounds like something started by a bunch of suburban housewives who then bake cookies and shit."

"Do you think they'd want a New Orleans chapter?"

"If they could find a sucker to do it, shit . . . sure. Why not? You'd just contact the guy in New York who runs the national committee. I actually remember his name. Vincent Lee. He'd be fucking thrilled. Just tell him where to send the credentials."

"*Byen mersi, mon ami.*" Ferrie hung up.

Ferrie got out a piece of paper and made some notes.

- *Have LHO start a chapter of the Fair Play Committee. Logistics? Write V. Lee in NYC. Office address for NOLA chapter?—Banister's office? Registration documents? (Gill)*
- *Prepare flyers.*
  - *LHO distributes flyers around town, out in open.*

- *Generate disturbances to get press, find some Cubans to fight LHO. Bringuier? Get LHO arrested.*
- *Get LHO on radio, TV*

Ferrie wrote several possible slogans for Oswald's flyers— "Be Fair to Fidel." "Hands off Cuba." "Let Cubans be Cubans." "Viva the Three C's: Castro, Che, Cuba."

Ferrie bussed to Lee Circle, walked up St. Charles, cut across Lafayette Square at Lafayette Street, and entered Banister's office in the Newman Building. Reading Ferrie's notes, Banister liked the ideas for Oswald, though he hadn't heard of the Fair Play for Cuba Committee. He made a phone call, chatted to someone, and hung up.

"That Fair Play Committee's legit. And the guy in charge *is* named Lee. Interesting coincidence, huh? There isn't much information about him except that he made some trips to Cuba from Florida in the fifties to help the rebels. He was a big Castro guy even back then."

"It sounds fucking perfect," Ferrie said. "Let's have Oswald set up a fake office in New Orleans for this Castro fan club. I can tell you, he'll love this shit."

"All right. Join me for lunch with Oswald tomorrow? You can help me lay this out for the guy."

"Probably not a good idea. He and I had some issues years ago. I had a good bullshit talk with him at the Lomalinda recently and he became almost friendly. But he was a little drunk. Sober, he might take a swing at me."

"Let's take that chance. I'm going to need you, and probably Jack Martin as well, to sculpt our new asset."

\\\\

They met Oswald the next day at the statue of Benjamin Franklin in Lafayette Square, near the Camp Street entrance to the Newman Building. Oswald had no problem with Ferrie joining.

Banister wanted to mix up the locations of the Oswald lunches. Who knew what eyes were watching out there? He, Oswald, and Ferrie walked a few blocks to Thompson's Restaurant on St. Charles between Common and Canal. Dutz had mentioned to Ferrie that Thompson's Restaurant had become an Oswald favorite. Oswald liked Thompson's "sophisticated" mix of American and Chinese food, Dutz had said. Oswald also was fond of a waitress there, Anna Lewis, who, coincidentally, was married to a man who'd worked with Banister and Jack Martin.

Oswald jumped at the idea of doing clandestine work for Marcello. He was tired of how his life was going—the wife, the kid, the nine-to-five job. He was destined to do more, he said. "I'm not going to be Ozzie Nelson. I'd rather be hanged like John Brown or fucking Nathan Hale than spend my whole life only doing what I'm doing now."

The plan to have him pose as a Communist activist excited Oswald—a James Bond challenge to appear to be the square opposite of what he was now, an anti-Communist. *He'd probably get to spy on dangerous lefties,* he thought. Oswald was so energized inside that he almost looked animated on the outside.

Anna took their orders, and then Banister and Ferrie laid out their plan to make Oswald a famous New Orleans Communist. Oswald had heard of the Fair Play for Cuba Committee from Russian émigrés in Dallas and even had some of the committee's literature. He was amused by the idea that *he* would found the New Orleans chapter.

The Camp Street address of the Newman Building was to be the official address of the new local Fair Play headquarters, not Banister's Lafayette Street address. Banister didn't need that exposure, but, he offered, he would give Oswald some space to use on his second floor.

"That space is a bit of a mess now," Banister said. "We store a lot of shit up there, including a bunch of guns. And a Cuban colleague of mine sometimes uses the space. You may run into him, name's Orlando Piedra. An old Batista guy.

"We'll straighten the space up and set up a desk so you can meet with new recruits if you need to."

Banister laid out the steps he and Ferrie had discussed— street activity with flyers, a manufactured fight, possible arrest, TV and radio exposure.

"Me on TV?" Oswald responded. "Shit. Excellent. Let's go."

"We'll get you on TV for sure, Lee," Banister said. "We have contacts with Edgar Stern, you've probably heard of him. His parents are loaded. Sears-Roebuck money."

Edgar's mother Edith was the daughter of Julius Rosenwald, one of the early owners of Sears and one of its first presidents.

"Edgar and his dad started Channel 6, WDSU," Banister continued. "Started a radio station too. The Sterns are part of the right-wing, rich-person web in this town. Interesting story. Edith's sister Marion got married to a man, coincidentally also named Stern, who later became a Soviet spy along with his second wife Martha. Martha was the nympho daughter of FDR's first ambassador to Nazi Germany. The Sterns' anti-Commie feelings only strengthened when they learned they had a family connection to agents of Stalin."

||||

"Let's get the registration going and the flyers printed," Ferrie said. "I've got some ideas for a slogan."

Ferrie handed Oswald his notes. "I'm fond of 'Hands Off Cuba.' It's simple but elegant. It suggests that there may be consequences if you beat up on Castro. Up to you, though."

Banister added, "Dave will be in frequent touch with you about details. Our colleague Jack Martin, who knows a lot about the pro-Cuban groups, will help as well. You'll like him, he's kind of strange, for sure. However, as you get to know him, you'll see he's pretty clever and big-time ballsy."

Martin wouldn't hear even a breath about the "JFK Affair," but Ferrie *did* need his help in turning Oswald into a known Commie. Martin's role would end after that was accomplished, Banister had told Ferrie.

"After we get the flyers printed up," Ferrie said, "I think you should do a practice run, handing out the flyers somewhere well away from the Quarter and making a nuisance of yourself. I was thinking a good place to practice would be down at the docks. You could annoy the sailors coming and going from the big Navy ship that's in port now."

"The *WASP*?" Oswald asked.

"That thing's gigantic," Banister said. "I like the idea. You'll get a lot of attention, Lee. The government has all kinds of eyeballs down there already. With the *WASP* here, there are even more eyeballs than usual. And maybe you'll get lucky and get beat up by some drunk sailors."

"It would be my honor," Oswald said, not joking.

"The next step," Banister continued, "would be to do some demonstrating in the business district. On Canal Street. And maybe in front of the Trade Mart. You'll get a bunch of pissed-off Cuban exiles flocking to you. Some of them will surely raise a stink about your little demonstration, maybe throw a punch at you, get the cops to come."

"What do I do now?" Oswald said.

"I'll have a lawyer at my office after you're done with work tomorrow. We'll start the paperwork for the committee. In the meantime, you should sketch out your flyer in your own handwriting and then take it to Jones Printing. Jones is right there by Reily. Start with a thousand copies."

Ferrie spoke up. "Lee, let's meet with Jack Martin at Pontchartrain Beach. At the lighthouse. Go over details. First Friday in August, eleven in the morning. The place'll be crowded, we won't be noticed. Bring some ideas with you."

Banister had one last proposition for Oswald, bearing in mind Ferrie's good idea that they might need Oswald on the "JFK Affair."

"After we create this public record that you're a Commie, Mr. Marcello may ask you to go even bigger to create a much more serious profile. One thing we've kicked around is to have you try to defect to Cuba."

"Shit, really?" Oswald asked.

"Yes, sir. You won't actually defect, of course. That's impossible. The goal is to make sure people notice your efforts and remember you. You'd then have the full credentials of a serious Commie. That could set you up for something really big for Mr. Marcello if he needs it."

"If Mr. Marcello asks you to do something big, like the Cuba thing, you okay with that?" Ferrie asked.

"Gentlemen, I'd sacrifice my life to do something epic," Oswald said assertively, with a steely smirk Ferrie had seen before.

CHAPTER 29

On June 10, 1963, an unusually hot June day in Washington, JFK motorcaded the five miles up Sixteenth Street and Massachusetts Avenue from the White House to American University to give the commencement address. He took this opportunity to talk about peace with the Soviet Union. The title of the speech was "A Strategy of Peace." He said that Russia wasn't "so evil that its people must be considered as lacking in virtue." We should, Kennedy said, "hail the Russian people for their many achievements in science and space, in economic and industrial growth, in culture, in acts of courage."

The anti-Castro community and the mob took notice of JFK's change in tone. Ferrie read excerpts of the speech the next day in the *Times-Picayune*. *Typical commencement-speech bullshit,* Ferrie concluded.

Six weeks later, though, Ferrie clicked on his TV on a slow Friday evening and watched another JFK speech, this one on the signing of a new nuclear test ban treaty with Russia. JFK spoke from the Oval Office on this new formal agreement with the enemy. The United States and Russia, JFK said, had agreed to stop testing nuclear weapons in the atmosphere, outer space, and underwater. Blood rushed Ferrie's brain.

JFK spoke in terms of peace. What Ferrie heard was capitulation. *What a pussy traitor.* He was actually going to stop improving our nuclear defenses—"in a spirit of hope." *But you can't "hope" the Commies away.* JFK was risking the country's security on the "hope" the Russians would keep their promises.

Fat chance, Ferrie said to himself. *Shit, the treaty was even negotiated in Moscow.*

Ferrie's phone rang.

"You watching this?" Banister asked.

"Fucking scary," Ferrie responded.

"Meet me at the Newman in an hour."

"Marcello and his mob brothers are fucking pissed," Banister said to Ferrie at the Newman. "Making nice with Russia, which means he's also really going to back off of Cuba. And, all the while, RFK continues to squeeze our stones like they were Kim Novak's tits."

"I heard he got his hands on those bad girls."

"RFK's not only trying to deport Marcello. You heard about Giancana, right?"

"A little."

"They placed him under FBI lockstep. It was obvious to Giancana's guys. A few weeks ago, the FBI even followed Giancana onto a golf course. Is nothing sacred anymore?"

"I don't give a shit about golf, what a fucking waste of time. JFK was right about one thing when he said, 'Show me a man with a great golf game, and I'll show you a man who's been neglecting something.'"

"I get it that you people don't play golf. But for us normal people, messing with this sacred activity isn't right. Giancana had one of his goons confront the FBI agents on the driving range. Giancana had the goon tell the FBI guys that if RFK wanted to talk to him, then call Sinatra—he'd set it up."

"Did RFK and Sinatra talk?"

"Nah, Sinatra and RFK apparently aren't getting along too well these days," Banister said. "But Giancana didn't just stand still and take this shit. That guy's as tough as a pine knot. He took the FBI and RFK to court!"

"Smart," Ferrie said.

"Giancana knew that this would make RFK cave. RFK couldn't risk having Giancana testify in public. He has way too much dirt on JFK. And on RFK, for that matter—including his private time with Kim Novak. It fucking worked. Giancana got a court order against the FBI to stay away from him. He doesn't actually expect them to go away, but they'll sure as shit stay off the golf course."

"Love it."

"Marcello's also pissed that JFK's moving ahead on all this integration stuff. It's getting out of hand. Look what they did to the good Governor Wallace. JFK fucking sent troops to Alabama to make Wallace let a couple of Negroes into his university. Now, watch—they'll try to integrate LSU next."

"Fucking scary!" Ferrie said sarcastically.

"Now on to more important things," Banister continued. "The 'JFK Affair' was already getting to the front burner, but it's boiling over now with this Russia shit." Banister had new intelligence to report about locations and schedules for JFK's campaign trips in the fall.

"Hit me," Ferrie said.

"Nothing's public yet. We have pretty strong information, though, that he's planning to go to the Army-Air Force football game in Chicago in early November—a thinly-disguised campaign trip. That game's on the second. Soldier Field. He'll probably do a motorcade on Michigan Avenue first. They can try to hit him there, or at Soldier Field. He'll be in the wide open."

"Good. Giancana's folks'll be able to get him before he goes to Texas."

"Let's hope so. That'd keep our asses clean."

"What else do you know?"

"If he's still alive, he'll do Florida and Texas just before Thanksgiving, probably the week of the eighteenth," Banister said.

"How do we know he won't do those trips before Chicago?"

"Don't know for sure. Our guys in DC noticed, though, that he's got a pretty packed schedule in October and mid-November. Plus he'll be sensitive to doing too many obvious campaign trips too early. In any event, our instructions are to be ready to go not long after the Army game, if he doesn't fly out of Chicago in a body bag."

"He will. Those Chicago hoods are good."

Ferrie's voice sounded confident, but the spirits that perpetually swirled around his brain were whispering to him that JFK would be alive until Dallas.

CHAPTER 30

O n the last day of July 1963, a Wednesday, Ferrie walked to Dr. Mary's apartment for an afternoon meeting. It was a temperate summer day, windy and partly cloudy. They sat outside on her patio, just outside her galley kitchen. As usual, she served tea—with scones this time.

"I've spent a lot of the last two months burning the midnight oil studying our problem killing monkeys," Dr. Mary began. "One night, it hit me. The answer was simple. The SV-40 virus is natural in the Asian monkeys we use. Thus, when you inject these monkeys with a cocktail of ground-up, souped-up tumors and the SV-40 virus, nothing severe happens. They already *have* the virus in their bodies. Their immune systems have learned to keep it in check. When they're injected, they still get cancer, but it's a weak cancer. Not deadly."

"Hmmm . . . Go on."

"We needed to find some animals that are similar but whose immune systems aren't accustomed to the virus. Dr. Ochsner suggested green monkeys."

"*Green* monkeys?"

"*Chlorocebus sabaeus*. Fresh from the wild. They're expensive and difficult to get. We couldn't get very many. Dr. Ochsner uses them occasionally, so we used his contacts.

"We had to use back channels and skullduggery to get them into the country," Dr. Mary continued. "Transported them through airports that don't normally handle scientific animals to avoid detection. And also to avoid any risk of contamination from other monkeys. The ones we got were shipped through

Madrid to the airport in Philadelphia. Dr. Ochsner sent a driver to Philly to pick them up."

"Where exactly did you get them?"

"They're from some forest park in the Republic of Senegal—a pretty new country in West Africa. They were flown out of the capital."

"Ah, Dakar. A bit of France in West Africa. *J'adore les francais.*"

"*Oui moi aussi.* And, as I'd figured, these guys hadn't been exposed to the SV-40."

"How *are* our little green friends doing?"

"I shot up two of them and they died damn quickly. *Au revoir singes.*"

"Jesus." Ferrie looked up at the sky for a few seconds. "Congratulations, ma'am. You did it."

"*We* did it, my friend. Congratulations to you."

"Dr. Carolyn know?"

"Yes. We had dinner last night."

"Our little project is about done?"

"No, sir." Dr. Mary turned solemn. "I'm sure you've guessed what's coming next. The really wrenching part. No way around it. We gotta try our little bioweapon on a human."

"I was still holding out hope we could avoid that, ma'am."

She patted him on the knee. "Me too. Believe me. Me too."

"How's this going to happen?" he asked.

"Friends of Dr. Ochsner's have arranged for us to get access to an inmate at Angola Penitentiary up by the Mississippi border. The inmate's going to be taken out of the prison and driven over to Jackson, about thirty miles away. The state mental hospital's there. That's where we'll meet the prisoner. He'll have gone through medical tests at Angola and then'll be checked by a doctor at the mental hospital. He'll have to be certified as being in good health, or we find another prisoner."

"Kind of ironic."

"Lest it not be clear to you, you'll be coming in with me. We won't be there long. We'll check him quickly, inject the man, and then get the hell out."

"When's this going to happen?"

"In about two weeks."

"You know I'm really conflicted, ma'am. My four brain lobes are fighting amongst themselves and with the cerebellum. I feel like I have one foot on the platform and one on the train."

"Ouch! Look, I know this is tough."

"Everything's a little upside down, ma'am. Can't Dr. Carolyn be your accomplice in this crime?"

"I really need a male. They're not used to lady doctors up there. They may not even let me in without a guy doctor. You'll be wearing a white coat like mine, by the way."

Though Dr. Mary had heard it before, Ferrie outlined his sacred dilemma. "I do believe that killing Castro is in America's interest and that it will improve the lives of the Cuban people. And I'm a scientist. This will be a scientific breakthrough. However, ma'am, being a bishop, the Roman Catechism guides me. *Do not slay the innocent.* This guy didn't do anything to us."

"I know. I know. Look at it this way. I've been promised that the only human subjects we'll be using will be the worst of the worst—murderers, maimers, rapists, dangerous drug dealers. Balance that against the poor innocent souls Castro is murdering as we speak. My view is that God would be okay with this."

"Maybe." Ferrie's eyes were cloudy.

"Hey, enough of this for now, my friend. How about this? You've been ribbing me for only going to fancy-pants places and only being with fancy-pants people. Missing out on the common-man experience. Let's go to a real New Orleans dive for dinner—some place you like. Show me something charming."

Dr. Mary wanted to get Ferrie's mind on something else.

"When people use the word *charming* to describe something, it's usually because it's shabby or run-down," Ferrie said, still somber. "But I do like the idea."

He dabbed his cheek, still troubled. Thinking of some of the scrungy places he could take the elegant Dr. Mary, however, he began to brighten. Ferrie had developed a strong, sibling-like affection for Dr. Mary.

He composed himself in Dr. Mary's bathroom and came out looking better. "I got the place. A landmark in world history. *Martin Brothers!*"

They took a bus from St. Charles through the Quarter to the northern border of the Marigny District. Martin Brothers had sat at the corner of St. Claude Avenue and Touro Street for over thirty years. Its claim to history was the invention of the "poor boy" sandwich, later shortened in most places to *po'boy*.

They sat at a wooden table with no table cloth. "Indulge me, ma'am. Let me tell you the history of this place and of the poor boy sandwich."

"I'm all ears."

Ferrie's lecture began. "Fifty years ago, two guys—Bennie and Clovis Martin—from a little bayou town called Raceland, not too far away, close to Houma. Came to New Orleans and got jobs as streetcar conductors. Their dream, though, was to have a restaurant. They left their conductor jobs after a few years and opened Martin Brothers' Coffee Stand and Restaurant at the French Market.

"There was a devastating transit strike in New Orleans shortly after that. 1929. There were massive transit strikes all over the country around that time."

"I know about the Milwaukee one in 1934," Dr. Mary said. "There were several days of rioting, a death or two."

"That was a short one. New Orleans's strike went on for three months, three ridiculously hot and humid months. Former trolley buddies of the Martins were in rough shape without pay.

"The Martin brothers wanted to help. They offered free sandwiches at their French Market place for the strikers. These strikers were beyond hungry, so the Martins made extra-large sandwiches and stuffed them with huge piles of meat and whatever else they had, cabbage, pickles, et cetera.

"The brothers worked with a baker on Touro Street to develop a different shape of French bread that was larger and didn't get narrow at the ends, allowing for more stuff in the sandwich. This even-ended bread also was easier to slice, and every inch of the loaf could be used to cradle the goodies inside. The brothers cut this new form of French bread into fifteen-inch and twenty-inch sandwiches.

"As the strike got longer and longer, they began giving these sandwiches away. When one of the strikers would approach the shop, the brothers would say, 'Here comes another poor boy.'

"Word of the large sandwich got around town pretty quickly to paying customers. The brothers started making money. They soon had enough to move to a real restaurant space—here!

"The Martins refined the sandwich at the restaurant using not only meat but also seafood, shrimp, crab, catfish, whatever people wanted. They began dressing the sandwiches with larger amounts of lettuce, cabbage, pickles, and added mayonnaise, mustard, Russian dressing, you name it. Some were served hot, like the roast beef ones, with gravy, and some cold. And here we are!"

Dr. Mary listened politely. "And the name *poor boy* stuck?"

"You got it. They still call them *poor boys* here. The copycats around town, however, adopted the shorthand name *po'boy* for reasons that are still unclear to me—probably just the lazy Cajun patois."

Dr. Mary had no choice but to try a "poor boy," opting for one of the less adventurous versions, the fried chicken breast. Ferrie went all-in with the most-New Orleanian poor boy—shrimp and crawfish. Both dishes came with the unique cubes of Brabant potatoes found only in New Orleans.

Dabbing her mouth, Dr. Mary announced, "Wow. Much better than I'd expected. From now on, my opera friends will sit in the Municipal Theater with poor boys in their tummies!"

Ferrie knew the hostess kept a camera in the hostess stand. He asked her to take a picture of him and Dr. Mary. They both said *"fromage."*

Dr. Mary then leaned forward, closer to Ferrie. "I have a question for you," she said quietly.

"Yes, ma'am."

"As you know, Dr. Ochsner and I spend a fair amount of time together. He's been ranting about JFK, that he's weak on Castro and Russia. He's not happy with JFK's civil rights stuff either. I mean . . . he's really irate."

"He's not alone."

"He's said a few things that suggest to me that he thinks Mr. Marcello is even angrier and is planning to do something. He hasn't said anything specific. One day, though, he did say that he thought Ray Gill and Guy Banister were working on a 'Kennedy project' for Marcello."

"They would be the guys."

"I know you're mixed up big time with Gill and Banister."

"We're working on Marcello's deportation case."

"Tell me you're not involved with anything else, no 'JFK project.'"

"Ma'am, you know I couldn't lie to you."

"So?"

"Lips are sealed. But no need to worry. I'll just leave you with this observation: *In this town—New Orleans—the craziest things make perfect sense.*"

It didn't take a rocket, or cancer, scientist to surmise, as Dr. Mary did, that Ferrie was in on a "Kennedy project"—and, worst case, that could only mean one thing.

"Okay. No more questions from me. Just be careful. Real careful. If you go down a rat hole too deep with these guys, you probably won't come out again. I'm concerned about you."

She began to wonder if she should be concerned about herself as well.

CHAPTER 31

Ferrie was especially busy as July turned to August in 1963. His final Eastern Air Lines hearing was set for the first week of the month, in Miami. Later in the month, the human test of the cancer virus would take place. And he had the Oswald-is-a-Commie work.

Ferrie, Oswald, and Jack Martin met at the Milneburg Lighthouse at Pontchartrain Beach Amusement Park, as planned, on Friday, August 2.

Unlike Ferrie, Oswald had plenty of free time. He'd been fired two weeks earlier from Reily, not a big surprise to those who knew him, including his wife. He hadn't been Reily's best worker.

Pontchartrain Beach, at the end of Elysian Fields, was more than an amusement park. Inside the front gate—which featured an animated sign containing a cherry-red 7-Up emblem and neon fish swimming among lighted bubbles surfacing up from the bottom of the sign—there were the expected rides, carnival games, haunted house, and bumper cars but also a well-known music venue that had hosted a performance by Elvis Presley seven years earlier. Fats Domino sang "Blueberry Hill" dozens of times at this "Beach Stage." A big draw for adults was the Polynesian restaurant, the Bali Hai. And there was putt-putt, one of the best putt-putt courses anywhere. The park also had a bath house, swimming pools, and a large sandy beach edging the lake.

The park itself had the best thrill rides in the South. Its signature ride was a gut-convulsing wooden roller coaster called the Zephyr. The Galaxy, the Music Express, the Wild Maus, and the Trabante produced adrenaline rushes. A new German-made ride called the Rotor, however, was the talk of the town the summer of 1963. It was a large cylindrical structure with a circle of flags on the top. Riders were strapped in and the cylinder would begin whirling around faster and faster. Through centrifugal force, the riders would be pressed against the wall as the floor dropped out beneath them.

Martin, as always, was wearing his trilby hat. "Good to meet you, Lee Oswald," he said.

The land on which the 1855 lighthouse stood had once been surrounded by water, but the city expanded the shoreline here in the 1930s with landfill. The lighthouse was now landlocked. It was one of the special attractions of the park, a real lighthouse on the midway. The lighthouse was the hub of the park.

The swimming area and sandy beach were separated from the amusement park by a seawall that was built when the shoreline was expanded. "Let's go over to the wall," Ferrie said.

Dozens of sunbathers of all shapes and sizes were lying on the sand on the other side of the seawall. "You good, Lee?" Ferrie asked.

"Tip-top. Ready to roll. As you guys suggested, I did try to pass out flyers down at the docks near the *WASP* about ten days ago. I know I got noticed because a security guy stopped me for a few minutes and gave me the third degree. Official-looking types were watching me the whole time."

"Any trouble?" Ferrie asked.

"A couple of Navy blockheads shoved me around a bit but that was it."

"You got off easy." Ferrie laughed.

"And I practiced my Commie sloganeering over in Mobile the other day."

"Say what?" Ferrie asked.

"My cousin, Dutz's son, asked me to come over to his Jesuit school there—part of the Harvard of the South, Spring Hill College—and talk about my time in Russia. Why not? I thought.

Particularly since Dutz agreed to pay for the trip. I took the wife and kid. It was easy. I made some notes and went out and lectured away for twenty minutes, with thirty minutes of questions. I didn't say anything too provocative. Made it clear, though, that I was a Marxist and hated capitalism. Shocked those Bible thumpers."

"Good initiative," Ferrie said. "Next Friday's the command performance."

"Rarin' to go."

Since Ferrie wasn't sure how long the Eastern Air Lines hearing in Miami would take, Martin had primary responsibility for managing last minute details before Oswald's performance. He'd been briefed in detail on Oswald and on the plan to make him look like a pro-Castro activist.

Martin, smoking a Camel, spoke up. "Lee, I'll meet you Friday at ten in the morning at Thompson's. You need to dress nice—white shirt, tie, nice trousers. Have your shoes shined. Dave'll try to join us if he's back in town.

"Bring the flyers with you," Martin continued. "As we get closer to lunch time, you'll head out on the streets, passing out the flyers and shouting out pro-Castro bullshit."

Ferrie handed Oswald some notes. "I'm sure you did well with the pro-Castro stuff over at Mobile, but, just for fun, I've jotted down a few ideas."

Oswald read the notes aloud. "The people of Cuba have spoken. They have chosen Fidel Castro, a man of freedom, as their prime minister. Respect the people. Respect sovereignty. Viva Fidel. Viva Fidel."

"I got it, gentlemen," Oswald said. "Actually, I think I can do a shitload better than this."

"You'll spend some time around the Trade Mart," Martin said, "and up and down Camp, up and down Common. Then you'll move to Canal Street and set up at several different places in the business district."

"You gotta generate confrontations," Ferrie said. "Some fights would be great."

"No problemo!" Oswald said. "Shit, I'm looking forward to this."

"I'd prefer not to leave confrontations entirely to chance," Ferrie said. "Here's what I was thinking. Sometime before Friday, go and meet some of the main *anti*-Castro folks in town. Say you're with them and want to help. Then, on Friday, at least one of them'll surely see you demonstrating *for* Castro. They'll fucking flip out. They'll think you're an infiltrator or a spy—or just an asshole."

"Sounds easier said than done," Oswald said.

"Nah," Ferrie responded. "We have one of the main anti-Castro guys on the payroll. He owns a place where those folks hang out."

Ferrie filled Oswald in on Carlos Bringuier. Bringuier and his brother-in-law now owned and operated the Casa Roca store at Canal and Decatur, facing the federal custom house, two blocks from the river. Bringuier deliberately chose that location to cater to foreign sailors, who had to pass through the custom house upon arrival in New Orleans. He sold large volumes of American blue jeans and "new underwear," items many foreign sailors couldn't get at home. The Casa Roca had become *the* meeting place for exiles. And the Cuban-run Havana Bar, a few doors up Decatur, had become the next stop for exiles to blow off steam after frequently vigorous discussions at the Casa Roca. Orlando Piedra regularly caught a drink or two there.

Articulate and bright, Bringuier had risen to the top of the exile community in the city. He continued to work the CRC, though that organization was weakening. In 1962, three months before the Cuban missile crisis, Bringuier was appointed to be the New Orleans delegate for a student anti-Castro group called the *Directorio Revolucionario Estudantil*. After the October deal with Russia, JFK began withdrawing support for the CRC, so Bringuier decided to spend the bulk of his freedom-fighting energy on DRE activities.

Banister had outlined for Bringuier the general plan for Oswald, to get him known as a pro-Castro advocate for use later, in some way, against Castro.

Oswald was directed to go to the Casa Roca, volunteer for the exiles' cause, and pledge allegiance to the anti-Castro movement. Then, on Friday, when Oswald would be performing his pro-Castro act, there should be some very angry exiles who would remember him. If a confrontation didn't happen on its own, Bringuier would make sure one did.

CHAPTER 32

Ferrie had to pivot quickly to his Eastern Air Lines case. Closing proceedings on his final grievances had been set to begin on Monday, August 5. Ferrie, Gill, and Banister flew to Miami Sunday evening, courtesy of Eastern's Flight 207. This hearing would be at a motel, the Crossway Inn, close to the airport.

Eastern had made its case more specific. It revolved around Ferrie's "moral turpitude" but also included claims of lies and omissions in his applications to the company and various and sundry other material misrepresentations to his superiors.

Unlike the February proceeding, this was a genuine, detailed exercise of due process—witnesses, cross examinations. The final outcome, however, was all but preordained. Ferrie surely would be permanently suspended from the airline. Nonetheless, Gill aggressively pressed the defense. He called a former cadet named John Irion, who had served in Ferrie's squadron in the mid-1950s, at the same time Lee Oswald served. And he called Ferrie's old friend James Lewallen. Lewallen had known Ferrie since 1948 in Cleveland. They had reconnected in New Orleans in the early 1950s. Ferrie's former CAP student, occasional roommate, and Houma raid colleague Layton Martens had earlier given a favorable deposition, which Gill produced as evidence at the hearing.

Ferrie testified nervously on his own behalf.

Banister's testimony, for the most part, was a summary of the results of his investigation into Ferrie's character. Eastern's lawyers William Bell and Sidney Wheeler forcefully pressed the airline's case and closely cross-examined each witness, particularly Banister. At the close of the four-day proceeding, the hearing officer announced that his formal decision would take six weeks.

The hearing ended just in time for Ferrie, Gill, and Banister to catch the daily 1:30 p.m. Eastern nonstop back to Moisant Field on Thursday. Ferrie was exhausted. He prayed. He went to bed early. He dreamed eerily about JFK. The president was smiling, waving. Then the dream turned suddenly dark. People were crying, wailing. Jackie's face appeared, stricken, blank. RFK was in the dream as well, painful sadness painted on his face.

Ferrie woke up in a sweat at 3:04 a.m. He thought immediately of the "JFK Affair."

What Ferrie didn't know at the time, at least not in any worldly way, was that at the same minute he woke, JFK's newborn son Patrick died at an Air Force base hospital in Buzzard's Bay, Massachusetts. Thirty-nine hours and twelve minutes old. The baby's death brought JFK and Jackie close together for the first time in years. JFK never cheated on Jackie again.

Ferrie slept fitfully the rest of the night.

CHAPTER 33

Friday was hot and thick in New Orleans. Martin was pleased to see Ferrie when he arrived at Thompson's that morning. Notwithstanding the swelter, Martin's trilby hat was perched on his head. Oswald, as directed, was wearing a white short-sleeved shirt and brown tie. Nice trousers and shoes.

Oswald was his usual high-and-mighty self. At the same time, he was unusually excited and talkative. "This thing's working, Dave, Jack. That Vincent Lee guy at Fair Play's headquarters in New York has welcomed me with open arms, said he wants to help! Listen to what he wrote me: 'We would be very, very pleased to see this take place and would like to do everything possible to assist in bringing it about.'"

Oswald had come armed with a stack of pro-Castro flyers and showed one to Ferrie and Martin. "Pretty good, right? Like you, Dave, I liked the "Hands Off" slogan the best. A little more eye-catching. And Mr. Lee uses the same phrase in his brochures. To mix things up, I stamped some of them with either my home address or my post office box. And the rest with Newman's main Camp Street address."

"The CRC was working out of 544 Camp last year. Bringuier had a fucking office there," Ferrie said. "He'll see the irony."

Oswald had also brought a homemade sandwich board with him. It wasn't the wearable type that hung over the shoulders but one you set on the ground in a triangle shape, two signs hinged at the top. Oswald had hand-written *Viva Fidel* on each side.

"You're on your own today," Martin said. "But next week, when you do this again, you'll have a couple of Cuban-looking helpers with you."

"Excellent," Oswald responded. He turned toward Ferrie. "As you requested, Dave, I hung out with anti-Castro folks on Monday over at the Casa Roca. Dressed nicely—it is a clothing store after all. Even wore a bow tie."

"Did you meet Bringuier?"

"Yeah, though no one used last names. He just introduced himself as Carlos. There were eight or ten other Cubans there. I mingled around the store, joined in talking trash about Castro. I told them, in various ways, that I wanted to get involved in their cause to free Cuba. They ate it up. A couple of them took me to their bar. They'll remember me there 'cause I ordered a lemonade—who does that in a bar?"

"How'd you like Carlos?" Martin asked.

"Seemed like a smart guy. Good English, though super strong accent. He *really* hates Castro. I felt at home talking with him. I offered to help. Told him I was a Marine and a good shot. I could train fighters. Would go to myself to fight Castro. I actually went back the next day and showed him my Guidebook for Marines."

"Sounds perfect, my friend. You're ready. Hey, enjoy it. Have fun!"

Ferrie paid the bill.

As part of the plan, Ferrie, with Martin's help, had organized an *anti*-Castro demonstration at the same time as Oswald's *pro*-Castro street activities. Ferrie's demonstration would be at least four blocks away from Oswald. "I'll get a good crowd of Cuban exiles," Ferrie said. "I'd rather have them with me than listening to Oswald. They might beat the shit out of him. We want him to get attention—but we don't want to get him killed."

Oswald started his leafleting on Camp and then Common but quickly got over to Canal Street, focusing on the 700 block in the business district, between St. Charles and Carondelet. One of Bringuier's Cuban friends Celso Hernandez spotted him right away. Hernandez had spent time with Oswald earlier in the week at the Casa Rosa. Hernandez was taken aback. Oswald—this supposedly fervent Castro foe—was loudly praising Castro and the Cuban Revolution and passing out pro-Castro flyers, though there weren't many takers. The *Viva Fidel* sandwich board was partially blocking the sidewalk adjacent to Canal.

Hernandez took one of Oswald's flyers. He scurried down Canal to Decatur, went to the Casa Roca, and filled Bringuier in. "That fuck duped us, Carlos."

Bringuier feigned anger. "Goddammit. An infiltrator, a mole, a Commie spy. I should have known. Christ, he's probably KGB. He's shit, a *pendejo*. C'mon, let's go have a chat with that prick."

He smiled to himself as he and Hernandez bolted up Canal to find Oswald. They were joined by another Cuban Miguel Cruz, who also had met Oswald at the Casa Roca. The three Cubans found Oswald at Canal and St. Charles. He'd moved his *Viva Fidel* board out on the curb.

Oswald tried to shake Bringuier's hand. Bringuier recoiled and yelled—"Traitor! Scum! Communist! *Cabrón!*"

A crowd began to gather, and Bringuier incited them. "Commie! This man's a Communist. Loves Castro. Would kiss his hairy ass. KGB! Spy! Traitor! Don't listen to this pathetic little man! Get him out of here! Go back to Moscow, you pinko pussy!"

Bringuier's two Cuban friends shouted similar things. One spat at Oswald. Bringuier conjured up a look of affected anger. He took his glasses off and raised his fists, preparing to hit Oswald. Steely as usual, Oswald confronted him. "Hey, Carlos, if you want to hit me, hit me. Do it."

The crowd egged Bringuier on. "Deck him, kick him in the balls!"

Word of the confrontation had reached Ferrie's separate demonstration. Many in Ferrie's anti-Castro crowd peeled off toward Canal and St. Charles. Ferrie headed there as well, joining Jack Martin on the trolley tracks in the median strip on Canal Street. They watched quietly.

Oswald was remarkably cool until Hernandez grabbed the
stack of "Hands Off" flyers and flung them into the air. Oswald
flushed. His voice began to sputter. When Bringuier called him
"Harvey," as Ferrie suggested, Oswald threw an empty punch.

A police car came up St. Charles and stopped. Two cops got
out and approached Oswald and Bringuier, side-handle batons in
their hands. Oswald complained to the policemen that Bringuier
and Hernandez had physically threatened him and taken his
property. He had done nothing, Oswald said, except speak out.

"This is America, officers. I got my First Amendment rights."

"Go to Russia, you Commie cocksucker," someone in the
crowd yelled. "Nikita wants you, we don't."

Bringuier told the police he hadn't touched Oswald. The
police took both of them off anyway, along with Hernandez and
Cruz, to the first district police station on the north side of the
Quarter. Ferrie and Martin followed. Ferrie chatted with a couple of the cops there, told them he was shadowing Oswald for
Banister. Every policeman knew Banister. Ferrie was allowed to
watch through the one-way interrogation room window. Oswald
appeared cold-blooded and confident. Not a bit nervous. He had
a familiar smirk on his face.

Oswald was charged with disturbing the peace. Bail was set
at twenty-five dollars.

Ferrie knew Oswald didn't have twenty-five dollars, so he
wasn't going anywhere for the time being. Ferrie and Martin
went over to the Newman Building to talk to Banister.

"Sounds like this is all going according to Hoyle, guys,"
Banister said. "When's the hearing?"

"Given it's Friday afternoon now," Ferrie responded, "not
until Monday."

Banister nodded. "I'll have Ray call Edgar and get WDSU-TV
to send someone over to cover the hearing. There's not much going on in this town in August except for the Africa-heat. What
else do they have to cover? And, Jack, I know you know Bill
Stuckey. He does a lot of Cuba interviews on Stern's radio station. See if he'll do Oswald."

"Already my plan," Martin said.

"Meanwhile," Ferrie said, "I should go bail Oswald out."

"Hold on," Banister said. "A night in jail because of his pro-Commie activity might be good for the picture we're painting. It'll give a little more *oomph* to the press accounts."

Ferrie met with Oswald in the jail. "Greetings, comrade," Oswald said.

Oswald had no problem spending the night in jail, though he asked Ferrie to call Lillian Murret and have her let his wife know. Dutz was out of town at a Catholic retreat.

"Nice place," Ferrie said. "I wish I could get a room."

"It's not that hard."

"Make the most of it. Make an impression on the cops. They'll probably interview you again in the morning. Pump up the Fair Play Committee. Have them think it's a real thing in New Orleans and has more members than just you."

"Sure."

"We'll get you out tomorrow and then you'll have Sunday to rest with your family before the hearing."

"I've been in a Navy brig but never a civilian jail. Not sure how things work. Can you see if your cop friends can get me something decent to eat?"

"I'm sure your comfort is their main concern." Ferrie smiled.

||||

Not wanting to create a record that he was in cahoots with Oswald, Ferrie had a friend of Dutz's named Emile Bruneau bail Oswald out Saturday afternoon. Ferrie met up with Oswald at Thompson's.

Oswald told Ferrie that he'd spun tales to the police about his background. He told exaggerated stories about the Fair Play Committee. It had thirty-five members. It had students from Tulane and Xavier. He said that some of the members were planning acts of violence. "I told the police they should have an FBI agent come over to hear what I had to say."

Creative idea, Ferrie thought.

Amazingly, it worked.

FBI Agent John Quigley visited with Oswald for an hour on Saturday morning. Oswald repeated the Fair Play exaggerations he'd told the police and added that a man named Hidell had ordered him to demonstrate and hand out flyers. Oswald had talked to Hidell several times and received notes from him, he told Quigley, but had never met him

"Who's Hidell?" Ferrie asked.

"He's me, *signor*. It's my alias—Alec J. Hidell. I use if for various things to confuse people. Like when I bought my guns. Bought by *A. Hidell.* Sometimes I put *Doctor* in front of Hidell."

"Hidell because it rhymes with Fidel?'"

"Hadn't thought of that. No, it's much cleverer. Alec was my nickname in Russia. J. Hidell was inspired by *Jekyll and Hyde*. You know, the book about the doctor who was a normal guy but could turn into a violent dark guy by taking a potion. A double personality. I've always kinda felt like I had some Jekyll and Hyde in me—am both a quiet, pretty good guy and, at the same time, can be a guy with a dark side."

"The unexamined life is not worth living."

"The FBI agent left scratching his head." Oswald grinned.

Ferrie put Oswald in a cab home. The wife wasn't going to be happy with his latest escapade, Oswald had said. She didn't like his continual rocking of their American life. She didn't want to go back to the Soviet Union.

Monday morning Ferrie sat in the back of a hearing room in the municipal court building on South Broad. The hearing was routine. Bringuier testified about the events from his perspective. Oswald offered no defense and pleaded guilty. He was fined ten dollars. The Cubans got off scot-free.

WDSU-TV sent a reporter-cameraman to the courthouse. He interviewed Oswald briefly on film outside the courtroom. "I'm a Marxist, not a Communist," Oswald said with determination. This short film clip appeared on the evening news.

Oswald breakfasted again at Thompson's with Ferrie and Martin on Tuesday morning. Banister joined them this time. "Fucking good work," Banister said to Oswald.

"I'm getting into it," Oswald said. "But, guys—I badly need some doubloons." With no job, Oswald was broke.

"Dutz'll drop off a hundred bucks later at your house," Ferrie said. "He's back in town."

"Let's keep this rolling," Banister said. "Lee, you'll be staging the bigger demonstration on Friday. This one should have more impact. Television cameras'll be there for sure. As Jack suggested last week, we're going to hire some guys who look like Cubans to dress up in nice shirts, just like you'll be wearing with your tie, and pass out flyers with you. You'll be the center of attention, though. You'll do the pontificating. It'll be in front of the Camp Street entrance to the Trade Mart at lunchtime."

"You'll be a star!" Ferrie exclaimed.

CHAPTER 34

Oswald, accompanied by Ferrie, found two men hanging around at the Louisiana State Employment Commission's offices at 601 Camp willing to pass out flyers with him, for a fee, pretending they were Fair Play members. "There actually were plenty of takers," Ferrie told Banister later, "given the two dollars we offered. There were only a few, though, who had the clean-cut, serious look we needed. And the dark complexion. One of them's got the un-Cuban name of Charles Steele—he's actually a local guy with olive skin. The other guy's a college-educated exile named Rafi. Don't know his last name."

The two were already dressed in clean, white short-sleeved shirts. Rafi, twenty-four years old, was wearing a tie. Twenty-year-old Charles was tieless but sharp-looking. Oswald's white short-sleeved shirt was tidy, as was his tie. He carried the flyers in a small folder tucked under his left arm, passing out leaflets with his right hand.

Ferrie watched this second Friday demonstration from the other side of Camp Street with Jack Martin, near Ralph Who's Arden Bar. Both Ferrie and Martin had heard dozens of "Who's-on-First' jokes in that Canal Street institution.

This performance was peaceful. With his two new "associates," the Fair Play group *did* look more substantial. Oswald, Charles, and Rafi were polite and respectful, though Charles left after only about fifteen minutes, the un-American goal of the effort finally dawning on him. The pamphleteering was displayed on that evening's WDSU-TV news.

Jack Martin had ensured that radio personality Bill Stuckey was in the crowd. As the demonstration broke up, Martin took Ferrie over to meet Stuckey. "What'd you think, Mr. Stuckey?" Ferrie asked.

"Interesting. *Mucho* interesting. This town is full of anti-Castro folks—lacking, though, in reprobates who actually like Uncle Fidel."

"Bill," Ferrie observed, "your show's getting a little predictable, with one anti-Castro guy after another. Mix it up by having a lefty on like Lee Oswald. You could cross-examine the shit out of him, maybe bring some right-wingers in to debate him."

"Not a bad idea. I like the debate idea, perhaps with the guy who assaulted him. I'd want a counter to this guy's radical bullshit."

"I know Mr. Oswald quite well," Ferrie said. "If you're serious, I can take you over to his shotgun house in the morning to discuss. It's on Magazine, 4905."

"This is a no-brainer," Martin chimed in. "You might want to do a show with Oswald before the debate, one on one. Let him spin out his story uninterrupted by his enemies. Then the debate."

"I'll think about it."

"Our boss Ray Gill heard about Oswald's tussle with the Cuban exiles and mentioned it to your boss Mr. Stern," Ferrie said. "They talked about how good it would be for the media to shine a light on this nut. It'll show how real the Castro threat is to us here in New Orleans. Ray told us Mr. Stern liked the idea."

"Well, as you say, Edgar's the head honcho. I can get Oswald on *Latin Listening Post* tomorrow night with just me. After that, we'll see about a debate. I *would* like to check him out one-on-one tomorrow morning."

||||

Ferrie, Martin, and Stuckey met for a cup of coffee Saturday morning at Crone's Bar at 5101 Magazine, a block and half west of Oswald's small shotgun house.

Ferrie gave Stuckey some background on Oswald, mentioning the Marines and his New Orleans childhood but omitting
the defection to Russia. Ferrie pointed out the store on the next
corner, at Dufossat Street and Magazine, where Oswald frequently strolled to get ice cream, one of his few current activities
outside the house.

"He's a serious guy, Bill," Ferrie said. "Spends most of his
time reading on his front porch. Takes a break to get ice cream
and then goes back to reading."

Ferrie showed Stuckey the way to Oswald's house, and Ferrie
and Martin followed from a distance, staying out of sight.

Oswald's house, 4905, ran parallel to and back from the
street and was fronted by a small courtyard. His place was
actually part of a larger duplex house on the west side, 4907
and 4911, which was positioned close to and facing the street.
Oswald's was attached to the back of the east side of this larger
house, running perpendicular to it, together forming something
of an "L" shape—it sometimes was called a "corner house." This
"corner house" was small, one-story with just two rooms and a
bathroom, and had a screened porch stuck on to the middle of
it providing access to Magazine down three steps leading to a
walkway through the courtyard that went out to a low metal
picket fence edging the sidewalk. Pedestrians on Magazine could
easily see people sitting on the porch.

A narrow driveway bordered the east side of the courtyard.

Though Oswald had been given a heads-up that Stuckey was
coming, he still was half-asleep. He heard the doorbell and trun-
dled out from the main room onto the screened porch, dressed in
fatigue pants and a white T-shirt. He let Stuckey in, gave him
another cup of coffee. They chatted. Stuckey could tell right away
that Oswald was book-smart and well-spoken.

Oswald gave Stuckey some background material on his "philosophy," including two printed Castro speeches and pamphlets
by Jean-Paul Sartre, an existentialist, and Corliss Lamont, a
humanist. Stuckey noticed a copy of Juan José Arévalo's *The
Shark and the Sardines* on Oswald's bookshelf. Stuckey was

well aware of the book. Written in 1961 by a former president of Guatemala, it was more of a political allegory than a philosophical tract. Strongly denouncing American imperialism in Latin America, the book had become required reading in Cuba.

There were blatant anti-Communist books on his shelf as well, including *What We Must Know About Communism*, by Harry and Bonero Overstreet, and *The Berlin Wall*, by Deane and David Heller. He told Stuckey he read all sides.

Surprisingly, a copy of *Portrait of a President*, by William Manchester, was out on the table.

Oswald agreed to meet Stuckey at five o'clock at the WDSU studios in the majestic 1816 Brulatour Mansion on Royal Street, which had the finest courtyard in the Quarter. The Saturday evening interview was soft and easy for Oswald. He gave detailed answers. He'd done his homework.

Was the Fair Play for Cuba Committee part of the American Communist Party? Oswald said that Fair Play had been investigated by Congress, and Congress had concluded that, no, it wasn't associated with the Communist Party.

The Fair Play Committee, Oswald said, was focused on "the narrow point" of Cuba and the belief that America should not intervene in the affairs of sovereign countries. Castro "is not a Russian puppet," he said.

Oswald argued that Castro was a Marxist, not a Communist. He explained that many countries emerging from a "feudal state," like Ghana for example, moved to a Marxist model. This was the stage Castro was in. He was an "experimenter."

In any event, Oswald said, a lot of countries have Marxist or socialist systems. "For that matter, Great Britain has socialized medicine."

However, "there will never be a capitalist regime again in Cuba," Oswald proclaimed.

Oswald waxed on about the definition of democracy, about the true meaning of capitalism, about the nature of revolutions, about the history of the sugar business in Cuba, about

Nicaraguan politics, about the book *The Crime Against Cuba*, and about the black market in the Soviet Union.

Gill, Banister, Ferrie, *and* Oswald were all pleased. Oswald was now squarely on the map as pro-Castro and, if not a pure Commie, a serious and smart lefty.

The debate on WDSU was set up for Monday evening, on a popular radio program called *Conversation Carte Blanche*. Oswald's "nemesis" Carlos Bringuier, along with the right-wing executive vice president of INCA, Ed Butler, were the opponents. The real debate, though, turned out to be between Oswald and the show's hosts, Bill Stuckey and his colleague Bill Slater.

Stuckey and Slater had researched Oswald, with Ed Butler's help, after his Saturday evening appearance on *Latin Listening Post*. They blindsided Oswald with questions about his defection to Russia and his attempt to renounce his US citizenship. They read excerpts from newspaper articles about his move to Russia.

Oswald was thrown for a loop but acknowledged these facts. The hosts then lobbed in razor-sharp questions, including whether his interest in Russia made him a Communist. They also tried to pin Oswald down on how he supported himself there, implying he'd been on the Russian payroll. Maybe was still on its payroll.

Bringuier implied that Oswald agreed with Castro that JFK was a "ruffian" and a "thief." And he declared that Cuba was now a "colony of Russia." Bringuier topped off the event by dramatically issuing a press release after the debate calling for a congressional investigation of Oswald, "a confessed Marxist."

Although Oswald made it through the debate, he'd been roughed up. It didn't really matter to the overall game plan, however. If anything, it painted a picture of a guy who probably was a sneaky Commie lying about his background and who'd actually pledged allegiance to Russia.

Viewing himself as a perfectionist, Oswald was depressed for not performing better. Ferrie agreed to accompany him home. But first Ferrie bought drinks at Oswald's favorite bar, the Napoleon House on Chartres Street in the Quarter. They each had the bar's signature drink, the "Pimm's Cup," a gin-based aperitif mixed with lemonade, 7-Up, and a sliver of cucumber. Oswald's mood softened. Ferrie smoked a cigarette.

From the Napoleon House, Ferrie sprung for a taxi to take the two of them back to Oswald's Magazine Street house.

The pregnant wife and the baby were asleep. Oswald invited Ferrie up to the screened porch for a beer. He came back from the kitchen with two Jax's and a scoped rifle under his arm. He didn't say much but seemed to get calmer as he mindlessly opened and closed the bolt on the rifle, as if he were practicing.

"Got this thing in the mail for $19.95. Or, should I say, A. Hidell got it. From a Jew store in Chicago. Whether I have a constitutional right to a gun or not, it *is* kinda fucked up you can get a deadly rifle by mail order in this country. No way that happens in Russia."

"The gun manufacturers in this great and kind land spend a lot of money to make sure you can easily shoot whomever you want," Ferrie responded.

"God bless them."

"What kind of gun did you get?" Ferrie asked.

"It's from the world-class Italian military," Oswald said sarcastically. "A surplus World War II bolt-action carbine, six-shot clip. Ordnance scope. Pretty accurate at 650 yards. State of the art—designed in the Gay Nineties! It's named after its inventor, Salvatore Carcano—a six-point-five-by-fifty-two-millimeter Carcano."

CHAPTER 35

Ferrie slept in Tuesday morning, a rare event. Dr. Carolyn was already at his apartment when he emerged from his bedroom. Only a few mice still remained.

"I'm about done here," Dr. Carolyn said. "Am heading over to Jefferson Highway in a half hour or so. Dr. Mary's there and wants to see you. Can you go now?"

"My pleasure, Doc."

They took a cab west to the new Ochsner Clinic, where Dr. Mary greeted them. She looked tense. "Dave, we have a volunteer from Angola Penitentiary. They want us there tomorrow."

Ferrie paused. "Yes, ma'am." He paused again. "Dr. Mary, what do you know about him? A dangerous criminal, I assume."

"I assume so. Probably a murderer."

Ferrie paused even longer. "God have mercy on us, ma'am."

Dr. Mary looked at Ferrie. She bowed her head for a few seconds.

"Come to my apartment at ten. I've got one of the clinic's cars. The mental hospital in Jackson's about a two-hour drive, a little north of Baton Rouge. I'll have the test tubes with me. Bring your satchel to carry them in."

"Yes, ma'am," Ferrie said solemnly.

Ferrie stayed home that night. He prayed the Compline—"O God, come to our aid."

He slept fitfully. He was jittery. He had a stabbing headache. He sensed that his blood pressure had skyrocketed.

Ferrie managed to get an early-morning appointment the next day with his doctor Richard Bagnetto. Dr. Bagnetto was treating him for a variety of problems, including chronic high blood pressure and hypothyroidism. That morning his blood pressure indeed was through the roof. Dr. Bagnetto upped Ferrie's dose of chlorothiazide, a relatively new diuretic drug that had proved to be quite effective in lowering blood pressure. The doctor made no adjustments to the dosage of Proloid, which boosted his thyroid hormone level.

Ferrie and Dr. Mary were on US 61 by ten fifteen on Wednesday morning. Since they weren't due in Jackson until 2 p.m., Ferrie talked Dr. Mary into cutting off Route 61 to Highland Road in Old South Baton Rouge for an early lunch at one of his favorite dives—the Cotton Club. Ferrie needed one of the Cotton Club's special Bloody Marys to help steel himself for the sinful act he was about to participate in. She readily agreed.

"I *am* a little peckish," she said.

Owner Louis Constantino greeted Ferrie and welcomed Dr. Mary. He took them to a table as far away as possible from the ringing pinball machines by the restrooms. Ferrie waved at bartender Jo-Jo.

Ferrie had filled Dr. Mary in on the restaurant's signature item, its homemade tartar sauce. It was a Cajun concoction that included relish, pimento olives, green onions, capers, and lemon juice, along with heavy egg mayonnaise. A notch less troubled than Ferrie about the day's venture, she got a large helping of the sauce to accompany her fried shrimp. He ordered crabmeat au gratin to accompany his single Bloody Mary. He only ate a few bites.

The East Louisiana State Hospital for the Insane was a half mile east of the Jackson town center. The facility was a dramatic Greek revival structure dating back to 1854, originally known as the "State Insane Asylum."

Earlier in 1963 the facility had gotten some unwelcome national attention from the famous fashion and fine art photographer Richard Avedon. Avedon took and had published heart-wrenching black-and-white pictures of broken and unkempt mental patients with blank and lifeless-looking faces.

The facility was obviously overcrowded and unsanitary. Avedon's photographs had been widely published, and the hospital was scrambling to improve its conditions and its reputation.

They turned off US 61 at St. Francisville and took Louisiana Route 35 to East Louisiana's main entrance. At the same time, a small convoy was driving the thirty-five miles west from Angola Penitentiary with the prisoner. Dr. Mary had insisted that the procedure be done at the hospital rather than at the prison, in case there were immediate complications that required medical help.

Striding between the solemn white columns at the front of the building, they entered the facility and were met by a hospital administrator in the large lobby. He took them to a smaller, separate facility behind the main building, a medical clinic used to provide routine healthcare for the hospital's employees. It had adequate equipment.

The prisoner was brought into the clinic. He was a thirty-ish, healthy-looking, brown-skinned man. The prisoner was accompanied by two guards.

"What can you tell me about this gentleman?" Dr. Mary asked the administrator, out of the prisoner's earshot.

"He's in good health, as you requested."

"What's he in for?"

"Robbed some Garden District houses. Rich bitches there pressed charges. In for a nickel—five years. Cuban refugee. He was selected, I assume, because he's been a bit of a rabble-rouser in the prison. I was just told to pick him and the guards up and bring them over here."

"He didn't volunteer?"

"I seriously doubt it. Angola isn't exactly a democracy."

Dr. Mary asked the prisoner if he was willing to participate in this experiment.

The prisoner had been told that he was part of a project to test a new version of the polio vaccine. He'd be contributing to society by showing this new vaccine was safe. He may be rewarded, it was suggested to him, with a shorter sentence. In any event, because of the vaccine, he was told, he'd benefit by being forever protected against polio.

Not understanding English, the prisoner just smiled, apparently happy to be out of Angola for an afternoon. All Ferrie's good Spanish could get from the prisoner was, *"Esta todo bien."*

"Ma'am, can we talk in the hallway for a second?" Ferrie's face was ashen.

In a shaky voice, Ferrie said, "This isn't right. The guy's not the worst of the worst. Not a murderer or a rapist. He doesn't seem to be dangerous at all. I can't do this."

"Let's take some deep breaths. We either got lied to or somebody screwed up. We're still doing the right thing, though. Look, there's a good chance this injection won't work. If it does work, remember what we talked about a few weeks ago. We'll be able to kill Castro and save the lives of tens of thousands of innocent people. Have you seen the latest reports of what he's been doing down there?"

"But . . . I don't know, ma'am."

"Dave. We've been given this assignment by some *very* powerful people. Dr. Ochsner told me that it's not only Mr. Marcello watching. His fellow mob bosses around the country are as well. To be crass, my friend, we can probably kiss our asses goodbye if we don't follow through."

"Can you gimme a moment?"

Ferrie walked to a corner, his back to Dr. Mary, made the sign of the cross, and bowed his head. He then recited the first part of the Devine Mercy Chaplet to himself—"O Blood and Water, which gushed forth from the Heart of Jesus as a fountain of Mercy for us, I trust in You."

He came back to Dr. Mary. "All right, ma'am. But I can hear an echoing voice in my head saying, 'Welcome to Hell, Mr. Ferrie.'"

"And probably, 'and you as well Dr. Sherman.'"

Dr. Mary and Ferrie reentered the clinic.

Ferrie's satchel contained two large test tubes. The cancer cells and virus resided in each of the vials, blended together with the centrifuged blood serum and glycol. Chymotrypsin, an enzyme that helps preserve cellular proteins, had also been injected into each test tube through the top.

Ferrie handed her one of the tubes. She began methodically, step by step, to administer the potion.

She removed the cap from the tube and wiped the rubber seal with an alcohol pad. She pulled the syringe plunger out and removed the needle cover. She inserted the syringe needle into the hole that had already been created in the top of the tube. She pushed the plunger of the syringe down, forcing air in rapidly. Turning the tube upside down, she pulled the plunger back. She then pushed the plunger forward very slightly to get rid of a few air bubbles.

For Ferrie, these steps occurred at a funeral pace. With each, he eerily heard the quiet yet chilling ringing of a church bell in his head. The ringing, he thought, sounded like it was emanating from the 1819 Paris-cast bell—*Victoire*—at the haunted St. Louis Cathedral overlooking Jackson Square.

Dr. Mary removed the needle from the vial and injected the prisoner in his cephalic vein. There was a hush, and then the prisoner asked if that was it.

"Yes, sir," Dr. Mary said. "Thank you so much." She was only going to give him one injection. That's all Castro would get.

Ferrie was still hearing the softly clanging church bell in his head.

"We'd appreciate it if you could tell the warden if you have any side effects from the shot, sir," Dr. Mary said to the prisoner. "You'll be brought back here on Monday. We'll be back too, to see how you're doing." The administrator translated Dr. Mary's words.

"Another break from that shithole," the prisoner said in Spanish. "Can't fucking wait."

||||

They climbed into the car. "By Monday—which is what, five days?—the guy'll still be alive, but he may be showing some negative signs," Dr. Mary said.

She was wrong. The prisoner died Friday afternoon, forty-eight hours later, of a galloping cancer.

CHAPTER 36

D
r. Mary visited Ferrie at his apartment a week later.
"I'm sorry, ma'am," Ferrie said softly. "No tea and scones here. I do have chocolate chip cookies."

"Perfect." She took a bite. "You doing okay?"

"Fair to middling. Praying for that poor bastard. But, I *will* say, it's sinking in that we have accomplished the impossible. All that work. Dr. Ochsner and his friends must be pleased."

"We wouldn't be where we are without you. In that spirit, I have a present for you."

Ferrie gently removed the wrapping around what obviously was a book. Expecting a medical book of some sort, he was surprised to see a book by Jean-Paul Sartre, *Being and Nothingness: An Essay on Phenomenological Ontology.*

"Read this. Remarkable. It'll clean out your brain for a while and fill it with grand thoughts. I can't pretend I have my head around all, or even many, of what the recent events mean for me—us—in the grand scheme of things. I do know this book's helped me. You'll find a concept of the 'great human stream' and how to follow that toward an understanding that, while life may seem empty at times, if you just dig deeper you'll see that you make your own life. Or something like that. You'll enjoy trying to figure out what he's saying."

"Sounds above my limited capabilities, but I'll give it a ride. Thank you, ma'am."

They chatted for a while about a range of things other than the cancer project. They talked extensively about Martin Luther King's march on Washington, which had just occurred. That spectacle likely would spur on the inexorable rush of the civil rights movement toward New Orleans. Just five hours away, the effort to desegregate the Birmingham schools was being met by violent opposition. The first day of school there had been canceled because of safety concerns. National States Rights Party mobs were roaming the city, and the KKK had exploded a bomb at the home of an NAACP lawyer.

Black leaders in New Orleans had been working nonviolently to desegregate lunch counters on Canal Street, largely unsuccessfully. But they were now talking about ratcheting up their efforts, like the blacks in Birmingham had done. Violent opposition was as sure to follow as night follows day.

"We already have some unhappy white folks in this town," Ferrie said. "They've been pissed ever since that little Negro girl with the pigtails was forced into the grade school over in St. Claude a few years ago."

"Amazingly tough little girl."

"She did stand up to those crackers over there. Her first name's stuck with me—*Ruby*. God bless her. Dr. Mary, I don't get the hatred against negroes, they're just people. But the KKK's inciting the racists with fear-mongering and paranoia. Like Woody Guthrie sang years ago, racists like to stir up the 'bloodpot of human hearts.'"

"People just get set in their ways, I guess. Only think about themselves. Sad."

They talked for a while about other issues of the day, including the dangers bubbling in South Vietnam. The government there had just declared martial law as North Vietnam was knocking on the door of Saigon, and Buddhist monks were desperately protesting religious discrimination by the South Vietnamese government, sometimes through self-immolation.

Dr. Mary then turned to her personal life. "I'm going to escape for a little while. Three weeks."

"Probably a good idea. Where to?"

"England. I need to get away. Decompress."

"Where does that leave our project?"

"This trip's not all play. I'm doing a little work first. There's a linear particle accelerator in England, just outside of Oxford. It's exactly like the one we have in New Orleans. I've gotten permission to use that accelerator for a few days. I'm going to try to make a few refinements to our product there.

"And *then*," she continued, "I decompress. I've booked into a lovely country inn. Not your style—an old hotel in the Cotswolds, in a little old English town with the unlikely small-town name of Broadway."

"No offense, but that sounds terrible, ma'am. What will you do there?"

"Stroll around town. Go to the Horse & Hound pub. Hike. You can hike several miles to a 150-year-old tower. And I'm going to sit in the lobby and the courtyard and read mindless James Bond books. England seems like a good place to read *On Her Majesty's Secret Service*."

\\\\\

Ferrie was too hyper to spend a week or two relaxing. And, in any event, he needed to turn his attention back to his work with Gill and Banister.

Banister was now focusing seriously on the idea of having Oswald attempt to defect to Cuba. This futile effort would be observed by various agencies of the United States and of state and foreign governments and by pro- and anti-Castro groups.

As with Oswald's street demonstrations, Ferrie and Jack Martin were put in charge of the Cuba defection strategy. The general plan was to get Oswald to Mexico City and have him try to get to Cuba from there. Mexico continued to have good diplomatic relations with both Cuba and Russia.

Ferrie drove out to Metairie one pleasant early September morning. He, Gill, and Banister had coffee outside by the murky Town and Country Motel pool.

"I've told him to get his wife and kid back to Dallas," Ferrie said. "Her friend in Irving is coming to get her. He needs a break from the wife."

"And we need his time," Banister said.

"Mexico City'll be time-consuming," Ferrie said.

"We need Oswald to run around all over Mexico City for a week," Banister said. "To Mexican government agencies, the Soviet and Cuban embassies, Cuban groups. He needs to pester the shit out of the whole city, yapping about his love for Fidel. Looking forward to some details from you and Martin."

"Aye, aye."

"Now listen up, hombre. If we are called on to get Kennedy," Gill announced, "Oswald *will* be the guy.

"And Marcello agrees. He'd actually heard about Oswald before I spoke with him. Sam Termine, the bodyguard, of all people, talked about him. Weirdly, Termine used to party around with Oswald's mother eight, nine years ago. For whatever reason, I don't want to know, he really liked her. He met Oswald then and then heard about it when Oswald came back to town recently after his world travels. When Termine learned about Oswald spouting Commie bullshit down by the USS *Wasp* in July, he got pretty interested in figuring this guy out. He's a former cop, he checked with the NOPD. They said Oswald was peculiar but seemed pretty smart.

"Termine suggested to Marcello that we should keep an eye on him, mentioned his Marine and Russia background, said the kid was obviously pretty brazen. The Little Man was all in when I mentioned using Oswald in the 'JFK Affair.'"

"Small fucking world," Ferrie said.

"Particularly after his upcoming Mexico adventure," Gill continued, "he'll be the poster child for a wild and crazy Commie. And an America-hater. If he gets caught—"

"Which he will," Banister interrupted. "Unlike Sergio, Oswald just *looks* like a murderer. Straight out of central casting."

"Okay. *When* he gets caught, the FBI will see a political motive, not a mob hit."

"Sounds simple enough," Ferrie said.

"I'm going to de-simplify it for you," Gill continued. "Let's say Oswald gets tagged as JFK's sole killer. That's what we want, of course. A Commie or just a loon. J. Edgar will buy that, nice and uncomplicated. And the public will buy it too—for a while. We're concerned, though, that after a spell, future investigators, professional and amateur, will come out of the woodwork. You know it's going to happen. Many of them just won't believe the great JFK was taken down by one lonely, fucked-up kook. They'll look for a plot. A conspiracy."

"Probably," Ferrie said.

"Mr. Marcello's no dummy," Banister said. "And he doesn't take chances. Dave, he's ordered us to make sure that if folks see a conspiracy in the future, they'll see a Commie conspiracy. Or a CIA one. Maybe CIA along with LBJ, or along with some wingnuts. Anything but a *mob* conspiracy."

"There's a challenge," Ferrie said.

"Yeah, a little tricky," Gill said. "The best idea we've had is to make it look like someone created a *second* Oswald, who was running around before the murder—intentionally to confuse people. This is a common spook tactic, the KGB and CIA do it all the time. They create a doppelgänger for the actual bad guy. They're good at obfuscation. Who did what? This is *not* a typical mob tactic. People don't think we're that smart."

"We're going to try to add a layer of mystery to Oswald that'll have investigators scratching their heads in the future," Banister said.

"The messier and more complicated he looks," Gill said, "the more they'll look at government operators pulling the strings. Not us. We're simpletons. We just shoot people in the face a bunch of times."

"Can't wait to hear these details," Ferrie said.

The three men continued to talk by the pool. They could talk freely because there was nobody around.

"Martin knows about the doppelgänger plan?" Ferrie asked.

"As much as you do," Gill said. "But obviously nothing about the 'JFK Affair.' In his mind, the Oswald-double scheme is a further step in shaping him for unknown future uses."

Gill gave Ferrie a week to knock around Mexico ideas with Martin. Gill and Banister would focus on the doppelgänger plan, working Arcacha Smith into the thinking. And then final planning would occur on September 24. The team—including Oswald, Martin, and Arcacha Smith—would meet all day on that Tuesday at the International House at 221 Camp.

Ferrie would be doing some flying as part of this venture, Gill told him.

It was Ferrie's job before the twenty-fourth, Gill instructed, to monitor Oswald, to make sure his wife leaves town, and to get him out of his house, all packed up, for the group meetings and the Mexico trip.

\\\\

The next day Ferrie swung by the shotgun house. He directed Oswald to leave his apartment by Monday evening and bus over to 221 Camp. He should plan to spend that night and the next day there. He would then be hitting the road Wednesday morning.

CHAPTER 37

Sam Giancana woke early, as usual, on the morning of Saturday, September 14. He was served a cup of coffee and a copy of the *Chicago Tribune* by his long-time housekeeper Ann DiPersio, caretaker Joe's wife. He was anxious to see the paper. He'd been given a heads-up about what was in it, and there it was on page 6 of Section 1— "Sinatra Silent On Whether He Knows Giancana." Giancana roared with laughter.

"Frank Sinatra today refused to say whether he knows Sam (Mooney) Giancana, Chicago hoodlum whom he was reported to have entertained recently at his Cal-Neva resort hotel in Nevada."

That was a fun fucking trip to Lake Tahoe, Giancana thought. He'd been there, even though he'd been banned from the State of Nevada, to see Sinatra and to spend some time with a long-time lover, the singer Phyllis McGuire. She was the youngest and sexiest of the harmonious McGuire Sisters, who had a huge hit in 1958, "Sugartime."

Giancana was amused by the article. He was, in fact, part owner of the magical Cal-Neva Resort, which straddled the border between Nevada and California at the top of Lake Tahoe. Sinatra had the controlling interest.

Cal-Neva attracted Hollywood stars, politicians, gangsters, and other rich folks to gamble and, frequently, to be entertained by various members of the Rat Pack, including Sinatra.

Sinatra had cleverly built luxurious underground tunnels— carpeted and lined with bricks—between some of the bungalows to attract movers and shakers who wanted to visit friends there who were not their spouses. The man could visit the lady's bungalow, for example, without being seen.

JFK had used the Cal-Neva tunnels on a number of occasions to spend private time with the sybaritic actress Marilyn Monroe.

Monroe was so attached to the Cal-Neva that, during the last weekend of July 1962, she tried unsuccessfully to kill herself there in Bungalow 52. Just a few days later, she successfully did so in Los Angeles.

On his recent visit to Lake Tahoe, Giancana had enjoyed spending time again with Sinatra. He'd asked Sinatra about Judy. Had he been in touch with her? "Radio silence," Sinatra responded. Giancana invariably got misty-eyed when he thought about Judy.

Giancana rifled through the rest of the paper. Unlike most days, this day's paper was chock full of news of interest to him. Henry "Scoop" Jackson, a hawkish Democratic Senator from the State of Washington, had announced his support for JFK's test ban treaty with the Russians. With Jackson's support, the treaty now looked like a lock. Another article reported that JFK had announced on Friday that he'd be addressing the United Nations for the first time in two years the following Friday to talk about world peace. *Chickenshit.* JFK was hoping the Senate would ratify the Russia treaty before his speech, the article said.

The paper had an article on the 1964 presidential election, "Goldwater Says G.O.P. Can Beat Kennedy," featuring a speech in Oklahoma by Barry Goldwater. "I say to you that the South today offers the Republican Party one of its most important advantages in many decades."

This is exactly what JFK is worried about," Giancana muttered to himself.

The paper also reported on a meeting between JFK's brother Ted and the wife of South Vietnam's President Diem's brother Nhu. She pleaded her country's case to the president's brother. The JFK administration, Giancana believed, had been slow to support South Vietnam's fight against Communism. *Just like Cuba.*

He turned to the movie page. He was thinking of seeing if his daughter Antoinette would go to the movies with him that evening. The movie choice was tough—there were several good ones. A new movie called *The Great Escape*, starring Steve McQueen as a POW in Germany during World War II, sounded interesting. And there was *How the West Was Won* and *The Thrill of It All*. *Johnny Cool*, with Sinatra's fellow Rat Packer Sammy Davis Jr., sounded up Giancana's alley. The lead character was described as "The Czar of International Mobsterism." But the clear winner for Giancana was *Cleopatra*. He had heard Elizabeth Taylor's splendid nectarine-shaped backside was on naked display in this blockbuster.

Not in the *Tribune*, and not in many papers outside of Texas that day, was news of the White House's official announcement the day before—Friday the thirteenth—that JFK would be traveling to Texas in late November. The omission of this announcement was of no moment to Giancana. He already was well aware of the president's plans for Texas, though he didn't expect JFK to be alive to take the trip.

CHAPTER 38

Eight days before September 25—D-Day for both the Mexico City and doppelgänger launches—Ferrie took the Napoleon Avenue bus south to Magazine and strolled west to 4905 to check on Oswald. He was on his front screened porch shirtless. Several books were stacked on a small outdoor table stand. The heat and humidity had returned.

"Hey comrade, everything good?" Ferrie asked.

Before Oswald could answer, his wife opened the front screen door and stepped on the porch. She looked to be eight months pregnant. Ferrie was surprised to see her—he thought she'd left town.

"This is my wife. Marina Nikolayevna Oswald."

She is *pretty*, Ferrie thought.

"Hello," she said with a heavy Russian accent. "Good to meet you." Marina then angrily barked something toward her husband in Russian. Oswald, who was fluent in Russian, just glared at her. She went back in the house.

"I thought she'd be gone by now," Ferrie said. "The clock's ticking."

"Her friend Ruth'll be here Thursday or Friday to take her back to Dallas. She'll probably wanna stay a day or two. I'll make sure they leave by Monday."

Ferrie took Oswald on the Magazine Street bus into the city to the Mexican consulate to get a tourist card. "What should I put down as my occupation?" Oswald asked Ferrie.

"How about 'spy'?" Ferrie joked. "Doesn't matter. Put 'photographer.'"

"Address?"

"Don't use your real address, make something up—640 Rampart, how about that? If they were ever to check it out, they'd see there's no such thing as 640 Rampart."

Armed with tourist card No. 24085, Oswald bussed back home by himself. Ferrie went into the Quarter.

Ruth and her kids arrived in New Orleans that Friday, parking her 1955 Chevrolet Bel Air station wagon in the narrow driveway extending back to Oswald's shotgun house. Oswald cheerfully helped Marina pack up and load the car over the weekend, and Marina, the little girl, and Ruth left New Orleans Monday morning. Early that evening, as instructed by Ferrie, Oswald jumped on a Magazine Street bus toward town, got off at Gravier Street, and walked to the International House.

"Try to make sure some neighbors see you leaving with the suitcases and getting on the bus," Ferrie had said to Oswald. "They'll assume you left town on Monday evening for parts unknown, should anybody ask in the future."

Oswald spent a quiet Monday night at the International House in one of its guest rooms.

Tuesday morning Ferrie drove the two-and-a-half miles to the Newman Building and parked in one of Banister's parking places along Lafayette Street. He walked to the International House.

Toward the end of World War II, a prominent businessman named Archie Jewell, looking to develop New Orleans as the country's major business hub for Latin America, organized the first "world trade center" in the United States. The International House. Its slogan—*dedicated to world peace, trade and understanding*—was written by Lindy Boggs, the feisty wife of local congressman Hale Boggs. The organization took over and remodeled a twelve-story Beaux-Arts building constructed in 1906 to house the Canal Louisiana Bank and Trust, one of the premier New Orleans financial institutions of the first half of the twentieth century. The address was 221 Camp, near the International Trade Mart, three blocks from Ferrie's parked car.

During the remodeling of the building, the front entrance was moved from Camp to Gravier Street.

One of the early presidents of the International House was Dr. Alton Ochsner.

Gill, Banister, Ferrie, Martin, and Oswald spent that Tuesday on the second floor of the International House in a conference room. Sergio Arcacha Smith had flown in and was there as well. He met Oswald for the first time.

The subject of the meeting was limited to the Mexico trip and the doppelgänger project. The 'JFK Affair' would be discussed with Oswald much later, without Martin.

Oswald was to arrive in Mexico City by bus on Friday morning. First, though, there'd be a whirlwind of multiple movements, feints, and deceptions that should flummox future investigators. *There had to be a second Oswald*, some would suppose. Martin would play this apparent second Oswald. The real Oswald and Martin would be in different places at the same time. They each would engage in activities witnesses should remember.

The coup de grâce of this plan would be to have the second Oswald meet with a prominent anti-Castro activist in Dallas at the same time the real Oswald was hustling off to Mexico. The activist Silvia Odio was a well-connected and wildly attractive Cuban exile. Arcacha Smith would be with Martin for this encounter.

The trickery would begin from the get-go. A ticket had been purchased on Trailways bus number 5121, leaving the station on Tulane Avenue on Wednesday at 12:20 p.m. for Houston. The real Oswald, however, would not be the passenger. Instead, Martin would be standing in for him on the bus. And he'd pick up Oswald's unemployment check, pretending to be the man, before boarding the bus.

Martin had cut his hair short. He'd wear a white T-shirt and camouflage pants. He was about the same size as Oswald. Though nowhere near the spitting image of Oswald, Martin's slightly altered looks would be close enough, particularly in the cloudy memories of his fellow bus travelers in the future.

Instead of taking a bus to Texas, Oswald and Ferrie would rise early at the International House on Wednesday morning and be driven down to the Houma-Terrebonne Airport—the blimp airport. They wouldn't be going to Houston, though. Their first stop would be Austin, where the real Oswald would be seen at the same time his doppelgänger would be seen on the bus from New Orleans.

Marcello's lieutenants had arranged for the use of a de Havilland Dove airplane owned by the oil services company Schlumberger, the owner of the Houma storage shed Ferrie and Arcacha Smith raided in 1961. Schlumberger had suspected the mob was involved in that raid but continued to allow Marcello, an important ally, access to the Dove.

Transporting Oswald on a private aircraft would make the trip impossible for future investigators to detect.

The Dove airplane was a workhorse post-war British twin-piston monoplane, fitted with two 340-horsepower engines. It had a range of almost nine hundred miles. The version Ferrie and Oswald would use had been designed to carry eight passengers plus a pilot and copilot. Because of its industrial use, this particular Dove had had four of the passenger seats removed to provide more room for cargo, not that Ferrie and Oswald needed the room.

Gill, Banister, Ferrie, Martin, Arcacha Smith, and Oswald continued to review the plans at the International House until late afternoon on Tuesday—they all would be staying in guest rooms there that evening.

Believing all was square as dusk began to fall, Banister proposed getting out of the building, taking a walk, and having a nice meal. They walked down the elegant marble staircase into the building's grand hall, paneled with Honduran mahogany, exited onto Gravier and strolled into the Quarter on Royal. A left and a right brought them to Galatoire's, a New Orleans fixture for sixty years on Bourbon Street. Oswald had walked past Galatoire's a thousand times over the years without once thinking he'd ever be inside.

Knowing full well about Gill's close connection to Marcello, Justin Galatoire offered dinner on the house. Accordingly, the group ordered heartily. Oswald went all in with the Oysters Rockefeller, turtle soup, and crabmeat ravigote, plus a side of onion rings. And bread pudding for dessert. He'd been told that he had to live cheaply in Mexico for appearances' sake, so he took advantage of this feast.

The dinner conversation was made more vigorous by the news that JFK's test ban treaty with Russia had been ratified by the US Senate. Eighty votes for, nineteen against.

As planned, Ferrie and Oswald lifted off from Houma early in the morning on the twenty-fifth. They flew straight over Houston, where Martin—the other Oswald—was going later in the day. They continued on to Robert Mueller Municipal Airport, just northeast of downtown Austin.

"Let's go over the Austin plan one last time," Ferrie said before deplaning. "Martin's on his way to Houston as Oswald Number Two. You, Oswald Number One, need to be seen and remembered here in Austin at the same time Oswald Number Two's en route to Houston. Your first stop'll be LBJ's Austin office on Congress Avenue in the Littlefield Building.

"Littlefield's an historic place, by the by," Ferrie continued. "When it was built fifty years ago, it was one of the tallest buildings in the United States. Built by a guy who fought at the Battle of Shiloh."

"You're full of useless information. Look, Professor, I fucking know what to do. I present myself at LBJ's front desk and drop off my letter asking for the okay to travel to Cuba."

"Here's some less useless information for you—LBJ's actually in the area today. At his cowboy ranch with a couple of cracker congressmen. They're spending tomorrow, get this, shopping for cows! You'd think they'd have something more productive to do back in Washington, like skimming budget money or going whoring with lobbyists."

"Maybe he'll hear about my visit."

"Doubt it. You're not famous—not yet, anyway."

"We then go to Governor Connally's office at the Texas Capitol," Oswald said. "The letter we drop off there will ask for his help in getting my dishonorable discharge from the Marines changed to honorable."

"You got it."

꠸꠸

The first two stops in Austin went as planned.

After leaving the Capitol complex, the two men took a long walk south through town and over the river to the orange-themed Trek Cafe on South Congress, *"Open 24 Hours,"* for a couple of cups of coffee and a bite of lunch. They made sure their waitress, who was wearing Woolworth rhinestone diamond earrings and a name tag saying "Florence," remembered Oswald by having him send his coffee back for supposedly having a hair floating in it.

Then the two walked back across the river to Seventh and Colorado to the Austin office of the Selective Service. It had reopened after lunch.

"Who can I talk to about my military status?" Oswald loudly asked a guy named Jesse at the front desk.

"What exactly are you looking for?" Jesse asked.

"The Marines screwed me when I left. Gave me a dishonorable discharge. There was *no* basis for that—check the records. One senior guy was pissed at me because I said Negroes should have rights. That's it. I gotta get the dishonorable thing removed. I can't get a good job, can't get a decent loan. It's crushing me, man."

"Okay. I hear you. Let me get Mrs. Dannelly. She's in today."

Lee Dannelly was the Assistant Chief of the office.

"How can I help you, sir?" Mrs. Dannelly asked.

"As I told Jesse, the Marines gave me a dishonorable discharge. For no reason. The guy who made the decision didn't like my politics, so he fucked me."

"Language," Mrs. Dannelly said.

"Oh, sorry. Excuse me, ma'am."

Good move, Ferrie thought. She'll remember Oswald.

"It's like there's a scarlet letter on my chest when I apply for anything. I need to get it changed."

"Okay, sir. What's your name?"

"Harvey Oswald," he fibbed. "I just left a request with Governor Connally to get an honorable discharge, but I know this won't get very far on his radar screen. He's probably cow-shopping with LBJ right now anyway."

"He's a good man," Mrs. Dannelly said. "But neither he nor I can help you. You need to contact headquarters in DC. I'll give you the forms to send in. You'll have to get some affidavits. Read the instructions."

"Are you absolutely sure? I really need this as soon as possible."

"It's protocol, sir. Send the forms in right away. They'll get on it in DC."

"All right. Thanks. And sorry about the bad language."

Ferrie and Oswald hightailed it back to Mueller Airport. They had two more stops before the end of the evening.

The 150-mile flight to Dallas took about forty minutes. They were met by Jack Ruby at Red Bird Airport in Oak Cliff. Ruby joined them for a quick cup of coffee at Casa Blanca in the airport.

The plan for the Dallas leg was for Ruby and Oswald to be seen together with some mob guys in a public place.

Ruby had been told that Ferrie was just passing through Dallas and Houston to get an update on Marcello's Texas operations. Oswald was with Ferrie, Ruby understood, because Marcello was doing a favor for Dutz Murret to try to get Oswald a job somewhere in the Texas organization. Dutz had asked that Ferrie take him with him to meet Joe Civello and Joe Campisi and see if they liked him. Ruby had no reason to question the story, though he didn't think much of Oswald.

Ferrie, Ruby, and Oswald drove to the Egyptian Lounge, which was just north of Red Bird. Owner Joseph Campisi greeted them. He took them to a table where the big boss Civello sat drinking a dirty dry gin martini with a protruding cucumber.

Oswald was able to be his regular anti-Castro self at this dinner. All present were committed to ridding Cuba of the Commies and returning gambling and pricey hookers to Havana. Civello and Campisi were not aware of the "JFK Affair" that had emerged from the Grand Isle meetings but, as Ferrie knew from past conversations, they clearly bore homicidal feelings toward JFK.

The dinner conversation indeed revolved largely around JFK—his betrayals, including his continued pursuit of Marcello and other members of the mob, his botching of the Bay of Pigs, and his subsequent kowtowing to Russia and Cuba. And his civil rights attack on the South.

After dinner Ruby drove Ferrie and Oswald back to Red Bird Airport. They lifted off and headed to Houston.

"Martin should arrive in Houston on the bus just before eleven," Ferrie said to Oswald during the flight. "We're going to have him call a big-time socialist who lives in Houston and ask for a meeting. We know the guy's out of the country, so they won't actually connect, but his wife might remember the call. Martin'll then spend the night at the Sam Houston Hotel, just up San Jacinto from the bus station. I got a room there too."

They landed at Houston Municipal mid-evening. Sergio Arcacha Smith was waiting for them at the airport, which was southeast of the city. Arcacha Smith had flown back to Houston from New Orleans earlier in the day.

The three drove into the city center. Oswald's bus to Laredo wasn't scheduled to leave until just after 2 a.m., so they had plenty of time for dinner. Arcacha Smith took them to Leon's Lounge on McGowen Street in mid-town, the oldest bar in Houston. The sign protruding out over Leon's entryway promised "BEER-POOL-SHUFFLEBOARD." A red London phone booth rested confusingly out front.

They sat at a booth and ordered beers. Lone Stars.

||||

Sucking down his beer, Ferrie said, "Thank you, Jesus. Long fucking day. Right, Alek?"

Oswald just nodded.

Ignoring the Alek reference, Arcacha Smith got down to business. "I'm meeting Martin tomorrow morning at the Sam Houston coffee shop. My new Cuban *bonco* Miguel Cruz will be with me. Remember him? He's one of the guys who went to jail with Bringuier on the day that made you famous in New Orleans, Lee. He needed a job, and I've given him some work with me in Houston. That Rafi guy from your second performance wanted a job too, but I declined. He's kind of a weird dick.

"I'll drive with Martin and Cruz to Dallas in my Impala," Arcacha Smith continued. "We'll check into the Cabana and then go over to Silvia Odio's place. We know she's in town. *And we know her sister's staying with her now*—provides another witness."

Silvia Odio was born in Cuba in 1937. Her wealthy father Almador was arrested and imprisoned in Cuba in 1960 for harboring an attempted conspirator against Castro. Silvia and her sister Annie fled to Miami and, from there, settled in Ponce, on the underbelly of Puerto Rico. She was comfortable in the United States, having gone to boarding school in Philadelphia.

In Puerto Rico Odio became an activist against Castro, motivated by her father's imprisonment. She worked with Castro's former minister of public works, then exiled in Puerto Rico, to form the *Junta Revolucionaria Cubana*—"JURE."

Odio moved to Magellan Circle in northeast Dallas, near White Rock Lake, in the spring of 1963. She worked energetically on JURE activities in Dallas and was promoted within the organization. She quickly gained stature in the broader Dallas anti-Castro community.

Arcacha Smith was in charge of the Odio plan. He had identified Odio a few weeks previously and recommended that she'd be a good anti-Castro witness for the "second" Oswald in Dallas. Odio—and, just by coincidence, her sister Annie—would observe Oswald Number Two up close and personal that Thursday evening. At the same time, the real Oswald would be riding a bus some four hundred miles away, around Laredo, on his way to Mexico City.

"What's the game plan for Odio?" Oswald asked Arcacha Smith.

"We'll have Martin looking as much like you, Lee, as we can. He'll have a little stubble on his face. Will smirk a lot."

"I smirk?"

"Does the Tin Man have a sheet-metal cock?" Ferrie asked.

"Huh?" Oswald's forehead crinkled.

"Miguel and I'll grease up our hair so we look more Mexican," Arcacha Smith said. "I'll lead the encounter and call myself 'Leopoldo'—will tell her we've joined JURE and want to see some action.

"Naturally," Arcacha Smith continued, "she'll wonder about the American guy. We'll introduce Martin as a fellow anti-Communist, a former Marine who's ready to fight. His name, we'll say, is *'Leon'* Oswald. We'll say the name several times. Later on folks might see our use of the name 'Leon' instead of 'Lee' as some kind of planned subterfuge."

"Very subtle." Ferrie grinned. "Inspired by the name of this joint?"

"Serendipity.

"We're going to repeat several times the fact that 'Leon' was a Marine. Martin's not going to say much. In fact, I bet he'll be gobsmacked by Odio's looks. But she'll remember meeting a white, smirky guy named Oswald."

"What *will* my doppelgänger say?" Oswald said.

"Just *'hola'* and 'happy to help,' nothing much more than that. We don't want him to make *too* much of an impression. If he did, Odio and Annie might realize later on that he wasn't the real Oswald."

"What are *you* going to say to her, Sergio?" Ferrie asked.

"That we want to help, we're members of her group, Castro has to go. Blah, blah, blah. I'm going to tell her that we're about to head to Miami. Is there anything we can do for her down there? I'll tell her we'll be back in Dallas soon and I'll call her. For my encore, I'm then going to call her on Friday, identify myself as 'Leopoldo,' and ask her what she thought of 'Leon.'

"I'll tell her on that call that Leon could be quite useful to the cause. A white American, ex-military guy can do things Cubans can't get away with. I'll make a big to-do that Leon is kind of loco and believes that if Cubans had any guts, they would've killed JFK after he tanked the Bay of Pigs."

"Wish I could be with you, sounds like fun," Ferrie said.

CHAPTER 39

The crowd at Leon's Lounge was beginning to thin out. Ferrie turned to Oswald and reviewed his next steps.

"It'll be ten, eleven hours to Laredo. Chat up some people on the bus. Tell them what you're doing, trying to get to Cuba through Mexico City."

"Before you cross the border," Arcacha Smith said, "you'll have a little time in Laredo—a charming little taste of Mexico in America. Get some posole. And go see the old San Agustin Cathedral. It's right there by the plaza. It'll make you believe in God. Man, it's something."

"Then you'll walk over the Rio Grande bridge to Nuevo Laredo and check through Mexican immigration," Ferrie continued. "It's a shame you won't have time to go to *La Zona*, Lee. 'Boy's Town.' *Anything* goes there, and I mean *anything*. Or to the Cadillac Bar—one of the most famous bars in North America. As *you* may say, it's epic. And, after the Sazerac Bar, it has the best Ramos gin fizzes on the planet. Maybe next time."

"The bus to Mexico City from Nuevo Laredo leaves at two fifteen in the afternoon. The tickets're in your satchel. The bus should be easy to find. Make a note that it's the Flecha Roja bus company, the only overnight bus to Mexico City. Number 516, $5.71."

"I got all of this down," Lee said. "I'm no retard."

"That remains to be seen," Ferrie joked. "I'm just being careful. Your Mexican bus'll come into the Flecha Roja terminal in the morning. Your hotel's close by, on the other side of a boulevard called Avenida Insurgentes and then south a block and a half. You can walk. The Hotel del Comercio, Calle Sahagún 19. I heard it's in a sketchy area, not too many Americans around, but it's cheap—$1.28 a night. You pay on a daily basis, in advance."

"Sí, señor."

"You'll be tired that morning," Ferrie continued. "But you need to leave your bag and go right away to the Cuban embassy on Calle Francisco Márquez, a couple miles south. It's in the same compound as the Soviet embassy. The lady who'll greet you will be a key person for you in Mexico. As the notes I made for you say, her name is Silvia Duran. She's from an important Mexico City family, serves as the secretary to the Cuban consul, a noxious former architect named Eusebio Azcue. The first thing you tell her will be a falsehood."

"One of my fortes."

"Tell her a guy named 'El Mexicano' arranged your trip and actually rode down to Mexico City with you."

"Who the Jesus is 'El Mexicano'?"

"You're going to tell her you don't know who he really is. Just that he's a Castro guy. Believe me, though, she'll know who he is."

"Who *is* he?"

"Just know he's a former Castro military captain, now a Cuban agent, living in Miami. His first name is Francisco, but he usually goes by Nicolas in the United States. He's working with Castro's former air force head in Miami to create mischief. The Cubans in Mexico City might pay more attention to you if they think 'El Mexicano' is supporting you."

"Weird that Castro's agent Francisco is a Mexican."

"He's actually Puerto Rican. Funny world.

"Then show Duran your packet of Commie shit," Ferrie continued, "like your Fair Play card and some clippings of your street shows in New Orleans. Tell her you want to get to Cuba by Monday. Make her feel sympathetic to you, try to make a connection. Our sources down there say she's a flirtatious, outgoing person—you should like her. About your age. That's not to say she's going to let you go to Cuba. I'm sure she's going to tell you that you need a Soviet visa to get into Cuba."

"When can I sleep?" Oswald asked.

"Not till later. After seeing Duran, you gotta go see the Russians, just up Calle Francisco Marquez. Ring the doorbell. When they let you in, make an impression. Give them your Russia story. *Demand* a visa, Lee. Pound your fist and *demand* one. They'll be a little taken aback—they don't get too many Americans wanting a Russia visa, particularly one who's actually lived in Russia. They'll probably have their main KGB guy deal with you. Kostikov. They'll say they need to check with Moscow."

"Then I can sleep?"

"Yep. But on Saturday you gotta go back to see the Russkies. They'll turn you down for a visa. Moscow would have checked your file by then and seen that you defected there and then defected back. They won't take a chance that you're either an undercover agent for the CIA or some other spook agency. Or you're just a crazy fuck.

"Then go back over to the Cuban embassy and make a ruckus, act desperate," Ferrie continued. "See the consul if you can."

"I'd love to be with you, Lee," Arcacha Smith said. "I'd slap that guy around."

"You may or may not see Azcue," Ferrie said, "but you really need to keep chatting Duran up."

"Another forte of mine," Oswald said sarcastically.

"It'll be a challenge for you, I get it. It'd be great, though, if you could get her interested in your plight.

"Call the Russkies several times on Sunday, see if you can reach somebody to keep pleading your case. Visit them again on Monday."

"Am I getting hardship pay?"

"One last thing, Lee," Ferrie said, ignoring the rhetorical question. "The CIA's man in Mexico almost certainly'll be on to you—he's always watching Kostikov, who's a really dangerous guy. Kostikov's been slipping into the country at San Diego. Not sure why.

"You won't even notice the CIA guy, Phillips. He's like a ghost, just blends in the background of things. Looks like an everyday guy, like Hugh Beaumont."

"I'm sure that reference flew miles over Lee's head," Arcacha-Smith said.

"Ha! I was looking in his eyes for some recognition. But—nothing. We need to buy him a TV so he can watch the Cleaver family, show him how a normal family acts."

"Get on with it," Oswald, growing annoyed, said.

"Just know that this average-looking guy is a player. He's the CIA guy who put Alpha 66 together—telling the exiles his name was Bishop. Before that, he was fucking undercover in Cuba during Castro's entire first year. He knows all kinds of shit.

"We don't think he's on to your charade in Mexico, but who knows with this guy? Here's the thing—if he were to contact you for some reason, don't get nervy. Just stick with the same story you're going to give Duran, that you're *simpatico* with Castro's revolution and you want to live there. He may not believe you. Doesn't matter—one way or another, you'll be in the CIA's records, which is a good thing.

"After your Monday visit to the Russian embassy," Ferrie continued, "you'll have some play time. Hit up Duran some more, she might really be feeling sorry for you by then, might invite you to one of her constant social events. Most of the Cuban community in Mexico City shows up to her parties."

"She has a lot of dance parties the Cuban exiles come to, including even Azcue," Arcacha Smith said. "Weirdly, she likes to throw 'twist' parties."

"'Twist' party?" Oswald asked.

"You really are quite a party guy," Arcacha Smith said. "Hey, you'll know it when you see it. *And* when you hear Chubby Checker singing."

"Chubby who?"

"*Come on baby*—be on red alert for those words. Listen to the opening notes. B-A-E," Ferrie advised. Ferrie hummed the notes.

"One more thing we picked up about Duran," Ferrie continued. "She's been having an affair with Castro's ambassador to the United Nations. This guy used to be the ambassador to Mexico. If we're lucky, she might tell him about a crazy but sad American named Oswald who was trying to get to Cuba. He'd remember something rare like that."

"I don't see how I get to know Duran," Oswald asked.

"This is a tall order for you," Ferrie said. "I know. But be charming. Ask her to lunch. There's a chain restaurant nearby called Sanborns. Offer that up, tell her you don't know anybody in the city and you'd appreciate it. They speak English at Sanborns."

"Hey, I'll try. Maybe I need some social lessons."

"We'd need a few years for that," Arcacha Smith joked.

"Just give it a go," Ferrie said.

"Duran has a particular friend you should try to meet," Arcacha Smith said. "A loud-mouthed Mexican woman writer named Elena Garro. Garro's an intellectual, but, for some reason, she likes Duran's twist parties. She's very well known in Mexico. Her recent novel, which I've read by the way, is the talk of Mexico City right now. *Los Recuerdos del Porvenir*—'Memories of the Future.'"

"I'll read it on the bus," Oswald said sarcastically.

"Garro used to be married to a famous poet who's now the Mexican ambassador to India," Arcacha Smith continued. "If you meet her, she's someone worth sidling up to and making an impression on. The Mexican press will listen to her in the future."

"If you can plug into Silvia Duran's social life," Ferrie said, "you might be able to plug into Duran herself, if you get my drift. She's supposedly a *caliente chica*. But if nothing develops with her, no worries. Just go to a bull fight."

"I'd prefer the bull fight. At least the bull has a chance."

"Or catch some jai alai," Arcacha Smith offered. "I saw a match in Miami, fastest game in the world."

"You have a ticket in your satchel on the Transporte del Norte bus to Nuevo Laredo Wednesday morning," Ferrie said. "Number 332. You'll cross into Texas and then go to Dallas. You won't get there until Thursday afternoon and, believe me, you'll be fried. Avoid your wife until at least Saturday. Go to the Y and get some rest. The Y'll know you're coming."

\\\\\

From the Leon Lounge, Ferrie rode with Oswald in Arcacha Smith's car to the new bus terminal at San Jacinto and McKinney. They dropped him off and drove the five blocks northeast to Prairie Street and the hotel.

Ferrie slept a few hours at the Sam Houston. The next morning, Gill called him to say that the final Eastern Air Lines grievances had been rejected. There was a thin silver lining, though—Eastern had awarded him a severance of $1,635.90.

Before meeting Jack Martin, Arcacha Smith got up early and drove Ferrie to Houston Municipal Airport. Like most Cubans, Arcacha Smith was raised to be a good host.

"I hope like shit they get JFK before Dallas," Arcacha Smith said.

"They will," Ferrie responded. "But Marcello wants us to be ready to go in case they don't. One way or another, we'll *have* to hit Oswald. He knows too much."

"Not my job, Dave."

"The good news for you—Ruby'll be the hitman. Not that he knows it yet."

CHAPTER 40

D r. Mary returned to New Orleans from England in early October. Ferrie had missed her.

She filled him in on her trip over tea and scones at her apartment. "I loved the Cotswolds, stayed at a lovely place called the Lygon Arms. Wow, what a classy, cozy inn. And there are so many cute towns nearby. It was pure relaxation. I really bonded with Bond!

"If you were a normal human being," she continued, "I'd say that you've gotta go there. But you're not a normal human being, I daresay. I've come to know you, my friend—you'd be bored silly with the charm, solitude, and relaxation."

"You *have* come to know me well, ma'am."

"More important, before the Cotswolds, the Oxford guys gave me lots of time with the particle accelerator. I was able to do some fine-tuning of our cancer weapon. Then, get this, I was able to separate out small pieces of the most virulent cells and turn them into a powder."

"Powder? How?"

"Basically, you freeze-dry the cells and the bovine serum. You put the results into a device with very low pressure. The liquid components sublimate—you know, evaporate. Voilà, you've got powder."

"The powdered version'll work?"

"It works like magic on the green monkeys. I tried it a few days ago over at the clinic."

"Jeez. Congrats, ma'am."

"So, we now can have a version of this weapon that can be taken orally, maybe even sprinkled in a drink—I'm sure it's tasteless."

"I assume we gotta try it out up at East Louisiana?"

"Here's the good news for you, Your Grace," Dr. Mary continued. "We can't try it on humans just yet."

"Thank you, Mother Mary," Ferrie said, raising his eyes up from Dr. Mary to the ceiling. "I'm not sure I even want to ask why."

"For better or worse, the whole project's on hold. Dr. Ochsner's instructions. I'm not sure why, but it appears that the bigwigs have other priorities over the next month or two—Marcello told him to suspend until January. I'm sure you know more about that than me."

"Believe me, the bigwigs don't always tell me what their priorities are. Further I'll say naught."

"I *do* need something from you now. I've got eight stainless steel test tubes with the powder in them. I've been told not to keep them on Ochsner property, and I just don't want them at my place. Keep them in your fridge?"

"Yes, ma'am. Of course. I'll make some room away from my milk, my Jell-O, and my takeout containers of chicken and sausage gumbo."

"Just don't mix them up." Dr. Mary smiled.

Ferrie took the tubes home in a cooler and put them in one of the door shelf bins of his pale blue Frigidaire.

Having these agents of death in his care, Ferrie felt a strong urge to pray. Donning his purple robe and black biretta, he faced the corner of his bedroom and shut his eyes. He started to recite the Golden Arrow while visualizing the face of Sister Mary of St. Peter but was interrupted by the ringing of his phone. It was G. Wray Gill. He sounded serious.

"I need you at the Town and Country tomorrow morning at ten. Marcello specifically asked for *your* help."

Ferrie slept fitfully that night. Direct assignments from Marcello were invariably formidable—and, not infrequently, hazardous.

CHAPTER 41

The meeting the next morning was just between Gill and Ferrie. No Banister. No Martin. Gill was in a no-nonsense mood. Though it was a muggy October morning, they still sat outside around the now half-drained motel swimming pool.

"Good to see you, Dave. Let's get down to it."

"Can't wait."

"Marcello has two critical assignments for you. Both requiring travel. Number one—Dallas. Number two—Guatemala."

"Not too excited about Dallas. However, Guatemala sounds good. I've always wanted to see Tikal."

"We'll chat about Guatemala later. For now, the first and higher priority is Dallas. The 'JFK Affair.'"

"Christ. Really?"

"We've been greenlighted to activate. It's a go."

"What the hell happened? What about Chicago?"

"The Chicago trip to the Army game's being canceled. The Secret Service's gotten tips about the plot. And they'd already determined that it would be hard to protect JFK on that trip. He was going to be driven eleven miles on the Northwest Expressway to the Loop. Part of that ride would've been through a warehouse district—between Grand and Lake. Warehouses scare the shit out of the Secret Service. Too many hiding places. And there usually are too few people in those buildings to notice a guy with a gun. Then, to get up to Soldier Field, there'd be a really slow turn on the ramp getting off the Expressway at the West Jackson exit. Easy shots from all directions."

"Florida?" Ferrie asked.

"The Florida trip's still on."

"Before or after Texas?"

"Before."

"How do you know?"

"Here's what we hear from Trafficante's folks in Miami. The Secret Service's been down in Palm Beach getting the Kennedy beach house ready for a weekend visit. We know JFK won't be there the weekend of the eighth—he'll be in New York the beginning of that weekend to give a speech, and then he'll need to be around DC for Veterans Day shit. Looks like Palm Beach'll be the next weekend, the weekend of the fifteenth. In fact, he's going to do a quick morning visit to Cape Canaveral on the sixteenth to get a briefing from that Nazi Wernher von Braun on the Saturn V and to watch them fire a Polaris. He'll work Palm Beach in around that.

"It's only logical that the Florida campaign trip will follow directly from there," Gill continued. "Starting on the eighteenth. The Texas trip will be at the end of that week. We know he won't do it the following week. Thanksgiving."

"Right. He's gotta be presented with a turkey in the middle of the week," Ferrie observed.

"Funny you mention that stupid tradition. He's going to do the turkey thing a week early, on the nineteenth. So we know he'll be back at the White House from Florida that Tuesday.

"*Ergo*, Dallas looks like it'll be that Thursday or Friday."

"What's he doing Wednesday?"

"Still at the White House. Has a party for the Supreme Court Justices. They say old Douglas is bringing his child bride."

"God bless him, he must still be cranking it up at sixty-five," Ferrie observed. "How *is* the Florida hit looking?"

"More and more unlikely. Trafficante's gotten really pessimistic, though he's cautious by nature."

"Why so pessimistic?"

"Security's going to be especially tight for that trip. There are hundreds of pissed-off Cuban exiles itching to throw a bullet JFK's way. Not just in Miami. Tampa too. As you know, Tampa has a long history of Cuban immigrants living there. Back to the cigar factory days. And they have a lot of bigots there going ballistic over the Negro stuff."

"Where would Mr. Trafficante try the hit, if he does?"

"Tampa. JFK's not going to be out in public much in Miami. However, he's doing a twenty-eight-mile motorcade in Tampa. The longest ever for a president, they say. From Al Lopez Field— where he'll surely give a speech to a big crowd—to the armory in West Tampa. He'll be driven pretty fast, though, except for a short circle through downtown on the way."

"Actually sounds pretty good for a hit. That's a shit-long drive, even if he's clipping along pretty fast most of the time. He'll probably have the top down the whole time. Why's Trafficante so doubtful it'll work?"

"Partly the increased security," Gill responded. "But he's also hearing that the Feds have been tipped off about the specifics of the hit. Trafficante has a high-placed mole in the Tampa police."

"What is, or was, Trafficante's plan?"

"We just know the basics. He's got a pro-Castro Cuban patsy named Lopez—not Al—all set up to take a shot from a middle floor of the Floridan Hotel as JFK goes south on Franklin."

"Ah, the Floridan. The tallest building in Tampa. I hear the hotel's really gone downhill since I lived there."

"This guy's our Oswald. He's been making himself a public nuisance around town, passing out Fair Play for Cuba shit just like your buddy. Is kind of a lost pony, like Oswald. Trafficante expects he'd miss and then get caught."

"Who's the second shooter?"

"A guy named Milteer's supposed to get the kill shot. He's going to be on Franklin, a little further down, between Zack and Twiggs."

"Near Jack Pendola's men's shop?"

"I don't fucking shop in Tampa."

"Did you say Milteer? *Joseph* Milteer?"

"Yeah. You know him?"

"He's done some work with Banister, for Marcello I think."

"News to me," Gill said.

"Big time KKK racist," Ferrie said. "A real cracker jerk."

"Yeah, that's what I heard."

"What's been leaked to the Feds?"

"They know about the Cuban," Gill said. "Been following him. That's not so bad, but Trafficante's now picking up signals that the FBI suspects Milteer's also involved. He should've picked less of a kook. Milteer was probably already on the cops' radar screen. Bottom line, Trafficante may just pull the whole effort."

"*Ergo*—looks like it's going to be Dallas."

"'Fraid so. The silver lining—"

"There's no silver lining."

"The silver lining's that a hit in Dallas might not be all that difficult. The Secret Service's going to be so focused on keeping JFK alive in Florida—which they almost certainly will—that they're not doing much to prepare for the Texas trip. And, we've heard, the Feds don't have any specific plot alerts about Texas. Nothing. They seem to believe that LBJ has so much control over Texas that he'll make sure nothing happens. Shows how much they know about LBJ."

Ferrie steadied himself. Hadn't thought this day would actually come. "What exactly do I do on this trip to the Big D, Ray?"

"You need to spend a lot of quality time with Sergio. He's there right now, getting ready. Crunching out the details. Go over his strategy, see if it makes sense. Make sure the logistics seem to work. How's the Oswald piece of it looking? And introduce him to Sparky."

"Take the Dove tomorrow morning from Tampa," Gill continued. "More horsepower than you need, but it's available. Sergio knows you're coming. Let him know when you'll be landing and he'll pick you up."

"All right," Ferrie said.

Ferrie's compliant demeanor betrayed a gathering storm roiling around his soul. He was getting actively involved in planning yet another murder. God might forgive him for one dead man, the prisoner. A second dead man, though—a president at that—probably not. Intellectually, he could justify this second murder to himself, like he did with the first murder, by thinking of it as being for the greater good. Helping get rid of JFK, ugly as that was going to be, would help in the fight against godless Communism.

Damn unlikely God's going to buy this excuse twice, though.

CHAPTER 42

Arcacha Smith picked Ferrie up in his Impala at Red Bird Airport early the next afternoon. A Tuesday. Ferrie was still stressed but was beginning to buck up.

They went straight to the Carousel Club. Ruby was surprised to see them.

"Jack, you look stronger than ever," Ferrie said.

"Strong as Samson."

"Meet my new partner in crime. His name is Sergio. A new Marcello guy."

"Good to meet you, sir," Arcacha Smith said to Ruby.

"Sure, likewise. What are you guys doing slumming around here?" Ruby asked.

"Sergio can't find any suitable entertainment in Houston, which is where he lives."

"No, really?" Ruby asked.

"Marcello wanted us to meet in Dallas to talk about some new business here. We chose your fine establishment for our meeting because of its ambience and because we need to run a few things by you later. Can you grab dinner with us?"

"Only if you're paying."

"Marcello's good for it."

"I'll get us a reservation at the French Room. Their crab cake with tomato—classic."

Ruby walked them back to his office. Ferrie caught a glimpse of the demur "Little Red-Headed Stripper" Joy Dale on stage as he passed through the club. Ruby had discovered her at the Texas State Fair where she was working in a tent show impersonating red-headed Hollywood stars like Piper Laurie and Deborah Kerr. Ruby had hired a number of employees from the fair, including Larry Crafard, his jack-of-all-trades at the club.

Joy was spunky-cute. Besides her hair, Ruby had said, her main attraction was her "cherubic" bottom.

There wasn't much of an afternoon crowd for the "Little Red-Headed Stripper," though her occasional lover Officer Tippit was there. She was going all out just for him.

Arcacha Smith and Ferrie entered Ruby's office, said au revoir to Ruby, and closed the door.

"I wanna walk through my thinking," Arcacha Smith said. "Then I think we need to figure out how to get Oswald a job on the motorcade route. It's going to be a lot smoother if he can shoot from a building he's supposed to be in rather than trying to have him sneak in somewhere unnoticed."

"Do we know there'll be a motorcade?"

"Trust me—there'll be a motorcade. Unless there's a *Wizard of Oz* tornado whirling through Dallas. And, unless it's pouring rain, the top will be off the car. Shit, the main reason for this trip is for JFK to be seen by as many Texas hicks and dress-up cowboys as possible."

"And we're sure he'll choose Dallas for a topless motorcade instead of somewhere else in Texas?" Ferrie asked.

"Ninety-nine percent sure. We now know he's flying first to San Antonio, then to Houston, then to Carswell Air Force Base in Fort Worth, all in the first day. He's giving speeches in San Antonio and Houston. There's not going to be much time on the first-day schedule for him to do a motorcade, certainly no more than a very short one. In any event, Dallas is the ideal city in Texas for a motorcade—it has a real downtown for him to ride through and be seen by lots of people."

"All right," Ferrie said. "Let's assume that's correct. How do we know the route?"

"No details have been released. However, we can figure it out with a pretty high degree of certainty."

"Talk to me."

"Let's start with two core, extremely logical assumptions. First, as I said, he'll want to get maximum eyeballs in tight on him—and on Jackie, if she comes with him. This means he'll do the motorcade through the heart of downtown. It also means he'll want to hit downtown at high noon. Lunchtime. Most employees in those office buildings only get thirty minutes for lunch, uniformly starting at 12:00 p.m. sharp. That's the sweet spot to get crowds.

"Second, JFK'll want to make a speech in Dallas in front of a respectful crowd. There are a lot of crazies here—"

"Duh."

"So, the speech will be indoors, where the audience will be by invitation only. No loud right-wing nut jobs. A business crowd. He'll want the speech to look good on Walter Cronkite. The options for a location for a decent indoor speech are pretty limited. There's the Women's Building at the state fairgrounds—easier to secure but it's not set up to handle large amounts of food. The Market Hall's still too small for this event, though it's recently been expanded. When you look around town, the obvious choice is the Trade Mart, which is in the same complex as the Market Hall. It's got a big atrium where you can put every mover and shaker in Dallas."

"Lunch or dinner speech?" Ferrie asked.

"Assuming I'm right about the motorcade being in the 12:00-to-12:30 window, dinner would be too many hours away. Too many hours for JFK to burn. He won't want to spend that much time in this crackpot town. Believe me, *I* don't want to spend that much time here."

"You think he'll do a lunch speech and then get the hell out of town?"

"*Sí.* It's only logical."

"His motorcade will come along here on Commerce?"

"It won't be Commerce," Arcacha Smith responded. "Though, frankly, it doesn't really matter to us. But all the big public parades go on Main Street. Main is the central downtown street, Elm on one side, Commerce on the other. It'll draw more eyeballs.

Plus it's a much nicer street than Commerce. It doesn't have the titty bars on it like Commerce does, including the shitty titty bar we're in now."

Arcacha Smith spread out a map of Dallas on Ruby's desk. He pointed to Love Field.

"They'll land at Love, here, in the northern part of the city, a little toward the west edge, not far from the Stemmons Freeway. Red Bird can't accommodate *Air Force One*. From Love, they'll either start with the motorcade or with the Trade Mart speech."

Pointing to the map, Arcacha Smith noted to Ferrie that the Trade Mart was fairly close to Love Airport, just a little bit south, three miles or so, right off the Stemmons. Downtown was another three miles south and further east. He marked each spot with a pen and then connected them with straight lines.

"A triangle," Ferrie observed. "If he does the downtown motorcade first, he'd do kind of a triangle, let's say circle, going to the east side of downtown, then traveling east to west on Main—he'd catch the Stemmons north, stop at the Trade Mart, and back to the airport."

"And if the Trade Mart's first, then the circle would go the other way, with the motorcade going west to east on Main," Arcacha Smith said.

"Right. Does it matter?"

"A little," Arcacha Smith responded. "This'll make more sense after we talk about the best location for the hit."

"Go."

"The best spot, no question, is a place called Dealey—Dealey Plaza."

"Sure. Just up Main. By the freeway."

"Yeah. Now, you *could* shoot him while he's on Main Street downtown. There are twenty-plus-story buildings that'll be right on top of him. The Magnolia Petroleum Building, for example. Main Street is so close-packed, though, it'd be hard for *me* to escape, not to mention Oswald, if we cared about that. And the odds of mistakenly shooting a bystander would be pretty high. We don't need that complication."

"Okay. Tell me about Dealey."

"The park is wide open, though not *too* big. About three acres. There are some good buildings on the northeast and southeast sides. There are also open escape routes, particularly on the north side."

"There's a railroad overpass too, right?" Ferrie asked.

"At the west border of the plaza. That could be useful."

"Okay. Dealey."

"Dealey is particularly spot-on if JFK's traveling east to west on Main, entering Dealey from Main. It'd be a bit more challenging if he goes west to east, getting off the freeway at Dealey and entering Main from Dealey."

"*Explique.*"

"If he enters Dealey from Main Street, he'll first turn right on North Houston then left to drive around the north side of the plaza on Elm Street, going toward the freeway." Arcacha Smith pointed to the map. "The two buildings in the northeast corner, the Dal-Tex and the Book Depository, would be excellent sniper locations while JFK is turning onto Elm or is already on Elm. Neither is a government building."

"I see," Ferrie said, studying the map. "His car will have to be going pretty slow to make the turn on to Elm. Probably an easy shot then from either of those buildings."

"Right. Also, the north side of the Plaza provides the best escape routes, particularly for me. On the north side, Elm runs along a small hill with a pergola on it, a memorial to John Neely Bryan."

"Ah, yes. The founder of this poor excuse for a city."

"Above the Bryan pergola, at the top of the hill, there's a five-foot-high fence. On the other side of the fence, down a hill, there's a railroad yard and parking lot. I could be up there behind the fence or behind the pergola. Or on the railroad overpass you mentioned. From the north side I can bolt out of the area pretty quickly. Shit, I could park a car in the parking lot if it's not shut off."

"If we get Oswald into the Depository or Dal-Tex," Ferrie recognized, "it'd be Oswald from the back and you from the front—JFK would be biangulated."

"Biangulated?" Arcacha Smith asked.

"It's a real word. Look it up."

"I will, believe me."

"So tell me what happens if JFK enters Dealey from the freeway and goes west to east."

"That's doable but much more cumbersome. Look at the map. The ramp from the Stemmons feeds easily onto Main. JFK'd be able to punch right through the middle of the plaza and would probably do that rather than curve up on Commerce and then have to make a sharp left and right to enter downtown on Main." Arcacha Smith moved his finger over the map.

"I'm guessing he'd be driven at a pretty good pace up to Houston. It'd be hard for me to be accurate as he went by. What would be more challenging is getting a lair for Oswald. It'd have to be in the federal post office building. With Kennedy in the traditional right-rear seat, Oswald'd have to be on the south side of Commerce, and that's the only option. But much more security than the private buildings around, probably couldn't get him in. And too far for Oswald to get anywhere close with a shot even if we did."

"All right. The $64,000 question. What's your best guess? Will the motorcade go *toward* the Stemmons or *from* the Stemmons?" Ferrie asked.

"Gotta be the east to west route downtown."

"Inform me."

"It's pretty obvious. If you were listening to me, you'd know he'll want to hit the lunch crowd on Main Street. If he does the lunch speech at the Trade Mart first, he'll be too late for the lunch crowd downtown. The speech would go to at least one-thirty, two o'clock. If he then went up Main Street, half the crowd would be back in their offices, chained to their desks."

"Pretty persuasive, Clarence."

"There's a subtler reason he'll do the speech second. We know he'll have that uncomfortable lumbar brace on for the motorcade, to keep his back erect. You know, his back's a mess from football and PT 109. He couldn't stay upright that long sitting on the soft car seat otherwise. He'll put the brace on in private on the plane.

"But then he can take the brace off at the Trade Mart, sit on a hard-backed chair. He can give the speech standing up holding on to the sides of the lectern. It would be pretty unwieldy for him to do the speech first and then take the time, somewhere out of sight, to put the back brace on for the car ride."

"A little more of a stretch," Ferrie said, "but I agree with the conclusion. East to west."

Ferrie was staring down again at the map. "But, Sergio—even if JFK goes east to west on Main, why wouldn't he just plow straight ahead through the middle of the plaza between the two pergolas and avoid the turn onto Elm? Like you say he would if he went west to east?"

"Brilliant question, professor. Easy answer. There's a concrete barrier extending way down Main toward the triple underpass that the entire motorcade would have to cut sharply around, awkwardly and extremely slowly, doing an S-turn to get over to the Stemmons ramp. Might not even be possible. In any event, the Secret Service would shit—the car would almost come to a full stop just feet from the underpass. The way the ramps are set up here, that wouldn't happen if he was going the other way. Eastbound, the ramp to downtown feeds right on to Main before it goes under the underpass."

"So much for that question. Nice work."

"*Gracias.*"

"*Ciertamente.*"

\|\|\|\|

"Here's a little tidbit for you, my Big Easy friend. The plaza is named after George Bannerman Dealey. His statue is right there at one of the east pergolas, sculpted by the same guy who did the Iwo Jima statue in DC."

"Okay."

"This guy Dealey was a true American success story, as you Yankees like to say," Arcacha Smith continued. "Born in England. Came to Dallas as a kid without much. Eventually started the *Dallas Morning News* and did a lot of civic things. One of Dealey's sons Ted eventually took over the paper. Unlike his father, though, Ted is a real prick—super right-wing prick. He detests Kennedy."

"Oh yeah, I know about this guy. He got up in Kennedy's face at the White House."

Ferrie was correct. Dealey rudely confronted JFK at a White House luncheon for publishers in 1961. He stood up and pointed at the president, loudly calling him and his administration "weak sisters."

We need a man on horseback to lead this nation, not a guy riding Caroline's tricycle.

"That's the guy," Arcacha Smith said. "Ted undoubtedly would be honored to have JFK murdered in his family's plaza."

CHAPTER 43

"Where does that leave us with Oswald?" Ferrie asked.

"We try to get Oswald a job in the Dal-Tex or the Depository," Arcacha Smith said. "Privately owned. Shots down on Elm from either place would be like shooting fish in a barrel. The Depository's the better choice. There are several floors that just store boxes of books—no offices or hallways, no people regularly there. Plenty of places to hide and maneuver around with nobody seeing you. It would be much tougher to get to an office window unnoticed in the Dal-Tex.

"And it'll be easier to get Oswald a job there," Arcacha Smith continued. "There's only one main employer, the Depository. Some of the book companies—mainly Scott Foresman and Gregg Publishing—have people there too but just a few. It's a busy season for school books, they're getting books in for the spring semester. They'll probably need extra bodies."

"So, the Depository?"

"Yeah, even though it *is* a little obvious—a warehouse right on the corner where the motorcade slows down to turn. Seems to stick out like a dick on a cow. However, Gill believes that the Secret Service's guard will be way down after the Florida trip."

"Maybe," Ferrie agreed. "In any event, they'll probably start relaxing after the motorcade leaves the packed downtown stretch."

"Oswald'll be able to blend in better at the Depository, just one of seventy-five employees who all look about the same—menial workers, basically white trash. The Dal-Tex has more of a mix of people—executives, oil guys, secretaries, seamstresses, basic worker bees, et cetera. There's a bunch of different types of companies there. A dress company, publishers, Belt Manufacturing, Eddie Mister, Dallas Uranium & Oil, Stanlea of Dallas."

"How do we get him a job there and get it quickly?" Ferrie asked.

"Ever heard of a Dallas rich guy they call 'Dry Hole'?"

"Byrd?"

"You know him?" Arcacha Smith asked.

"I know *of* him," Ferrie responded. "Rich guy. He helped found the Civil Air Patrol. You know, the Boy Scouts for young wannabe pilots that I've worked with."

"Lucky for you and your immoral lifestyle he did. And fucking lucky for us—Byrd owns the building the Depository's in. They leased it from him a few months ago. And he's heavily wired into Civello. Also wired into the rich Dallas righties. *And,* by the by, into LBJ."

David Harold "Dry Hole" Byrd was one of those wealthy, conservative oil men who ran Texas and controlled Texas's politicians. These oilmen, including Clint Murchison, H. L. Hunt, and Sid Richardson, had been in bed with the mob for decades. Back to the Piranio brothers.

Byrd was born in the very first year of the twentieth century in Texas in a small town with the out-of-place name of Detroit. He started making increasingly big money in oil in the 1920s and '30s. He was tight with his cousin Senator Harry Byrd of Virginia, a right-wing powerhouse in DC. Another cousin was the explorer Richard E. Byrd.

In 1961 "Dry Hole" and partners formed a successful electronics and aerospace firm known by its initials, LTV.

"The stars are aligning over the Depository," Ferrie said. "Shining brightly."

Ferrie called Civello, told him that Marcello needed Civello to contact Byrd and get a guy a job at his Depository building. Ferrie also requested Civello to meet him and Arcacha Smith for lunch the next day.

Ferrie and Arcacha Smith emerged from the back office at the Carousel Club. Beverly Oliver, an attractive seventeen-year-old singer from Ruby's main competitor, the Colony Club, was paying a neighborly visit. Ruby and his new red-hot stripper Jada were sitting at a table with Oliver. Jada was wearing a mink coat and high heels, her trademark off-stage look.

They joined the table in the midst of a colorful story being told by Jada. She'd recently driven her 1963 white Cadillac, with "J A D A" imprinted on the side door and Louisiana plates, to Mexico. Returning with two hundred pounds of marijuana in the trunk, she got through the border crossing unscathed by "accidentally" exposing her bulbous breasts to the border guards. Distracted, they waved the car through, closely inspecting only the driver's chest.

Jada opened her mink and flashed Oliver. "My not-so-secret weapons." The entire table laughed, including Oliver.

"Spectacular tits!" Oliver exclaimed.

Ferrie and Arcacha Smith grabbed Ruby while he was still laughing, and the three went over to the nearby French Room at the Adolphus.

Gill had instructed both Ferrie and Arcacha Smith to fill Ruby in on the "JFK Affair" and to start setting him up for the Oswald hit. They were to explain this to Ruby in a way that didn't freak him out. But, at the same time, they had to gently send the strong message that there'd be consequences if he didn't follow orders.

After a round of drinks at their isolated back table at the French Room and the ordering of crab cakes with tomatoes, Ferrie waded slowly into the subject of the "JFK Affair" by telling Ruby that Marcello was interested in any intelligence Ruby was picking up about the JFK visit to Dallas. Ruby likely would have heard something from his Dallas police friends. The cops would get early confidential details on the presidential visit.

Ruby indeed had some intelligence. A police source had confirmed that JFK was arriving mid-morning on Friday, the twenty-second, from Fort Worth. JFK would later go on, no doubt reluctantly, Ruby had heard, to Austin to pay homage to LBJ at his small ranch.

"Mr. Gill asked me to ensure that you'd be in town the weekend of the twenty-second," Ferrie said.

"Of course. My business almost never closes. Why?"

Ferrie lowered his voice to a whisper. "Jack. Marcello and his colleagues are done with JFK. They're going to take him out. Here. Dallas."

Ruby swiveled his eyes from Ferrie to Arcacha Smith and back again. "Jesus. I'm not totally surprised, but Jesus—you mean here? Really? *Oy gevalt!*"

"We won't get you too tarnished by the details. Just know you're going to have a role. Congratulations."

"Holy Moses. Why? What role?"

"Here's what you need to know—your old friend Lee Oswald, remember him?"

"Unfortunately. He was back in the club last night, seems to have gotten a lot stranger, which is saying something."

"He'll have a role too," Ferrie said. "A big role. The shooter. Assuming he's still alive after the murder, we'll need to take him out too—for obvious reasons."

"None of this is obvious," Ruby said. "Oswald's a weirdo and a loser. If you're relying on that guy to hit JFK, you *schlubs* have really lost your minds. It won't happen, he'll fuck it up."

"We're taking that chance," Ferrie said. "You *might* be right. If you're not, though—if Oswald gets JFK, lives, and gets caught before he leaves Dallas, which he probably will, we're in serious trouble. After a few days, he'll start blabbing like a high school girl. Marcello's decided you're the guy to stop him from blabbing."

"What? Me? C'mon, you guys have much better assets for this than me."

"If things go like we think they will, Oswald'll be held with the city cops, at least for a few days," Ferrie noted. "You're the best person to do it because you have full run of their offices. You can get him."

"I don't know. What happens to me then, assholes? They'll arrest me and put me on trial."

Arcacha Smith chimed in. "They won't put you on trial. You'll be a national hero. Oswald'll be a pariah. People love Kennedy. In any event, Civello will get you out. Marcello guarantees it. Trust us. You'll be okay."

"Shit. I gotta think this over, fellows. Shit."

"You're a good man," Ferrie said. "While you're rolling this around in your brain, add this to the equation—Marcello's prepared to take care of your tax debts. We know they're weighing you down."

"Fucking IRS."

"You remember Paul Roland Jones?"

"Known him for years. 'PR,' they call him. A Hoffa guy."

"He'll bring you a check. Seven grand."

Not too subtly, Ferrie then asked Ruby about his sister Eva and his cherished dog Sheba. "God bless them," Ferrie said. "We know you'd do anything for them. Whatever it would take, right Jack?"

CHAPTER 44

Ferrie and Arcacha Smith met Civello Wednesday at the Egyptian Lounge for lunch. Campisi greeted them at the door and took them to a private table in the back.

Civello had acted quickly on Ferrie's request for help from Byrd, knowing that Ferrie was acting for Marcello. "Byrd wouldn't piss me off for something so minor," Civello said. "But he was curious about the request."

"Kind of understandable," Ferrie said. "Why would the mob want to put a guy in that crummy building so badly?"

"He asked me if Marcello was going to hit a judge working in the Criminal Courts Building. Or spring someone loose from the jail.

"I told Byrd I was just acting on orders from above," Civello continued. "I didn't know what Marcello was up to, probably just trying to get a guy in the Depository to do some surveillance on the courts or on one of the other buildings in sight."

"And Byrd said?" Arcacha Smith asked.

"'Of course.' But he said he had a bad feeling about it. He just thought it sounded suspicious. He wished me luck and said he'd help as long as I never mentioned his role to anybody. And he then said he was leaving town for a while. He's going big game hunting in Africa all of November and December. Don't know if that was already planned. I just know I'm not supposed to bother him."

The three men finished their pizzas. Arcacha Smith and Ferrie drove back to the Cabana. They needed to spend one more night in Dallas. They were meeting with Oswald the next day.

That night, Ferrie called Civello to check in on any further developments with "Dry Hole."

Byrd had directed the man who ran the Depository, Roy Truly, Civello said, to interview and accept any applicant named Oswald. Can hire him as a temp, Truly was told. Byrd also told Truly, if asked later on, to say nothing about his involvement. Truly was just to say he liked that Oswald had just gotten out of the Marines and that he seemed like a nice young fellow.

Truly would never disobey Byrd, but he in fact did need some short-term help.

There was a second Depository warehouse in addition to the one on Elm Street, at 1917 North Houston Street, four blocks north of the motorcade route. Truly was told to make sure Oswald wasn't placed there, even though that was where most temporary employees were assigned.

Ferrie and Arcacha Smith met with Oswald late the next morning, the tenth, at the Copper Cow, which was on Commerce, close to the Neiman Marcus building. Ferrie had been there one night about a year earlier on Ruby's recommendation. Oswald had taken the bus into town across the Trinity River from the apartment he was staying in near Lake Cliff Park.

"My Russian ball-and-chain and my daughter are staying with Ruth Paine out in Irving, fifteen miles from Dallas," Oswald whined. "She wasn't real thrilled with the Mexico City trip, to say the least. Sent me to town to get a job and to give her some space. I just signed on to move next week into a fucking boarding house in Oak Cliff. That's what my life's come down to. A wife and kid, another kid about to pop, unemployed—and living in a group home. Loser."

"Things'll be coming up roses soon," Ferrie said.

Ferrie and Arcacha Smith described the Depository job. Oswald balked. Surprisingly, he said he in fact had already rejected the idea of working at the Depository.

"One of Ruth Paine's dullard neighbors works there and likes it," Oswald said. "She's been all over me to apply to that hell hole. Filling book orders all day. Christ."

Instead of the Depository, or other places pushed by Ruth Paine like Manner Bakery and Texas Gypsum Company, Oswald was fixated on getting a job in TV or radio. After all, he'd done so well with the media in New Orleans in August. He also had a strong interest in working for Trans Texas Airways. He was close to getting a job as a cargo handler there. In his application for that job, he trumpeted his experience in the CAP in New Orleans from back in the 1950s.

Ferrie told Oswald that they finally had *the* epic assignment for him. However, to carry out the assignment, he *had* to be working at the Depository. And, if he completed the assignment successfully, there would be some *dineros* in it for him, more than enough to buy a car.

"Start shopping," Ferrie said.

That was enough for Oswald. "Then the fucking Depository it is. I won't let you down, sirs."

"Fantastic," Ferrie said. "That Ruth Paine is also pushing the Depository is kismet, boys. She can be a layer of protection for us. Lee, do this. Agree to have Mrs. Paine check this out for you. Have her call a guy at the Depository named Roy Truly. You'll be all set. Epic is coming your way."

CHAPTER 45

The upcoming trial of Marcello was an offshoot of RFK's thirty-month pursuit of him. The deportation case itself had been stalled by several years of back-and-forth litigation and appeals.

RFK had decided to take a different approach to try to get Marcello—rather than deport him, lock him up. RFK now claimed that Marcello had criminally asserted a fraudulent birth certificate showing he was born in Guatemala. Marcello perpetrated this fraud, RFK argued, to avoid being deported to Italy. This argument bore a couple of ironies. First, RFK actually had *relied* on the fake certificate to deport Marcello to Guatemala in 1961. The other irony was that Marcello was born in neither Guatemala nor Italy. Though his parents were Sicilian, Marcello's country of birth was Tunisia.

A few days after Ferrie returned from Dallas, he met with the Marcello trial team at Gill's Pere Marquette office. Jack Martin was present, as was DC lawyer Jack Wasserman, who was going to try the RFK case along with Gill.

Guy Banister was there as well, though he seemed a little out of it. He was pale, with dark bags under his eyes. He looked worried. His eyes shifted slowly back and forth. *Something's wrong with him*, Ferrie thought.

"The case is before Chief Judge Christenberry," Gill said. "Native New Orleanian, real Creole. A decent guy. He's got one life-long flaw, though—a hair-trigger temper. He's known to throw books and other shit at lawyers when they're making arguments he doesn't think much of.

"Because of this flaw," Gill continued, "Christenberry's a great draw for us."

Gill explained. Marcello had known Judge Christenberry since the early 1940s, when Christenberry was the US Attorney in New Orleans. Marcello had made a point to sidle up to Christenberry as he rose through the mob ranks.

Unable to manage his bursts of anger, Christenberry got into scrapes with some powerful people in New Orleans during those years. He made enemies. After he was put on the federal bench by President Truman, Christenberry rendered some decisions that a few of these enemies weren't happy with. There were periodic threats against Christenberry and his family. He was concerned enough on more than a few occasions to reach out to his influential acquaintance Carlos Marcello. Marcello used his pull in town and his web of connections to keep the judge and his family safe. Christenberry never forgot Marcello's efforts.

"Dave, there's no rest for the weary," Gill said, switching subjects. "We need you to get going down to Guatemala. Need some reconnaissance down there for the trial."

"Tikal?" Ferrie responded.

"Maybe next time," Gill said.

"Let me give you the background on the tangled tale of Marcello's 'birth' in Guatemala." Wasserman said. "In the 1950s the Feds wanted to deport Marcello because of his 'dangerous business activities.' They assumed he was born in Italy. Mr. Marcello, of course, didn't want to get deported, but he *really* didn't want to go to Italy. Nor did he want to be deported to his real birthplace. It'd be difficult or impossible for him to keep running his New Orleans businesses from as far away as Italy or Tunisia. And difficult for him to ever sneak back to New Orleans from across the Atlantic."

Gill picked up the story. "We looked for a more suitable country for Marcello. We'd then make up a birth certificate there. Neither Italy nor Tunisia would take him if we showed he was born somewhere else." Gill had lived through this entire saga. "We decided on Guatemala. An odd choice, you may think. But it actually seemed perfect. It had a corrupt government that would give Marcello flexibility to do his thing. At least, that's what we thought at the time. Also, Guatemala is a busy trade partner with New Orleans. Cargo ships from New Orleans have an easy ride down through the Yucatan Straits into Puerto Barrios. Smaller fishing boats out of New Orleans often troll as far south as Guatemala, looking for shrimp. Those waters along the coasts of British Honduras, Guatemala, and Honduras are also flush with tarpon, snapper, and wahoo. We envisioned that, at the appropriate time, Marcello could be picked up by a fishing boat and then taken back to Louisiana through a remote bayou."

Gill finished the story and then defined Ferrie's assignments.

"Got it," Ferrie said.

"And, sorry to say, but you gotta fly commercial. I know you'd like to fly the Dove down there, but it'd probably end up taking more time and be riskier. In any event, we don't need you to be tired when you arrive," Gill said.

Gill wished Ferrie luck. Wasserman, Martin, and Banister each shook Ferrie's hand.

Ferrie left for Guatemala City on October 11, taking Delta Air Lines through Atlanta to La Aurora Airport, which was a few miles south of Guatemala City. He cabbed the four miles to the Hotel Maya Excelsior, smack in the middle of the city.

Guatemala City was the most beautiful city in Central America. Even though a civil war was beginning to rage in the countryside—leftists versus the government—Guatemala City itself was peaceful and fun-loving.

Ferrie had his first evening free. He walked around town, slowly heading up Calle 13, crossing the Parque Central to the Metropolitan Cathedral. The main cathedral in the city, the Metropolitan was 150 years old and magnificent. Its interior was sparse but arresting. To help prepare for the long couple of days ahead, Ferrie prayed the rosary. Making the sign of the cross, he started with the Apostles' Creed. Praying out loud, he finished with, "Glory be to the Father." He lit a candle.

On the way back to the hotel, he ate at an old Basque restaurant called the Altuna. He had a traditional tuna pot sitting at a table on Altuna's stunning skylighted patio.

After a good night's sleep, Ferrie met Mike Maroun—the lawyer who had trudged around Central America with Marcello in 1961—at the Maya Excelsior coffee shop. Maroun had been a close associate of and lawyer for Marcello for more than twenty-five years. Based in Shreveport, Maroun not only practiced law there but also ran Marcello's Shreveport motel on the east side of the Red River—a motel with the familiar name "Town and Country." Maroun had clients in Guatemala and knew the country well. He'd be driving Ferrie around Guatemala in a black Lincoln.

Ferrie had two main jobs in Guatemala.

\\\\

In the 1950s Marcello and his brain trust sent an emissary to Guatemala to figure out a way to create a record of Calogero Minacore—Marcello's real name—being born in the country on February 10, 1910, Marcello's date of birth. The emissary was a trusted con man named Carl I. Noll. Noll was trained as an electrical engineer but spent much of his time as a street-smart petty criminal and small-time gangster.

Noll was able to work his miscreant magic to persuade the prime minister and his law partner to have a birth certificate created and certified attesting that a Calogero Minacore had been born in 1910 in a small Guatemalan mountain village. The prime minister and his law partner were well-rewarded thereafter and had remained close to Marcello over the years.

Maroun arranged for Ferrie to meet with these two gentlemen—former Prime Minister Eduardo Rodriguez-Genis and his law partner Antonio Valladores—and persuade them to deny any involvement with Noll in this effort. Ferrie was authorized to offer money. That was Ferrie's first assignment.

Ferrie's other job in Guatemala was to spy on an FBI agent working for the RFK prosecution team. What evidence from

Guatemala will RFK have at his disposal? Wasserman had been tipped off about this FBI guy, and Maroun had had little trouble locating the man.

"The FBI agent is at the San Carlos Hotel on Avenida la Reforma, near the American Embassy. He just got here yesterday," Maroun told Ferrie. "Diuguid. John Diuguid. He was a federal prosecutor in the Northeast, and then RFK put him in charge of watching the South. In particular Marcello. Diuguid is down here trying to get evidence to corroborate what Noll is going to say on the stand in the trial. The RFK folks are worried about relying on Noll's word alone because of his shady past.

"I've lined up a meeting with Rodriquez-Genis and Valladores tomorrow morning. They haven't met with Diuguid. And they assured me they won't meet with him before they meet with us. They fear Marcello more than the US government, believe me."

"Couldn't see them today?" Ferrie asked.

"No. They're up in Huehuetenango on a case. Today we're going to follow Diuguid. He almost certainly's going to the village where the books were cooked. San José Pinula. It's about fifteen miles away on crazy-winding mountain roads.

"Carl Noll paid off the main local government folks there," Maroun continued. "He got them to hand-write an entry for Calogero Minacore on the page of the town's births ledger for February 10, 1910. Noll had them use an old pen and mimic the handwriting style of the other 1910 entries on the page."

Ferrie and Maroun cut over to 10a Avenida in the Lincoln, headed south until it turned into Avenida La Reforma, passed the Botanical Garden, and parked at the corner of 8a Calle and 1a Avenida, close to the San Carlos Hotel. A black car similar to Maroun's, obviously for Diuguid, was parked along 8a Calle.

As they left the outer rim of Guatemala City, discreetly following Diuguid, the road climbed into the Sierra Madre Mountains and turned zig-zaggy and dangerously narrow. They stayed several curves behind Diuguid. The people in the small villages on the way were clearly dirt poor, but they didn't look unhappy. Probably knew nothing better. Naked kids stood beside the road with their hands out as the cars went by.

Two large black cars coming into San José Pinula didn't go unnoticed. Ferrie could see curtains being pulled back in the wooden houses along the main street, 1a Calle. Lawyer Diuguid stopped at the Iglesia Antigua on 5 Calle. Ferrie and Maroun stopped a block away.

After a solid hour, Diuguid came out of the small cathedral carrying the briefcase he'd gone in with. He drove off.

"Follow him?" Ferrie asked.

"Nope. We need to see if he found anything of use to him in there. This cathedral holds the birth records. What Noll says is that he and several former government accomplices went around from village to village to find a church ledger that had a blank line on the page for February 10, 1910."

"I take it they found one here."

"That's Noll's story. I assume Diuguid was confirming that and looking for evidence that the handwriting was done more recently than 1910."

The priest's curate greeted them. Maroun said he and Ferrie were working with a man to check certain old birth records in the cathedral, but he was in a separate car and they'd lost track of him on the drive from the city.

"He was just here," the curate said.

Could they look at the records the man had looked at? Ferrie asked the curate. The curate spoke good English.

The old musty record book for 1910 hadn't yet been put away. The curate put it on a table in the cathedral's records room.

"We don't want to waste your time and duplicate our colleague's efforts," Ferrie said. "Do you recall what he was doing with the records?"

"It was a little unusual, I would say. He had a magnifying glass and stared for some time at one page from 1910. He then appeared to take some pictures with a small device unlike anything *I'd* seen before. The last thing, and I almost stopped him, he appeared to be taking a scraping from the page, with a small knife. He put some flakes of what I assume was from the old ink into a small clear bag. I began to approach him, but he said very politely that he was finished. I let him go, with the bag. What are you looking for?"

"We all work for a man who believes his father was born here, that's all," Ferrie said.

"Well, I can't be of much help to you. That was a little before my time on this Earth. But here you go." The curate opened the book to the page Diuguid had examined. He left the room to greet a parishioner.

The page for February 1910 had an entry on the tenth for "Calogero Minacore," born at nearby Palo Blanco—son of "Guisepe" Minacore and "Suigia" Farrugia, slightly misspelled versions of the names of Marcello's real parents. It appeared to fit right in with the other entries both in the penmanship and in the shade and appearance of the ink.

"It was clear what Diuguid was doing," Ferrie said. "He's going to have the photos analyzed to see if some expert will say the handwriting is different from the other entries on the page and done with a more modern style. And he's going to test those flakes to see if that type of ink was available in 1910."

Ferrie took his own pictures. "To me, the writing looks indistinguishable from the other handwriting on the page. I'm sure we could get some expert to say that."

"Agree," Maroun said. "The jury won't be able to detect any difference in the handwritings—the experts'll just cancel each other out. I wouldn't bother to take any of our own scrapings. We don't want to irritate Mr. Curate. But my bet is the age of the ink will be in the ballpark. I was told that Noll's a shit, but he's not stupid."

Ferrie and Maroun met Rodriguez-Genis and Valladores the next morning at an office the government kept for the former prime minister in the Post Office Building.

The Post Office Building had a stunningly ornate archway. With high ceilings and elaborate cartouche molding on the walls, the prime minister's office was similarly ornate.

The prime minister and his colleague spoke perfect English. "Gentlemen, it is an honor to meet you, and we are grateful for your time," Ferrie said.

"Certainly," Rodriguez-Genis responded. "How *is* our friend Carlos—'El Hombrecito'?"

"He's fine and confident that this case will be dealt with satisfactorily," Ferrie said. "Through me, he's asking for your help."

"You know we are named defendants in the birth certificate case as well," the prime minister said. "Of course, your attorney general Mr. Bobby Kennedy can't force us to join the party in New Orleans, and we have chosen not to."

"The right decision, Your Honor," Maroun said. "Have you been approached by our Justice Department for affidavits or depositions in connection with Mr. Marcello's birth certificate?"

"An FBI fellow named John something-or-other left a card, that's all."

"Mr. Marcello has kindly asked that you not talk to the Justice Department or FBI," Ferrie said. "And he wonders whether you would provide affidavits supporting his case."

"Our memory is pretty clear on this. Mr. Noll was working for Carlos at the time. He met with me and Mr. Valladores and several of my government colleagues. He showed us a picture of an old birth notation from San José Pinula for an odd name he said was Carlos's real name. Mr. Noll was persuasive in convincing us to accept this record without further investigation, which we decided to do. Based on that, I directed the government to work with Mr. Valladores to issue a certificate of birth. I assume that is not what you want the affidavit to say?"

Ferrie shook his head. "Not exactly. We've prepared affidavits for both of you, at Mr. Marcello's request, that essentially say you've never met Mr. Noll, have no knowledge of any of his activities in Guatemala, have no knowledge of anything related to Mr. Marcello's birth certificate."

"Mr. Ferrie, we have great respect for Mr. Marcello and will consider his request. Please give us a little time to consider this and review your draft papers."

"Absolutely. Mr. Marcello greatly appreciates your kindness. He's authorized us to pay for your time at a handsome rate. He knows how valuable your time is."

After some further conversation, Rodriguez-Genis and Valladores agreed to a fee. They also asked for a gentleman's agreement that Mr. Marcello would look favorably upon any future requests that *they* might make of *him*. They signed the affidavits. Ferrie agreed to return in a week or so with their compensation.

He returned to Guatemala on October 30. This time he flew on Taca Airlines through San Pedro Sula in Honduras to La Aurora Airport. He met an agent of the prime minister's the next morning at the Hotel Maya Excelsior and gave him a satchel.

His flight back home wasn't until the next day, so he had the afternoon to go visit the National Palace, nicknamed the "Big Guacamole" because of its greenish tint, and the nearby National Library of Guatemala, with its magnificent representations of Mayan codes. Soon after his return to New Orleans, he found that $7,093 had been deposited into his bank account.

What Ferrie had accomplished in Guatemala was one of the three main foundations of Marcello's defense. With Maroun's vital assistance, he had taken Rodriguez-Genis and Valladores out as potential affiants or deponents that could corroborate Noll's story.

The second foundation for Marcello's trial team was to eviscerate Noll's character, veracity, and mental health through an aggressive cross-examination inside the courtroom. And, for good measure, to shake him up a little *outside* the courtroom— make sure he understood that testifying against Marcello wasn't a healthy thing to do. Banister was in charge of this outside-the-courtroom effort.

So as to leave nothing to chance, the third foundation was to eliminate any possibility of a unanimous verdict. Jack Martin was assigned to find a juror who could be enticed to go Marcello's way.

With these three efforts, coupled with the judge's favorable opinion of Marcello, the result of the trial was foregone.

‖‖

The RFK court case would do more than clear Marcello—it was going to provide the entire trial team, including Ferrie, a convenient alibi for the day of the JFK hit, whether it happened in Tampa or Dallas. The trial was scheduled to go through the week of November 18. The White House had now publicly confirmed that JFK would make his campaign visits to Florida and Texas during that week.

Though Ferrie's efforts on the Marcello trial were winding down, his work on the "JFK Affair" wasn't. If the assassination were to happen in Dallas, he'd have one last project. He'd be hitting the road to Texas hours thereafter.

CHAPTER 46

The RFK-Marcello trial went as planned. Wasserman julienned Noll with sharp questions about his extensive criminal record and mental stability. Noll was particularly wobbly on the stand one morning after a visit the evening before from a Marcello associate from Mississippi.

Wasserman then called a man named Ben Probst to the stand. Probst testified that Noll had swindled him out of $10,000 and lied about things he was supposed to be doing for Probst in Guatemala related to leasing construction equipment to the Guatemalan government. "He swindled us out of all of it." A woman named Yvonne Klein testified that Noll had fleeced $13,000 from her, also in connection with Guatemala-related projects. He was "a con man," she told the court.

Sealing the victory, Jack Martin, through intermediaries, approached a juror named Rudolph Heitler, a clerk at the Krauss Department Store. Heitler—whose name, along with the other jurors' names, was published in the *Times-Picayune* on November 6—was willing to vote not guilty in exchange for a generous contribution.

Marcello, Ferrie, and Gill spent the weekends during the trial—November 9–10 and 16–17—at Churchill Farms, supposedly planning trial strategy. In fact, trial lawyer Wasserman stayed at Gill's offices in the Pere Marquette and did that work. At Churchill Farms, the business was the "JFK Affair."

The White House had announced during the trial that JFK's visit to Florida would be only one day, the eighteenth. He'd do both Tampa and Miami on that day. And the turkey presentation at the White House indeed would be on the nineteenth, the Supreme Court visit the next day. Texas after that.

Trafficante called Marcello the night of the fifteenth to say that the heat was on in Tampa, he was an inch away from having to pull the plug.

\\\\

On Saturday morning, the sixteenth, the phone rang at Churchill Farms. Gill picked up. It was Sergio Arcacha Smith calling from his Houston home.

"Ray, I hired some guys to watch Love Field for any signs of a presidential advance party. Didn't tell them why. *Bingo.* There were FBI or Secret Service guys there on Thursday. And in addition to checking out the airport, they clearly were surveying a motorcade route."

Two Secret Service officers indeed had been in town. They met with local officials at Love Field. The two men—Winston Lawson and Forrest Sorrels—then got in a black car and, at a slow pace, drove out of Love. They did *not* go directly toward the Stemmons and the Trade Mart. Instead, they headed a little east and over to Lemmon Avenue, headed south along Turtle Creek to Cedar Springs Road, and then turned right on Main Street from North Harwood Street. They motored, still slowly, west on Main Street.

Lawson and Sorrels made a right on Houston Street and then turned left on Elm, skirting the north side of Dealey Plaza. They went down the slope of Elm Street and entered the Stemmons there, just past the Texas School Book Depository. Once on the Stemmons, they sped up and went to the Trade Mart.

"They had to be rehearsing and timing a motorcade route," Arcacha Smith said over the phone.

The rehearsed routing is what Arcacha Smith had predicted earlier, Gill thought.

Gill hung up the phone and filled Marcello and Ferrie in. Things were beginning to move quickly. The clock was ticking.

"Dave, it's time to activate Oswald," Gill said.

Ferrie called Arcacha Smith back.

"*Cómo te va?*" Ferrie asked.

"I'm good. Am lunching with Ruby at the Egyptian Lounge on Monday."

"Where's Oswald today, do you know?"

"He's at the boarding house. The wife told him not to come to Ruth Paine's house this weekend because there's some Paine family birthday party there. I guess they're afraid Oswald will scare the kids."

"He'd scare *your* kids, wouldn't he?"

"Actually, he scares *me* a little!"

"I need to call him, it's time to wind him up. He needs to be ready to go. The chances of getting JFK in Florida are looking slim. They've really tightened things up on that trip, with all the surly Cuban exiles down there. Can you meet Oswald on Wednesday to give him the details?"

"Yeah," Arcacha Smith said. "I'll be back and forth between Houston and Dallas all week—the boss thinks I have a deal going in Dallas."

Ferrie called Oswald at his rooming house on North Beckley Avenue in the Oak Cliff section of Dallas. Arcacha Smith had given him the phone number. WH3-8993. Housekeeper Earlene Roberts answered. He asked to speak to Mr. Lee—Mrs. Roberts knew Oswald only as "O. H. Lee." She called him to the phone. Ferrie announced that the time had come for his epic assignment.

Oswald hadn't heard about the upcoming JFK trip to Dallas. In fact, the two Dallas papers—the *Dallas Morning News* and the *Dallas Times-Herald*—wouldn't feature the trip until Tuesday, the nineteenth. The articles that Tuesday would describe the motorcade route precisely as Arcacha Smith had predicted, passing right in front of the Depository.

Ferrie didn't tell Oswald about the JFK trip during the call on the sixteenth. He'd learn soon enough. What he did tell him was to meet Sergio Arcacha Smith after work on Wednesday at Ruby's Carousel Club office to talk about the details of the "epic" assignment. Arcacha Smith, he instructed, would be Oswald's hands-on point person on this adventure.

He did forewarn Oswald that he'd need to bring his Carcano to work on Friday morning.

"Why?" Oswald asked soberly.

"I'll let Sergio fill you in, but you'll like the plan, I guarantee it."

"Man! Sure. It's out in Ruth's garage, I'll need to get out to Irving Thursday night."

"Fine. You still good for this? Still ready for something special to help Mr. Marcello and fight the Commies?" Ferrie asked.

"Yes, sir." In a voice outwardly as cold as ice, Oswald said, "My heart's racing faster than Man o' War."

CHAPTER 47

One week after Arcacha Smith's November 16 call to Churchill Farms, Ferrie was in Houston, deeply distraught. The fact that JFK had actually been murdered was sinking in deeper and deeper. Ferrie, effectively, was one of the murderers. He'd never before leaned on Mother Mary for forgiveness as much as he did that day. He was also growing edgy and fearful that his role in the assassination would be discovered.

He hid his anxiety from his travel companions Al Beauboeuf and Melvin Coffey. As dusk was settling over the Winterland Ice Skating Rink in Houston that Saturday, Ferrie was standing nervously by the outdoor payphone, waiting for a call, a call that never came. After a time Ferrie made two calls. The first was to the Carousel Club in Dallas. After ten minutes of lively conversation, he popped the hook switch down and let it quickly pop back up for a second call. He rang Gill in New Orleans. They spoke quietly for five minutes. Ferrie then slowly replaced the handset.

"Let's go boys. I wanna show you Galveston." He wasn't going to go straight home after what Gill had told him on the phone. Jack Martin, Gill had said, was spreading stories around New Orleans and to the cops that Ferrie was close to Oswald. And that Oswald had his library card on him when he was arrested in Oak Cliff. Ferrie had hypnotized Oswald, the rumor mill was whispering.

Gill had assured Ferrie that nobody would believe an alcoholic criminal like Martin and that the cops didn't believe the hypnotism tale. But, nevertheless, it would be prudent for him to take his time getting home. Ferrie needn't stay at the skating rink, Gill had advised. Arcacha Smith would not be coming there.

Around eleven o'clock, after a slow trip that included a stop at the NASA facility in Nassau Bay and some other sightseeing, Ferrie and his traveling buddies checked into room 117 at Galveston's Driftwood Motel on the Seawall, 32nd Street and Beach Boulevard.

"The clerk was named Mary, I never forget a Mary," Ferrie told Gill later. "And her last name rhymed with Mary. Doveri. Mary Doveri. Ha!"

He was too antsy to go to sleep. "Let's hit a few bars."

They popped in and out of three or four near-empty beachy bars on the Seawall and spent a half hour in Sonny's Place on 19th Street. The town was quiet and mournful. Before heading back to the Driftwood, he showed Al and Melvin the remains of an iconic Galveston night spot, the old Balinese Room, perched precariously on a six-hundred-foot pier that had been severely damaged by a hurricane in 1961. "This place used to be world famous," Ferrie told the guys. "Always full of stars, including Sinatra a few times. Gangsters and gamblers. I've got a great story about this place."

Here comes another lecture, Melvin thought.

"There was a bartender here named Santos Cruz. A giant among bartenders. One of his favorite customers was the famous singer Peggy Lee."

"Never heard of her," Al said.

"You fucking moron. Blonde, sweet voice. You've heard the song 'Fever'? Or 'Mañana'? Ah, she was so alluring—she purred her songs. *'Mañana is soon enough for me!'*" Ferrie tried to sing the song. Poorly.

"Okay, sure," Melvin said. "Go on, Professor."

"Santos Cruz invented the fucking margarita right *here*—for Peggy Lee. He called it *margarita* based on the name Margaret, the formal version of "Peggy"—*Margarita* is the Hispanic name for Margaret."

"Fascinating," Al said.

"I'm not done yet. Here's the really interesting thing: The name *Margarita* isn't really a Spanish word. It was adopted by the Spics from—drum roll, please—*German*! The German word for Margaret, *Margareta*, became *Margarita* in Spanish! So, boys, when you drink a Margarita, think German, not Mexican. *Prost, meine Freunde!*

"We're just lucky Cruz didn't use her real name for the drink. Norma Deloris."

The three returned to the Driftwood at about 1 a.m.

They delayed their departure from Galveston on Sunday to watch the continuing assassination news. Ferrie wanted to witness Ruby's execution of Oswald.

After that successful spectacle in the Dallas Police basement garage, the three men left Galveston and drove through Orange, Texas, to Vinton, Louisiana, about twenty-five miles west of Lake Charles. They stopped in Vinton at Buster's Bar and Grill, a rustic crawfish place. Ferrie knew the owner. Melvin ordered boiled crawfish for the group while Ferrie used the payphone to try Gill. No answer.

The next stop was Alexandria, squarely in the middle of the state. Out of the way for getting back to New Orleans but requested by Al Beauboeuf because he had relatives there. The three could stay overnight with the relatives if necessary.

Ferrie tried again to reach Gill several times from an Esso gas station on North Bolton Avenue in Alexandria. He was growing increasingly dark about what might be happening in New Orleans. Unable to reach Gill, Ferrie called his own apartment in New Orleans. His old CAP and CRC friend Layton Martens, who had helped him in Houma and in his Eastern case, was likely to be there. Martens stayed with Ferrie off and on when he was on breaks from studying music at the University of Louisiana at Lafayette. Ferrie and Martens shared an interest in, among other things, musical composition.

Martens answered. In a quavering voice, he asked, "Where the fuck *are* you?"

"In Alexandria. I've been trying to reach Gill today but no luck. What's going on there?"

"Damn, Dave. There are TV guys on the street waiting for you. There's a WWL truck right out front."

"What? What do they want?"

"Apparently, the cops heard you knew Oswald, and the news guys got wind of that. The cops are probably lurking about waiting for you too. And there are reports around that your library card was found in his wallet."

The cops had actually believed Martin? Ferrie worried.

Shaking, he hung up the phone. He crossed himself, deciding not to spend the night in Alexandria but instead to drive toward New Orleans, two hundred miles away. He corralled Al and Melvin, who were instead ready to get off the road and party.

He stopped the Comet at several gas stations on the way to use public phones, trying to reach Gill. He finally connected.

"Things have heated up—you now gotta get back to New Orleans," Gill said. "It'll make things worse if you appear to be in hiding. They're ready to hunt you down. You may avoid having to wear an orange jumpsuit if we go down to Camp Street voluntarily."

"What's the latest with my library card? That asshole didn't have my library card. It's in my apartment."

"I'm checking that out," Gill said. "Jack Martin's been panicking, trying to get the cops focused on you and not him."

"Appears to be doing a shit-good job."

"I'll take care of this, Dave."

"What about the story that I hypnotized Oswald?"

"That's been killed. But I need you here pronto."

Notwithstanding Gill's new message of urgency, Ferrie wasn't in a big hurry to get back to New Orleans. And he was hungry. He and his companions drove to the Cotton Club in Old South Baton Rouge for crabmeat au gratin with the famous tartar sauce and Bloody Marys. He took comfort in the fact he'd been there in August with Dr. Mary. Bartender Jo-Jo gave the three a free round.

Ferrie was fortified but near hysteria as he approached 3330 Louisiana Avenue Parkway. He dropped Al there to check with Martens, see what was going on. Ferrie then sped off north and dropped Melvin off at his home on North Pierce.

He doubled back to Broadmoor and dialed Gill from a pay-phone on South Dorgenois, close to his apartment. He reached Gill on the first try this time.

"Things are going to hell in a hand basket, Dave. Your buddies Beauboeuf and Martens were arrested immediately after you dropped Beauboeuf off at your place. They called me for help. Martens said the cops, a bunch of them, broke into your place a few days ago and took tons of stuff from your apartment. Books, notes, passports, bags of crap, weapons. Garrison, Klein, other DA guys were there."

"Shit, shit, shit." Ferrie was agitated. His only thought was getting out of town. "*Shit.*"

He hung up—and fled. He drove back to Baton Rouge and then tacked east about fifty miles to Hammond, arriving hours after midnight.

He'd decided where to go on the fly. Another of his young male friends from the CAP was a student at Southeastern Louisiana College in Hammond. Seemed a safe place for the time being.

Believing that he was being followed, Ferrie stopped a few miles south of Hammond in Ponchatoula, turning sharply left and right on streets laid out in a grid around a rectangular park in the town and then parking the car on a side road called Wayne Street. He turned the car off and slouched down in the front seat, ruminating there for an hour and a half. He was too wired and scared to sleep. After being satisfied he in fact hadn't been followed from New Orleans, he drove up to the college to crash with his friend. He'd work on next steps there.

Thomas Compton boarded at Hollaway-Smith Hall. Ferrie had no idea how he remembered that little tidbit, but he was able to get in the new-looking dorm and knocked on Compton's door at about 5:30 a.m.

"What the hell?" Compton mumbled.

"Let me in. Fast."

Ferrie was shaking and near tears.

"I'm royally fucked. Six-feet-under fucked. I just need a place to crash for a bit."

"Sure. What's going on?"

"Believe me, you sure as shit don't want to know. All I'll say is that the cops and the fucking FBI are at my place taking stuff and waiting there to haul my ass to jail. I haven't done a damn thing wrong but there are forces at work here that are out of my control."

Compton pulled a bottle of illegal absinthe from under his bed. Ferrie gulped down a few shots and slept for several hours. When he awoke, Compton gave him a piece of plain toast. And a Mountain Dew, for the caffeine.

He called Gill.

"Dave, stop being a dumbass, you're making things worse for yourself," Gill said.

"I'm pissing in my pants."

"Just settle down and get your dumbass back here. The cops don't have anything on you. You'll be fine. And you can take some of the pressure off of your buddies Beauboeuf and Martens by clearing some things up with the cops here. Like the library card. They're being squeezed about you. Deny all the Oswald stuff. Obviously."

"God-fuck-it. All right."

"Meet me in the office downtown. I'll be there all afternoon waiting."

Ferrie left Hammond around 1:30 p.m. Stopping quickly by his apartment, which was free of cops and cameras at the time, he put on a fresh shirt. He then drove to Common Street and Gill's office.

"Look what the cat finally dragged in." Gill shook his head. "You look like the wreck of the Hesperus."

"I've had a couple of rough days," Ferrie said.

"I'm sure. But you need to compose yourself damn quick. We need to scoot. I told the local prosecutors I'd get you in as soon as you got back. Thankfully, the new DA himself—Garrison—won't be there. He's a piece of work, by the way. Got some screws loose. And he leaks like an eighty-year-old man."

Gill took Ferrie to the police department's first district station on the edge of the Quarter. He was formally arrested for being a fugitive from Texas, an absurd placeholder charge. Assistant DA Frank Klein began questioning him. Pershing Gervais, a former crooked street cop, was present. Ferrie had known Gervais since the fifties.

The Feds arrived and quickly took over the questioning. FBI special agents Wall and Shearer began by walking Ferrie through his background, with special emphasis on his CAP experience. He said he didn't know Oswald and had no recollection of him being in the CAP program. He was shown pictures of Oswald—profile, full face, and full length.

"The profile picture has a vague familiarity to it, but the other two don't ring any bells."

The FBI agents reviewed Ferrie's recent employment history with Eastern Air Lines and his work on Carlos Marcello's defense team in the RFK case.

The questions moved to the night of the assassination. The police and the FBI knew about the odd trip to Houston.

"It was the beginning of the weekend. I'd been busting my balls on the trial for over a month. It was finally over. So, I decided to get a couple of buddies and go somewhere to relax. We didn't have a specific plan, maybe go hunting, do some drinking. The one thing I definitely wanted to do was to check out a skating rink in Houston."

"Skating rink?" SA Wall asked.

"Needed to figure out a new way to make an honest living. I can't do airline flying any more, and Mr. Marcello's deportation cases are over. I heard this rink in Houston was for sale. It's ridiculously popular—thought maybe I could make some money there. I called Mr. Rolland, the guy who runs the rink, and he said I could come by to see it."

"You don't seem like an ice skater."

"Did a little in Cleveland as a kid but never liked it, sir. I've heard it's a good business, though."

"Who told you it was for sale?"

"Hmmm . . . I think it was a guy from Houston I met one night in the Quarter."

"Name."

"I'll have to rack my brain to come up with the name."

"You got the money to buy this rink?"

"I have some savings and a line of credit with a banker— Herbert Wagner. Call Herb."

Ferrie described his time at Winterland in some detail, including meeting with manager Chuck Rolland, and said he visited another skating rink in Houston called Bellaire for comparison's sake.

"We left Houston Saturday evening and drove to Galveston. We actually stopped at the Space Center for about twenty minutes, looked around, got back on the road. It's not a long drive to Galveston. We checked into a motel—the Driftwood, I believe. Hit a couple of bars, went to bed."

"Why Galveston?"

"I've had some fun there over the years. I thought the boys would like it."

"And then?"

"And then we thought it would be relaxing to drive back to New Orleans along part of the Gulf coast from Galveston. If you haven't done that trip, by the way, you should. It's stunning, sir."

"Fine. More detail?"

"We got up pretty early on Sunday, had breakfast, watched a little news, including the Oswald thing—and then hit the trail. We took the ferry over to Port Bolivar to pick up the coast road to Port Arthur. We made some stops. You can check on those. We had to stop to get new spark plugs for the Comet. It was a Gulf station on the left side of the road, just past Port Arthur on

87—Gulfway Drive. Called Weeks Service Station, I think. We were there for about a half hour. In fact, they had the TV on and I watched some of JFK lying in state at the Capitol."

"That raises my biggest question about your little trip," SA Wall stated. "The whole country's dazed and grieving. And you and your buddies go lollygagging over to Texas, in the middle of the night, to have some kicks? Don't make sense."

"I get that, sir. I liked the guy, Kennedy, and I was really sorry it happened. But there was nothing we could do about it. I knew I just had to get away for a spell. And I'd made the arrangements. Didn't think too much about it."

"Where else could we check your story out?"

"Let me think. So we crossed into Louisiana from Orange and stopped for dinner at a place in Vinton. Buster's Bar and Grill. Mr. Gill has a client there that I've done some work for. This guy owns Buster's. I spoke with him for quite a while about a case Mr. Gill's working on for him in Lake Charles."

"What's his name?"

"Marion James Johnson."

Ferrie then described the next stop 120 miles northeast at Alexandria and his call to Layton Martens. Martens had told him, he related, that he was being tied to the assassination based on information Jack Martin was providing to authorities. Martens said there were TV trucks in front of his house. He then detailed the trip through Baton Rouge, to New Orleans, to Hammond, and back to New Orleans. As soon as he got home, he said, he told Mr. Gill that he wanted to go straight to the authorities. He had nothing to hide.

Gill chimed in, "Jack Martin is flat out lying."

Martin had often used false names, mainly "Jack Suggs," Ferrie told SA Wall. Ferrie had heard that Martin had been charged with murder years ago in Texas. He was a career thug and fraudster, Gill added.

"Martin said my library card was found on Oswald," Ferrie complained. "How he came up with that bullshit story I don't know, but you can find my library card in the stuff you guys took from my home. Check the property room." Gill had earlier confirmed that the card was there among the material seized from Ferrie's apartment.

"I can only guess that Martin is scared you'll come after him on the assassination, so he made all of this stuff up," Ferrie continued. "Probably while he was drunk. Must've come up with the hypnotism lie too."

What do you know about Cuba groups in town? Ferrie took a chance and volunteered Arcacha Smith's name, but said he was anti-Castro and Ferrie had had only some brief contacts a year or two ago. They didn't seem to care about Arcacha Smith. *The Fair Play for Cuba Committee?* He had no recollection of it. *Know Ruby?* No.

There were no questions about Carlos Marcello, though Ferrie was known in town as a Marcello associate. The presence of Gill, Marcello's lawyer, confirmed Ferrie's importance to the New Orleans mob network. But still no questions.

The police held him overnight, though not in an orange jumpsuit, and then released him on Tuesday. Gill agreed that he would submit to a further interview the next day and that he wouldn't leave the environs of New Orleans. The second interview was shorter. The FBI agreed to conduct it at Ferrie's apartment. Gill had retrieved the library card from the property room in the station on the edge of the French Quarter and brought it with him. New Orleans Public Library card #ML89437 in the name of Dr. David Ferrie.

Thirteen days later, Ferrie provided a two-page statement dated December 10—personally typed on his Olivetti—to Regis Kennedy, the senior FBI agent in New Orleans, drilling in on his key points.

> I have no records, or recollection, to my knowl-
> edge, to show that LEE HARVEY OSWALD was,
> or was not, a member of . . . the Civil Air Patrol.
> To my best knowledge and belief I do not know
> LEE HARVEY OSWALD, and have no personal

recollection of ever having met him. If I ever did meet him it was very casual and to my best recollection have not seen him in recent years.

I have not frequented any night clubs in the city of Dallas in the last fifteen years. To my knowledge, I have never met JACK RUBY who, I understand, from public sources, operated a night club in Dallas, Texas.

A student of a CAP squadron that had been a member for a complete course would not have received enough training with firearms to enable him to develop any proficiency in the use of a gun, in my opinion. Instructions were never given, to my knowledge and recollection, to use a telescopic sight on a rifle.

I have for years been a student of hypnotism. From my study and knowledge of the effects of hypnotic induction and the subsequent hypnotic states, I do not believe it would be possible to induce a post-hypnotic suggestion, ordinarily, which would last long enough without a series of repeated suggestions, to enable an individual to commit a crime, especially one involving a series of discretionary judgements.

That said, the FBI never again sought out Ferrie.

CHAPTER 48

The next Saturday night, Ferrie ran into Jack Martin, trilby hat and all, gambling at the Lomalinda. Feverish with anger, he confronted Martin about his false allegations.

"Settle down, Dave," Martin responded. "It's not at all what you think. Let's talk."

"Talk to your mother—she's the only one who'd believe your fucking bullshit." Ferrie balled his fist.

"She's dead."

"You probably killed her, wouldn't surprise me."

"C'mon. Give me a few minutes. I'm beggin' you."

Ferrie reluctantly agreed to go with Martin over to the Hotel Monteleone, where it would be a little quieter.

They settled into a booth in the lounge area at the back of the Hotel's Carousel Bar, away from the hullabaloo emanating from a couple of drunks at the revolving bar. The booth was close to the large model ship. One of Don Lamond's insane but brief drum solos in Bobby Darin's finger-snapping version of "Beyond the Sea," sounding like drums falling down a flight of stairs, was in the air as they stared at each other.

"Here's the deal," Martin started. "I went with Banister to have some drinks the afternoon Kennedy was shot."

"Nah. He was at the court and then at the party here."

"Nope—you probably just assumed that. He told me he didn't feel like it. He said he'd fucked with a witness for Marcello and it was eating at him. Wasn't in the mood. So we went to the Katz 'n Jammer for a couple of shots. We then went to his office. Delphine was there."

"Where's this going?"

"You probably know that Banister's been acting kind of weird for a while. Disturbed."

"Stay focused. Why did you try to fuck me?"

"Let me finish. Back at his office that afternoon, Banister was tense, nervous—then became nutso. He started yelling at me—crazy shit. Out of the blue, he said I'd been making too many expensive long-distance calls on a case. What? He then started screaming about the assassination. He said people were going to take him down—because he worked with Oswald so recently, I assumed. He said he might go to the cops. Might tell them about everyone who was with Oswald over the summer. Get it over with. I was thrown for a loop."

"Jesus, Jack. But why rat me out?"

"I told him to calm down, asked him why the fuck he'd do that. He went shit-ballistic. Ranting about how much trouble he was in and repeating that he'd turn us all in. He said I'd have to watch my back for the rest of my life. He was wild-eyed.

"He then took his .357 Magnum out of his holster," Martin continued. "Held it by the butt and started beating me on the head with the barrel. Christ, I was stunned. Literally. I started bleeding like a Russian princess. Delphine saw it all."

"Great story. But meaningless to me."

"Just hold on. I blew outta there, blood flowing down my face, and made a beeline to Charity Hospital. I got patched up and went home. I was fucked-up, man. I couldn't think straight. I called the cops on Banister, though I didn't plan to press charges. I was beginning to hallucinate about being hung for conspiring to kill Kennedy. I don't know shit about the Kennedy thing, but I couldn't think of anything else. I called this guy in the DA's office. Herman Kohlman. Said someone might say I had something to do with the assassination. I swore I didn't.

"I was scared, Dave. To save my ass, I guess, I just blurted out that they needed to check you out because you knew Oswald really well."

"Weak. Fucking pathetic. Shit, Jack. That guy Kohlman knows a lot about me, he used to be a reporter."

Perry Como's "Papa Loves Mambo" was now playing.

"I was in a swivet. I didn't know what I was doing. And I'd had a few drinks by then. I must have just had telephone-itis, just kept talking out of my ass. But, look, here's the important thing. I've now told the cops that the calls I made about you were the result of shock and brain injury and that nothing I said was true."

"I'm sure they already knew you have brain damage. Jack, they could've roasted me on Gruesome Gertie based on what you said. Where did the library card story come from?"

"I swear, I'm really not sure. I thought I heard something on the news about somebody's library card being found on Oswald. No idea why I thought it was yours, maybe was the booze talking to me. But *I* never told the cops anything about your library card. I did mention it to Hardy Davis—you know, the bail bondsman. But not the cops."

"Davis's a prick.

"And I hypnotized Oswald to kill JFK?"

"Have no fucking idea where that shit came from," Martin said. "Not a clue."

"Well, notwithstanding your miserable treachery, you asshole, the cops and the Feds have cleared me."

"Hate me all you want, but I'm not your problem. Banister is cracking. I could see it weeks ago, well before he beat the shit out of me. He's feeling the pressure big time. He's going to end up squealing to the cops about *all* of his Marcello work, not just the Oswald stuff. He can deep six Marcello and Gill for a hundred things *and* take you down with them—whether or not you guys had anything to do with Kennedy."

Sinatra's 1961 swing rendition of "That Old Black Magic" was winding down as the two men left the bar.

CHAPTER 49

rank Sinatra was in the Rosedale Cemetery in West Los Angeles on the day JFK was gunned down. A scene for a Gordon Douglas movie, a musical called *Robin and the 7 Hoods*, was being filmed there. Just before he heard the news, Sinatra had noticed a grave stone near the filming location for a John F. Kennedy, born 1873, died 1940.

Judy Campbell was five miles away at the Beverly Crest Hotel, at South Spaulding Avenue and Wilshire Boulevard on the eastern edge of Beverly Hills. "Luxuriously furnished, swimming pool, patio dining, completely air-conditioned, complimentary television, radio, complete food and liquor service, under cover garage." A nice place to hunker down, which is what Judy was doing.

Sinatra and Campbell had been incommunicado for some time, but their affection for each other hadn't diminished. Nor had their affection for JFK, though each had been estranged from the president for some time.

Sinatra's strain with JFK had been caused by RFK, who didn't want JFK seen cavorting with a man who associated with gangsters. Push came to shove when JFK had been scheduled to stay with Sinatra on a West Coast swing in the fall of 1962. Sinatra was excited, even going to the trouble of having a helipad built at his Palm Springs house. But RFK nixed the visit with Sinatra at the last minute. Instead, he lined JFK up to stay in Palm Springs with Sinatra's long-time friend and role model Bing Crosby. Sinatra was enraged at the Kennedys. He threw several champagne glasses against his living room wall.

Upon learning of RFK's action, he asked fellow Rat Pack member Peter Lawford, the president's brother-in-law, to intercede. Bing Crosby, though honored to have JFK as a house guest, also went to Lawford on his friend Sinatra's behalf. Lawford failed to make any difference, though Sinatra suspected the weak-kneed Lawford put little effort in to trying. Miffed at Lawford, he vetoed Lawford's scheduled role in *Robin and the 7 Hoods* as Allan A. Dale, a good-guy member of Robin's Merry Men. Lawford was replaced, at Sinatra's direction, by none other than Bing Crosby, rewarded for his fidelity.

Douglas's movie was well-stocked with stars in addition to Sinatra and Crosby—Dean Martin, Sammy Davis Jr., Peter Falk, Victor Bueno, Hans Conried, Tony Randall, Edward G. Robinson. The graceful but beginning-to-age brunette Barbara Rush played Marian, who ended up running off with Allan A. Dale at the end of the movie. The song "My Kind of Town" was introduced to the world in this movie and later nominated for an Academy Award.

Judy's strain with JFK was more serious. She'd last slept with JFK in December 1962. That visit had been matter-of-fact, and Judy began to believe that JFK was taking her for granted. She also sensed at that time that, with his successful conduct of the missile crisis, he was increasingly confident about winning a second presidential term. Consequently, he'd stick with his icy wife at least through the election.

Unable to live like that, Judy had been considering giving JFK an ultimatum when her life was seismically rocked in January 1963—she learned she was pregnant with JFK's baby. She waited a couple of weeks to tell him.

Invariably poised and unflappable, JFK had been shaken by this news. After quizzing Judy to make sure it was his baby, he composed himself and offered to support whatever decision she made about the baby. But his body language clearly sent a different message. She promised JFK she'd keep their little secret. JFK's political career hung in the balance. He promised to make it up to her later.

Judy reluctantly aborted the baby at the end of January. Though the procedure was illegal, Sam Giancana pulled some powerful strings to have it done at Chicago's Grant Hospital. Judy had lied to Giancana and said the baby was the product of a drunken one-night stand in New York.

Giancana's feelings for Judy had grown exponentially over the previous twenty-two months. In an emotional moment before the abortion, Giancana offered to marry Judy and help raise the baby. Stunned, and appreciative, Judy kissed him gently but declined. She still saw JFK in her future.

However, this was not to be. Judy and JFK had had a few cursory contacts in the spring after the abortion. Judy did engineer an encounter at the Mayflower Hotel in May, but, even though she'd sported an elegant, sexy Audrey Hepburn look, there were no sparks. JFK went back to the White House after a couple of drinks. He cut off all contact after Jackie miscarried baby Patrick in early August.

||||

Both Judy and Sinatra were thunderstruck by the assassination.

Sinatra immediately stopped the filming in Rosedale Cemetery. He walked around the cemetery for several hours by himself. Director Gordon Douglas offered to stop for the day, but he declined.

"Let's do the damn thing. I don't want to come back again."

After the day's shoot was finished, Sinatra was driven by his valet George Jacobs at high speed the 111 miles to his Palm Springs home. He then virtually disappeared for three days, grieving alone.

When Judy heard the news from Dallas, she fell to the floor in her Beverly Crest Hotel room. She didn't leave her room for a week. Just drank, cried, and slept. Except for speaking twice on the phone with her older sister Jacqueline, a former movie and TV actress who had performed under the stage name Susan

Morrow, Judy spoke to no one. Her "Uncle" Armand had broken contact after she'd left Trafficante's colleague Giancana.

As Judy was coming out of her week-long funk, she called Sinatra in Palm Springs. She needed to see him, even if for just an hour or so. Sinatra agreed. Giancana's mob colleague Johnny Roselli, who had become friendly with Judy, drove her the two hours to Palm Springs. Roselli had booked two rooms at the swanky Riviera Hotel on North Indian Canyon Drive. His girlfriend Dorothy Towne would be sharing his room.

Sinatra met Judy and Roselli the next day, November 30, at the Canyon Country Club, five miles south of the Riviera on the southern edge of this man-made city in the desert.

Surrounded by a cloud of smoke, Dean Martin and ten others were seated at a long table with Sinatra at the Country Club's restaurant. Sinatra jumped up from the table when he saw Judy, snubbing out his cigarette in an ashtray.

"Hey doll, my Jude," he said, hugging her. "Johnny, can I take Judy for a bit? Go up and sit with Dean. He's in his funny-drunk phase."

Judy and Sinatra went into a side room. They hugged again.

"You okay?" Sinatra asked.

"Drained, empty. How could this happen, Francis?"

"Who knows, babe. I don't. Jesus. I've had a rough time with it, really rough for a few days. I'm trying to get on with things now, but it's trying."

"Francis, I took envelopes of stuff back and forth between Jack and Sam. Do you know what that was all about? Sam ended up getting really pissed at Jack."

"I don't. And sure as shit don't want to know."

"I feel like Sam had something to do with Jack's death. I think there was something in those envelopes that angered him. Shit, Francis. I may have blood on my hands."

Sinatra hugged her more closely. "Nah, babe, don't torture yourself. But Christ, it did look like a mob hit, didn't it? I don't believe the lone-nut crap. And then the hit on Oswald. C'mon? Here's my advice. Lie low, don't talk to anybody about any of this again. Never. *Mai più*! Live a quiet life somewhere. Get married. Have a kid. Learn how to golf."

They broke their hug and parted. Roselli drove Judy back to the Beverly Crest, where she stayed in her room for another week.

〣〣

Ten days after saying goodbye to Judy, Sinatra picked up his phone in Palm Springs. He didn't recognize the low male voice on the phone. "Mr. Sinatra?"

"Yep."

"Greetings, sir. News item for you—we got your son."

"What? Who's this?"

"Are you listening? Your son's with us. Kidnapped. He's okay for now, Big Frankie. A little bruised but okay. He'll stay okay if you pay attention to us."

"Let me talk to him."

"I'll put him on. For five seconds."

"Dad," Frank Junior said nervously. "I'm all right. Love you and mom. Don't worry."

"Where are you, Frankie?"

Sinatra heard the phone rustle around. "That's it from Little Frankie," the man said. "Here's what we want, Mr. Sinatra. Two hundred and forty thousand dollars. Simple. You probably got it in your fat wallet. If not, get the dough quick. Or the bruises turn into . . . dead."

"Where are you?"

"All I can tell you is that we are at a very nice gas station. Not too far away."

"Why's he bruised? How'd you get him? Where—in Tahoe?"

"This ain't an interview, Mr. Sinatra. Though I will say we did the crowd at Harrah's a favor. Little Frankie's singing was annoying everybody, so we took him away and went on a car ride."

The kidnapper hung up. Sinatra called the FBI. He thought about calling RFK, but RFK was too grief-stricken, so he called

RFK's Deputy Attorney General Nick Katzenbach. Katzenbach advised him to pay the ransom. The FBI, he said, would arrange for currency that could be tracked by serial number.

News of the kidnapping leaked out pretty quickly. One of the first callers to Sinatra was Sam Giancana. "Shit, what a nightmare. I'm sorry, *mi hermano*. Anything, and I mean anything, we can do, just name it. We can help you get these punks. Frankie will be fine."

"*Paisano*, God bless you. I'm not fucking around with Frankie's life. These assholes just want money. I'm going to pay, maybe even more than what they've asked for. I just want the kid back."

Several hours later the kidnappers called again, from a different gas station. "Mr. Sinatra, what say you on the 240 large? Your Frankie is getting nervous. I think he just pissed his pants."

"Put him on."

"Frankie," Sinatra heard the kidnapper say. "Daddy wants you. Keep your blindfold on. You can say two words, 'I'm okay.' That's it."

"Dad," Frank Junior said. "I'm okay."

A voice in the background yelled, "We said *two* words, you pussy." Sinatra could hear a thump, probably to the back of Frank Junior's head.

The kidnappers told Sinatra to have a courier with the money go to a specified payphone the next morning.

The voice streaming from the earpiece on the payphone's handset the next day told the courier, an FBI agent, to go to another payphone two miles away. The agent ended up going to a total of five payphones around LA before being ordered to drop the money off between two buses parked at a Texaco station in Sepulveda.

Not long after the FBI made the drop, one of the kidnappers let Frank Junior go by the side of the Mulholland Drive overpass on the San Diego Freeway. Disoriented and scared, Frank Junior made his way south into the ritzy Bel Air section of LA.

He waved down a security guard patrolling the neighborhood. The guard stowed Frank Junior, at his request, in the trunk of his car to avoid the press and drove him to the nearby home of Nancy Barbato, his mother.

When the news of Frank Junior's release reached Sam Giancana, he called Sinatra. "Hallelujah, baby. He's fine?"

"Thanks be to God."

"*Si, mio amico.*"

"Sam, I gotta ask. You must know something about this kidnapping. You know everything. Is it 'cause the Kennedy's kept coming at you folks?"

"You kidding, right? Francis, my friend—I know nothing. I love you and the kid. But I gotta think you should take this as a message. A message from somebody. You're a powerful guy, Francis. Your hands are in many different things. You know a lot of shit about a lot of people. You got power. Someone wants you to be careful, be smart. You and your family were lucky this time. *Non dimenticario mai.*"

"Sam, Sam, *si, lo so*. Please, I'm not a threat to nobody."

"*Intesi*. Understood my brother. Go to your son, kiss him on both cheeks for me. Hug him close."

Giancana hung up and dialed Los Angeles. "Johnny. *Va bene*. I'm damn sure Francis got the message—*silenzio* about me, us, JFK, Judy. And he should've tried shit-harder to stop the Kennedys from fucking with me and Carlos, shouldn't've let Bobby push him around."

"*Magnificu*, Sam."

CHAPTER 50

Sunday, December 1, 1963, was Ferrie's first free day since preparation for the Marcello trial had begun in earnest in October. For the first time in many weeks, he had the time to hold a mass in his apartment. Eight of his followers attended. Ferrie prayed for the soul of President Kennedy, pointing at his American flag. And he prayed for Oswald's soul. He also honored Officer Tippit, whom Oswald had incomprehensibly gunned down as he was trying to escape. Ferrie then gave Holy Communion.

After the mass he hung up his black robe and decided to call Dr. Mary. She'd previously left several messages for him at Gill's office.

"Ma'am, I've been meaning to call but have been tied up with Mr. Gill on some legal things. How are you?"

"Just fine. I'm working too hard, but I do have today off."

"Excellent. How about some tea?"

"Sure, come on over."

"Ma'am, how about this? Let's go over to the Roosevelt, have tea and scones there. My treat."

"No oranges all the way from China?"

"Let's see if the Roosevelt can do that."

They greeted each other warmly several hours later at the Roosevelt. The Roosevelt always had a cream-of-the-crop crowd for afternoon high tea, which was provided in the Blue Room. Demurely dressed tea girls, all white, worked with the waiters and waitresses, all black, to make sure the customers, all white, were well-served.

On the night of November 22, after telling Ferrie at the Hotel Monteleone to be careful and then returning to her home, Dr. Mary had opened the Town and Country envelope he'd put in her hand. *"Dear Dr. Mary. If we don't see each other again, keep me in your heart for a while. DWF."*

Short and sweet, Dr. Mary thought to herself at the time. *And scary.*

As soon as she'd heard about the assassination, Dr. Mary suspected Ferrie was involved in some way. That's why she tracked him down at Marcello's victory party that Friday. She saw dread in his eyes when she found him at the front door of the Monteleone. He was jumpy. Beads of sweat on his brow. When she read the note later, her suspicion that he was connected to the murder was all but confirmed.

She was grateful to lay eyes on Ferrie at the Roosevelt that Sunday afternoon. He looked calm and happy to see her. She decided not to bring up the assassination on this pleasant occasion and focused on seeing how he was doing.

"Everything's A-OK, ma'am. Though I do miss Topolinia!"

"I'll take you to Disneyland."

"Frankly, I'm as stress-free as I've been in years. I've got some time on my hands for the first time in a long time. I'm planning to hang out my shingle as a therapist—use that PhD from the prestigious Phoenix University in Bari, Italy! I'm going to devote more time to my religious stuff, too. And flying, of course."

"I've been worried about you, so I'm really glad things sound good."

"What about you, ma'am?"

"I've got some new interesting projects at the hospital. And, like you, I seem to have more free time. I'm seeing my lady friends more often, doing dinners, soaking in operas. Life is full."

"You have a guy, ma'am?"

"No guy. Look at all the trouble guys cause!"

CHAPTER 51

After two weeks of radio silence, Gill called Ferrie and asked for a meeting to catch up. "This Friday okay? Ten a.m. at my office? Sergio'll be here too. We'll get lunch afterwards."

The meeting was on Friday the thirteenth. Ferrie entered Gill's office in the Pere Marquette Building from Baronne Street.

"My *bonco!*" Arcacha Smith said. They vigorously shook hands and clapped each other on the shoulder.

"Not the best idea to meet on Friday the thirteenth, Ray," Ferrie said. "Bad luck."

"You've apparently forgotten that Ray's a rational man," Arcacha Smith said.

"Castro was born on Friday the thirteenth. Now that's bad fucking luck," Ferrie continued.

"Not for him," Arcacha Smith joked.

"Things've settled down for you, Dave?" Gill asked, ignoring the banter.

"No TV trucks on Louisiana Avenue Parkway lately."

"And you, Sergio?" Gill asked.

"Living the dream. Good—and quiet."

"I asked you two here to go over your recent activities in Texas in more detail, now that things have settled down," Gill said. "There's a big pow-wow in about ten days with an LBJ guy. This guy's going to meet with Marcello and the other mob bosses. I'd like to be fully up to speed."

"Of course," Arcacha Smith said. Ferrie nodded.

"First and foremost, Sergio, congratulations on the hit in Dallas. Marcello's very pleased. I'd like to hear a play-by-play."

"It actually went surprisingly smoothly, guys. We got some luck with the rain stopping in the morning. We heard from the police radios that Kennedy would have the top down.

"Dave and I made sure Oswald took the Carcano in with him Friday morning. He had to go out to Ruth Paine's in Irving the night before to get it. Got a ride into town the next morning with a neighbor of Ruth's. He must've wrapped the rifle in a blanket or a sheet or something. I didn't have to get ammunition for him, he already had a clip of six full-metal-jacket, rimless bullets designed for the Carcano.

"He was to stash the rifle on an upper floor of the building when he got to work and then just go about his business until lunchtime. Not many employees in the building went to the upper floors on a regular day. And, with Kennedy coming by, nobody would be up there then. They'd all be down on the street to get a peek.

"I parked early in the morning in the railroad parking lot behind the Depository, on the other side of the hill that borders Elm Street. Brought a new really nasty pistol from Remington. Hard to get. They call it a .221 Remington Fireball XP-100. It's like a cut-down rifle—has a long barrel for a pistol. I fitted it with a Leupold scope and put it in a briefcase, along with fake Secret Service and Dallas police badges. I was nicely dressed, gray poplin jacket."

"You're always nicely dressed," Gill said.

"Indeed. I thought about setting up on the railroad overpass over Elm. It would've been an easy pot shot from there. But it was too open, and there were some Dallas cops policing it from time to time. Funny—but there were no Secret Service guys anywhere, as far as I could see.

"I could tell as soon as I got there that the better spot was on the top of the hill between Elm and the parking lot, behind and to the side of the pergola. There's a fence up there. Nobody was around. No cops. No spectators. *Nadie.* I took my sweet time setting up behind the fence, got the Fireball out of the briefcase, put it in my pocket. And waited. The grass was still wet from the overnight rain."

"How far away were you from the street?" Gill asked.

"It's much closer than I had thought it'd be. I don't know, maybe fifty feet. That entire plaza is smaller than it looks on television. Even Oswald's shot was easy, right there for the taking."

"Television makes it look like a tough shot," Ferrie said.

"Nah, not really. The only minor issue is an oak tree between the window and the street. But a decent sniper easily could work around that, at least with a decent rifle.

"The hardest thing for me was just waiting around, hoping nobody saw me. I paced around the grass, getting my shoes muddy. I had to go down and scrape them off a few times on the closest car. After a while I could hear the crowd and saw the motorcycles turn off Main onto North Houston. I looked up toward the upper floors of the Depository to see if I could see the barrel of the Carcano. I couldn't see shit, though. The sun'd come out and it was glinting off that big-ass Hertz sign. Right in my eyes.

"The whole sequence of events that followed unfolded in slow motion for me," Arcacha Smith continued. "Was kinda surreal."

"Did Oswald actually hit Kennedy?" Ferrie asked.

"Surprisingly, he did, though his first shot missed by a mile. Maybe it clipped a branch of the oak tree, or maybe he was just anxious. But it was a wild shot, way over the limousine and way down the slope to the base of the middle part of the triple underpass part of the railroad bridge. Out of the corner of my right eye, I could see a guy over there reach up and grab his face, hit by shrapnel or part of the curb."

"Oswald's next shot landed?"

"Yeah. About half way down Elm, as the car came out from behind a sign momentarily blocking my view, it was clear that JFK had been hit in the upper back. The bullet must've hit his spinal cord. His elbows quickly raised up parallel with the ground, as if he were starting the chicken dance. This is a common, involuntary reflex to a sharp punch to the spinal cord."

"Ah, the Thorburn Position," Ferrie stated.

"Shit if I know what it's called. I just know it happens. Anyway, JFK started to show he'd been hit—his smile disappeared, he looked . . . quizzical.

"I saw this all pretty clearly," Arcacha Smith continued. "Which was pretty surprising, I thought I'd be rushed. Why wasn't the car speeding up right away? Why weren't the cops and Secret Service guys shooting their rifles in the air, which they're supposed to do?

"Frankly, I felt for Kennedy. And I really felt for his wife. She looked like a model—just beautiful. But I had a job to do. I waited a few more beats for JFK to get a little further down Elm. Before I raised my pistol, I heard a third report from the Depository. That one hit Connally." Arcacha Smith paused.

"Go on," Gill said.

"I started to look through the Leupold scope on the Fireball—remember, things were really moving in slow motion for me. As I was taking aim, I saw a little prick of blood on the front of JFK's neck, near his Adam's apple. Was puzzling because there weren't any other shooters, at least as far as I knew. Must've been a piece of the bullet that ricocheted back from the Connally shot. Or maybe a piece of something in the car kicked up by that shot."

"That probably confused the poor bastards trying to do the autopsy," Ferrie said.

"That's only a good thing—confusion. You got off one shot?" Gill asked.

"That's really all I could take, no time to reload. JFK was right in front of me just as Connally was hit. His back brace probably made the shot easier, he was still sitting upright even though he'd been hit in the back.

"Jackie was turning to look at him. There was a strange silence for a few beats. Eerie. I took my shot, aiming for his right eye. I was about an inch off because JFK jerked his head slightly forward as I pulled the trigger. Got him in the right temple. His head just exploded. Tough to watch."

"What ammo did you use?" Gill asked.

"I chose the Fireball because it can shoot .222 ammo with a mercury load—awesome. Basically a longer, souped-up version of a .22 shell but stuffed with mercury. The copper jacketing depresses against the much harder mercury core and shatters into fragments on impact. The forensics guys won't be able to tell what kind of bullet shattered JFK's head."

"Oswald got off three shots," Gill summed up. "That's consistent with what I'm told the cops found at the Depository, three shell casings on the floor. One shot hit Kennedy but not fatally. One hit Connally. One missed. The Feds'll know the head shot came from a second shooter."

Arcacha Smith agreed. "They'll know."

"They'll move heaven and earth to cover that up," Gill said. "The world can't know there was another shooter who got away. The Feds, the Dallas cops, LBJ—they'll wanna get this behind them as quick as they can."

Ferrie chimed in. "They're going to have to put on a magic act to conclude that Oswald did all the shooting."

"Man, I hope Houdini's ghost helps them out," Arcacha Smith said.

Arcacha Smith continued his story. "My poplin jacket was reversible. Right after my shot, I turned it inside out. It went from a grey to a plaid jacket. I rushed down the hill to the parking lot. There were people hurrying up the other side of the hill from Elm. I'm sure some of them had heard my shot.

"There was a Dallas cop in the parking lot. The cop stopped me. I admit, I was scared shitless. Before he could say anything, I whipped out my fake Secret Service badge. He quickly eyeballed it and just waved me on. I didn't see any other badges in the area—and saw zero guys who looked like real Secret Service."

"The Secret Service wasn't at its best, as we predicted," Gill said, "And I heard most of JFK's agents were hungover that day.

Virtually the whole detail had closed down a Fort Worth club the night before. The Cellar. Funny thing. The owner of the Cellar's a crooked friend of Ruby's named Kirkwood."

"Obviously, the Dallas cops were no better," Arcacha Smith said. "Yukking it up with each other, smoking cigarettes, acting like it was a day off. Most of them hated Kennedy, maybe that's why. They just didn't give a shit."

Gill responded, "Regardless. What you accomplished was incredibly impressive. I can assure you Mr. Marcello is very pleased."

"No hay problema."

"What you didn't know at the time, Sergio," Gill continued, "is that we had three of our guys in the railroad yard, in a boxcar, keeping an eye on you and ready to jump in if there was a problem."

"You guys are good. Who were they?" Arcacha Smith asked.

"Small-time crooks. Guys who knew what we could do to them if they didn't do as they were told. One of the guys, named Holt, was in on the Bay of Pigs. Another, Harrelson, is a real-life contract killer. We have a lot of stuff on that guy."

"Probably better that I didn't know about this," Arcacha Smith said.

"By the way, Dave, the third guy told us he was in that boy's flying club at Moisant Field when you and Oswald met," Gill reported. "He knew both of you."

"Name?"

"Chuck Rogers."

"Yeah, yeah. Brainy guy, taught the kids how to use radios, probably in his thirties then. But I don't get it. He had a good job, for one of the oil companies, I think. What happened to him? He must've royally fucked something up to be working for you guys now."

"Long story," Gill said. "Let's just say for now that he's a really savvy psychopath, will probably murder somebody someday."

"We of course wanted Oswald to get caught," Arcacha Smith resumed. "But we told him we'd get him to a safe house if he bolted the building right away and got down to the parking lot. There was a door on the north side that opened out onto the dock area and four overhead doors on the north and west walls.

"I'd told him he had five minutes to get there, I couldn't wait any longer. But I knew that'd never happen, there'd be too much commotion for him to make it down that quickly. Not taking any chances, though, I didn't even wait a minute. I just beat it to the safe house."

"Didn't matter, he never made to the parking lot," Gill said. "According to what Campisi learned from DA Wade, Oswald got held up by Truly and some reporters rushing into the building. So, he just sauntered out the front door of the building. The cops didn't seal the building right away. He walked east about seven blocks and then took a bus west on Elm heading back toward Dealey Plaza."

"That's another example of the great job the Dallas police did," Ferrie said sarcastically. "I heard traffic started flowing through Dealey pretty soon after the shooting. That whole plaza should've been a crime scene."

"Of course," Gill said. "The traffic was a tangle going back into the plaza. Oswald got off the bus at Elm and North Lamar and grabbed a cab to his boarding house on North Beckley. We think he took this weird trip to Oak Cliff to see if there was a message for him there about what he should do next. Of course, there wasn't."

"So he decided to go out and shoot a cop?" Arcacha Smith's asked acerbically.

"Wade told Campisi that Oswald grabbed a jacket and his pistol and started walking southeast. Where was he going? It looks like he was heading down to Jefferson Boulevard to get another taxi to take him to the Greyhound station downtown on South Lamar. From there, best guess is that he was planning to take a bus south, follow the same route he did in September. Laredo, Nuevo Laredo, Mexico City. He knew his way around Mexico City. Oswald didn't know Dave was in Houston on a rescue mission."

"But the cop got in Oswald's way," Ferrie said.

"As you know," Gill responded, "the cop, Tippit, was a regular at Ruby's place. My thinking is that Tippit recognized Oswald from the club and just stopped him to chat. Oswald freaked and shot him. Jackass."

"The cops said Tippit stopped Oswald because he matched the description of the suspect given to the cops," Arcacha Smith said.

"That's what they say. But, c'mon. The description was of a white guy in his early or mid-twenties, five feet nine-to-eleven. Wearing a windbreaker. There are a thousand guys in Dallas that meet that description. Tippit was a farm-dumb guy, just driving around and saw somebody he knew," Gill said.

"If Oswald had had an ounce of composure, he would've casually chatted with Tippit and then made it to the bus station," Ferrie said.

"He'd be drinking mojitos and screwing Silvia Duran while listening to 'La Cucaracha' as we speak." Gill smiled.

"Instead," Ferrie said, "like John Brown's body, Oswald's is 'a-moldering in the grave.'"

CHAPTER 52

"You went straight to a safe house?" Ferrie asked Arcacha Smith.

"Civello's guys have a place on South Ervay Street, down near Beaumont. Near Ruby's Silver Spur Club," Arcacha Smith responded.

"Wait," Ferrie said, surprised. "Ruby still has that club? He never told me about that one."

"Not surprising," Gill said. "He runs that outside of Marcello's orbit. He has a long history with it. Sleazier than his other clubs. It's by an old movie theater called the Ervay that Ruby used to run in the fifties."

"I parked about four blocks away, took off the plaid jacket, put on a blue blazer and a clip-on tie, grabbed a briefcase I'd stowed in the car, and walked to the safe house. Some cop cars whizzed by. But I guess I didn't look like a killer."

"That's a big reason why we chose you, señor," Gill said.

"The plane was all gassed up and ready to go in Galveston," Ferrie said. "Just waiting for you, Sergio."

"We would've had fun in Guatemala City. No doubt. But I wasn't identified by anybody. I guess they weren't looking for an older guy who looked like a snooty sommelier, they only went after a white-trash young guy. And things cooled off like magic when Oswald was caught at that theater. Shit, the guy was locked up within ninety minutes of the killing. Imbecile. The cops just cashed it in after that. By two thirty, it suddenly was like nothing'd happened in Dallas. No more dragnet, nothing. I know it's a shitty police department, but, God Almighty, it was the president. They apparently felt they had caught their guy. Case closed.

"I thought, what the hell? I just took off. Got in my car. Drove back to Houston and my family. Got there for dinner. Easy."

"Out of curiosity, what was the plan if it'd kept raining on Friday and the top would've been on the car?" Gill asked.

"We would be up shit creek but maybe with a paddle," Arcacha Smith responded.

"Can't wait to hear about this," Ferrie said.

"There's nothing in that car that's bulletproof. The top's plexi-glass. The windows are standard two-ply glass. Don't know why that is, but it gave me a chance to hit him pretty easily where I was. I would've made a game-time decision whether to shoot, was hoping he'd have the window down even if it was raining."

"And Oswald?" Gill asked.

"Yeah. So, I told him not to shoot at the car if the top was up. He couldn't have seen Kennedy anyway and probably would've hit one of the ladies. He was to shoot three or four shots above the car, into the air right after the turn. People would've probably froze for a second or two and then my shot would come, while Oswald was still firing. The cops still would've looked first at the Depository Building."

"One last thing, Sergio. What is your alibi for where you were that Friday?"

"My boss—a goofy guy with a goofy name, Cal Clausel—will say I was at our office in East Houston on November 22. I'd told him I'd met a girl in Galveston and was going to spend the day with her. He was a little surprised I would cheat on my wife—which I don't do, by the way—but he was fine to cover for me. I'd covered for him once on a cheating weekend he enjoyed a few months back at the La Posada Hotel in Laredo with a Mexican waitress. I knew I could count on him."

"Anybody else who'll say you weren't in the office?"

"No. I told old Mrs. Magee, Clausel's secretary, the same story, very sheepishly. She'll say I was there—she wouldn't want to hurt Shelia's feelings by saying I was screwing around on her."

"And you came home to your wife just like it was a normal day?" Gill asked.

"Yeah, like clockwork. She was glued to the TV watching the coverage, pretty upset. She frankly didn't pay much attention to me."

"Goddamn amazing," Ferrie said. "Maybe God *was* with us!"

"I would've had some 'splaining to do if I'd gone to Guatemala or spent the weekend in Dallas. I was going to say it was a secret project for Marcello, I couldn't talk about it. But she's no dummy. She would've wondered. But it did seem we were blessed on this thing."

"Good." Gill turned to Ferrie. "Tell us about the Ruby hit on Oswald."

"I did a quick check-in call with Ruby from the Monteleone lobby during the Friday party, to make sure he hadn't blown town. Then I talked to him longer when we got to Houston in the middle of that night. I made sure he was ready to go and that he'd do it before Oswald was transferred out of the city jail. He pushed back a little on whether this was really necessary, but he knew he had to do it. He'd gotten the message that his sister and dog were otherwise at risk.

"I reminded him he'd be seen as a hero, that no jury would convict him."

"Ruby was in the Oswald press gaggle on Friday night at the police offices in the Municipal Building," Gill said.

"Yeah, I heard that. That was even before my call from the skating rink."

"Later," Gill said, "they brought Oswald out for a kinda press conference in the basement assembly room, just outside where they do the lineups. Ruby was down there too. it looked to me like Oswald recognized Ruby, he seemed to shoot Ruby a smirk. And then, when Wade answered shouted questions from reporters, Ruby fucking spoke up and corrected the name of the Fair Play for Cuba Committee."

"I saw footage of that in Galveston," Ferrie said. "Stupid. He looked good, though. Nice suit, pocket square, horn-rimmed tinted glasses. No doubt had shaved for a second time that day and had lathered McLean's hair lotion all over his head."

"That hairy bastard always shaves twice a day," Gill said.

"I could use some of that hair." Ferrie grinned.

"He'd sell you some, he'll do anything to make some dough."

"The next day, Saturday, was a dead day for Ruby getting any access to Oswald. They took him for a lineup, but they had him pretty well surrounded in the hall, and otherwise he was locked away. I called Ruby again when I went back to the skating rink Saturday afternoon. He said he'd get the prick Sunday morning, that they were moving Oswald then. Pat Dean had told him."

"He made it look impulsive," Gill said.

"*He* came up with that charade, trying to make sure he avoided the chair I assume. He told me he was going to drive from his apartment near the zoo, park his white Oldsmobile in a lot at Main and Pearl, and go to the Western Union office, right by the Municipal Building. That would be the reason he was downtown on Sunday, to wire some money he owed a stripper. He said he often wires twenty or twenty-five bucks to girls, often poor 'Little Lynn.' Then, so his story will go, he suddenly realized he was by the police station and decided to see what was going on.

"He was surprisingly clever. It was his idea to leave his mangy dachshund in the car. He'd never do that if he knew he was going to be locked away, right? He'd planned to call George Senator later, have his roomie get the dog."

"But why go to the police garage?" Gill asked.

"He thought that through too. He knew there'd be activity around the garage ramp—not just police but media too. Dean'd told the press about the Oswald transfer to the county jail. On the spur of the moment, he'll say, he decided to go down and survey the scene."

"Letting the press know—Texas idiocy."

"Yep. Dean told the press to be in the garage by 10:00 a.m. He told Ruby, though, that Oswald wouldn't actually be moved until 11:20, 11:30, after some additional questioning."

"What then?"

"I didn't talk to Ruby again after my call with him Saturday afternoon. But I got a debrief on the rest of the escapade from Campisi. They're pretty good friends. Campisi visits Ruby in the jail.

"Campisi told me about a second clever thing Ruby did, in addition to the dog. Ruby timed the Western Union wire for very close in time to when Dean told him Oswald would appear in the garage. He kept the time-stamped receipt in his pocket—added to the *mise en scène* of a spontaneous act."

"How'd Ruby get into the garage?" Gill asked.

"People think Ruby went down the ramp," Ferrie continued. "He didn't, though he's saying he did. He left the Western Union office and jogged down the alley between the office and the Municipal. There's a door in the alley into the first floor of the Municipal, just a couple of hundred yards away. From there it's an easy walk down a fire escape stairway to the garage. Only took Ruby two or three minutes to get down there—he moves damn well for a fifty-two-year-old thug—which is good because Oswald came out of the jail office closer to 11:20 than 11:30."

"How'd he enter without being seen?" Arcacha Smith asked.

"That fire-escape stairway enters the parking garage on the opposite side from the jail office and the ramps to Main and Commerce. Everybody down there had their eyes trained on the jail office doors waiting for Oswald. Ruby came from behind them, climbed over a small railing, and was right there at the bottom of the ramp to Main, pistol in his right pocket, brass knuckles in his left. He told Campisi he saw a cop drive a car up the ramp and out to Main Street just a minute or so before they brought Oswald out."

"Did Ruby leak anything about the plan in advance?" Gill asked both Ferrie and Arcacha Smith.

"Don't think so," Arcacha Smith responded. "I did hear that Jada tried urgently to leave Dallas for New Orleans that Friday morning. But, unbelievably, she ran over a guy at Lemmon and Atwell with her white Cadillac—a TI employee, by the way. She never made it out of town that weekend. Was she trying to flee because of something Ruby said to her about the upcoming events of the day? He *had* grown pretty close to her, even though she'd stopped dancing at the Carousel a few weeks before.

"But she's not said anything."

"She did a TV interview with ABC after Ruby shot Oswald," Gill said. "She didn't say much, certainly nothing suspicious. In fact, she helped us out by saying Ruby was perfectly capable of an impulsive act like shooting Oswald."

CHAPTER 53

"Now, Dave, give us a brief status report on the Dr. Mary project," Gill requested.

"No offense, but should Sergio leave the room?"

"It's all right. He's cleared to hear this. And he knows the project's been yellow-lighted."

"The short of it is that we have a magic potion that's ready to go. We tried a version on a prisoner in August—the guy was dead forty-eight hours later.

"Dr. Mary then devised a version that's taken orally, crushed into a powder. The oral concoction works fantastically on green monkeys. On humans too? Probably, but we won't know for sure until they turn the light green again—pun intended."

"Where's the stuff now?" Gill asked.

"I've got eight vials in my fridge."

"Keep them, for now."

||||

Gill got up and paced back and forth. "We're obviously in a new phase now. Sergio, I need you to go back to Houston and resume your everyday life. I'll definitely need you for some things down the line, but you can relax with your wife and all those kids for now."

"Great. I genuinely miss selling air conditioners."

"On the other hand, Dave, we need *you* now."

"Lay it on me."

"We need your piloting skills for a 'come-to-Jesus' meeting with an LBJ guy. You gotta fly me and Marcello to the meeting."

"Sign me up."

The three men then had lunch a few blocks away at the Acme Oyster House. Fried oyster platters all around. Sides of jambalaya and grilled smoked sausages. Bloody Marys.

Two days later Gill and Ferrie had breakfast at the Royal Castle, a fast-food restaurant near the Town and Country Motel, in a booth in the back, away from other patrons.

"Our guys and the LBJ folks need to talk about where things are going to go in the future on a wide range of things. Castro, Russia, civil rights. And, most important, the Kennedy war on the mob—RFK's still around. LBJ's sending his closest advisor, Tommy the 'Cork' Corcoran, to review the bidding with us. Tommy Corcoran's been around for decades, back to FDR and the war. He's *the* Washington power broker.

"The 'Cork' *made* LBJ," Gill emphasized. "LBJ was a backbencher before he hitched his wagon to Corcoran's ass. Corcoran was impressed with LBJ. He saw a young senator who was savvy beyond his years and ruthless, so they say. Corcoran got Speaker Rayburn to be LBJ's mentor. LBJ rose quickly in the House and then later in the Senate. The 'Cork' convinced him to run with JFK in 1960, which wasn't an easy sell.

"Representations made by the 'Cork' will be as if they were made directly by LBJ," Gill continued.

"Never heard of the 'Cork,'" Ferrie said.

"You'll meet him soon—in West Virginia."

"West Virginia? I had hoped to go my entire life without ever being in that hick-ass state."

"Corcoran wants the meeting to be in driving distance of DC. Even though he's a private citizen, he's so close to LBJ that he's under a constant microscope. Reporters are much more geared up after the assassination to actually do their jobs.

"Corcoran doesn't want to draw their attention by heading out to National Airport with a briefcase," Gill continued. "If he looks like he's going off on White House business, eyes will be on him. He wants to drive in his own car on a Friday morning with his wife, like they are taking a weekend trip. He'll drop the wife off in Charlottesville at a new inn on the way."

"Where exactly are we going?"

"About a four- to five-hour drive from DC is a large resort in the middle of nowhere called the Greenbrier. The 'Cork' wants to go there. Though it's remote, the resort is huge. Rumor has it that there's a massive bunker below the main building in case there's a nuclear war, big enough for the White House, Congress, *and* Supreme Court to escape to."

"Shit, *West Virginia?*"

"It's *barely* in West Virginia, just over the border from Virginia. There's an airfield close by. You'll fly me and Marcello there and join us at the resort. The meetings with Corcoran will be in a private room with just Marcello and his colleagues. And one advisor each. I'll be Marcello's advisor."

Marcello arranged to use Schlumberger's de Havilland Dove for the trip. Ferrie, Gill, and Marcello were driven down to the old blimp airport in Houma very early on Friday morning, January 10.

White Sulphur Springs, West Virginia, where the Greenbrier was located, was more than a thousand miles from New Orleans. The Dove, with its nine-hundred-mile range, thus required a refueling stop. Ferrie chose an airport in Tennessee, the McGee Tyson Airport just south of Knoxville, 610 miles from New Orleans. A convenient and resourceful place to stop. McGee Tyson Airport served the Air National Guard, as well as Alcoa, which had a large smelting plant nearby.

From there it was 313 miles to the Greenbrier Valley Airport.

Set on eleven thousand acres, the Greenbrier had a large main building with cottages and golf courses sprinkled around the grounds. The main building was stately and historic—dating back to 1930. It was sparkling white. Its predecessor hotel, the Old White, had been built in 1858. Robert E. Lee and his family spent summers on the grounds of the Old White after the Civil War. JFK's parents honeymooned there in 1914. The Duke and Duchess of Windsor were frequent visitors to the present 1930 structure.

The interior of the Greenbrier was bursting with colorful pastels, dominated by cantaloupe melon, forest green, carnation pink, and cobalt yellow. The resort was suffused with southern hospitality and elegance. After sunset, men wore coats and ties, and the women wore tasteful, soft-hued dresses. At the time of these meetings, the resort was still adorned with Christmas ornamentation. Ferrie, Gill, and Marcello were greeted with glasses of champagne.

Tommy the "Cork" Corcoran had already arrived. Santo Trafficante, Sam Giancana, and John Roselli would arrive shortly, with their advisors, in private planes.

Marcello began to head to his suite. "Ferrie, good job—we see you when da meetings done."

"We should be finished by ten or so," Gill said. "You and the other guys can meet us for a drink later."

The bosses and their advisors met with Corcoran in the Washington Room. With time to kill, Ferrie grabbed a quick bite at the classy Old White Club in the resort's southeastern wing. JFK and three of his sisters had attended the opening of the Old White Club in April 1948. Ferrie listened to a few songs performed by the club's longtime combo, the Populaires, and then repaired to the upper lobby to reread his well-worn copy of G. K. Chesterton's *St. Francis of Assisi*.

At ten thirty Ferrie and his fellow pilots were called into the Washington Room for a nightcap. The faces of Marcello and his colleagues, and of Corcoran, looked satisfied but serious. Giancana raised a toast. "To the President of the United States, Lyndon Balls Johnson!" The next morning, the mob chieftains had a final meeting over breakfast in the Crystal Room with the "Cork."

Retracing the air lanes back to New Orleans, Ferrie, Gill, and Marcello landed at Houma in the late afternoon on Saturday.

"Thank you again, my friend," Marcello said to Ferrie. "*Bon prudi.*"

"Get some rest, Dave," Gill said. "Take tomorrow off, catch up on other things, and then let's get together for a discussion of the meetings with Corcoran on Monday out at Churchill Farms. I've called Sergio in for this. Plan to spend the night."

CHAPTER 54

Ferrie picked Arcacha Smith up at the Town and Country Motel Monday morning in his Comet. Arcacha Smith had spent the night at the motel after flying in from Houston the night before. The two drove the eleven miles to Churchill Farms. Gill was already at the farmhouse.

"You guys ready to start?" Gill said, wasting no time.

The two friends nodded. They each noticed that Banister wasn't there.

"Mr. Corcoran was clear that LBJ would back off the mob. Not a big surprise. LBJ's been taking mob money in Texas for years."

"He'll take money from anybody," Arcacha Smith said.

"But we need to play ball with him. LBJ wants three basic things from us," Gill said.

"Bad luck comes in threes," Ferrie whispered to Arcacha Smith.

"First, he wants full support for the proposition that Oswald killed JFK and that he acted alone. Whether that's true or not is irrelevant, Corcoran told us. LBJ doesn't want his administration to be distracted by conspiracy craziness and the ghost of JFK."

"What does he want us to do?" Ferrie asked.

"LBJ assumes the mob had something to do with the murder. He's no idiot. He believes the mob sent Ruby to silence Oswald. It's the mob's MO, after all. But he really doesn't give a shit. He just needs us to make sure that anybody who knows anything doesn't talk. All lips need to be sealed. Whatever it takes."

"What's LBJ going to do to keep the dogs off of us?" Ferrie asked.

"He'll push RFK out, which won't be hard. RFK's a mess. And LBJ's Warren Commission will do a snow job on Oswald. And it'll do it quickly," Gill said.

"The commissioners'll have to consider Castro, with the Bay of Pigs and all," Ferrie said. "That'll bring them to Oswald's Castro street performances here. And to us."

"They're going to do a half-assed look at Castro and then accept his denials. He had no reason to kill Kennedy. Shit, Kennedy agreed to stay away from Cuba. The 'Cork' says they have reason to believe he's not crazy, which he'd have to be to do this."

"They still worry the shit out of me," Arcacha Smith said.

"Corcoran assured us the commissioners won't go rogue,'" Gill said. "LBJ and Hoover have fixed it. They're definitely not doing a deep dive on Castro, the 'Cork' was clear, so don't sweat."

"I wouldn't be so sure about Earl Warren, that bastard. He just took the goddamn Bible out of the schools. Can't trust him." Ferrie was starting to raise his voice.

"LBJ forced Warren to chair this thing," Gill said. "Warren has no interest in the investigation and begged LBJ not to be involved. Typical LBJ, he announced to the press that Warren was chairing the commission shortly after Warren had turned him down."

"Who else is on this thing?" Arcacha Smith asked.

"LBJ also coerced that southern bigot Senator Russell to be on it. Russell has no interest either. He hates Warren, believes he's committed treason. But Russell's an extremely close friend of LBJ's. They're like family—LBJ calls him 'Uncle Dick.' He agreed as a favor to LBJ, but he won't spend hardly any time on it. He's frenzied about Negroes getting the same rights as the rest of us. He'll do whatever LBJ wants on the commission, hoping LBJ'll give him some breaks on Negro issues.

"The other members are weak," Gill continued. "The old CIA guy, Dulles, is losing his marbles. There's a congressman named Ford from Michigan who isn't the brightest guy in the world. They say he played a lot of football without a helmet. Hale Boggs also is a commissioner, but we know he won't buck Marcello on anything. Shit, he wouldn't be our esteemed second district congressman without Marcello. And he'll do whatever *LBJ* wants—he's known around Washington as 'LBJ's Man in the House.'"

"McCloy, Cooper?" Ferrie asked.

"Ah, you've done your homework," Gill responded. "McCloy in fact could be a burr in Warren's ass—fucking smart Harvard lawyer. But he'd get out-voted on anything of significance. I don't know about Cooper. He's a pretty competent guy. A Republican but a reasonable one. He and LBJ were Senate friends, and he actually did some secret work for JFK. He liked JFK. I think he'll want to close this thing up for the family."

"You'd think J. Edgar would want to investigate all leads," Ferrie stated.

"Christ, no," Gill said. "Hoover wants to get this over with just as much as LBJ. Wants to paint Oswald as an odd duck and deep-six the fact that the FBI probably fucked this up. They should've been on to Oswald, and Hoover knows it. Corcoran told us that the FBI had Oswald right in their crosshairs. Oswald actually went to the FBI offices there and left a note—two weeks before the murder. We don't know what it said because Hoover had it destroyed."

"Jesus," Ferrie exclaimed.

"And Hoover didn't lift a finger to check out any Dallas gangsters or wingnuts in advance of the visit."

"I got it," Ferrie said. "Hoover'll want to have his fat homo ass covered in the commission's final report."

"It'll be covered," Gill said. "Hoover can control the commission because they have to rely on him for most of the facts. LBJ's made sure the commission has a tight budget, so it won't have many experienced lawyers nor much ability to do independent investigating."

"All good for us," Ferrie said.

"And you think the public will buy the commission's white-wash?" Arcacha Smith asked.

"Most will for a while," Gill said. "But that'll probably start to crack in a few years. In fact, there's already a busybody Jew lawyer named Mark Lane—real name, Mark Levin—asking tough questions and making some news. Some of our guys think the KGB is using Lane to start stirring this pot, get people thinking the government is covering something up."

"Seems possible," Ferrie said. "The Russkies are always looking for ways to use some narcissistic idiot to rattle gullible Americans, make them question the system."

"The worm'll turn on the commission's report," Gill continued, "when that home movie of the murder gets played out in the public, which it will."

"Where the assassination photos in *Life* came from?" Ferrie asked.

"Civello heard from one of his Dallas FBI sources that you can see the head shot clearly in a couple of frames *Life* didn't publish and that there's no doubt the shot came from the front and right. But by the time the movie comes out, leads'll be drying up. It'll be hard to do a serious investigation."

"What's LBJ's second request?" Ferrie asked.

"LBJ wants to pivot away from Cuba. He wants all efforts against Castro—including ours—to stop, at least for the time being. He believes that Castro is contained and that Russia is focusing on other things. He doesn't wanna upset that messy apple cart."

"What? That's half the reason why we took JFK out. To get someone in the White House who'll be serious about taking out Castro," Arcacha Smith said.

"Hold on, let me finish. This is a bit of a chess game. The third thing is that LBJ believes he has no choice but to continue JFK's civil rights policies. He's gotta be seen as keeping some of JFK's legacy. And he needs the Humphrey part of the party in the election. We can't get in the way of any of his efforts on Negroes.

"The righties and southerners will go berserk when they see LBJ continuing Kennedy's civil rights policies. To soften them up, LBJ has found a big new shiny object they'll marvel over. The *Chinese* Commies! These Commies are way nastier than the Russians. As we speak, the Chinkerbells are trying to take over all of Southeast Asia, starting with South Vietnam."

"JFK was already turning to Vietnam," Arcacha Smith observed.

"The righties believe JFK was doing that just to get re-elected, that he would've let the Chinese have South Vietnam after the election," Gill said. "But LBJ's telling them he'll fight the bastards to the death."

"Sergio's right about Cuba," Ferrie said. "Why doesn't LBJ use those resources to take Cuba back?"

"The wingnuts, for the time being, are losing interest in Cuba. They feel it's too far gone. LBJ's being clever. Southerners will have an orgasm going after the Chinese. That'll soften the blow of the Negro stuff. The good news for us, we're told, is that taking care of these Asian Commies will be pretty easy and can be done quickly, while civil rights is getting done, and then LBJ promises he'll take Castro out. We'll get our casinos back and, Sergio, your people will be freed. It's just going to take a little longer than we'd thought."

"It'll be tougher than they think to beat these Orientals in their own jungles," Ferrie said.

"They're going to burn the jungles," Gill said.

"Good luck with that," Ferrie said.

"The anti-Castro stuff simply has to stop," Gill said adamantly. "Including Dr. Mary's project."

They broke for lunch. Once again some great food from Frank at Commander's Palace had been sent over—this time, Creole gumbo and griddle seared gulf fish.

||||

Things got more serious after lunch.

"Based on the messages received at the Greenbrier, Marcello has some tough action items for us," Gill said. "But first he wants to assure both of you of his confidence in you and that he knows you'll be radio-silent about the assassination. He doesn't trust many people, but he trusts you two. You've both been loyal through some pretty tough times."

It appears our lives are safe—at least for now, Ferrie thought. *Thank the Lord for having me rescue Marcello from Honduras.*

"This is rough business, as you thugs know," Gill said. "We're simply going to have to get rid of a few likely leakers. Those are the instructions."

"As in kill them?" Ferrie asked.

"Yes."

There was a moment of silence reminiscent of the meetings the previous June. All quiet except for the ticking clock. Tick. Tick. Tick. Then Gill spoke.

"You may think that an obvious dead man would be Jack Martin."

"No great loss," Arcacha Smith said.

"It wouldn't be. But Marcello wants us to hit only where necessary. He's a pretty good Catholic, you know. Wants us to be humane. Believe it or not, murder is always a last resort for him—Kennedy was a last resort. I've had extensive interviews with Martin, and I think he'll be quiet, for now anyway. And he really doesn't know anything except that we fucked around some with Oswald last summer and fall. He's clueless on the 'JFK Affair.' And on the Dr. Mary thing. We'll keep an eye on him. If he starts blabbing, we may need to change course."

"Jada?" Ferrie asked.

"Thought about that. Still possible that Ruby said something to her, given her attempt to escape Dallas right before the assassination. She could be holding on to something. But we don't think so. She's hidden herself away in New York and has been quiet. We've got people watching her up there."

"I'm sure you had no problem getting guys to watch *her*," Arcacha Smith said.

"But there are a few must-haves for now. The first, I'm sorry to say, is Banister. We all respect the guy, an American hero for a lot of his life. He's done good work for Marcello. But he's running out of steam and, frankly, there's something wrong with him. Look at his pistol-whipping of Martin. Marcello's worried."

"There's no way he'll talk, Ray," Ferrie said. "Let me go see him."

"No can do. The orders have been given. And *you* have to do it. We need you to use one of the Dr. Mary tubes in your fridge on him."

"Ah, shit. I can't do it."

Gill ignored him. "And it's gotta be done soon. If I understand this magic potion correctly, it should kill him in a few days. They won't do an autopsy on a guy his age who looks like he died of natural causes. They'll just call it a heart attack."

"God help me," Ferrie said.

"Target two's going to be even tougher for you, Dave.

"Marcello sees no option but to get rid of Dr. Mary."

Ferrie bent over, looking like he was about to throw up. He said nothing for a couple of minutes. Tick. Tick. Tick.

"You're fucking shitting me."

"I genuinely wish not. It'll be tough, I know."

"Nope. She's not getting killed by anybody. Why kill Dr. Mary? She's not going to talk. Talking would ruin her life, her career, everything. I'm beggin' you. Ray. Please. I'll watch her."

"Marcello's not comfortable with letting her go. She knows we were planning to hit Castro—and how. You and Dr. Mary are the only persons alive who know the complete picture and details of the bioweapon. Dr. Ochsner knows only the broad strokes, and Marcello'll never worry about him. Carolyn Talley's in the dark.

"If this thing got out, LBJ's fury would rain over all of us like nuclear fallout. People'd believe that Castro got wind of the work and assumed it was a CIA plot. They'll definitely throw away the Warren Commission Report then and conclude that Castro beat us to the punch, got JFK first. The dominoes would fall from there. LBJ'd be pressured to turn back to Cuba, flipping

his agenda upside down and probably getting him in a mess of
a war with Cuba. He'd be pissed. He'd figure out who was really
doing the bioweapon and then turn RFK's mob-hating acolytes
loose on us.

"And Marcello himself would pay a hefty personal price
with LBJ."

"Fucking crazy, rank speculation," Ferrie shouted.

"Maybe, but it's Marcello's crazy, rank speculation. Look,
Dave, he knows you won't leak—nor Ochsner. Just doesn't know
about the doctor, doesn't know her."

Ferrie bowed his head and prayed. *Mary, the Mother of
Forgiveness, help me to recognize my sins, know better the effects
of my sins, and realize that I had a part in Jesus's crucifixion
and death.* Ferrie was thinking of both Mother Mary *and* of Dr.
Mary.

"Keep the prayers coming, Dave, because Marcello wants *you*
to administer the magic potion to the good doctor, in addition
to Banister."

"No, sir. Christ, no."

"Yes, sir. Christ, yes."

"There's no shot in shit."

Gill paused. Ferrie stared at him and then paced around the
room. He threw a glass, which shattered against the fireplace.
Gill stared out the window. Arcacha Smith stared down at his
feet.

Ferrie was breaking down. Gill shut his eyes and thought
for a minute.

"I tell you what," Gill said. "We're not doing either of these
hits immediately. I might get my ass chewed out, but I'll revisit
Dr. Mary with Marcello at the appropriate time. Probably to no
avail, my friend, but I'll try. In the meantime, you do need to
monitor her."

"What did Mr. Marcello have in mind in terms of timing?"
Arcacha Smith asked.

"This isn't the time to take any risks with the Ruby trial
coming up," Gill said. "The trial starts around the third week

of February. The judge, Brown, is not a bad judge for an elected judge, but he's freaked out by having to do this. He'll bend over backwards to make sure Ruby has a fair trial, so he'll let the defense put anything in the record they want. Including any relevant suspicious deaths post-assassination, I'm sure. We gotta be careful until the jury comes back."

"Hard to see how Ruby doesn't go to the electric chair," Arcacha Smith observed.

"Probably will," Gill said. "But Ruby's gotten a hot-shot California lawyer named Belli. They say Belli's tenacious and ambitious. He'll be a legal god if he gets Ruby off after the whole world saw him off Oswald. He'll turn over a lot of rocks, so we need to lie low. If Belli gets even a hint that the mob threatened Ruby in to doing this, Ruby may walk, and the government will be all over us."

"Message received," Arcacha Smith said.

"Sure," Ferrie said somberly.

"One last thing," Gill said. "Ruby's a momma's boy at heart and at some point will squeal unless we put him out of his misery first. Don't need to do it now—he thinks he'll get off because the jury will say Oswald deserved it. So, he won't talk about us yet. But, as long as Belli doesn't find out about our role some other way, Ruby'll be convicted. And then he'll start panicking.

"Once he's convicted, we're adding him to the magic potion hit list."

CHAPTER 55

During the first quarter of 1964, Ferrie tried to clear his mind of the jumble of bad and scary thoughts running around it. Not being constructed for downtime, though, he spread himself out in multiple different directions, pursuing a crazy array of absorbing activities.

The most out-of-character of these activities was investing in a gas station in Metairie. Unlike the ice rink in Houston, this business opportunity was a serious one for Ferrie. His friend Al Beauboeuf invested as well. It was a Gulf station at the corner of Veteran's Highway and Metairie Heights Avenue, on the way to Moisant Field. They cleverly renamed the station Dav-Al's.

Behind this surprising entrepreneurial move was Ferrie's increasingly severe need for income, now that there was a lull in his Marcello activity. But the station had another benefit for Ferrie, an unintended benefit. It gave him a chance to help out some young men who needed jobs, like a new friend named Tom Clark, who also needed temporary housing. Some of his other young hires similarly needed a place to stay. Ferrie was invariably happy to oblige.

More consistent with his intellectual interests, Ferrie set about to establish a practice as a psychologist, using his PhD from Phoenix University as a basis for this endeavor. He rented a small office near Moisant Field at 1302 Clay Street. He had business cards made up, put an ad in the *New Orleans States-Item*, and identified himself in the New Orleans phone book as Dr. David Ferrie.

Another diversionary activity for Ferrie was to get back to flying professionally. Neither Eastern Air Lines nor any other commercial airline was an option for him. Fortunately, he'd found several charter companies that would hire him to do freelance flying. One client was particularly easy for him to get—United Air Taxi, a Marcello firm.

Ferrie also renewed a relationship with an old friend at Lakefront Airport named Al Crouch. Crouch ran a company called Saturn Aviation, which, luckily for Ferrie, chartered planes *and* conducted pilot training. Ferrie was hired to do some of both for Crouch. Ferrie in turn hired Tom Clark to work with him. Clark began living with Ferrie off and on.

And, naturally, he devoted energy to his religious life. He decided to attend mass at as many Catholic churches in New Orleans as possible. He went to St. Mary of the Angels in the Florida Area of the city, on the eastern side, to Our Lady of Guadeloupe Church by Basin Street on the edge of the French Quarter, to St. Joseph Church near St. Louis Cemetery No. 2, in mid-city. In the area called the Tremé, populated mainly by poor blacks, he participated in several raucous masses at St. Augustine Church. Particularly inspirational was his visit to the historic Immaculate Conception Jesuit Church right by the Pere Marquette on Baronne and across from the Roosevelt Hotel in the central business district. From the outside, the style of this church's building was bracing, a wild mix of Gothic, Moorish, and Byzantine Revival. Inside, Ferrie prayed long and hard at the main altar, staring up at a solid marble statue of the Blessed Virgin perched high above in a marble bay, "Mary's Niche," two halos of white lights appearing to encircle her head. The statue was hand-carved for the last queen of France, Marie Amélie. He felt Mary's love.

And he made up for lost time at the Holy Name of Jesus on St. Charles near Tulane University. He owed the nuns.

Ferrie celebrated his own mass once a week at his apartment, attended by various friends, vagabonds, trespassers, tempters, and martyrs.

This busy but enjoyable life for Ferrie, away from the often grisly and complicated world of the mob, was sharply interrupted just after dinner on March 13, a Friday. When Ferrie's phone rang that evening, he had a feeling it'd be G. Wray Gill on the line. It was.

"Ruby was found guilty today. Poor sucker, but obviously no surprise. The good news is that nothing bad for us came out in the trial. In fact, Belli didn't even attempt to argue that others made Ruby kill Oswald. He pegged his entire case on Ruby's mental state and the impulsive nature of the act. Belli called Ruby a 'village idiot, a village clown.' Nice try—but the jury didn't buy it."

Ruby hadn't been helped by his police friend Patrick Dean. Dean testified that Ruby decided to murder Oswald late on the night after the assassination "when he noticed the sarcastic sneer on Oswald's face." So much for no premeditation.

Belli countered with a parade of experts on mental health—a Yale professor, a University of Texas neurologist, a Maryland expert on criminal psychology. They all testified that Ruby, for various reasons, didn't understand that what he was doing was wrong.

The jury didn't buy the experts. It deliberated for just over two hours and found Ruby "guilty of murder with malice, as charged in the indictment." It assessed his punishment "at death." Texas used the electric chair as its preferred method of capital punishment. Ironically for Ruby, Texas's chair had been called "Old Sparky" since it was first plugged in in 1924. Ruby's sister nicknamed him "Sparky" in their childhood.

"Next steps?" Ferrie asked.

"We're still going to lie low for a few weeks. Need to get through the post-trial legal maneuvering. But go ahead and get a plan ready to go for Banister. Be ready to execute it ASAP. When I give you the word."

Banister and wife Mary had separated over his relationship with his secretary, Delphine Roberts. He'd shown signs of unsteadiness for some time before the separation, but he began a more pronounced downward spiral thereafter. He was arrested for violently arguing with three young men at a bus stop and then following them onto a bus brandishing a gun. His private detective business was tanking, and he hadn't paid rent on his offices in the Newman Building for over a year. Old Man Newman was trying to evict him.

Increasingly paranoid and unpredictable, Banister was rapidly becoming a greater and greater risk to the Marcello organization. He could fall apart and start talking to the authorities or the press at any time.

Ferrie reached Banister by phone at his Newman Building office in mid-April. "It'd be great to catch up," Ferrie said.

Banister responded that he was swamped. Ferrie knew this was false but still expressed his sympathy. Lunch would have to wait a couple of weeks, Banister said.

Ferrie and Banister finally met for lunch at Mancuso's at the beginning of May. They talked about old times, current politics, the Ruby trial, the Beatles on Ed Sullivan, IBM's new "System/360" mainframe computer. Banister mentioned his marital breakup but only in passing. He said he was moving his office out of the Newman Building to Delphine's basement.

His hands shuddering, Ferrie emptied a full vial of cancer virus into Banister's beer while he was going to the bathroom. Banister drained the beer quickly. He then said he had to get back to work.

The cancer took longer to work than Ferrie had expected. Banister was still a physically strong man at sixty-three. It took two weeks for him to die.

Delphine Roberts found Banister face down on his apartment bed, wearing only his white Fruit of the Loom briefs and clutching a bath towel, on June 6. He was supposed to be moving things into her upscale Garden District home at the time but hadn't shown up. Coroner Dr. Nicholas Chetta chalked up his demise to a heart attack.

Learning of Banister's death, Ferrie, at Gill's request, went over to the Newman Building to see if Banister's office was still accessible. Gill was concerned that Banister had left incriminating files behind.

Ferrie was able to get into Banister's office. He went straight to the file cabinets. Quickly opening each of the four drawers, he was taken aback. They were empty. No files. No documents. The drawers had been cleaned out.

He *did* find a small box on the floor of the office with a few randomly placed index cards in it. These cards appeared to describe the subject matters of what had been in Banister's files. Most of the cards had names that weren't familiar to Ferrie. But he did recognize some of the cards. Among the titles were "The CRC," "Sergio A Smith," "TACA Air—Guatemala," "Dutz M."

Ferrie called Gill and filled him in. Gill told Ferrie that, coincidentally, Delphine had just dropped off some Banister files at his office. But these files related only to Ferrie's Eastern Air Lines case. She had thought, she said, that Gill would want those, since Gill had been Ferrie's lawyer. There were lots of other files in the office last time she'd been there, she said.

"Sometime after Delphine left the office with the Eastern files," Gill said, "someone obviously went in and packed up the rest of the files. I'll talk to her about that—and to Mary Banister. But my bet is that we're not going to find them."

"FBI take the files?"

"Who knows? Just bring me those cards you found. We'll lock them up."

A week later, Gill paid a visit to Ferrie at his apartment. A rarity.

"I've heard the state police has Banister's files," Ferrie said.

"Heard that too. I'm talking to my friends there. But let's discuss Dr. Mary."

"Shit. I beg you, for Christ's sake. She won't talk, she hasn't talked. I've kept an eye on her. Fuck. Fucking threaten her with something, like you did with Ruby. But don't . . ." Ferrie's voice trailed off, his head dropped down.

"Calm down, little girl. Look, Marcello likes you, you know that. He's heard your plea for Dr. Mary and thought more about it. He's prepared to commute her death sentence. Frankly, he also realized that Dr. Ochsner would be royally unhappy if we took his favorite doctor from him. Ochsner's a Marcello friend, as you know. We'll watch her. But she's okay for now."

Ferrie raised his head and looked up to the sky. "By God's grace," he said. Looking back down at Gill, he simply said, "Thank you, sir. Say *grazij* to Mr. Marcello."

"Certainly. But, one thing. Marcello has asked that you stay away from her for a while. He'll be more comfortable if the only two people who know everything about the Castro cancer virus don't interact with each other for now. Okay?"

"If it'll save her . . . yes, sir, absolutely."

"All right. Call me if you have any other thoughts about Banister's files. What do you think's in them? What do those cards indicate? What do you remember? Anything? Crank your brain up on these questions."

Gill left. Ferrie put on his clerical robe and lit some candles and incense. He knelt.

"Father of Jesus, we praise you and give you glory for the wonderful things you do for us—for life and health, for friends and family, for this splendid day."

CHAPTER 56

In April the Warren Commission's light shone on New Orleans in the form of two staff lawyers in the city to take depositions. Albert Jenner and Jim Liebeler. Notwithstanding the "Cork's" promises about the ultimate outcome of the commission's work, Marcello was nervous about this visit. But in fact there was nothing to worry about. Jenner and Liebeler didn't seek out a single Marcello-related witness. Dutz Murret *was* deposed but only because he was Oswald's uncle. The lawyers also deposed Dutz's wife, daughter, and athlete son "Boogie."

Rather than fish around for conspirators, the deposition-takers focused solely on Oswald's life history and personality. Thus, in addition to the Murret family, they interviewed Oswald's junior high classmates Ed Voebel and Bennierita Smith, several neighbors of Oswald when he was a child living in the Bywater section of New Orleans, a couple who had been friends with Oswald's mother, Oswald's landlady and a neighbor from his time on Magazine Street, the man who owned the garage by Reily Coffee, and Carlos Bringuier, who had been seen with Oswald on Canal Street and in the Casa Roca. Two teenagers who were in the Casa Roca when Oswald visited on August 5, 1963, were also deposed.

Dave Ferrie wasn't contacted, even though he was known in town as having Marcello ties—*and* reportedly had consorted with Oswald. There were no depositions of Marcello, Gill, *any* Marcello lieutenant or relative, Martin, Beauboeuf, Coffey, Martens, *any* Ferrie friend, Ochsner, Reily, or Butler. Nor of the radio men Stuckey and Slater, who could have testified about

Ferrie and Martin's role in the Oswald shows. Nor of any of the New Orleans officials, including Jim Garrison, who were involved in Ferrie's arrest and interrogation in November 1963. The Warren Commission never contacted the people in the Big Easy who mattered in what really happened.

Nor, for that matter, was there a single question put to the deponents about Ferrie, Marcello, Banister, or Gill—no questions about anybody in Marcello's orbit. Even Dutz, a known Marcello associate, only got Oswald questions. These depositions were soft, mainly exploring Oswald's personal history and habits, his TV and radio adventures in New Orleans, and his views on Communism. There wasn't the slightest interest in testing whether Oswald had had confederates.

Though he'd been a good soldier, staff lawyer Liebeler was becoming uncomfortable with the commission's quick parade toward an Oswald-only verdict. Before the April trip, he had lobbied the commission's general counsel, Lee Rankin, a former US Solicitor General, to broaden the net in the Big Easy, but he was rejected. No "frolics and detours," Rankin had said, toeing the line that had been drawn for him by Warren.

Wesley "Jim" Liebeler was a flaky though sharp oddball on the staff. Unlike virtually every other staff member, Liebeler was an inveterate conservative—a card-carrying member of the John Birch Society, a right-wing group that was even too extreme for conservative icon William F. Buckley. Among JFK-lovers on the staff, Liebeler made it clear that he'd be voting for Barry Goldwater in the fall.

But Liebeler was no buttoned-down Republican stiff. Notwithstanding being married with two sons at home in New York, he was a champion partier and serial philanderer. He roamed the bars of DC virtually every night, drinking copious amounts of alcohol while looking for—and often bedding—attractive women. He wasn't shy in bragging about his conquests the next day at work. The late nights and alcohol only seemed to energize him in the office.

His rebellious streak was evident in the scruffy reddish beard he grew during the investigation. Chief Justice Warren had requested staff to dress well and be clean-shaven. The beard drove the Chief Justice crazy. Despite his liberal judicial opinions, Warren had little tolerance for slovenliness and disorder.

Without the knowledge of Albert Jenner, the staff colleague with him in New Orleans in April, Liebeler met informally with a well-known, larger-than-life Big Easy lawyer named Dean Andrews. At 340 pounds, Andrews was hard to miss. He dressed as if every day were Mardi Gras. Andrews could've been a character in a Damon Runyon story, a fat, southern Sky Masterson—an over-the-top, braggadocios, devil-may-care character. Like Masterson, Andrews was an accomplished raconteur and gambler. He wore sunglasses all the time, even indoors. He talked like a Cajun version of Maynard G. Krebs, embroidering his stories with words and phrases like *swinging like sixteen, swinging cat, fuzzrod,* and *juiceman.* He referred to FBI agents as "Feebies."

The Feebies had talked to Andrews after the assassination about his astonishing claims that he'd had contacts with Oswald and had been asked to represent Oswald in Dallas, but they paid him little mind. Liebeler was determined to hear directly from Andrews. When he did, he got an earful.

CHAPTER 57

As the deadline was approaching for the final report, Liebeler raised a racket. He begged to do some more depositions, begged to explore some of the hundreds of tips that had come into the commission about possibly nefarious Oswald associations. This time Rankin relented. With the probe coming to a close and the report already being written, he saw little harm in giving Liebeler a bone. But Rankin put him on a short leash. Only a handful of depositions were authorized. One was of Andrews.

Liebeler also got the okay to go to Dallas to interview Silvia Odio. He was interested in hearing her story about Oswald's possible visit to her apartment in the fall of 1963. He was equally interested in viewing her reported great beauty firsthand.

He arrived in New Orleans on the evening of Monday, July 20. His depositions were the next day.

The Marcello organization had information on every commission staff lawyer, including multiple pictures of each. Liebeler's presence in New Orleans was thus immediately known throughout the organization. Not that he was trying to be secretive. He spent most of that night roaming around the French Quarter, drinking and looking for action. He was noticed in the 500 Club, the Sho-Bar, and the Old French Opera House. Pete Marcello himself served Liebeler a roast beef po'boy at the Sho-Bar's long wooden bar. Frank Caracci gave him a free drink at the Old French Opera House.

By the end of that evening, sources in the clubs had learned from a woozy Liebeler why he was in town and whom he would be talking to. Marcello's people were pleased with the list. Liebeler's leash wasn't slack enough to give him the range to directly poke the mob bear. Unlike the other lawyers on the staff, however, Liebeler wasn't prepared in his own mind to take the mob completely off the table.

Liebeler was tailed by one of One-eyed Pete's bouncers out Chartres Street to St. Philip and the Chateau Motor Hotel, where Liebeler finally went to bed well past three in the morning.

Gill called Ferrie early Tuesday morning to tell him about Liebeler's planned deposition of Andrews.

"What? Why?" Ferrie asked.

"God only knows. The commissioners are either confused or, more likely, just happy to get Liebeler out of DC. We hear he's not a good team player and making it tough for LBJ and Warren to close their show."

Ferrie *had* heard that Andrews was seeking attention by making wild-eyed claims about Oswald. His main fabrication was that he'd done legal work for Oswald related to Oswald's undesirable discharge from the Marines—Oswald must've in fact wanted the "undesirable" label removed. He hadn't been acting, at least on that point, in Austin.

Ferrie knew for certain that Andrews had never met Oswald. He, Dutz, and Martin had kept track of Oswald's every move while he was in New Orleans.

"If nothing else, Andrews will entertain Liebeler. You need me for anything on this?" Ferrie asked.

"No, just thought you'd want to know. Andrews may say Oswald had associates here, but I'm sure he knows nothing about our project."

"Good. I'm going flying." It was still early in the day.

Before he could leave for Lakefront Airport, Ferrie received a call from Dr. Carolyn Talley. She was crying uncontrollably. Her voice was whimpery.

"She's, she's . . . dead. Dr. Mary. Mare, my Mare.

"Oh, my God. Dave. I'm so, so sorry."

Ferrie had been holding a tea cup. His grip immediately loosened. The cup fell to the floor and shattered. Dr. Carolyn's words didn't compute. "What?"

"She was found in her apartment dead, murdered." Dr. Carolyn was hysterical. "Brutal. She was stabbed, burned. Shit, Dave. I'm gonna throw up."

Ferrie was silent. Speechless. Immediately numb.

"Are you there?" Dr. Carolyn asked.

"Am I here? Christ. No. Not really. Jesus. What the fuck happened?"

"I don't know," she sobbed. "Don't know."

Ferrie rushed over to 3101 St. Charles. The charred and punctured body had been taken away. New Orleans police filled up the curved driveway in front of the entrance to the complex, blocking nonresidents from entering. A crime scene van was parked on Harmony Street. All Ferrie could get from the cops was a shake of the head and a "no comment." Ferrie returned home and called Gill.

"You fucking lied to me. You killed her. God-fucking-dammit. Shit, Ray. They mutilated her. Christ to hell." Ferrie's voice trailed off.

"Dave. Who?"

"You fucking know who. Dr. Mary. God—"

Gill interrupted. "Hold on. Hold on. What? Shit . . . what? Are you sure? Where? When?"

"Ray. I know you assholes did this."

"Christ, Dave. Of course not. Christ. Get a grip. Jeez, come over. I'll make some calls now."

"You fuck. My Lord." Ferrie was drained. "Mary."

He slammed the phone down, cracking the cradle.

After a few hours, Ferrie gathered himself and went to confront Gill.

Ferrie walked into office 1707 of the Pere Marquette Building. He refused to shake Gill's hand.

"Drink?" Gill asked. Somberly.

"No."

"Am so sorry. You know I knew her too. Knew her well. Knew her for quite a few years, as did my wife. My wife's devastated. Dave, we'd never hurt her."

"Of *course* not," Ferrie said sarcastically.

"We didn't do it. You must know that. *Think.* If nothing else, you know we don't mutilate people."

"You could've mutilated her to disguise that you bastards did it."

"C'mon. You know—you fucking *know*. Damn it, we don't mutilate people. And she was a close colleague of Dr. Ochsner's. Do you think Marcello would've done something like that to Ochsner? Not to mention that Marcello wouldn't go back on his word to you."

"You never know in this fucked-up gangster world."

"I've been working the phones. You might not believe it now, but I *am* pissed. We're going to find out what happened.

"But here's what I'm hearing," Gill continued. "You surely know that Dr. Mary had a number of lady friends. I'm told that some of them were more than just friends. After her husband pulled the plug, she gave up on men. She took comfort in being with women."

"We never discussed anything like that," Ferrie said.

"The rumor going around right now is that one of her lady friends found out about another lady friend and went ballistic on her. I have no idea why this lady, or whoever did this, would burn Dr. Mary after shooting her. Maybe she thought she could cover up bullet evidence or fingerprints or something."

"Women don't kill women—certainly not like that."

Whether it was an act or not, Ferrie could see sadness in Gill's eyes. Gill said, "My sources with the cops tell me that there were no signs of a break-in. And that Dr. Mary's white purse, jewelry, and prescription drugs were still there. Dr. Mary almost certainly knew the killer."

"Shit."

"Her car, the white 1960 Valiant, was gone. The cops found it an hour ago on Chestnut Street, near Commander's Palace. They found a tube of somebody else's lipstick and a perfume dispenser on the street by the car."

Ferrie had had enough and left. He wasn't convinced in the least that a lesbian lover had killed Dr. Mary. Nor was he convinced that whoever killed Dr. Mary wouldn't be coming for him.

When he returned home, he picked up his copy of the afternoon paper, the *New Orleans States-Item*. The paper had a large picture of Dr. Mary and a screaming headline across the top of the front page: *ORLEANS WOMAN SURGEON SLAIN BY INTRUDER; BODY SET AFIRE.* A sub-headline read, *CLUES LACKING IN KILLING OF DR. SHERMAN.*

Ferrie was emotionally exhausted and deeply despondent. He lit a candle and said a brief prayer. "Eternal rest grant unto her, O Lord, and let perpetual light shine upon her. May her soul and all the souls of the faithful departed, through the mercy of God, rest in peace."

The bizarre sacrificial nature of Dr. Mary's death made Ferrie think of New Orleans Voodoo, a subject he'd studied. Ferrie often used elements of Voodoo, which itself incorporated aspects of Christianity, in his masses. Voodoo is a healing religion, with rituals largely designed to ward off bad luck. There's an element of Voodoo, however, called *gris-gris*, that involves casting evil spells, usually using a talisman. Sometimes these spells sought deadly results.

Ferrie didn't actually believe Dr. Mary's was a Voodoo killing. But perhaps a Voodoo-oriented prayer could help Dr. Mary's soul. *Shit, why not try?* he thought.

Ferrie recited the end of the Our Father—which Voodoo priests and priestesses often said as part of their services—and then sang the first part of the Voodoo "Priye Ginen," which opened most Voodoo ceremonies.

"Car c'est à toi qu'appartiennent le règne, la puissance et la gloire, aux siècles des siècles. Amen."

Blowing out the candle, Ferrie walked into his kitchen, where the makeshift lab had been, and made a cup of tea. He drank the tea and ate an orange that had come all the way from China. He laid down on the bed. His eyes were heavy, but sleep wouldn't come.

CHAPTER 58

Andrews's singular personality came through in the deposition in June. When asked if Oswald was gay, Andrews colorfully replied, "I couldn't say. He swung with the kids. He didn't swish, but birds of a feather run together. I don't know any squares that run with them."

When asked about the "kids" he saw Oswald hanging out with, Andrews said those boys were definitely gay. "They were what we call *swishers*. You can just look at them. All they had to do was open their mouth. That was it. They can swing better than Sammy Kaye."

Andrews told Liebeler that Oswald had come to his office several times in the spring or summer of 1963 with men who looked as if they were "Mexicanos." Oswald wanted some work done on his "undesirable" discharge from the Marines, Andrews said.

Sometime after the office visits, Andrews ran into Oswald as he was passing out leaflets in front of the historic Maison Blanche building, where Andrews's office was located. The two men chatted briefly there. Oswald told Andrews that he was being paid to pass out the leaflets, that this was a "*job*." The leaflets were "kooky Castro things," Andrews told Liebeler. "They extolled the virtues of Castro, which around here doesn't do too good. They have a lot of guys, Mexicanos and Cubanos, that will tear your head off if they see you fooling with these things."

Andrews then relayed a particularly stunning and dubitable story. Right after the assassination, Andrews said, a man named Clay Bertrand called him and asked him to defend the arrested

Oswald. Andrews declined, in part because he was sick at the time and in part because he was suspicious whether Bertrand—whom Andrews had met two years before—in fact was acting on behalf of Oswald.

Liebeler asked Andrews whether Clay Bertrand was a homosexual. "Bisexual. What they call a *swinging cat*," Andrews replied. Later that day, Liebeler called an associate in DC to have him start researching Bertrand.

After Andrews, Liebeler deposed two Cuban exiles—Orest Pena, the owner of the Habana Bar, a Cuban hangout near the Casa Roca store, and the bar's main bartender, Evaristo Rodriguez. They both testified that Oswald had come in the Habana on at least one occasion. He had been in the company of a Spanish-speaking person.

Pena and Rodriguez clearly remembered Oswald. He was white, for one thing. And he ordered lemonade. Nobody had ever ordered lemonade at the Habana Bar—Rodriquez had to be shown how to make it. Oswald was wearing a bow tie, moreover, though the neck of his shirt was open. The bow tie was clip-on, just hanging from the collar. After being served, Oswald had complained loudly about the price of the drinks. He shouted at Pena.

Though Liebeler expected these depositions to be interesting, he was surprised how squarely they supported his conviction that there was more to Oswald than just being a crazy loser. Oswald had spent time in an *anti*-Castro bar with a Hispanic friend, probably Cuban. He was dressed strangely, at least for that venue, and had ordered an unusual bar drink. This all appeared to be designed to make him stand out. And he yelled at the owner to boot. Yet, according to Andrews, Oswald had been paid to be a public *pro*-Castro advocate with his leafleting on Canal Street. And his subsequent appearances on radio and TV had to have been directed by others as well, Liebeler concluded. By whom? The Hispanic with him at the Habana Bar?

The next day Liebeler deposed Silvia Odio in Dallas. Odio's testimony, Liebeler had urged, could indicate a conspiracy. He didn't tell Rankin that his other reason for this endeavor was to see Odio in the flesh—he had heard she was dangerously attractive. The intelligence on her good looks was true. Distracted by trying to work out in his mind how to get her out of her tight dress and into his bed that night, Liebeler mumbled the opening questions incomprehensibly.

Once the interview got rolling, Silvia Odio testified clearly about the visit in late September 1963 by Leopoldo, another Hispanic man, and Oswald. They were all identified as anti-Castro activists interested in joining Odio and the opposition. They told her they were making a "big movement" to buy arms for the cause. They said they couldn't stay long because they were about to go on a trip. The next day Leopoldo had called her and asked what she thought of the American. She said she "didn't think anything." Leopoldo told her that Oswald was "great" but "kind of nuts."

The scenario described by Odio smelled to Liebeler like a staged scene to paint Oswald as a "nutty" Castro-fighter. But Liebeler also knew that the Odio visit occurred at a time when the FBI had pegged Oswald as being on his way to Mexico. Was there a plan to make it look like there was an Oswald impostor? *Why?* Liebeler wondered.

The deposition sowed seeds of further intrigue for Liebeler. What really made Oswald tick? What were his politics? Where did he really stand on Castro? *Who was really pulling the strings?*

Back in Washington, Liebeler lobbied for more time to finish the commission's investigation. There was much more to Oswald than just being a lone nut who was out to make a name for himself in history, he argued to Rankin. He knew, though, that this was a futile effort. In fact, he had said to Silvia Odio over dinner in Dallas, after a few drinks and before being turned down for sex, that the Chief Justice had ordered the staff "to cover this thing up."

While Liebeler was on the right track, the commission was on a different, and faster, track. On September 24, 1964, a year to the day after the final meetings on the Oswald doppelgänger and Mexico City plans, LBJ was presented with the final 888-page "Report of the President's Commission on the Assassination of President Kennedy" in a ceremony with the commissioners at the White House. It was released to the public three days later.

"The Commission concluded that there is no credible evidence that Lee Harvey Oswald was part of a conspiracy to assassinate President Kennedy."

The mob was implicitly exonerated. And the report said that any possible foreign involvement, including Cuban involvement, had been thoroughly investigated and rejected. The commission's conclusion that Castro was not to blame, buttressed by senior staffer William T. Coleman Jr.'s personal observation that Castro was "not a crazy man," was correct. Not correct was the statement that the investigation had been thorough. Given LBJ and Hoover's tight reins on the inquiry, and the unreasonable deadline for a final report, numerous suspicious leads weren't followed. An aggressive look at a possible connection between Cuba and Oswald would've inexorably led to a serious scrutiny of New Orleans in the summer of 1963—of Oswald's pro-Castro demonstrations, of Ferrie, of the Marcello network.

There were no dissents from the report.

J. Wesley Liebeler, for one, though, continued to believe the work was unfinished, a belief that was fueled by the June depositions. The next year Liebeler would help one of the quickly growing number of critics of the report, Edward Jay Epstein, a Cornell University graduate student. Epstein wrote the first book critiquing the Warren Commission Report in detail—*Inquest: The Warren Commission and the Establishment of Truth*—published in June 1966, while Epstein was still a graduate student, by the Viking Press. The book used, in large part, confidential information provided by Liebeler.

Criticism of the Warren Commission Report grew over the next two years. As public restlessness with the Oswald-only conclusion began spiraling more intensely in 1966, a DA in New Orleans, a flamboyant, unstable man named James Carothers Garrison, was presented with information that inspired him to exploit this restlessness. A number of the new potential suspects people were starting to talk about were located in his jurisdiction, and Oswald had spent the summer before the assassination there.

Garrison's tenure as the DA of Orleans Parish hadn't been going well at that point. Starting the first criminal prosecution of the JFK assassination could be the tonic to distract folks away from his incompetent and feckless nature. It also could have the bonus of bringing him fame and fortune. He craved attention— and a place in history.

By the end of 1966, he was obsessed with this new project. As Garrison's investigator Lou Ivon told others later, once Garrison dedicated himself to a course of action like this, he wouldn't "crawfish"—a New Orleanian's way of saying that he would never back down.

CHAPTER 59

Dr. Mary's murder was never solved. This crime became the biggest modern-day mystery of the ever-mysterious New Orleans.

For the next three Decembers of his life, Ferrie paid reverence to Dr. Mary after his annual trip to donate toys to the Crippled Children's Hospital, where he had first met Dr. Mary. Since she had not been buried in New Orleans, Ferrie performed this annual ritual where Dr. Mary lived and died. He would kneel at the entrance to the Patio (or the Patios) Apartments and say the same words of grace.

"Eternal rest grant unto her, O Lord, and let perpetual light shine upon her, May she rest in peace. *Et verbum caro factum est et habitabit in nobis; et vidimus gloriuam elus gloiram quasi Unigenti a Patre, plenum gratiae et veritatis.*"

He would then leave a new toy.

CHAPTER 60

At about the time the Warren Commission Report was being released to an anxious public, there was a knock on Ferrie's door. Not expecting any visitors, and never knowing if he'd been put on Marcello's hit list, Ferrie was on high alert. He crossed himself and opened the door slowly. It was Gill—another rare unannounced appearance at Ferrie's apartment.

"Can I come in?"

"Yeah, sure. And pardon the mess."

Gill brushed aside a ratty blanket on the couch and the crumbs that were underneath and sat down. Gill refused the cup of tea Ferrie offered.

Ferrie, in his fidgety mode, sat across from Gill. He had softened on his knee-jerk view that Gill was involved in Dr. Mary's death.

"I want to talk about Dutz. Have you seen him lately?"

"I heard he moved up to Lakeview. Have *you* seen him? What's going on?"

"Haven't seen him but I heard he's having a tough time. He's being harassed left and right because he was Oswald's uncle and because he put Oswald up in New Orleans before the killing. He's not well. Frankly, people say he's becoming unglued."

"What do you mean?"

"We're watching him. He's drinking—outrageously. He's spending way too much time in the bars on Lakeshore Drive. And he's starting to ramble on about Oswald and Oswald's friends. We're worried about him. You know better than anyone that he knows a lot of stuff that could bring us down."

"Sure."

"We know he's told some fellow barflies that his nephew was set up. We know he's getting pressure from his wife to publicly defend Oswald. More so, his wife's kooky sister, Oswald's mother, is shitting all over Dutz for not telling the press what a great guy her miserable son was, that he'd never hurt a fly. He's just inches away from cracking. It's just a matter of time. We're afraid he's going to go to the FBI or Garrison."

"Nah, he won't talk. He worships Marcello."

"We can't take the chance."

"Oh, shit. Dutz? Ray, please. He's harmless. Loyal. You guys owe him. Let him live out his golden years. I'll talk to him."

"I'm sorry. Marcello's sorry. Dutz has just become too big a risk to all of us. It's just the way it is. If it's any solace, I don't think Dutz's going to live much longer anyway. He's racked with anxiety, weakening quickly. The old Dutz is already gone."

"What are you saying? I've gotta feed him the monkey virus?"

"Soon."

"You can't get someone else to do it?"

"You're the expert. And, as a religious man, you can be an instrument of Christ's mercy for a dying man."

"You must have practiced that fucking bullshit line several times in front of a mirror."

||||

In early October Ferrie reluctantly traveled up to the Lakeview neighborhood of New Orleans to visit Dutz and Lillian. They had a nice visit.

On October 13, 1964, the *Times-Picayune* published Dutz's obituary.

"DEATH CLAIMS SPORTS FIGURE. Charles F. 'Dutz' Murret, well-known New Orleans sports figure, died Monday at 6:30 p.m. in Southern Baptist Hospital after a brief illness. He was 63. A Requiem Mass at St. Dominic Church will be followed by interment in St. Roch No. 2 Cemetery."

CHAPTER 61

As 1965 began sadness suffused the lives of Frank Sinatra, Judy Campbell, and Sam Giancana.

Sinatra was back at the curved Fontainebleau Hotel in Miami Beach, performing with rubber-faced, actor-comedian Joe E. Brown. Professionally, he had had a blockbuster year in 1964. His movie *Robin and the 7 Hoods* was a hit. The feature song in that movie, "My Kind of Town," was nominated for an Oscar. As a singer Sinatra put out his second album, "It Might as Well Be Swing," with the iconic Count Basie and his orchestra. The LP was arranged by a talented young jazz producer named Quincy Jones. It was destined to be a classic.

Notwithstanding his professional successes, Sinatra hadn't recovered from the shock and agony of the assassination. In his personal life, he had become disconnected from his mob friends after the kidnapping of his son. And his Kennedy-connected friends would have nothing to do with him. His snub of Peter Lawford hadn't been forgotten in the Kennedy camp—and RFK had a growing gut feeling, rumor had it, that some of the mob leaders Sinatra palled around with may have had a hand in JFK's murder.

The Fontainebleau Hotel always brought back a swirl of memories to Sinatra, most clearly the 1960 visit for the Timex show with Elvis Presley. He remembered all too well that Judy had been with him. He remembered their lovemaking fondly—and her "headlights." But he was haunted by the fact that he had introduced her to Sam Giancana during that visit. That introduction and the ensuing triangle that developed—JFK,

Judy, Giancana—had probably affected history, Sinatra had come to believe.

In the midst of his early-1965 appearances at the Fontainebleau, Sinatra agreed to do a rare radio interview. He didn't do many interviews and did this one only as a favor to his friend the famous comedian Jackie Gleason, who'd moved his TV show to Miami Beach the year before. The interviewer was a thirty-one-year-old local radio and television broadcaster named Larry King.

King was nervous about the interview but was efficient and direct with his questioning. He got Sinatra to open up, at least a little bit, on a number of topics, though Sinatra seemed to be in a poor mood. He was particularly sour when King asked him about the treatment he got in the press. "These people live off the real or imagined fortunes or misfortunes of those with much greater talent than them," he said.

King found Sinatra to be fascinating but, deep down, "unhappy, complicated, lonely."

While Sinatra was at the Fontainebleau, Judy was in Beverly Hills getting some unwelcome news. She had spent most of 1964 in a funk—alcohol, drugs, one-night stands, paranoia.

In January 1965 she learned that, again, she was pregnant. Father unknown. She was flooded with memories of her pregnancy by JFK two years before. The decision to abort that baby had haunted her every day since. *What if she'd had JFK's baby?* News that JFK had fathered a child outside of his marriage would've leaked out and caused an uproar. It would've been particularly shocking and shameful because Jackie had gotten pregnant at around the same time. Party bosses would've stopped him from running for reelection. He would be alive today.

Judy decided she would have *this* baby. She couldn't live with another abortion. She would put the baby up for adoption.

Giancana hadn't been on his game since Judy had cut him off in favor of JFK. He spent an increasing amount of time trying to mask his angst by globetrotting. And relentlessly chasing skirts.

There was no shortage of women willing to spend private time with Giancana.

His mind wasn't on his work. He was inconsistent in carrying out his job as Chicago's mob boss and, in fact, wasn't spending much time in Chicago. In private and sometimes in public, he was increasingly prone to bright flashes of anger.

Though Giancana outwardly had performed well at the meetings at the Greenbrier early in 1964, he actually had been tired and unfocused. He sensed thereafter that he was no longer being treated as first among equals by Marcello, Trafficante, and Roselli.

Just a few days after returning to Chicago from White Sulphur Springs, he had been jolted when he picked up the *Chicago Tribune* on the morning of January 16, 1964. There was an article on page three with the headline, "Inside Story Of Meeting To Fire Giancana."

The article reported on a meeting of regional gangsters the previous December that had been called to discuss concerns with Giancana. The gangsters made a decision at that meeting—"Giancana will be demoted." Among the reasons cited were "his temper" and his "behavior as a playboy."

The author of the article had had good sources. The December meeting, he reported, had been led by mob elders Anthony ("Big Tuna") Accardo and Paul (the "Waiter") Ricca, both of whom had been leaders of the Chicago mob before Giancana. The article listed the other participants—Sam ("Teets") Battaglia, William ("Willie Potatoes") Daddano, Felix ("Milwaukee Phil") Alderiso, Rudolph ("Rudy") Fratta, his brother Frank ("One Ear") Fratta, and Albert ("Obbie") Frabetta.

Stunned by this article, Giancana did take comfort in the fact that the meeting didn't include any of the senior mob bosses from other parts of the country. In fact, the article specifically said that the decision to demote Giancana had to be approved "by the national brotherhood of crime."

Giancana tried to up his game during the rest of 1964 to prove to his peers that he deserved to continue as Chicago's mob boss. When the national mob leadership became concerned about caporegime Joe Bonanno's disruptive activities in New York, Giancana volunteered to help calm things down. Bonanno, one of New York City's up-and-coming mobsters, had been moving in on territories controlled by the Buffalo bosses, including Buffalo itself and Toronto. An informant had ratted out Bonanno's plans to hit Don Carlo Gambino, a plan that hadn't been officially sanctioned.

In the fall of 1964, Giancana organized several Bonanno enemies, including one of Bonanno's cousins, to kidnap Bonanno in front of his Park Avenue apartment building on October 21, 1964.

The Bonanno kidnapping pleased the other mob bosses, but at the same time they were hearing more and more about Giancana's lack of attention to his day-to-day duties in Chicago and his frequent absences from the city. In a meeting not long after the Bonanno kidnapping—held at Giancana's home away from home, the Armory Lounge in Forest Park, Illinois— Giancana was ordered to appoint what amounted to a chief operating officer to run things in Chicago on a daily basis.

Mooney "Sam" Giancana's power completely slipped away when the mob "Commission" concluded that the JFK assassination was a mistake, the biggest one since the poor planning of the Apalachin summit meeting of mob leaders led to a cop bust in 1957. Nothing good came from hitting JFK. Contrary to the "Cork's" representations, LBJ—with Vietnam becoming a much bigger problem than he had envisioned, particularly after his mischievous Gulf of Tonkin stunt—was distracted and had indefinitely back-burnered Cuba. And what spare time LBJ had was taken with his struggle to convince his southern friends on civil rights. Maybe JFK would've actually gone back after Cuba, as he had promised to Giancana, after the election? He certainly wouldn't be bogged down in Vietnam or on civil rights issues like LBJ, the mob believed.

More disturbing to the mob leadership, LBJ didn't have the time to notice the continued RFK-inspired crusade against the mob. Jimmy Hoffa was fighting bribery and fraud charges. Vinny Rao was convicted of perjury. Giancana himself was facing criminal charges in New York and Chicago, which would soon land him in jail.

As 1965 was winding down, the Commission was beginning to blame Giancana—who, at the time, had been the operational "first among equals"—for the mistake of November 22, 1963. Not only did nothing good come from this mistake, the leadership believed, but, to the contrary, the mob was worse off, for it now had to live under the ever-present threat that its role in the assassination would be discovered and the wrath of civil society would come down on it.

Had the Commission known that Giancana's urge to get Kennedy had been fueled by an emotional recoil from Judy Campbell's rejection, it would have levied the ultimate punishment upon him at that time, instead of imposing this levy a decade later, when Giancana was under subpoena to testify on the assassination.

\|\|\|

The JFK assassination proved to be personal debacles for Giancana, Sinatra, and Judy. Giancana had lost power and was sliding toward prison. Sinatra was depressed and increasingly disconnected from formerly powerful friends in the mob and the Kennedy clan. Judy had lost the love of her life and was in an emotional tailspin, about to have a child she would never know. Sinatra and Judy both were weighed down with the thought that, because of the president-mob courier relationship that went sour, they unwittingly played a role in JFK's death.

The three would never see each other again.

CHAPTER 62

District Attorney Jim Garrison was not a normal or stable man. A doctor diagnosed him in 1951 as having a "severe and disabling psychoneurosis of long duration" that "interfered with his social and professional adjustment to a marked degree. He is considered totally disabled from the standpoint of military duty and moderately incapacitated in civilian adaptability."

The doctor concluded, "His illness . . . is of the type that will require a long-term psychotherapeutic approach."

Garrison's personality disorder manifested itself in a complex of traits, most notably a conspicuous narcissism mixed with chronic insecurity. These conflicting properties created a driving urge to be the center of attention. His fractured mind grew out of a troubled childhood. His father Earling was a lifelong fraudster and criminal. Garrison's mother, Jane Anne, divorced Earling when son Jim was two. Earling then kidnapped young Jim. Jane Anne got him back and struggled to raise him and his sister Judy with odd jobs, including selling corsets. It was an angry household, mother Jane Anne full of hate for her husband and the life she had been given.

Notwithstanding his personal defects, Garrison graduated from Tulane Law School and became a competent, though indolent, lawyer. He worked for the FBI and then for four years with the law firm of Deutsche, Kerrigan, and Stiles in New Orleans. After several years as an assistant district attorney thereafter, he ran for Orleans Parish District Attorney in 1961. A longshot, he barely won in a crowded field—though in future years he always claimed it was a huge victory.

Immediately after Garrison took office, Marcello's network learned through sources that Garrison was planning to order raids on strip joints and gambling clubs. He wanted to make a splash with the local press by launching a public crusade to "clean up" the Quarter.

Garrison's raids were carried out with much fanfare and bravado.

In an exceptionally rare move for Marcello, he decided to meet with Garrison in person. Marcello summoned him to the Town and Country. Garrison knew he had no choice but to go to Marcello and not the other way round.

The meeting was cordial. Thereafter, though Garrison continued with his raids, they had little teeth. Virtually all the strippers, club managers, and hookers who were arrested were let go and not prosecuted. The Quarter didn't get any cleaner.

Another result of the Marcello-Garrison meeting was that, during his entire twelve-year tenure as DA, Garrison never acknowledged publicly that there was organized crime in New Orleans. Whenever he was asked specifically about Marcello, even knowing about RFK's relentless prosecutions of him, he always referred to Marcello as just a "local businessman."

In his second year in office, just several hours after JFK was murdered, Garrison heard about Ferrie's association with Oswald from Assistant DA Herman Kohlman, the recipient of Jack Martin's betrayal of Ferrie and an old Ferrie acquaintance. He directed local police to turn Ferrie's upstairs apartment upside down for evidence while Ferrie was traveling in Texas—a scene that he and another Assistant DA Frank Klein personally observed. And he ordered that Ferrie be arrested upon his return to New Orleans.

At the first district police station, accompanied by G. Wray Gill, Ferrie was interrogated by Frank Klein. Before long the FBI joined and took over the questioning. The FBI had Garrison release Ferrie the next day.

Over the next three years, Garrison had little interest in the JFK assassination. He was indifferent to the Warren Commission's conclusion that Oswald had acted alone.

Garrison won reelection in 1965, with the quiet support of Marcello's operation. For most of 1966, he celebrated his victory by not working very much. He visited Las Vegas frequently, usually staying at the mob-owned Sands Hotel and Casino. Marcello lieutenant Mario Marino, the long-time showroom captain and social host at the Sands, who grew up with Marcello and his brothers in New Orleans, often paid Garrison's bills and gave him large lines of credit.

At home Garrison spent much of his time at the old New Orleans Athletic Club on North Rampart Street, where John L. Sullivan had boxed and Johnny Weissmuller had swum. Garrison spent hours with his elbow on the elegant mahogany bar at Vaughn's Pub in the club, often with celebrities like Robert Goulet, Art Linkletter, and Tennessee Williams. At other times he would hold court in the French Quarter at Felix's Oyster Bar before visiting the Playboy Club next door. The Playboy Club was on Iberville in an old carriage house, sandwiched between Felix's and Moran's Restaurant. Right across the street from the Acme Oyster House. Garrison was on a first-name basis with Geri, the Playboy Club's "Door Bunny." And he routinely bought drinks for the club's incredible house trio, jazz pianist Ellis Marsalis, bassist Robert Prado, and drummer Joe Martin.

Toward the mid-point of the first year of his second term, he began to hear chatter about his inattention to his job. Criticism galled him. The chatter was all "fake," he told friends. The city was relatively peaceful—people should be admiring the beautiful job he was doing. *Results trump personal conduct, right?* He needed a new public crusade to divert people's attention away from his unusual behaviors, to remind them of his fundamental greatness. The perfect project fell fortuitously into his lap.

Spurred by the growing public discourse over the merits of the Warren Commission Report, and miffed that his Oswald stories were getting little play, the corpulent lawyer Dean Andrews rang up Garrison, an old law school chum, in October of 1966 to bear his witness on the subject of JFK's assassin. Garrison was more than willing to meet with Andrews. He had long delighted in Andrews's tales and his amusing relationship with the English language. Plus Andrews had offered to take Garrison to Broussard's, which, along with Galatoire's, Antoine's, and Arnaud's, was one of the four Grand-Dame restaurants in the Quarter.

Twenty years later, Garrison wrote a deluded description of this lunch, portraying himself as if he were Dostoevsky's Grand Inquisitor and Andrews as if he were a paranoid witness, scared he would get a bullet in his head from some dark source if he talked too much. In truth, Andrews was his usual carefree and forthcoming self. And Garrison was a clueless, lazy listener—at least at the beginning of the session.

In his distinctive, jivey lingo, often calling Garrison "Daddy-O," Andrews reviewed his plotline. He'd met with Oswald and several of his gay "Mex" friends. Oswald was looking for legal help concerning his discharge from the Marines. He'd seen Oswald thereafter passing out pro-Castro leaflets on Castro, *paid* to do so, Oswald had told him.

Andrews related the Clay Bertrand saga. Bertrand, whom Andrews had met a couple of times, called the Saturday after the assassination to see if Andrews would represent Oswald in Dallas.

"Couldn't swing going to cowboy town, was laid up sick in the deluxe room 202 of the funky Hotel Dieu Hospital."

"What's Bertrand look like?" Garrison asked.

"Numero uno, he's clearly a homo, or at least bats from both sides of the plate. Not that I keep score. I just know he swishes. The guy's tall. He stood up when I saw him once at Cosimo's, over on Burgundy. I could eyeball then that he was about six two, six four. Bright sandy hair, blue eyes. Well-dressed cat. Talked pretty."

"*Clay* Bertrand sounds like *Clay* Shaw." Shaw was the well-known former head of the International Trade Mart.

"Can't say he is, can't say he ain't."

Thinking of the arrest of Ferrie on November 25, 1963, Garrison asked, "Know Dave Ferrie?"

"We both did some Marcello jobs, so I ran into the dude, but I don't bum in those circles."

"Would Ferrie've hung out with Oswald?"

"Can't put my hand on the Bible on that, but, yeah, most likely, Jolly Green Giant. Ferrie slummed a lot with Oswald's uncle, as did young boy Lee."

"Did Ferrie hang with Shaw?"

"They both gravitate toward a certain type of fringy joint. And, hey, you know what they say about birds of a feather."

Garrison looked up at the egg and dart molding on the ceiling protecting the Napoleon Room at Broussard's, then took a sip of his third French 75 and smiled at Andrews.

Gill had little trouble getting a briefing on the lunch conversation. He filled Ferrie in. "You know Clay Shaw, the Trade Mart guy?"

"Know who he is," Ferrie responded. "Quite a sexy older gentleman. CK that he's gay."

"Andrews kinda hinted that Shaw sometimes calls himself Clay Bertrand, and, as Bertrand, he contacted Andrews and asked him to represent Oswald."

"Ha! No one in their right mind would hire Andrews for more than getting out of a traffic ticket. He probably made the whole thing up, was just jerking folks around. I doubt there even *is* a Bertrand."

"Whatever, but Garrison now's looking at Shaw, Oswald, and you—you're all part of a suspicious New Orleans homosexual cabal. This gay chorus somehow pranced over to Dallas and took JFK out."

"That's breaking news to me."

"Nevertheless, Garrison was intrigued by what Andrews had to say. So much so that he took Andrews to Broussard's for lunch a second time. Sprung for the bill himself this time. But

Garrison's got a short attention span. Wait for him to move on to something else. He will."

\\\\\

Though even Garrison knew that Andrews was usually full of shit, he had his staff do some digging around the Quarter, and a number of bartenders confirmed that Shaw sometimes used the name Bertrand, particularly when he was in offbeat bars with other men. As Garrison thought more about this sensational information and Andrews's story, a fire was lit—exactly when his reputation needed a jolt. Energized, he went to the New Orleans Public Library and read the "Summary and Conclusions" chapter of the Warren Commission Report and skimmed the recent conspiracy books by Edward Jay Epstein and Mark Lane.

He convinced himself that, as Epstein and Lane had already concluded, there'd been a conspiracy to kill JFK. But he'd use his official position to dramatically expand from Epstein and Lane. Based on Andrews's intimations, Oswald, Ferrie, and Shaw undoubtedly worked together as part of the conspiracy, Garrison told his staff. And each of them, Garrison had heard, was homosexual, or at least a "swinging cat." Jack Ruby was probably involved as well. He'd heard rumors that Ruby was gay, and, after all, Ruby lived with a guy. *What a story*, Garrison marveled to himself.

His faultily constructed brain hit on it. The assassination was, as he told his staff, "a homosexual thrill-killing." This would get worldwide attention. There it was. Garrison's esteem would get a seismic bang with this bombshell. His constituents would marvel. Once again, he would get the admiration he deserved. He's a stable genius, his people would say.

He decided to focus this new investigation first on the "fairy" interrogated as a potential conspirator shortly after the assassination, David William Ferrie.

He also decided that he wanted, needed, this to be a national story, covered by the elite publications. On background he informed Richard Billings of *Life* magazine that he was start-ing a JFK investigation. He called an old acquaintance Martin Waldron of the *New York Times* Houston Bureau and told him the same thing—but added that he was focusing on Ferrie and that Ferrie had been arrested after the assassination.

Waldron acted immediately on the leak by preparing a memo to help Garrison, resembling a set of litigation interrogatories. It was dated a day short of the three-year anniversary of the assassination. The memo consisted of thirty-two numbered ques-tions about Ferrie and Oswald based on confidential suggestions made by Garrison.

> Does Mr. Ferrie have a police record for, or was he purported to be, a sex deviate? If so, what kind?
>
> Did the New Orleans Police Department vice squad know or have reports that Mr. Ferrie and Oswald had been associating together?
>
> There have been reports that Mr. Ferrie has been acting as a pilot for Carlos Marcello, reputed to be involved in various shady enterprises in Southern Louisiana. Is there any truth to this?
>
> Do New Orleans police officials know why the staff of the President's Commission to Investigate the Assassination of President Kennedy did not call Mr. Ferrie as a witness?
>
> *Do New Orleans police officials have any reason to believe that Mr. Ferrie may have been instrumental in suggesting or urging Oswald to commit violence, in particular the Kennedy assas-sination? If so, please explain.*

Garrison played the press artfully over the next few years, sometimes by sharply clashing with it, to fuel the public's inter-est in his work on the JFK assassination, notwithstanding his work's frequent lack of integrity.

CHAPTER 63

After Dr. Mary's death, Ferrie grew increasingly paranoid and nervous that he'd suffer the same fate. He had chronic headaches and insomnia. Everywhere he looked, he saw portents. He last felt this way before he tried to commit suicide after being thrown out of St. Charles Seminary in the 1940s.

He decided to buy a grave site, choosing St. Bernard Memorial Gardens in St. Bernard Parish, a historic area specifically mentioned in President Lincoln's Emancipation Proclamation. He also asked his lawyer, a middle-aged man named Gerry Aurillo, to write a will.

The only way he knew to deal with his anxiety was to keep as busy as possible. He increased his contract piloting work with Saturn Aviation and United Air Taxi. His gas station had tanked in late 1964, so he started his own sideline piloting business flying fishermen in his Taylorcraft out to Freemason Island, a tiny, pristine strip of land in the Gulf about eighty-five miles east of New Orleans. A friend of Ferrie's named Eustis Veazey ran a commercial fishing camp there. He also supplemented his income by training young pilots at Lakefront Airport, mainly for Al Crouch's businesses. Tom Clark continued to work with Ferrie on training and lived with Ferrie for two months during 1966.

To avoid having any free time at all, he poured energy into his work as a psychologist, seeing patients at his home in addition to his office on Clay Street in Kenner. He continued to list himself as Dr. Ferrie in the phonebook.

His remaining small slivers of waking time were used for his periodic Catholic masses at his apartment.

Ferrie had become closer to Dr. Carolyn Talley in the two years since Dr. Mary's death. As the holiday season of 1966 began, thinking about his annual pilgrimage to Dr. Mary's apartment, he suddenly felt a need to see Dr. Carolyn.

Dr. Carolyn was classy, as Dr. Mary had been. She suggested a formal meal at Antoine's on St. Louis Street in the Quarter.

They took a table in the back of the ornate, green-and-gold Rex Room and ordered Oysters Rockefeller, which had been invented at Antoine's in 1899.

"I've gotten some news that's starting to sink me." Ferrie spoke softly.

"Talk to me."

"You know how edgy I've been since Dr. Mary's death. Shit, I've hardly slept. But recently, after two years of safety, I was starting to breathe a little more slowly. I was actually sleeping more than a few hours a night. And then . . ." He paused.

"It's okay," she said. "Just talk to me."

"They're coming after me."

"Who? What's up?"

"Our looney bug-eyed district attorney is looking at me and some others as somehow being involved in the JFK killing. He sicced one of his dogs on me recently—a young legal beagle named Volz. Made me go over to Tulane Avenue. I checked with Quigley at the FBI if he could quash this, but he said I had to go ahead. Garrison had a fucking subpoena served on me. And Volz recorded the interview."

"What'd Volz ask you?"

"Mainly about a trip I took to Texas the weekend JFK was killed, leaving from the celebration party at the Royal Orleans. Took a couple of guys to a Houston ice skating rink."

"Ice skating?"

"Righto. My family skated on the Old River in Cleveland, a couple of times anyway. And I'm a big Dick Button fan."

"I think you just like saying 'Dick Button.'"

"I described this trip in excruciating detail in '63, so no big deal. Told Volz the same story. Ice skating rink was a business opportunity. The rest of the trip was to relax after the trial, drink, shoot geese with buckshot. I told him we had shotguns with us."

"You told me the victory party was at the Monteleone."

"What? Yeah, shit. Right. It was. I think I'm losing my marbles."

"No biggie."

"Gill told the FBI in '63 that it was at the Royal Orleans, that's probably why I said it. Gill intentionally fuzzed up some of the details of that Friday."

"What else with Volz?"

"Quizzed me about the trip home. We stopped in Alexandria. That's when this guy Layton Martens told me I was in big trouble, because of some rumors going around town.

"Then out of left field, Volz asked some questions about Morris Brownlee."

"Who's he?"

"May be hard to believe, but he's actually my godson. He was one of my trainees in the fifties. Wanted to be baptized and, apparently impressed with my eloquence, asked me to preside— and be his godfather. Nice thing. Good guy. Has a bit of a drug problem, but I'm working on that. Volz asked me if I took him hunting, did I take him on any trips? I didn't understand what Volz was getting at—at least not then. I'll come back to that."

"That it?"

"He asked if I knew Oswald, even whether I knew him when he was a teenager. No—no recollection, anyway.

"I did tell him a guy I'd known went to the FBI after the assassination and said that he and Oswald were in my CAP squadron in the fifties. I said I couldn't remember the guy's name, just that he worked in a flower shop on Canal. I'm pretty sure, though, that it was Ed Voebel. A school classmate of Oswald's. But I didn't want them chasing him down."

"Tangled web."

"A Marcello thug named Jack Martin really tangled me up back then. Volz asked a lot about things Martin had said about me, mainly that I knew Oswald. A new one from Volz was that I taught Oswald how to shoot a rifle. *Moi*? C'mon. I told him Martin's a psychopath. He likes attention. You'll like this—I told Volz that Martin tries to get close to the bride at every wedding and the corpse at every funeral."

"Cute."

"Volz's last question was whether I'd take a polygraph," Ferrie finished. "I said yeah, had no hesitation at all to do that."

"Doesn't sound all that bad."

"It's bad. I could tell he was skeptical of everything I said. And I know he's been interviewing people about me all over town. Particularly friends of mine. He dragged in the guys I took the Texas trip with, Al and Melvin, and grilled the shit out of them. Melvin called me a few days ago. He first thought they were just fishing around, mainly interested in the trip.

"But then, Melvin said, they had a bunch of weird questions about homosexuality that didn't make sense to him," Ferrie continued nervously. "They asked him whether he was a homo and which of my friends and associates were homos, including Morris. That's why they were asking me about Morris and tak-ing trips with him. He's as straight as a Louisiana flag pole, by the way. And they had a bunch of questions about Dean Andrews. Whether I socialized with him. Whether he was bi."

"Dean Andrews?" Dr. Carolyn asked.

"He's an obese, mouthy lawyer in town. He's like the class clown of the French Quarter. At every Mardi Gras party. A profligate. He prowls around the Quarter and sometimes over to Frenchmen Street. He particularly likes a joint called Cosimo's on Burgundy and sometimes holds court at the flaming-fountain patio at Pat O'Brien's. He's actually kind of a funny guy. I don't know him personally, but I heard him rant about a judge once at the Napoleon House—said the judge 'was picking me like chicken, shucking me like corn, stewing me like an oyster.' He jive-talks like a hipster."

"Like a Big Easy Lord Buckley?"

"Very good—Andrews *is* known to talk about 'cats' and 'kitties.' He went to school with Garrison, he's been blabbing to him."

"What else did Al say?"

"That, other than yours truly, they were fixated on a guy named Clay Shaw—and whether *he's* gay."

"Shaw's the guy who ran the Trade Mart, right? Was Rex once? Kind of a handsome, sophisticated-looking guy?"

"Yep. But I hate to tell you, he actually *is* a homo, so keep your knickers on," Ferrie joked, not very successfully.

"No worries, he's not exactly my type. But if he's gay, why's he always with Muriel Francis?"

"Oh, please. She's a rich-bitch cover for him. You need one of those if you're a big-shot gay in the South.

"Look, I don't have any fucking idea why they were asking about Shaw. I've never even met the guy."

"What else did Melvin say they asked?"

"Whether I ever had a sexual relationship with Shaw? Was Oswald a homo? Did I have sex with Oswald? What did Shaw have to do with the assassination? Did Oswald have pansy friends or associates who were also involved in the assassination? What about Ruby? Light in the loafers?"

"You need to take a few deep breaths. It's just all too crazy to be believed. I'm sure Garrison's trying to get some press time and then he'll drop it. That guy couldn't find his own ass with a map and a flashlight."

"Nice language, Doc. He's *not* moving on. A reporter friend called me last night and told me that Garrison had just given a background briefing to the press. He announced—dramatically, my friend said—that he had a suspect in the assassination. He didn't identify the suspect, but he described a guy who sounded a lot like a certain polymath you know."

"How so?" she asked.

"He described a homosexual who's done a lot of flying for Marcello. And get this. Garrison's assistant, a pudgy waste of space named Lou Ivon, has paid a guy to get a job with me. A spy!

"It turns out it's a guy I know, a mechanic who used to work for me out at Lakefront. Jimmy Johnson.

"He's also instructed Johnson to ask me to put him up for a while. Ivon knows I often let guys from the airport crash with me."

"How do you know all this?"

"The best way possible—from the spy's own mouth. Johnson's a crook at heart. He's just gaming Ivon and Garrison. He needs the money. And he wants to get in good with the cops for any future trouble he might get into."

"If Garrison's going to the trouble to have a crook paid to monitor you, then you're probably right—you're a target. But again, Garrison's inept. I just wouldn't worry too much about it."

"Why the homosexual questions?"

"You'll lose your faith in God if I answer that."

"It's already been lost . . . Mare's murder."

Ferrie paused and then whispered, "Lord Jim's got a thing about gays. Thinks we were after JFK. We can talk more about this but not here. Too many nosy ears in Antoine's. Come by my house sometime."

"Can't wait."

"By the way, you'll see the aforementioned Jimmy Johnson there. I *did* let him move in. He's actually not a bad guy. I had an opening."

\\\\\\\\

The phone rang shortly after Ferrie got home. The voice on the line surprised him. It was Gill. His contacts with Gill in the previous two years had been infrequent. He was nervous whenever he heard Gill's voice.

"We need you, Dave. When can you get over here?"

"Now?" Ferrie asked nervously.

"Yes."

Ferrie assumed that Marcello had decided to take him out before Garrison could get to him. He recited a prayer for the dying.

"God of power and mercy, you have made death itself the gateway to eternal life."

He left his apartment to learn his fate.

CHAPTER 64

Ferrie took the South Claiborne bus to Camp and Common, made the short trek to the Pere Marquette, and decided to walk up the seventeen floors to Gill's office. The stair-climbing helped to clear his head.

"How's life, my friend?" Gill asked.

"Couldn't be better, sir. You?" Ferrie's voice carried a small tremble.

"Never a dull moment," Gill said. "We need to talk about a new project for Marcello."

"Of course, sir." Ferrie was relieved that his head didn't appear to be on the chopping block. At least not yet.

"But first, what more do you know about what Garrison's doing?"

"Nothing you don't know, I'm sure. He had Volz talk to me about the Houston trip. Pretty plain vanilla interview, but since then he's been all over friends of mine. I hear from them he's fixated on people he thinks are homos. Including me. He's really obsessed with Clay Shaw."

"That's what I heard. He's spinning out a theory that JFK was killed by homosexuals, for some reason. It makes no sense. Except for the fact that Garrison is a lunatic."

"And, apparently, phobic about homos."

"Do you know whether he's gotten his hands on Banister's files?"

"No. Shit. I hadn't thought of that."

"We'll find out. In any event, Dave, you know we have full confidence that you'll be discreet. 'We' includes Marcello."

"You have no worries, sir."

"Garrison will end up making a fool of himself. Forget him, let's focus on important things."

"What do you have for me?"

"It's time to shut Ruby down. Jack is starting to ramble to visitors and even a few reporters. He's losing it. We think he's getting dangerous. Sooner or later he's going to slip out something big. As the British would say, he's completely lost the plot."

"My job?"

"Put him out of his misery. You still have some of that magic potion left, right?"

"Yeah, some."

"Is there enough left to get Ruby."

"I think so. I'm sure it's lost a lot of punch. But it should work, I would guess, on two or three more victims. Particularly if they aren't in good shape."

"Good. Ruby's in poor health. Jail's not been kind to him. Even a little pinch of the cancer powder should end it."

Relieved that *he* wasn't on Marcello's hit list, Ferrie was more than happy to take on another mission for Marcello. He liked Ruby, but, one way or another, he knew Ruby would be exiting this planet soon. "What's the scoop?"

"The Texas Court of Appeals has given Ruby a new trial. It was kind of a screwy decision saying that Ruby—who everybody in the free world saw murder Oswald on TV—couldn't possibly have gotten a fair trial in Dallas because that's where the crime occurred. The decision was unanimous, though. Weird, crazy world. They ordered a new trial in Wichita Falls."

"That hick city up near the Oklahoma border?"

"Yeah. They must think those folks don't have televisions."

"It can't be any better for him there," Ferrie said. "The Oswald murder was probably the first time those crackers had ever seen a Jew. They're not going to let a Jew murderer go."

"Well, no matter. This trial simply can't happen. Ruby would crack this time.

"A couple of days ago," Gill continued, "Ruby was moved from the Dallas county jail to Parkland Hospital. He's got a bad cold, maybe pneumonia. You need to get in there ASAP and give him a dose. Can you leave tomorrow?"

"Sure. I'll have to cancel some things, but sure. How do I get into Parkland?"

"I'll have Campisi pick you up at Red Bird. He's been visiting Ruby, he's known the guy for fourteen years. He'll take you there. They always let him in."

"What does Campisi know about what I'll be doing?"

"He won't know. I just told him that Marcello values your powers of observation and your scientific background and wants you to assess Jack's condition up close. He'll just think you're helping Marcello gauge the chances Jack will actually make it to his trial. It's supposed to start in February."

\|\|\|

Ferrie flew commercial to Dallas this time. He had one of the steel tubes in his overnight bag. Joe Campisi picked him up in a sleek, brand-new, two-door, eight-cylinder Thunderbird with a Landau top.

"Nice wheels."

Campisi smiled and nodded. "We're going straight to Parkland." Parkland was twelve miles from the airport.

The work at Parkland was surprisingly easy. The cop outside Ruby's door knew Campisi and let them in the room. Ruby was awake and eating his lunch. Campisi kissed Ruby on both cheeks.

The formerly strapping Ruby, usually wearing a sharp suit and a gray Fedora, now looked pathetic and wan, draped in a polka-dotted johnny gown. "He has that going away look," Ferrie whispered to Campisi.

The hospital room, like most hospital rooms, was sadly stark. A bed, a sink, sterile-looking medical equipment, a five-year-old black-and-white TV. Ruby was attached to an IV tube.

"Jack, you remember Dave Ferrie, right?"

"Dave, *shalom*. Quite a mess I'm in, huh?" Ruby said.

Ruby got a bolt of energy from having visitors. He began to raise his voice well above a whisper. He claimed that "they" were trying to kill him. "They" loved to torture and kill Jews, he said. "Guys, you gotta get me out of here. Get me to Washington. I got a lot to say, but not here. *They'll* kill me."

Ruby harped on and on about Jew-haters being after him. The memory that Ferrie and the mob had gotten him to kill Oswald apparently had left him, at least for the moment.

"We just need to get you better, Jack," Campisi said.

"Shit, I'll never be better until I get the truth out. Get it off my chest. But it's gotta be in Washington. I need to talk to the big mockers there. Johnson, Warren, Hoover."

"Jack," Campisi said. "Rest up here in the hospital and then I'll see what I can do about going to DC."

Ruby raised his voice further. "I told the truth to that lady on that TV show *What's My Line*. I love that show. That Bennett Cerf's fuckin' funny. She was my favorite, though. You know, Dorothy Kilgallen. Cute, smart broad. Classy. New Orleans gal, by the way. She visited me. Nice ass for a fifty-year-old city broad. Better than most of my strippers, I tell you.

"I told her everything," Ruby continued. "But then some goons whacked her last year when they found out—CIA, probably. Fuck, I was sick to my stomach when I heard that. I need to talk to Hoover."

"Kilgallen was murdered?" Ferrie asked Ruby.

"Better believe it, guys. They fuckin' drugged her."

Frank Sinatra popped into Ferrie's mind as soon as he heard Dorothy Kilgallen's name. Kilgallen had angered Sinatra with a series of articles about him that aired a lot of his dirty laundry. Sinatra and Kilgallen had been friends, so these articles stung Sinatra. *Sinatra and his associates would've had nothing to do with Kilgallen's death, right?* Ferrie thought. *Right?*

Nah. Had to be one of Giancana's Brooklyn thugs. Right?

"I gotta piss like a racehorse," Campisi said.

When Campisi went into the bathroom, Ferrie dumped a tablespoon full of cancer powder into Ruby's coffee.

As Campisi rejoined them, Ruby began railing wildly about New York City's supposed mistreatment of Jews after he killed Oswald. "They injected cancer into Jews. Hundreds of them. Because of me. Shit. Like Nazis. Did you know that?"

"We'll look into it," Ferrie said.

"They've fuckin' got me too. I'm shit sure of it. They brought a doctor in from Chicago a couple of days ago. He injected me over and over, said it was penicillin because of my cold. Lying fucker. Shit, those goddamn cancer cells are swirling around me now. I can feel them. Tell someone, Joey. Christ, get me out of here."

It was pure serendipity that Ruby began talking about cancer being forced into him just minutes after Ferrie actually had forced cancer into him. "Jack," Campisi said, "no one is trying to kill you. You're in a hospital, *putz*. They don't kill people here, at least not on purpose. Get some rest."

"I'll never make it to that new trial, guys. It'll be another fuckin' show trial anyway. Like they do in Russia. Fuck me. They might as well line the casket up in the hallway here."

Ruby was running out of steam. It'd all be over for him soon.

"Go to sleep," Campisi said. "I'll see you soon. You'll be back to turning tits and ass into money in no time."

Ferrie whispered quickly in Ruby's ear, though Ruby was nearly asleep. "Bless you, Jack. Your ride's almost here. You'll be with your god soon. And you'll meet my Jesus. I commend you, my brother, to the Almighty. I give you over to the care of Him, whose creature you are." Ferrie crossed himself.

Ruby shot Ferrie a bemused look. "There ain't no fucking Jesus, you *schmoe*," he whispered and then shut his eyes. He fell dead asleep.

Campisi and Ferrie left the hospital. This had been the first time Ferrie had ever been to Parkland Hospital—where both JFK and Oswald died, soon to be joined by Ruby.

Though it was the wrong direction from Parkland, Campisi wanted to treat Ferrie to a late lunch at his Egyptian Lounge before heading back to Red Bird. Campisi insisted on the restaurant's signature dish for both of them. The Combination Plate—spaghetti, lasagna, meat ravioli, and meatballs. Heavy Italian food wasn't exactly Ferrie's style, but, feeling drained after the Ruby visit, he cleaned his plate.

Back in New Orleans Ferrie went straight to the Crippled Children's Hospital for his annual trip there to give presents to sick kids. Dr. Carolyn joined him. Afterwards, though, Ferrie wanted to go alone for his ritual visit to the Patio (or the Patios) Apartments. Dr. Carolyn understood.

Kneeling by the front door of the apartment complex, Ferrie bowed his head to pray but could only cry.

CHAPTER 65

The next day, a few days before Christmas, Ferrie had a surprise visit from Sergio Arcacha Smith at 3330 Louisiana Avenue Parkway.

Ferrie was happy to see him. He liked and respected Arcacha Smith. A strong bond had been forged between them, grounded in their shared adventures and shared terrible, historic secrets. He served tea and scones, still thinking of Dr. Mary. Arcacha Smith sat on one of Ferrie's two cruddy couches.

"What're you in town for?" Ferrie asked.

"I've got a few projects for Mr. Marcello," Arcacha Smith said. "I'm on my way over to the Town and Country from the Quarter and thought I'd stop by."

"It's good to see you, my friend."

"You look like you need some sleep. How're things?"

"I *am* beat. Lots of pressure."

"Heard you're in Dallas now."

"*Sí*. They moved me there a couple years ago, got me another air conditioner job, doing export work this time but only to cover my real job—following Civello and Campisi around, learning the business."

"Must be weird living in Dallas after all you've been through there."

"I find myself drawn to Dealey. Just find myself there without thinking."

"Like you're under a Voodoo spell."

"The other uncanny thing is that the house they have me in now, out by White Rock, is damn close to where I introduced 'Leon' Oswald to Silvia Odio."

"That little masquerade party has done its job. Conspiracy junkies are having a field day with it. They see one Oswald in Dallas at the exact time another one is bussing from Nuevo Laredo to Mexico City. Black magic!"

"I've heard about the lame District Attorney and would like to hear more. But first tell me about Ruby. Gill told me you've made sure that Ruby wouldn't make it to his next trial. The monkey powder, I assume?"

"I saw Jack in the hospital and put some in his coffee. That'll do the job. He's pretty weak."

"That stuff still works?"

"It should work. It's weakened for sure, but Ruby just needs a little nudge to get to the other side. I'm almost out of the stuff. Just one tube left in my fridge. I don't want it too close to anything I actually consume, so it's in one of the door shelf bins."

"How long do you give Ruby?"

"He won't see much of 1967."

"He's probably better off. Beats getting fried. *And* he'll get to miss the rough years coming up in this country. We're in for some shit times, Dave. I'm telling you. Americans getting chewed up in Vietnam. Riots here over that stupid war. More Negro battles with cops. Hippies getting beat up by George Wallace bigots. There'll be some serious death and destruction, Your Grace, I'm sorry to say.

"Thanks, Captain Optimism."

"This Vietnam thing *is* daft. It was supposed to be easy, but now LBJ is upping the troops over there to five hundred thousand. Christ. He's gone native on this war and forgotten his promises to us about Cuba."

"Fuck him. Nothing we can do now. Change subjects. I want to show you something. Be back in a second." Ferrie went back to his bedroom. When he returned to the living room, Arcacha Smith had moved from the couch and was sitting at Ferrie's piano. He was playing an old Cuban children's song, "Duérmete Mi Niño."

"Fucking sweet, piano man." Ferrie took a big sip of his tea.

"I hear *you're* the piano man, Liberace."

"My mother taught me that song when I was a kid," Arcacha Smith continued. "In English, the title is 'Go to Sleep, My Child.'" He sang in English, "Sleep, my love; sleep, piece of my heart."

"I could use some sleep," Ferrie said.

"Just relax a little, Dave. You'll sleep, I know it."

Ferrie showed Arcacha Smith a framed picture Dr. Carolyn had given him. It was of Ferrie and Dr. Mary at Martin Brothers Restaurant.

"Nice. Something to remember her by. I was so sorry to hear about her death."

"They still haven't found her killer."

"At this point, I bet they never will, my friend," Arcacha Smith said. He finished his tea.

"It really doesn't matter. It won't bring her back."

Arcacha Smith put his jacket on and left.

The visit was a nice break and diversion for Ferrie. He felt calmer. The Cuban children's song in his head, Ferrie did sleep well that night.

||||

It took Ruby a couple weeks to die, on the third day of 1967. The *Dallas Times Herald*'s evening edition on that day reported in a large banner headline: "RUBY IS DEAD–Oswald's Slayer's Death Peaceful. CANCER CONQUERS."

CHAPTER 66

The calm Ferrie felt after Arcacha Smith's visit was short-lived.

Jim Garrison's glare began to penetrate deep into him in the new year. He grew acutely fearful and anxious. On more than one occasion, he couldn't conduct flight training or piloting assignments because of crippling headaches. Colleagues or students at times would find him with his head down on a desk at Lakefront Airport, barely able to open his eyes.

Garrison's investigation was gearing up. He'd gotten hold of the complete home movie of the assassination—the "Zapruder Film," named after the Dallas dress manufacturer who took the movie—from an assassination researcher. The most consequential home movie ever taken, it comprised just six feet of celluloid. It was shot with a $167.50, eight-millimeter Bell & Howell Zoomatic 414PD Directors Series camera.

The film had never been shown publicly, though thirty-one black-and-white frames had been included in the November 29, 1963, edition of *Life* magazine. Selected color frames were published by *Life* in its December 6, 1963, October 2, 1964, and November 25, 1966, issues.

Shortly after acquiring the Zapruder Film, the FBI had assigned numbers to the relevant frames, starting at the point where the motorcade was making the turn onto Elm. The frame numbers went from 1 to 486. The FBI determined that every 18.3 frames of the film represented one second of time. The Warren Commission Report included frames 171 through 207 and 212 through 334 in its eighteenth volume, exhibit 885, though the printed copies were small, black and white, and blurry.

Sources within the DA's office had told Gill that they had the movie. The movie confirmed, they said, that there was a conspiracy, that there clearly were two shooters. The film showed that the head shot came from the front and side, not from the Depository behind JFK. JFK's head snapped backward not forward. Though the Warren Commission had published a poor version of the frame showing the head shot, frame 313, the true picture of the snap-back impact of the blast was only clear when viewed in motion.

When Gill filled Ferrie in on this fact in a January meeting at the Pere Marquette, Ferrie was struck by the frame number, ending in thirteen, an unlucky number. He said to Gill, "It's kind of Voodoo creepy that JFK was killed on a Friday at frame 313, his Dallas trip was announced on a Friday the thirteenth, Castro was born on a Friday the thirteenth. As the ghost of Marie Laveau and I know, it's an ominous day, the day God threw Adam and Eve out of the Garden of Eden. Been all downhill since then."

"I know you have some Voodoo in you, mixed in with all that Catholic bullshit," Gill responded. "But I deal with facts. *You* can channel the ghost of Marie Laveau if you want, but here's a more important fact the movie apparently shows."

"*Alions.*"

"They say that frames 337 and 338 are the smoking guns. At that point, Kennedy's body had fallen to his left after the shot, leaning against Mrs. Kennedy. The back of his neck and head are cleanly visible. There's no sign of an entry wound. Nothing. No blood, not even on his collar or jacket. Every hair in place.

"This will chill you—the FBI only gave the Warren Commission frames up through 334. Hoover had 337 and 338 *but held them back.* Why? You tell me, Sherlock," Gill continued.

"Obviously part of the whitewash. Jesus!

"So, Garrison really does know there was a second shooter."

"If he had any doubt about that after seeing those things," Gill said, "here's the capper. Let's go back to the famous frame 313. Three thirteen and the next two frames show JFK's head exploding into a cloud and streaks of whitish red matter. We'd seen these frames in *Life*, but they say you really do have to see the movie. The head just shatters."

"So?"

"Oswald was shooting full metal jacket bullets. If *he'd* hit the head, the bullet would have passed right through. No explosion. Still would've killed Kennedy but no explosion. There had to be another type of bullet hitting the head, one that fragments on impact. Frangible ammo they call it. *Had* to be another gun. The DA's guys see that."

\\\\

Ferrie called Dr. Carolyn on Monday, February 6. "Please come over. Jimmy's not here. I'm by myself. I'd like to talk."

"You're not getting ready for Mardi Gras?" she asked.

"Skipping this year, too freaking cold. Plus I'm not fond of the King this year."

"And that is?"

"Morgan Whitney—a fucking banker who turned me down for a loan once for no goddamn reason."

Upon her arrival, Ferrie made tea for Dr. Carolyn. She hadn't been to his apartment for a couple of years and had forgotten its eccentricities, smell, and clutter.

"Good to see your rat hole again."

"Speaking of rats, it's all over town that Garrison is going after me. I can't go out without people staring at me. People are watching my apartment. And, shit, it's not just our friends from the *Times-Picayune* or the *New Orleans States-Item* anymore. There are out-of-town guys here from the *New York Times* and the *Washington Post*. God knows who else."

"What is Jimmy Johnson telling you?"

"It's unbelievable. Garrison is still aroused by the homosexual angle. But he's not a complete idiot, though he's pretty damn close. What I hear is that when he goes public—which could be any day—he's going to say the CIA did it, or at least elements of the CIA. He'll say many in the CIA thought JFK was a pussy, too soft on the Soviet Union. Garrison's going to try to paint a picture of the CIA organizing people like me, Oswald, Ruby, maybe Andrews, maybe Clay Shaw as part of what was basically a coup d'état."

"It's all bullshit, right?" Dr. Carolyn asked.

"Of course. Nobody's really going to believe it. It's crazy. Why would the CIA use a few homosexuals in New Orleans and Dallas when they have infinitely better assets? But Garrison's going to wreak some havoc along his way."

"You'll be okay. His story's too nutty. Sounds like he's outlining the script for a shitty movie. Some fools would actually believe it if it were in a movie. There's a sucker born every minute. You know who said that?"

"P. T. Barnum. Shit, I'm in the crosshairs of fucking P. T. Barnum."

"That's actually a myth, Professor. Ever hear of Hungry Joe?"

"I've heard of Sloppy Joe."

"P. T. never said 'there's a sucker born every minute.' But I wouldn't put it past some guy who thinks he's like P. T. Barnum to pay Garrison for the rights to make this into a movie thriller. Like the *Manchurian Candidate*."

"Sinatra's finest."

"Garrison would insist that he be played by Sinatra."

"Actually, Sinatra could play himself."

"What?"

"Never mind," Ferrie said.

"Is he going after Marcello?"

"No way. He needs Marcello on his side. I bet part of this bizarre crusade is to divert suspicion away from Marcello, earn some brownie points. Lane and Epstein have unleashed hordes of folks working on assassination stories, a few are sniffing around the mob."

"*Was* Marcello involved?"

"*No lo sé* about that."

"But what the hell should I do, ma'am. I can't think straight."

"You've never known Clay Shaw, right?"

"Right. I've seen him on TV and in Mardi Gras parades and a few soirées, that's it."

"And you don't know Dean Andrews?"

"Like I said before, everybody who parties in this town has seen him at various festivities and at bars in the Quarter. But, no, I don't know him personally."

"I assume you don't know anybody from the CIA?"

"The way things are going, I wish I did. But the answer is no."

"How about this? Why don't you just call Garrison up, or maybe that guy you mentioned the other day, Ivon. Have them come here, tell them you don't know Andrews or Shaw and then just answer their questions. You're clean, right?"

"Right. I'm as unblemished as a virgin's maidenhead. But talking to them would only make things worse, I just know it. What a fucking nightmare. Fuck."

"Just do it. They're going to call you in at some point soon anyway. Beat them to the punch. If nothing else, you might avoid them focusing on just you when they go public."

"Christ. I just need this to go away."

"It will, it will." Dr. Carolyn gently patted his knee.

"Dr. Carolyn?"

"Yes, Dr. Ferrie?"

"My mind's blown. And, more importantly, my soul. I've given my life to God, but I've committed so many sins. Bad sins. I've had to do some things that, I think, were good for people in general but were . . ."

"Hold on, Mr. Priest. You Catholics have a thing called justification, right?"

"You must be thinking of my favorite council," Ferrie responded. "The Council of Trent in the sixteenth century."

"Hmmm . . . Yeah, sure was. My favorite too."

"They put out a canon on justification, but it's freaking ambiguous. Bottom line—your sins are washed away if you're infused with sanctifying grace. Whatever that is. What is more understandable, to me anyway, is the concept explained by Saint Augustine in the *City of God*. Eleven hundred years before Trent. He talks about 'just wars.' You can engage in these to help reach the City of God. But frankly I'm not really sure any of this fits my bad acts."

"Close enough for jazz."

"But I've committed some mortal sins, Dr. Carolyn. You don't know about them, and you don't wanna know. But I don't think the Holy Spirit's grace can cleanse so much wickedness from one soul."

"God is good. You know that better than anyone."

"Yes, yes. But have I been fighting a *just* war or an *unjust* war? God's not big on forgiving mortal sins. Can mortal sins be just? That's the question."

Ferrie struggled with this question big time. Murders usually are mortal sins, but here the ultimate result of the most heinous act he had helped commit was getting rid of a nonbelieving, soft-on-Communism leader—and a chronic sinner—and replacing him with a fierce anti-Communist. A God-fearing man who often quoted from the Bible. The world would be a better place. At least that's what drove the heinous act at the time.

"I don't know what all you've done," Dr. Carolyn said. "But, though you're the religious expert, I believe all sin can be forgiven by a loving God."

"The only hope for me, Doc, is to go all in on the Sacrament of Penance."

"I skipped that class in medical school."

"Starts with contrition. As they said at your favorite council, 'contrition is sorrow of heart and detestation for sin committed, with the resolve to sin no more.' And then, relentless confession. I need to recognize my sins and intensely tell an agent of God about them and that I'm repentant. Over and over. Usually you tell a priest, but I'm going higher—as I've done most of my life—straight to Mother Mary."

"Sure. Go for it. Makes sense to me, Father."

Ferrie said a full mass that night at his apartment. Just for himself. He took communion. He confessed sin after sin. He fell asleep by his makeshift altar in full vestments, his biretta lying on its side by his hairless head. Wooden crucifix by his side.

CHAPTER 67

Ferrie decided to take Dr. Carolyn's advice. He called Pershing Gervais in the DA's office a week after that year's unusually cold and unusually violent Mardi Gras. He'd known Gervais since the 1950s. Gervais had attended the questioning of Ferrie after the assassination. He was a good investigator—and a better con man.

Gervais, a friend of DA Garrison's since before World War II, refused. He didn't want to get between Garrison and Ferrie. He suggested that Ferrie call Lou Ivon. He did so, and Ivon agreed to come over to his apartment during the afternoon of Saturday, February 18. He said he would be bringing a colleague.

But things went pear-shaped before this meeting took place. On February 17, the *New Orleans States-Item* ran a story by three reporters with the headline, "DA Here Launches Full JFK Death Plot Probe." The article's intended focus was on Garrison's unreasonable overspending in office. "Mysterious Trips Cost Large Sums." But the real breaking news in the article was that the "mysterious trips" related to a heretofore unknown investigation of JFK's murder.

Ferrie wasn't mentioned in the article, but he still was deeply unsettled by it. The investigation had finally become public. It was only a matter of time before his name would be brought into what was certain to be relentless public attention. He had to do something right away.

The lead reporter on this ground-shaking story was named Rosemary James. There were two other by-lines. Jack Dempsey had had the original tip on the story, but the paper gave it over to James because Dempsey had had a long running feud with Garrison. The third reporter was a squirrely guy named David Snyder. Snyder, an acquaintance of Ferrie's, had been at the Sho-Bar with Pershing Gervais the night Ferrie and Al had gone to see Jada perform for the first time after her arrest for lewd behavior in 1963. Ferrie picked up the phone and dialed the *New Orleans States-Item*. He told Snyder that he had information that there in fact was an active investigation into the assassination—and that in fact *he*, wrongfully, was a target.

Ferrie offered to tell everything he knew. But, he said, he wasn't feeling well. Snyder would have to come to 3330 Louisiana Avenue Parkway.

Snyder's office was nearby. With his appearance at Ferrie's apartment that Friday evening, the clock marking the last weekend of Ferrie's life began ticking. Tick. Tick. Tick.

Ferrie met Snyder out front, and they walked slowly up to the second-floor apartment. "I've got encephalitis," Ferrie said in a soft and wheezy voice. "And a terrible headache." Ferrie was pale.

"Hey, no worries, take your time," Snyder said.

Settling onto one of the ratty couches, Ferrie said, "Mr. Snyder, believe me, I wasn't involved in any way with the assassination. But I know Garrison believes the opposite. He thinks I was a conspirator. It's all crap. The guy's crazy, you know."

"Clearly," Snyder said. "I'm surprised how much attention my little article got. I mean, he *is* a crackpot. But I've been getting calls from all over the country. Even one from Scotland! It's looking like we're gonna see a lot of out-of-town reporters in the Big Easy over the next few days."

"There are some already outside my fucking house. Shit." Ferrie put his head between his knees.

Snyder and Ferrie talked for four and a half hours. Ferrie laid out what he knew of Garrison's "case," including the homosexual angle and Garrison's focus on him and also on Clay Shaw. "All bullshit," Ferrie said. Garrison apparently had a "hard-on" for Shaw and for him.

Ferrie also talked at length about Jack Martin and how Martin had lied to Garrison's office about Ferrie right after the assassination. Martin, Ferrie said, was a "whack-job alcoholic."

"Martin has admitted he fabricated the story about me and Oswald," Ferrie said. "When this is all over, I'm going to sue the shit out of Martin *and* Garrison."

Ferrie continued, lying. "Mr. Snyder, I never, ever, met Oswald. *Never.* Before November 22, if I'd bumped into him right on Bourbon Street at high noon, I wouldn't have had a clue who he was."

Snyder left around ten thirty. Ferrie's phone rang within minutes. Other reporters frisking their sources in the DA's office had been hearing that Ferrie was a target. Sam DePino, Channel 12's crime reporter, was on the line. DePino had had information on the secret Garrison investigation for several months but not enough to go on the air with it. His sources had told him that Ivon was going to interview Ferrie soon.

Ferrie talked to DePino for twenty minutes and then said he had to crash. He gave DePino a CliffsNotes version of what he'd told Snyder.

Saturday morning, the eighteenth, Ferrie's life began slipping faster off the rails. The *Times-Picayune*—the morning sister paper of the afternoon *New Orleans States-Item*—featured a front-page article confirming the DA's investigation. "What allegedly sparked the investigation is the possibility that a well-organized assassination plot involving local residents may have been hatched in 1963, prior to Oswald's departure for Dallas." Implicitly identifying one of the "local residents" as Ferrie, the paper said, "A man arrested in New Orleans as a Texas fugitive on November 26, 1963 (four days after the assassination) was kept under surveillance for the district attorney for a 24-hour period last month." Ferrie's arrest on that Tuesday in 1963 as a fugitive from Texas had been reported at the time by the *Times-Picayune*.

Ferrie was beside himself. *Fucking Garrison*, he thought. And he was scared. He called Burt Johnson, a young pilot he was training. "You see the paper? I'm in as much trouble as a hog waiting in line in the Chicago Yards. Shit, man."

"Comin' over," Johnson said.

"Good. Two of Garrison's finest are visiting me this afternoon. It'd be good to have a witness here."

The Saturday edition of the *New Orleans States-Item* came out shortly after Johnson arrived. Information Ferrie had passed on to Snyder, on background he thought, appeared in the article, including the specific news that Ferrie was a target of Garrison's inquiry.

Mid-afternoon on that Saturday, Lou Ivon and his colleague Anthony Sciambra arrived at Ferrie's apartment. Sciambra, an assistant DA, coincidentally had known Ferrie in a previous life when Sciambra had worked as a security guard at Lakefront Airport.

"Long time no see," Sciambra said, shaking Ferrie's hand out front on the sidewalk.

"I'm thrilled to see you again, Moo Moo," Ferrie said sarcastically. Sciambra's nickname was "Moo Moo."

He led the investigators up the steps, moaning and groaning with each step. Ferrie told them he was "sick and weak" and hadn't been eating.

Burt Johnson was sitting on the piano bench. Sciambra had met Johnson in the past at Lakefront and didn't object to Johnson being present. Jimmy Johnson—no relation to Burt—wasn't there.

Ferrie laid down on the sofa, two pillows under him, in the front room. He was wearing brown corduroy pants and an unbuttoned white work shirt over a Hubba-Hubba T-shirt.

"Okay, what's the story, Morrie?" Ivon asked.

"I'm concerned about your investigation," he said. "I've heard you guys are about to arrest me. That true? I'm unemployed. Broke. Sick. Fuckin' scared. I'm hounded all day by reporters and other assholes. Can't you guys lay off?"

"We're just gathering facts," Ivon said. "We have zero plans to arrest you—of course, unless you confess!" Ivon and Sciambra chuckled.

Garrison's guys focused on the details of Ferrie's November 22 trip to Texas with Coffey and Beauboeuf. Ferrie gave his well-rehearsed reasons for the trip—to relax, hunt, explore a possible business opportunity.

"Who shot the president?" Sciambra asked.

"Oswald, obviously, but shit if I know who the other shooter was."

"Other shooter?" Ivon asked.

Ferrie asked Johnson to get him books from another room on anatomy and pathology. He then got out a few pieces of paper and launched into an educated description of key facts about the shooting. He drew a map of Dealey Plaza and marked the trajectory of the shots.

"As an amateur scientist and investigator myself, I couldn't help but analyze the event," Ferrie said.

He began a detailed lecture on the Warren Commission's "magic bullet" theory. He started with JFK's neck wound. "If you look at Commission Exhibit 386, which supposedly is a drawing of the top of JFK's back on the autopsy table, you can see that the wound was where the back joins the neck. Now, I have information that the wound was actually lower, but even if you take the drawing at face value, the magic bullet theory just doesn't work. The bullet had a downward trajectory, obviously, from the sixth floor of that book warehouse. For the magic bullet theory to work, the bullet would've had to hit Kennedy in the top of the back, again heading downward, then zig back up to exit the middle of the front of his neck, and then zag back down to hit Connally. *Are you fucking kidding me?*

"The rules of physics would have to be suspended for that to've happened," Ferrie continued. "LBJ and Hoover just didn't want to complicate their lives, so they had Arlen Specter, one of the lawyers, come up with this fiction to account for the fact that Oswald fired only three shots and one missed. Specter twisted himself in knots like a Hindu yogi to try to show that only two bullets did all the damage."

Ferrie also discussed the speed the bullet would've had to travel out of JFK's neck to hit Governor Connally and do damage. In the course of this discussion, pointing to pages in the books Johnson had fetched for him, he identified virtually every bone in the body and every hard and soft muscle. He talked about the dermis and epidermis.

"And even if the bullet had moved from JFK's neck to the governor," Ferrie explained, "it would've been slowed down so much from passing through layers of hard and soft muscle in JFK that it would've just bounced off of Connally's leg onto the floor of the car. But we know Connally's back wound had a lot of air in it, meaning the striking bullet had mucho velocity."

"Kinda confusing, Mr. Wizard," Ivon said.

"Okay. I'll give you a simpler story then, Curly. One even a stooge like you can understand. Set aside everything I just baby-fed you. The fact of the matter is that the bullet that hit Kennedy in the back never even exited the front of him. *Ergo*, it couldn't have hit Connally. That's what the FBI wrote—officially wrote, mind you—just two weeks after the hit. Ace agents Sibert and O'Neill. I have this on good authority. The good doctor Humes, the FBI says, found there was no exit path for that bullet. To the contrary, sir, the entrance tunnel was shallow, ended a finger's length into the tissue. And the doc saw that the bullet hole in the back was too low and at too steep an angle to have passed out through JFK's neck in any event. No magic."

"Everyone knows there was an exit from the neck," Sciambra pointed out.

"We really don't know, Detective Moo Moo—his neck got mucked up by the butchers at Parkland. He may've just had a nick from flying debris kicked up by Oswald's third shot. Or who knows by what?

"Hoover surely knew there was no 'magic bullet,'" Ferrie continued. "I'm told the Zapruder movie shows that the head shot clearly didn't come from the rear. Nor did it come from

Oswald's Carcano. Hoover certainly saw that. He knows there was another shooter. But, again, he and LBJ didn't want any muss or fuss with this thing."

"The FBI *did* do a shitty job," Ivon said. "We're on the same page there."

"Yeah, but be shit-careful about pissing off J. Edgar," Ferrie warned.

Ferrie made the case that there was a second shooter because he was certain Garrison was already convinced of this fact. It would *not* be in his interest, he assumed, to argue his innocence by pointing to the Warren Commission's conclusion that Oswald acted alone. There was a conspiracy, he would acknowledge, but he wasn't part of it. He in fact was in the courthouse on Royal Street at the time of the murder. They should be looking for the second shooter.

"You've said before you didn't know Oswald," Ivon asked. "Wanna change that?"

"I've never told a lie."

"Let me ask you this—you ever have relations of any sort with Clay Shaw?"

"I've never met Clay Shaw," Ferrie responded.

"Dean Andrews said you knew Clay Shaw—that you *really* knew Clay Shaw, if you get my drift," Sciambra said.

"Dean Andrews is a professional screwball and liar—a teller of tall tales. It wouldn't surprise me if he said he had information that Jackie Kennedy did it. You know how Dean Andrews is."

"You know Sergio Arcacha Smith?" Ivon asked, out of the blue.

Holy Jesus. The FBI didn't seem to care about him in 1963. What had Garrison's slobs heard?

"I met him once or twice, didn't really know him."

"How'd you meet him?"

"He was an anti-Castro guy, did some work with Guy Banister. Banister introduced me to him. Just once or twice."

"Know Ronnie Caire?"

"Ronnie who?"

"He and Arcacha Smith worked together in some 'free Cuba' group. We talked to Caire last month. He said some interesting things about Arcacha Smith, that he worked with the Cuban underground, he stole explosives from the Houma blimp field, he committed other criminal acts."

"I don't know anything about what Arcacha Smith did."

"Nothing about the blimp field explosives?"

"Never been to Houma."

"Okay. We'll talk to Arcacha Smith. If we can get him out of Texas."

"I'm trying to help you guys, but this is bullshit." Ferrie stopped the interview and said he wouldn't talk to them anymore. He would only talk to Garrison in the future. "Call me only if Garrison wants to talk," Ferrie said to Ivon.

Ivon and Sciambra left. Ferrie felt that they'd been playing with him in talking about Andrews and Shaw. But Arcacha Smith? What did these guys *really* know? Did they have the Banister files? What was Martin telling them? *I should've probed these assholes more*, Ferrie thought.

\\\\\\

The next day, Sunday, Ferrie remained edgy. His neck hurt. He canceled a flight instruction appointment. Reporters and newsmongers were keeping vigil up and down Louisiana Avenue Parkway and on South Roman Street. The *Times-Picayune* had published another Garrison story, which it would each of the last four days of Ferrie's life.

"Garrison Predicts Success for Probe—Convictions Will Result, He Declares." The second half of this article was all Ferrie.

> — *David W. Ferrie, a pilot and sometimes investigator, called the Garrison investigation "a big joke." Ferrie said he has been pegged as the get-away pilot in an elaborate plot to kill Kennedy.*

— *"Our route [back from Texas after the assassination] brought us back by Alexandria on the Sunday after; and it was there I learned that 13 law officers, including Garrison and former assistant district attorney Frank Klein, had broken into my home and carted off books, photographs and some other personal belongings."*
— *When he returned, Klein questioned him and his companions, said Ferrie. "We were all thrown in jail and booked with being fugitives from Texas," said Ferrie bitterly.*
— *Ferrie denies knowing Lee Harvey Oswald.*
— *Ferrie has been looking into possible local tie-ins to the assassination on his own. . . . Ferrie said, "My assessment of Oswald is that he would be incapable of any interpersonal relationship, especially anything as delicate as a conspiracy to kill."*
— *Ferrie said he had been ill at home for about three weeks with encephalitis.*

The *Times-Picayune* feature on the Garrison investigation included only one picture. Not of Garrison. Not of JFK. Not of Oswald. Not of Ruby. On page two at the top of the third column was a sinister-looking view of Ferrie, from the side and looking slightly down on him. Being in black and white gave Ferrie the appearance of a film-noir character. He was wearing a fedora pulled down in the front down to his eyebrows.

||||

Ferrie left his apartment late that afternoon. A throng of reporters shouted at him.

"Don't get a boner guys. Just going down to the drug store. You can continue hounding me in a few minutes when I return." Several reporters followed him anyway.

He walked down Louisiana Avenue Parkway to South Roman, turned left toward Washington and entered the Broadmoor Pharmacy. Passing directly through to the back door, he exited and snuck through a parking lot to rejoin Roman a little farther east, out of sight of his pursuers. He took the South Claiborne bus to Canal and Camp and walked the several blocks to the Hotel Monteleone.

Reaching Lou Ivon from the same payphone he had used to call Dallas on November 22, 1963, Ferrie nervously asked where things stood after their meeting and when he could see Mr. Garrison. Ferrie said he was ready to talk in more detail but not at his apartment.

"The dickhead press and stalkers are harassing the flaming hell out of me. I'm fucking scared for my life. You need to come get me, guys. I'm at the Monteleone. I'll be riding on the Carousel Bar, drinking a Vieux Carré."

"Yippee-I-oh-ki-ay!" Ivon said. "Don't fall off."

"Asshole."

"How about this? Let's get you a room in a hotel for a few days, away from the madding crowd."

"Jesus, you've actually heard of Thomas Hardy?"

"Shit, yeah. One of the Hardy Boys."

"Bingo. Sure, a hotel stay sounds good. I need a vacation. Book me a massage too. With a male, of course."

"Why not? If you're not too dizzy, get your candy ass off the merry-go-round stool you're riding on and wait for us out front on Royal Street."

CHAPTER 68

After praying to Mother Mary from his bar stool, Ferrie exited the Monteleone and got in Ivon's 1960 Rambler American on Royal Street. Ivon had a different investigator with him this time, a guy Ferrie didn't know—a guy with a girl's first name, Lynn Loisel.

"Where's my hotel, boys? Hawaii?"

"Yeah, how'd you know? The big pink one on Waikiki."

"My lucky day! I'm going straight to the Mai Tai Bar when I get there. Their Mai Tais are historic, as I'm sure you know. And unique. They throw in orange juice."

"Been there many times," Ivon said.

Pretending to check his notes, Ivon continued, "Oh, wait. I got it wrong, sorry Dave. We have you at the equally exotic Fontainebleau Motor Hotel."

"Splendid. Miami Beach!"

"Close. But no. Tulane Avenue. We have a beautiful room for you there. And don't worry, it's under an alias. And we'll pay for it! *And*, better than the Mai Tai Bar—they have the world-famous Hawaiian Luau Restaurant and Lounge."

"In return for this treat," Ivon continued, "we need some more chat time with you. Garrison then'll meet with you in a day or two, I promise."

"I'll take it."

The Fontainebleau was at Tulane and South Carrollton Avenue, in mid-city, near Xavier University. It was a large complex with three swimming pools and a "palm-lined patio." It billed itself as the "South's Largest and Finest Motor Hotel."

Garrison often put witnesses there and recorded them with hidden tape recorders. The mob had connections there as well.

Lou Ivon reinterviewed Ferrie in his hotel room. The pressure was getting to Ferrie. *Why Arcacha Smith?* He'd become increasingly panicky. His sky-high anxiety had put him in a confessional state of mind. To Ivon, Ferrie seemed to be scared, even wild. His impulse control disorder seized him.

Most of what Ferrie said now was different from his earlier statements—and wasn't true. He now said that he in fact *had* known Clay Shaw. They'd had relations. Shaw told him he worked for the CIA. And Shaw had spoken angrily about JFK, Ferrie lied. Clumsily, Ferrie was frantically trying to save himself by providing support for Garrison's fixation on Shaw.

He was worried about what was in Banister's files. So, he admitted he'd met Oswald but said it was just briefly at a bar in the French Quarter in the summer of 1963. However, he held the line on Arcacha Smith—didn't know much about him, he told Ivon.

Ivon left, leaving Loisel to guard Ferrie. With his overheated brain spinning in circles, Ferrie grew disturbed that he'd said all the wrong things. *Shit,* he wondered. *Have I fucked myself?* He had to get away from these guys.

When Loisel left his post to get some cigarettes, Ferrie slipped out of his Fontainebleau room and bolted from the "South's Largest and Finest Motor Hotel." He took the Tulane bus to the Lake Forest line and walked up to Lakefront Airport. He would spend the night there.

Airport operations were closed down for the night that Sunday, but the historic 1934 Art Deco terminal was open. Entering through the two-story atrium, he peered up at the Xavier Gonzalez murals, noting in particular his favorite one, the one that depicted the giant dirigible the USS *Akron* flying over New York City in March 1933 before making an historic voyage to the Panama Canal. The *Akron* crashed off of the New Jersey coast a month later, the largest dirigible accident in history, killing seventy-three people. This crash spelled the beginning of the end of the US Navy's dirigible program.

Looking up and down the hallways, Ferrie saw only one person, a janitor.

"Dr. Ferrie, how you doin', sir? What can I do for you?"

"Satch, my friend. I've got *mucho* problems I need to get away from. I'm going to crash on Crouch's couch."

"Sounds like a Zydeco song, Dr. Ferrie."

"*Oui, mon ami.* Clifton Chenier gave me that line."

"Awrite, sir," Satch said, smiling widely.

Neither Dr. Ferrie nor anyone else at the airport knew the janitor's real name. All referred to him as "Satch" because he looked like the ageless former baseball player Leroy "Satchell" Paige, a star in both the Negro and Major Leagues. Paige was a beloved, good-natured figure everywhere but especially in the Deep South, having grown up and started his career in Mobile, two hours from New Orleans. The Lakefront janitor had Paige's lanky physique and enthusiastic personality.

"Anybody else around tonight?" Ferrie asked.

"Mr. Campbell. Doin' some paperwork, I think."

As Satch began walking slowly back toward the janitor closet at the other end of the airport, Al Campbell came walking by. Ferrie had known Campbell for years, ever since Campbell had worked for him and Jack Martin to ferret out Commies at New Orleans colleges. Campbell now was Bell Helicopter's point man at Lakefront.

"You look like shit," Campbell said.

Since the beginning of the year, Ferrie had lost what was left of the military, ramrod demeanor he'd had when he was younger. He was beginning to slouch.

"Been a rough couple of days."

"I read about you and Garrison in the paper. Sounds like bull."

"Total nonsense. I need a night away from all the freaks and clowns. Am bunking in Crouch's office tonight."

"Sounds comfy. Good luck. Pleasant dreams."

Campbell shook Ferrie's hand and took off.

Ferrie went out to the tarmac and found his Taylorcraft L-2, which he'd moved back to Lakefront from Moisant Field. He circled around it a couple of times. He then slowly rubbed and patted the nose of his plane, as others would do to a pet dog or prize horse. After one last pat, he said, "See you later, alligator."

He flopped down on Crouch's couch. He tried to sleep, but the last ten years of his life swirled around his turbocharged brain. Cuba. Ruby. Guatemala. The 500 Club. Blaze Starr. Jada. The Lomalinda. Arcacha Smith. Winterland Ice Rink. *Marcello. Garrison. Dr. Mary. Cancer. The 'JFK Affair.'*

It then dawned on him that Campbell, his last human contact of the day, was an old school chum of Oswald's. *Fucking Oswald.*

He tried to focus just on Dr. Mary, the best person he'd known in his forty-nine-year, garbled life. He rolled off the couch and knelt on the floor. He prayed for Dr. Mary, "Lord, those who die still live in Your presence; their lives change but don't end." He then prayed the Ave Maria. The closing words seemed to comfort and calm him: "Holy Mary Mother of God, pray for us sinners now and at the hour of our death. Amen."

Contrition. Confession.

Returning to the couch, exhausted and calmer, he was able to sleep for a few hours.

CHAPTER 69

Ferrie woke early at Lakefront on Monday, February 20. That day's *Times-Picayune* story about Garrison's quest was titled, "Arrests Planned, Garrison Repeats." The article had one brief mention of Ferrie as being the get-away pilot. A related squib on the front page said, "Press Calls Pour From Over Globe."

After only a nervous skim of the article and the squib, Ferrie bussed south toward town. He had a full morning agenda. Though creaky, he moved peripatetically around town.

He first went to his doctor, Dr. Richard Bagnetto, to talk about his headaches, nervousness, and fatigue. He told the doctor that these symptoms had exacerbated since the first of the year. Dr. Bagnetto had treated Ferrie for high blood pressure and a hyperactive thyroid for years. The doctor easily determined both conditions had worsened. He prescribed higher doses of Proloid for the thyroid and of chlorothiazide to protect the heart.

"See me in a week," Dr. Bagnetto said.

From there, Ferrie sought out several prized associates to tell his side of the story to. He walked to the FBI's office to see Regis Kennedy, pleading his innocence. Kennedy had known Ferrie since the Marcello trial in November 1963. They had met in the courthouse during that long trial and had had multiple contacts for various reasons since then. Ferrie had given him a statement related to the assassination on December 10, 1963.

He then moved on to see Carlos Bringuier. On Canal Street in the summer of 1963, Carlos Bringuier had fake-tussled with Oswald over Fidel Castro. Both had been arrested. Bringuier, he knew, had been deposed by the Warren Commission and would surely be called on by Garrison.

Ferrie finished up with lawyer Gerry Aurillo, both a former flying student of his *and* a former Garrison assistant. There, in addition to rebutting Garrison's emerging conspiracy theories, he discussed a possible lawsuit against Garrison. And against Martin as well.

He was exhausted but pleased he'd accomplished these meetings with the FBI, Bringuier, and Aurillo that Monday. He knew all hell was breaking loose. He returned to his home through a small but vocal phalanx of reporters and onlookers.

At about the same time, at the Fontainebleau Motor Hotel, Garrison was holding his first press conference on his JFK investigation. The DA had been forced to come out publicly after the Dempsey-James-Snyder article the previous Friday in the *New Orleans States-Item*. Garrison didn't mention any details. But his tone was aggressive and confident.

"There is no question there will be arrests of individuals, charges, and convictions.

"The investigation is no longer routine."

Ferrie wasn't specifically mentioned. Implicitly, though, Garrison referred to him in an ominous way. In criticizing the press's handling of his investigation—Garrison tended to savage the press when he wanted to distract from his own foibles—he answered a question by saying that "the irresponsible handling of this story by the newspapers yesterday and this morning in New Orleans *has placed the life of one witness in such jeopardy that I think there is a real question as to whether he'll live or not."*

Back at his home, Ferrie's head was splitting deeper and sharper. He was exhausted. His mood was black and blue. It got worse when the phone rang. Lou Ivon.

"We've missed having you at the Fontainebleau. Had hoped you'd want to watch Garrison's show."

"Had places to go."

"Given the newspaper leaks, our beloved DA felt it was his obligation to give his people a status report."

"He only feels an obligation to himself."

"Heads up—you're the next news. We'll be coming to get you in a day or two. The warrant's being written. Clean your place up. *Please.*"

Unsurprised by this bulletin, and now concerned that his time on this planet would be over soon, Ferrie lifted his Olivetti onto his kitchen table and somberly composed two notes, the keys of the old typewriter sticking on every tenth letter. He twisted the feed roller and pulled out the first sheet of paper containing the words he'd written—a personal missive to a specific friend. He then punched out a second note, one with words of anger for the predicament he was in. He folded the sheets of paper, put them in two separate Town and Country envelopes, and left them on the kitchen counter. He moved the typewriter from the kitchen to his piano stool.

Tuesday morning brought headlines and television reports about Garrison's press conference. Under a picture of an agitated Garrison kicking a reporter out of the room, the *Times-Picayune* headlined that the DA was "Confident He Can Show JFK Killing Was Plotted" and "Believes No Foreign Nation Involved."

Ferrie left the house early in the morning after a cup of coffee, waved at the several scribes skulking around out front, and went again to the Broadmoor Pharmacy. This time he had real business to do there, picking up his prescription for Proloid. As he had before, he then snuck out the back door.

He stayed away from his apartment for much of the day, visiting Bringuier again and spending some time at the main public library on Loyola Avenue. He took the time to skim through, not for the first time, several of the twenty-six volumes of the Warren Commission Report.

Walking the four blocks to Baronne Street, Ferrie had lunch at the coffee shop at the Roosevelt Hotel. He people-watched in the lobby thereafter for a couple of hours. Toward the end of the afternoon, he called David Snyder to see if he had any news. "*Anything?*" Snyder had nothing.

He returned home as the afternoon morphed into evening on Tuesday, the twenty-first. There was a note conspicuously taped to his door from a reporter named George Lardner.

"Mr. Ferrie. Sorry you were out. If at all possible, could you give me a ring at my hotel or leave a message as to where and when we might get together." In addition to signing his name, Lardner identified his affiliation, the *Washington Post,* and provided a phone number.

He wondered if this Lardner was related to the famous short-story writer Ring Lardner. He enjoyed Ring Lardner's stories and decided to call George Lardner because of the possible Ring Lardner connection, even though he was exhausted. He dialed the number Lardner had provided. 573-5251. It was almost midnight when Lardner arrived at Louisiana Avenue Parkway by a Metri taxi.

Ferrie greeted him at his front door. Yesterday's headache had moderated a little, but he still didn't feel well. Lardner later told investigators that Ferrie was "moody."

"Greetings, Mr. Lardner. Sorry about the mess." He was back in his brown corduroy pants and white work shirt over the Hubba-Hubba T-shirt. No shoes. He sat on his couch. Lardner sat on a living room chair.

\|\|\|\\

"No worries, Mr. Ferrie. I'm just glad you were able to see me. I know it's late."

Lardner looked like a typical gumshoe investigative reporter. Frumpy, ill-fitting clothes. Five o'clock shadow on the verge of becoming a short beard. He fit right in with Ferrie's junky apartment.

"One question for you, Mr. Lardner. Are you Ring Lardner's grandson? I'm a big fan."

"Glad you like him. He's one of my heroes. My great uncle."

"I particularly enjoyed the short story 'Some Like Them Cold.'"

"Some Like Them Cold" was a cynical tale about an egotistical songwriter. Ferrie saw a mix of ambition and gloom in that story. He identified with a life of ambition and gloom.

"Actually haven't read that one," Lardner said.

"You should. And I read *'The Ecstasy of Owen Muir'* by Ring Junior. Your second cousin?"

"Yep."

"Deep novel. Kinda picaresque. Wow—I enjoyed it thoroughly. Many of his criticisms of my religion, Catholicism, were well taken. Not all of them, mind you, but many of them."

"I'll pass that on to him. You know he wrote that novel because he was on the Hollywood blacklist. He would've much preferred to be writing movie scripts."

"Ignorant fascist assholes. This novel was the only good thing that came out of the fucking Un-American Activities Committee.

"If you don't mind, I'm going to stretch out on the couch. I'm a little slow tonight." His headache coming back, Ferrie rubbed his right temple.

"But first, want some coffee?" Ferrie offered.

"You betcha, shoot me up. Thanks."

Ferrie filled two cups and put them on saucers. He put Lardner's on an end table. Ferrie's went on the coffee table. He slumped down on the couch.

"I'd like to get your take on this Garrison thing," Lardner said. "Just briefly. You must be beat. I'm sure you're not living a life of relaxation right now."

"No shit, Dick Tracy." Ferrie chuckled and then coughed.

Ferrie sat opposite Lardner, on the couch against the wall.

"What can you tell me?" Lardner asked.

"Well, you don't have to be Sigmund Freud to see that Lord Jim Garrison is a clinical narcissist. He's a publicity whore who in his own mind is never wrong. In terms of new facts, something he's not big on, he's got nothing new, zippo, *nada, rien*. But you gotta understand, sir, this isn't always a logical city. As our beloved *Picayune* paper put it in 1851, 'Everyone in this good city enjoys the full right to pursue his own inclinations in all reasonable, and unreasonable, ways.'"

"Catchy."

"That little quote's so spot-on, man, that after I first heard it I went and found a copy of the original paper and made some notes." Ferrie pulled a piece of paper out of a side table.

"This seminal quote was published on Ash Wednesday, ten years and a month before Fort Sumter. The great Swedish soprano Jenny Lind was finishing a tour of the city, under the watchful eye of P. T. Barnum. She was like the Beatles wrapped up into one person. It was Jennymania in town—Jenny Lind hats, Jenny Lind gloves, Jenny Lind sausages. That evening she was set to perform her supposedly stunning version of the cavatina from the *Barber of Seville.*

"The paper, then called the *Daily Picayune,* noted how much fun Mardi Gras'd been that year. 'Much social enjoyment and amusement prevailed all over the city.' The parade, the 'neat and showy costumes,' the 'fluttering banners,' presented a 'magnificent and spirit-stirring spectacle.' The ladies on the balconies and in the windows 'lent an additional charm to the gay scene.'

"Lent was upon us now, the *Picayune* said, and some folks'll be more soberly focusing on religion. But here's the thing, Mr. Lardner. What the paper then said is that the mischief doesn't have to stop just because it was Lent—it *never* stops in New Orleans, people always do what they want. 'Little diminution, however, will ensue in musical, social and theatrical entertainments.' And everyone'll still have—even though its Lent—the right to be unreasonable.

"Nothing's new. We're in the middle of Lent now but Garrison and his merry band don't need to act soberly 'cause, shit, we're in the Big Easy. Why look for reason in what they're doing?"

"You're expecting to be arrested?"

"Sure. Soon—day or two. As the *Picayune* suggested long ago, this is not a city that is prone to knowing what it's doing before it arrests people. But, eventually, people'll see Garrison's a fraud. I just pray to Jesus and Mother Mary that he doesn't destroy too many lives along the way. Including mine."

Ferrie's voice was soft but firm.

Lardner asked, "Why the focus on you?"

"Lord Garrison had me arrested a few days after the assassination," Ferrie responded. "He'd heard I knew Oswald. He also heard about a trip to Texas I'd made that Friday night. The FBI stepped in, thank God, and saw nothing was there. They made Garrison let me go. But three years later, bored I guess, he had a divine revelation, based on nothing but fairy dust, that I'd been ordered to go to Houston to fly one of JFK's shooters out of Texas. You know I'm a pilot?"

"Used to be with Eastern, right?"

"They canned me. I wasn't quite their type of straitlaced guy."

"I wanna hear about that sometime and about this alleged second shooter. But, for now, tell me about the Texas trip."

"I was in a courtroom in New Orleans that Friday supporting Mr. Marcello on a trial brought by RFK. The judge announced that JFK had been shot. The case ended successfully. I'd worked my ass off for months on that case and was ready to get away. Frankly, I didn't pay much attention to the assassination. I know I should've, but I just had to escape.

"There was a celebration of the court victory at the Carousel Bar at the Hotel Monteleone," Ferrie continued. "I attended for a little while but cut out early. I picked up a couple of buddies, and we went to Houston and Galveston to hunt geese and party. I never got close to Dallas.

"The FBI looked at Oswald's time in New Orleans and found I had no tie to him or to any suspicious JFK-haters. They had no trouble concluding that Oswald acted alone—that he was just a misfit looking for the spotlight. Oswald's got that in common with Garrison."

"That's the reason Garrison's doing what he's doing?" Lardner asked. "Attention?"

"Bingo. His favorite quote—"If you want to get a mule's attention, hit him with a piece of stovewood.

"He really *is* deranged. He's been diagnosed, I've heard. Thinks he's as infallible as Jesus. But there's something else. He's insanely freaked out by homosexuals, particularly successful ones. His targets are all homosexuals, including me."

"Why? Do you think deep down he may believe he's a homosexual, and he's fighting it?"

"Good question, Sigmund. Maybe. I do some therapy work, and I've seen that kind of thing."

"But what does this phobia have to do with the assassination?"

"Garrison gets it in his head that Oswald was a homo. He heard that Oswald didn't spend much time with his wife or any other women, that he was lousy in bed. Then he hears that Oswald was close with Clay Shaw."

"Shaw's used to head the International Trade Mart." Lardner had done his research.

"Yeah. He's a big muckety-muck in this town, but, unlike most of the big muckety-mucks here, he's not a panty-hunter. He's as gay as me. Garrison can't stand that a powerful guy in New Orleans is a poof.

"He hears that Shaw tried to hire a lawyer to get Oswald off, and he already thinks that I knew Oswald and was involved in a JFK conspiracy," Ferrie continued. "He figures that, since I'm a homo and I get around, I must've known Shaw. Garrison's tinged mind puts two and two, and two, together. He starts to see Oswald, Shaw, and yours truly as not only friends but as members of a murderous Friends of Dorothy gang."

"Why would a band of homosexuals want to kill JFK?" Lardner asked

"Who the fuck knows? Maybe looking for a thrill? Or upset we have a womanizer as president? There's no sane reason I can think of."

"This'll be a shit-hard sell for Garrison."

"He's going to dress it up by attacking the Warren Commission and showing there was a second shooter. He thinks he can do that with the Zapruder Film. Oswald, *ergo*, was part of a conspiracy. And then he'll ask, who was Oswald with in the months before the assassination? Why, it was Shaw, Ferrie, and a few of their male friends in New Orleans. Voilà!"

"A stretch."

"Again, no shit, Dick. Even crazier, I hear one of his real objectives is to get an interview in *Playboy*. I'm serious. He already spends a lot of time at the Playboy Club here. He believes that if he can be in *Playboy* and if he can be photographed hanging out with Hef and a few of his big-titted, air-brushed gals at the Playboy Mansion in Chicago—particularly with Margaret Lee, an often-naked local celebrity—he'll be viewed as a man's man."

Ferrie was weakening but willing to go late with Lardner. Lardner took advantage, quizzing Ferrie in detail about his background, his friends and contacts, his range of interests, and his views on a second shooter. It was pressing four in the morning on Wednesday when Lardner left.

〰️

Later that day, after learning of Ferrie's death, Lardner wrote that his visit with Ferrie just hours before showed him that Ferrie "was a man of parts, . . . [H]e was fluent in several languages, trained in psychology and medicine and showed the assimilation of many of the 3000 books he had scattered through his rooms."

He "seemed in good spirits, not like a man about to kill himself."

CHAPTER 70

Ferrie's rush of energy speaking with Lardner fizzled quickly. He was now groggy and anxious to lie down. But first he opened his fridge and took out a bottle of Brown's Velvet milk, poured a glass, and put it back in the fridge. The single remaining steel vial of cancer powder stared up at him from the side of the fridge.

Though blurry-eyed, Ferrie could tell that the tube was out of place. It was in the upper door shelf bin. Ferrie, however, always kept the tube in the lower bin, as far away as possible from the top interior shelf where he kept his Jell-O, milk, and takeout containers. He picked the tube up and twirled it around. *I gotta deep-six this*, he thought. *Garrison's goons will be ripping the apartment apart . . . again . . . soon.* He knew there was still enough material in the tube to kill another person or two.

Ferrie decided to empty the stainless steel tube and put the tube itself at the bottom of his garbage bag. He slowly and carefully twisted off the top. *Lefty loosey, righty tighty,* he reminded himself. He looked inside one last time, immediately shuddered, and lost his grip on the tube. It dropped and clattered on the floor. Ferrie's face froze. He crunched his eyes shut. Blood rushed his brain.

The tube was empty.

His mind sprung to life, racing to and fro. *How could the fucking tube be empty?* He racked his brain.

It quickly came to him. Only one person knew about the monkey virus and that there was a little left. And knew where it was—in a steel tube in the side of his Frigidaire. This person had visited Ferrie five or six weeks before. His mind tumbled.

He wobbled around his apartment, banging his fist on the piano, shifting the carriage back and forth on his old Olivetti typewriter on the piano seat, punching a garage-sale throw pillow. He rubbed his face. He looked in the mirror. The image staring back at him was pale and disheveled. Through his cloudy eyes, his reflection looked almost translucent.

Ferrie had no doubt where the contents of this tube ended up.

He began to hear a church bell in his head, like the one he heard at East Louisiana Hospital several years before. The old nineteenth-century bell of St. Louis Cathedral—Victoire. *Bong. Bong. Bong.* But these knells were fainter than before, as if they were literally coming from Jackson Square. Then they stopped. *The bell'd rung out.*

Fatigue was now cascading through Ferrie's body. He believed he could feel his cells dividing and growing, growing and dividing, spinning out of control. Metastasizing. *"God give me strength,"* he whispered to himself. Tired. So tired.

Tired. But, suddenly, the anger he'd been feeling turned into peacefullness as he began to visualize Saint Augustine's City of God. Saint Augustine's teaching that wise men sometimes had to do bad things to earn a place in the City of God comforted him. *The City of God.*

He slowly stripped off his clothes and donned a thin white robe. He grabbed his plain olive-wood crucifix. He was too wiped out to take off his wig and fake eyebrows. Slipping under the sheets, Dr. Mary appeared to him. Her face then morphed into the face of Mother Mary. "Mary," he whispered. "Forgive me."

He fell fast asleep. He dreamed of flying, wispy clouds above him, bayous below. He was in control. Content.

||||

Jimmy Johnson decided to go by Ferrie's apartment on Tuesday morning, George Washington's birthday. He first glanced at the morning's *Times-Picayune*. Below the fold on page one there was an article describing the support of Louisiana Senator Russell B. Long, son of Huey Long, for the Garrison probe. In a press conference on Tuesday in DC, the paper reported, "Long said that Garrison had under arrest one suspected conspirator" in 1963 but had to let him go. "I'm convinced that Jim Garrison has some information the Warren Commission didn't have." The noose was tightening on Ferrie. But it no longer mattered.

Johnson found the body, draped in what appeared to be a white shroud, at eleven forty-five that Wednesday morning. Johnson had been let into the apartment by the landlord after he found the apartment locked and heard nothing from inside, even with his loud battering of the front door.

There was an untroubled look on Ferrie's face. His eyes were wide open.

CHAPTER 71

D r. Nicholas Chetta, the coroner of Orleans Parish, performed an autopsy on Ferrie's remains, starting around three o'clock Wednesday afternoon. He was assisted by pathologist Ronald Welsh. Garrison insisted that Lou Ivon be present. Working his way up the body before dissecting the brain, Dr. Chetta found little of note. Ferrie had a few marks on his upper lip but no deep hemorrhages or swellings. The marks could've been caused a hundred different ways.

The brain, though, was altogether different. It was awash with small tumors. Dr. Chetta could see that the tumors were fresh and had grown quickly. "Ferrie died of brain cancer," Dr. Chetta reported definitively to Ivon.

Ivon went out into the hallway and called Garrison. Watching Ivon through a glass window separating the morgue from the hallway, it was obvious to both Chetta and Welsh that Ivon and Garrison were having an animated conversation. Ivon hung up the phone and reentered the autopsy room.

"Mr. Garrison believes you need to look harder. He's convinced this had to be either a suicide or a murder. We've had eyes on him all the time—he's shown no sign of cancer. In fact, for God's sake, he'd been active, running all around town, hanging out at the airport, talking to reporters until all hours. Maybe he's been a little tired. Who wouldn't be? He knew he was in big trouble, was stressed for sure. You can tell if someone has brain cancer. The person has trouble speaking, loses memory, has seizures.

"It's obvious, Nicky. He was scared shitless and decided to give up the ghost. Or someone didn't want him telling us the truth."

"I saw what I saw. There were numerous small tumors. They'd grown into his brain. Several clearly had been oozing blood."

"Let me put it this way. Mr. Garrison's demanding you conclude this was a suspicious death. You can say it could've been suicide. Maybe murder."

"C'mon. I took a fucking oath. Shit, they'd have my license. And Ron's."

"You losers need to do *something* here for Mr. Garrison. Or, frankly, you won't need your licenses. Look, we're trying to find out who killed our president. We think we know who was behind it, but we'll be able to get there quicker and with more leverage if it looks like Ferrie died under suspicious circumstances. That'll show people that our investigation is serious. It'll show there are people who didn't want Ferrie to talk to us."

"Christ, Lou. Goddamn it. Gimme some kind of break here," Chetta said.

Ivon called Garrison again.

"Garrison would be okay if you leave it kinda ambiguous— say some general stuff that may indicate he was given some poison or bad drug, mention the marks on his mouth, don't use the word 'cancer' anywhere. Just think of something. *Capisce?*"

"*Capisce*, you fuck," Chetta said. "*Strunzo.*"

"Draft your thing and I'll take a look at it. We know Ferrie took Proloid, maybe he overdosed on that—by force or voluntarily. It can cause heart issues, right?"

"I'll do something, but I'm not mentioning Proloid," Chetta said. "That wouldn't kill him, too fucking slow-acting."

"Garrison likes the Proloid angle, has a nice ring to it," Ivon said.

"He can say what he wants. The fucker actually used to take Proloid himself, maybe he knows more than a certified doctor.

Just don't quote *me* on Proloid. Anybody who knows anything about this stuff will know it's bullshit."

"What about the diuretic Ferrie took, can you overdose on that shit?"

"Oh, sure—too much of that maybe could dehydrate someone to death. If he took a bucket full. Incredibly unlikely in the real world, but go for it if you want."

Chetta had Welsh write the report. It classified the death as "natural" but had enough other things in it to satisfy Ivon. Welsh was willing to bend the truth, writing that there was bleeding in the brain caused, not by tumors, but by a "berry aneurism," though he didn't say this was the cause of death. In fact, berry aneurisms, which occur at the base of the brain where key arteries join at the Circle of Willis, seldom are fatal. Dr. Bagnetto would've noticed symptoms of ruptured aneurisms when he saw Ferrie on Monday.

And, to please Ivon, Welsh wrote that he and Chetta had found "pulmonary edema and congestion." Pulmonary edema results from excessive fluid in the lungs. That can be caused naturally—or can be caused by certain toxins or medications.

In the "external examination" section of his long report, Welsh noted that there was "a lesion in the upper lip" and a marking on the lower lip. Garrison could point to these observations and say these may have been the result of a tube forced into his mouth. Or by him clumsily ingesting handfuls of pills.

||||

With this incompetent autopsy report, Garrison hinted privately to reporters that Ferrie died as a result of foul play. He told the public it was probably suicide.

"The apparent suicide of David Ferrie ends the life of a man who in my judgment was *one of history's most important individuals.* Evidence developed by our office had long since confirmed that he was involved in events culminating in the assassination of President Kennedy."

CHAPTER 72

A few days after Ferrie's death, Sergio Arcacha Smith met with G. Wray Gill and Carlos Marcello at the Town and Country.

"I hated dis whole thing. You know—hitting Ferrie. We had ta, Smith, after da DA got a chubby for 'im. But I liked dat Ferrie guy."

"Me too, Mr. Marcello," Arcacha Smith said. "Me too. I've asked the Lord to heal me and bless me. And also you, sir."

"*Grazie*, my friend. *Molte grazie*."

"Tell us first about Dr. Sherman, Sergio," Gill requested.

"I'd met her with Dave, sir. He thought she was the nicest lady he'd ever known. He thought she'd be world famous, probably cure cancer. I know you had to make a tough decision on her, sir. I respect your resolve."

"*Ti ringrazio tanto*. But sad," Marcello said.

"I made sure it was a gentle death."

"Yeah? Dey told me she was a mess."

"We didn't use the cancer stuff, didn't want to get Dave involved in any way. I knocked on her door, which was on the patio side. Since she'd met me before with Dave, she let me in. Got me some tea. When she put the cup in front of me I grabbed her arm and injected her with potassium chloride. Her heart stopped quickly. No pain. She went peacefully."

"*Molto bene*."

"I *wanted* the scene to be messy, like a crazy person did it— as far away from looking like a mob hit as possible. I stripped her and laid her down by her bed on the floor. I made sure she was dead. Then, gently, I stabbed her in four or five places and splattered some blood on the wall. I probably went further than I really needed to, burned part of the body and her mattress. The cops won't be able to figure it out. It could've been a robbery gone wild. It could've been a thrill kill by a lunatic."

"Makes me sick to my stomach," Gill said. "Your approach isn't my cup of tea, but we had to put her down after she started to leak a little to Talley."

"Since there was no break-in, they'll think it could've been done by somebody she knew, maybe a sex partner. She *was* naked. Or maybe she was burned at work by that machine at Public Health Dave told me about—someone she worked with could've taken her burned body home. Who knows, right?"

"Just you, only you," Marcello said. "Even when you six foot under—*only* you."

"Not that you can actually get six feet under in this town," Gill said, trying to inject some lightness into the session.

Arcacha Smith got Marcello's message loud and clear. *Silencio.*

"The one thing it *didn't* look like, sir, was a hit you would've done. Mr. Marcello, you have too much class to have had that mess made."

"*Sì.*

"Now talk ta me about Ferrie," Marcello instructed.

"Dave was nervous and unhappy. He was tortured by the JFK thing and Dr. Mary. And he knew his life was going to be a nightmare because of Garrison. I think he was ready to give himself over to God. That made it a little easier for me to do.

"When I visited him near Christmas," Arcacha Smith continued, "I emptied the last tube of that monkey powder into his tea when he was out of the room. I put the tube back in the fridge. It was a steel tube, so he couldn't see that it was empty without opening it."

"It took him a while to die," Gill noted.

"The powder was losing its magic. We saw that with Ruby. It should've popped Ruby off almost right away, but it took a few weeks. It would've taken longer than it did with Dave if he'd been stronger."

"Pain?" Marcello asked.

"I heard he had some headaches that were probably caused by the tumors, but I don't think he was in much other pain. Dr. Chetta told me he died peacefully."

"*Grazie Dio.*"

"Sergio, you've done your duty," Gill said. "We're retiring you from our little business. And know that you're safe from us, safe as houses. You just have to lose your memory of the 'JFK Affair.' We'll send you some money and then you're on your own to lead a happy and prosperous life in Houston with your family."

"Thank you, sirs. God bless you."

"You're *not* free from others, though," Gill pointed out. "Garrison's going to come up your ass soon. Stay in Texas, he can't get you there. In the future, you may have others on you as well—your name'll probably come out. But, knock on wood, so far all the misdirection we organized has kept the conspiracy sleuths largely away from us."

"I'll just tell anybody who wants to know that I was working on secret Cuba stuff with my good friend Bobby Kennedy up until the assassination. And it's illegal for me to provide any detail."

"*Pazzo,*" Marcello grumbled.

"Yeah, crazy," Gill said. "But maybe *so* crazy some folks may believe it."

Marcello poured out three shots of limoncello made specially for him in Rome by Giorgio Pallini based on a family recipe going back to 1899. "To Ferrie," Marcello said. "Â *Saluti.*"

"Â *Saluti,*" Gill said.

"Â *Saluti,*" Arcacha Smith responded. "Cheers."

Carlos Marcello bowed his head and crossed himself. "*Buono reposo, Davide.*"

WEDNESDAY, FEBRUARY 22, 1967

The notes David William Ferrie left behind on his counter were found by the New Orleans Police on the afternoon of his death. Beaten down by his difficult and extraordinarily complex and challenging life, and knowing he may not survive the unhinged crusade of Jim Garrison, he had first written a short note to Al Beauboeuf, with whom he'd recently had a falling out. "[Y]ou treated me as you did because I was the one who always got you in trouble. . . . All I can say is that I offered you love, and the best I could."

He wrote the second note for the ages:

To leave this life is, for me, a sweet prospect. I no longer find anything in it that is desirable, and on the other hand everything that is loathsome. . . . A somewhat messianic district attorney has proved himself utterly unfit for office, just as he proved that an electorate cannot be depended on to pick the right man. . . . When I was a boy my father preached that in the "American way of life" you are innocent till proven guilty. No greater lie has ever been told. . . . If this is justice, then justice be damned.

Goodbye
Dave

SATURDAY, JULY 15, 1967

Though Jim Garrison's notions about the JFK assassination were flights of fancy, his most basic conclusion that there was a conspiracy was correct. Speaking to a national audience on NBC-TV five months after Ferrie's death, Garrison lucidly painted this bottom-line truth.

"Tonight I'm going to talk to you about truth and about fairy tales, about justice and about injustice.

"As children, we become accustomed to hearing fairy tales. They're always pleasant stories, they're comforting to hear because good always triumphs over evil. At least this is the way it is in fairy tales. Fairy tales are not dangerous for our children. And are probably even good for them up to a point. However, in the real world, in which you and I must live, fairy tales are dangerous. They are dangerous because they're untrue. Anything which is untrue is dangerous.

"And it is all the more dangerous when the fairy tale becomes accepted as reality simply because it has an official seal of approval.

"The conclusion of the Warren Report that President Kennedy was killed by a lone assassin is a fairy tale.

"The people of this country don't have to be protected from the truth. This country wasn't built on the idea that a handful of nobles located in our federal agencies in Washington, DC, should decide what was good for the people to know and what they should not know. This is a totalitarian concept which presumes that the leaders of our federal government constitute a special elite which by virtue of their nobility and their brilliance empower them to think for the people.

"I say that the day has not yet arrived when the only reality is power and the ideals on which our country was built are merely words printed on paper.

"I believe that in this conflict between truth and power, and this is exactly what it is all about, that power cannot possibly smash truth out of existence. The people in this country will *not* let that happen."

POSTSCRIPT

The main characters in this tale continued to lead intriguing lives or, in several cases, experienced suspicious deaths, after Dave Ferrie died.

\\\\

The most impactful death was RFK's. RFK had come to believe that his nemesis, the mob, was responsible for his brother's assassination. In 1968 he ran for president and, by mid-April, had become the favorite to succeed LBJ. As president he would've had the power to renew his crusade against the mob, including closely investigating the mob's role in the assassination. RFK was gunned down in the kitchen of a Los Angeles hotel in June of that year after winning the California Democratic primary. A "lone nut" was blamed for the killing, though conspiracy theories have abounded ever since, and the ballistics evidence indicates that there was a second shooter. RFK is buried at Arlington National Cemetery.

\\\\

Sam Giancana was shot to death in his home on South Wenonah Avenue in Oak Park, Illinois, on June 19, 1975, eleven months after returning from eight years of self-imposed exile in Mexico and five days before he was to testify in Washington before the Senate Select Committee on Intelligence, known informally as the "Church Committee." Subject areas before the

Church Committee included JFK's assassination and efforts by the mob and/or the CIA to kill Castro. Giancana's mob assailant, a "friend," put a bullet in the back of his head and then six more in his mouth and face, while Giancana was making the two of them a meal of sausage, escarole, and beans. Giancana is buried at Mount Carmel Cemetery in Hillside, Illinois.

John Roselli's legless body was found floating in an empty fifty-five-gallon oil drum, heavy chains coiled around it and holes punched in the side to make it sink, in Dumfoundling Bay near North Miami Beach on August 9, 1976. He'd been asphyxiated. Roselli *had* testified before the Church Committee—just days after Giancana was murdered and then again the following April—about mob involvement in attempting to kill Castro. Roselli's damaged and incomplete body was cremated.

After several decades of effort, the government finally was able to jail Carlos Marcello in 1983. Suspicious of Marcello's ability to break the law even from behind prison walls, the FBI planted an informant close to Marcello in a federal maximum-security facility in Texas. According to a March 7, 1986, FBI report: "On December 15, 1985, [the informant] was in the company of Carlos Marcello and another inmate at the Federal Correctional Institute, Texarkana, Texas, in the courtyard engaged in conversation. Carlos Marcello discussed his intense dislike of former President John Kennedy, as he often did. Unlike other such tirades against Kennedy, however, on this occasion Carlos Marcello said, referring to President Kennedy, 'Yeah, I had the son of a bitch killed. I'm glad I did. I'm sorry I couldn't have done it myself.'" After several strokes, and suffering from Alzheimer's, Marcello died in his sleep on March 2, 1993. He is buried at Metairie Cemetery, which is also the final resting place of Jim Garrison, Louis Prima, and Sam Saia.

Four days before he passed away, Santo Trafficante Jr. spoke in Italian about the Kennedys with his lawyer Frank Ragano. "We shouldn't have killed John, we should have killed Bobby." He died on March 17, 1987, of complications during surgery.

Trafficante is buried at L'Unione Italiana Cemetery in Ybor City, Florida.

\\\\\

Jada, whose real name was Janet Adams Conforto, was mowed down from behind by a school bus, empty of passengers, while riding a motorcycle in Albuquerque, New Mexico, on May 9, 1980. The bus driver, a woman named Donna Beeman, had an unobstructed view of the motorcycle as she sped over it on East Central Avenue, in the 12800 block. The local police concluded it was an unfortunate accident. Jada was forty-four. She is interred in an unmarked crypt at Lake Lawn Park Cemetery in Metairie.

Coroner Nicholas Chetta died mysteriously at the young age of fifty at Mercy Hospital on May 25, 1968. He'd just been elected president of the Louisiana Medical Society. Not being able to diagnose the cause of death, doctors concluded that he died from a heart attack. Chetta's death came after he'd testified at the preliminary hearing on Clay Shaw's arrest on March 16, 1967—he spoke then only about the mental fitness of a witness against Shaw. His death came before the Shaw trial, which started on January 29, 1969, where he would've been asked about Dave Ferrie's death. He'd told NBC in 1967 that Ferrie died of "natural causes," but at the same time said it was "possible" that there were deadly drugs or other substances in the body that couldn't be detected. He is also buried at Lake Lawn Park Cemetery.

Judy Campbell led a relatively quiet life for over a decade after the assassination. She married professional golfer Dan Exner in April 1975. Her quiet life ended a few months after the wedding when she was required to testify before the Church Committee. Though her testimony was confidential, the Republicans on the committee leaked to reporters that she said she'd been an intermediary between JFK and Giancana. Over the following ten years, she told the story of her affair with JFK, in varying ways, to television and print reporters, and she wrote a book. In the book she also claimed that JFK had cavorted with prostitutes in the White House swimming pool. And, in an interview with ABC's Lynn Sherr in late 1996, she disclosed her role as a courier between JFK and Giancana: in April 1960, she said, JFK "showed me a satchel and it was full of money. And he said will you take this to Sam." She also disclosed her abortion of JFK's baby: "He said I want you to know if you want to have the baby, have the baby." When she said she thought she should abort the baby, JFK responded, "Do you think Sam could help us." Judy died of natural causes in 1999. Her body was cremated.

Frank Sinatra never reconnected with the Kennedy family after the brouhaha over JFK's proposed stay at his house in 1962. He never again engaged with the mob after his son's kidnapping the following year. And the break with Peter Lawford, JFK's brother-in-law, effectively dissolved the Rat Pack. After the 1968 election, he turned to the Republicans, actively supporting Richard Nixon and then Ronald Reagan. Sinatra continued performing and making movies. His last public performance was in December 1994 in Japan in the Fukuoka Dome. The FBI released 1,275 pages of previously confidential memos, case files, and other documents on Sinatra in December 1998. This "dossier" contains detailed information about Sinatra's links to the mob. "Sinatra enjoys surrounding himself with hoodlums." There are repeated references to his relationship with Giancana. "Giancana has been a guest at various places owned or operated by Sinatra and at Sinatra's home in Palm Springs, California." Sinatra's bond with JFK is also addressed, including reports of the two being at "indiscreet parties in Palm Springs, Las Vegas and NYC." One informant expressly told the FBI that "notorious hoodlums" were using Sinatra to gain "an entrée to the Senator." Sinatra died six and a half months before the release of the FBI dossier, of natural causes. He is buried at Desert Memorial Park in Cathedral City, California.

\\\\\

Dr. Mary Sherman's murder investigation remains open. On the fiftieth anniversary of her death, a jazz funeral was held in front of the Patio (or the Patios) Apartments, led by British jazz trumpeter Clive Wilson. Her burial location is not publicly known.

ǀǀǀǀ

Sergio Arcacha Smith was never interviewed formally or informally by the FBI nor by any investigator or lawyer associated with the Warren Commission or Jim Garrison. Garrison *sought* to depose Arcacha Smith, but this effort was half-hearted, for reasons that remain unclear. When Arcacha Smith agreed to an interview but on the condition that the session take place somewhere other than New Orleans and that he have a lawyer present, Garrison quickly backed down. The House Special Committee on Assassinations did depose Arcacha Smith eleven years later, on July 7, 1978, in an office building in the heart of Little Havana. During the course of this light-touch, eighty-eight-minute interview, conducted by Chief Investigator Gaeton Fonzi, there was only one question about the assassination. Q: *On November 22, 1963, do you recall where you were and what you were doing?* A: *Working in Houston with Mr. Calvin Clausel.* There was one question about the Houma raid. The other sixty-four pages of the sixty-six-page transcript covered questions and answers about people Arcacha Smith had known in New Orleans in the early sixties. He *had* known Ferrie, Gill, Banister, Bringuier, Martin, Caire, and Novel. He had *not* known Oswald or Ruby. He was asked about Orlando Piedra, the former head of Batista's Bureau of Investigation and later an exile in New Orleans. Piedra, Arcacha Smith had said, was rich and just laying low in New Orleans. However, "he used to come to me and give me money every time a [poor] Cuban came [for help], to buy shoes for them or blankets or things like that."

Arcacha Smith lived out his years peacefully, dying on July 5, 2000. His burial location is not publicly known.

‖‖

The role David William Ferrie may have played in JFK's assassination was investigated extensively by the House Select Committee on Assassinations between 1976 and 1978, to no firm conclusion. The HSCA found that Ferrie was "philosophically and politically complex," "a devout Catholic," and "rabidly anti-Communist." He and Arcacha Smith were "eager partner[s] in counterrevolutionary activities." Ferrie knew Oswald, the HSCA determined, meeting for the first time when Oswald was a teenager. However, "the nature of the Oswald-Ferrie association remain[s] largely a mystery." Ferrie rests peacefully in the cemetery plot he bought in 1964 at St. Bernard Memorial Gardens, Chalmette, St. Bernard Parish—exactly thirteen miles from the grave of Carlos Marcello.